BLIND SPOT

SEE NO EVIL

BLAMELESS

SHATTERED ECHOES

BLIND SPOT

BARBARA SHAPIRO

HarperPaperbacks
A Division of HarperCollinsPublishers

▲ **HarperPaperbacks**
A Division of HarperCollins*Publishers*
10 East 53rd Street, New York, N.Y. 10022-5299

This is a work of fiction. The characters, incidents, and
dialogues are products of the author's imagination and are not to
be construed as real. Any resemblance to actual events or
persons, living or dead, is entirely coincidental.

ISBN 0-06-101150-9

HarperCollins®, ▲ ®, and HarperPaperbacks™
are trademarks of HarperCollins*Publishers,* Inc.

Cover photo by © 1998 by Dean Siracusa/FPG

First printing: July 1998

Printed in the United States of America

Visit HarperPaperbacks on the World Wide Web at
http://www.harperpcollins.com

❖ 10 9 8 7 6 5 4 3 2 1

To Dan

ACKNOWLEDGMENTS

Thanks to the usual suspects: Diane Bonavist, Jan Brogan, Floyd Kemske, Donna Baier Stein and Nancy Yost. Thanks to the family: Robin, Scott and Dan Fleishman. Thanks to the experts: Michael Bogdanow, Steve Corr, Bernie Fleishman, George Foote, Ronnie Fuchs, Gary Goshgarian, Gail Grodzinsky, Phyllis Kaplan-Silverman, Leslie Metge, and my anonymous, generous forensic psychologist. Thanks to my readers: Margie Bogdanow, Deborah Crombie, Tamar Hosansky, Pat Sparling, Vicki Steifel and Kelly Tate. And thanks to the editors: Carolyn Marino and Robin Stamm.

CHAPTER ONE

MCI-Watkins sits on an asphalt island between the north and southbound lanes of Interstate 95 like a barricaded rest stop from which there is no exit for those who reside within. This prison houses only women inmates; its male twin is about twenty miles down the road. No matter how many prisons Suki visited, she always had the same reaction. As she came within sight of the building, every law she had ever broken came roaring back at her: the marijuana she'd smoked in college, the time she'd accidentally made two IRA contributions in one calendar year, the expired inspection sticker currently attached to her windshield. As Suki carefully parked between the two yellow lines of a designated visitor's spot, she cast an apprehensive glance over her shoulder. Guilty as charged.

Although she hadn't had enough time to prepare for this meeting—nor, if she decided to take the case, was she going to have the pretrial preparation time she usually demanded—she was more resigned than concerned. Resigned, because as a forensic psychologist with a fairly new private practice, a nonsupportive ex-husband, two teenage children and maxed-out credit cards, she wasn't in the position to be too choosy about her clients. Unconcerned, because over the years she had conducted more initial assessments than she could count: in courthouses, in psychiatric hospitals, in fancy drug rehab centers—and in just about every prison in New England.

Yesterday afternoon, Mike Dannow, possibly the best defense attorney in the state, had called. "Know this is short notice," he told Suki in the clipped way he always spoke, as if he were just too busy to complete his sentences. "But I need a favor. Big one. Got a major murder trial coming in three weeks. Retrial of one of my own from a decade ago. Very complicated. Interesting. But my shrink's leaving the country to receive some big mucky-muck award in Amsterdam, or some such place, and I need a replacement. Need the best. Need you." Suki didn't ask why he hadn't hired her first.

According to Mike, his client, Lindsey Kern, had always maintained a ghost killed her boyfriend, but he hadn't allowed this into evidence during the first trial, fearing an insanity verdict and assuming—incorrectly—that the jury would accede to his argument of accidental death. It had taken him almost ten years, but he managed to dig up a piece of evidence the prosecution had failed to disclose, and then use it to petition the court for a new trial. No one ever said Mike Dannow wasn't a smart operator. "And now Lindsey's gotten worse," he had explained to Suki. "Nine years in the can and she thinks she's clairvoyant. Floats around seeing things going on miles away. Believes she knows what'll happen tomorrow."

As Suki recalled Mike's words, the shadow of the boxy prison fell over her, and she shivered in the early spring air. He had no way of knowing how close this case cut, nor how frighteningly seductive it promised to be. Pulling her coat tightly around her, she looked up at the barbed wire riveted to the top of the mean-looking metal fencing, then hurried to the entrance.

The front door to the prison was unimposing, and Suki entered a room that was strongly reminiscent of a small-town bus station with its vinyl flooring, plastic chairs and row of vending machines. But the corrections officer—for some reason, in Massachusetts, the designation "guard" was considered politically incorrect—at the front control was also behind a wall of bullet-proof glass. He spoke through an intercom which made his voice sound as if he were five hundred miles away. "Dr. Suki Jacobs?" he muttered, pulling out a grimy piece of paper. He ran his hand down the typed list. "No Suki Jacobs here."

"How about Suzanne Jacobs?" she asked. Her real name was Suzanne, but her father had nicknamed her Suki when she was a toddler and it had stuck.

The officer patiently read his list once again. "Still not here," he rasped through the static.

"I'm taking over for Dr. Nathan Breman," she pressed. "I have an appointment to meet with one of the inmates at two o'clock. Lindsey Kern."

"Shrink, huh?" he asked with a slight smirk.

Suki pointed to her watch. "It's almost two."

"I suppose it's possible you have an appointment, *miss,*" he said, emphasizing the "miss" in place of the "doctor." "But I can't let anyone in whose name isn't on my daily roster." He touched his finger to the bill of his hat in a way that clearly indicated she was dismissed.

Suki reached into her briefcase and pulled out an envelope. She pushed it through the small space below the window. "It's from Superintendent Rizzo," she said, "authorizing me to visit Ms. Kern at any time I wish." Suki had played this game long enough to know to come prepared. Even in a women's prison, it was a male world, and neither women nor psychologists were highly regarded.

The officer skimmed the letter and grunted, then said he would have to check. While he called the superintendent's office Suki walked to the bank of pay phones next to the vending machines and called her service. She asked that they hold all her messages, with the exception of emergencies, until further notice. Suki felt it was rude, as well as therapeutically undesirable, to allow one patient to infringe on another's time. Just as she hung up the phone, the officer called her name and motioned her through the metal detector. She retrieved her letter with a smile. He ignored her.

After the metal detector there was a trap, a small room in which the door in front of you can't be opened until the one behind you is locked shut. The air in the trap was overheated and stale. Suki was glad when an officer ushered her through, even though he immediately barked, "You don't have to go to the john, do you?"

When Suki said no, the officer softened. "It's real easy to hide drugs around plumbing," he explained. "If you had to go to the john, you'd have to go back to the front area and then I'd have to take you in again." He shook his head. "Bill always forgets to ask people before he sends them through." Then he led Suki down a corridor lined with small interrogation rooms. He pointed into one. "They'll bring her to you in a couple of minutes."

Suki looked into the room. It was dark and small, and held nothing but two chairs. There was no window. Although Lindsey Kern, with her college degree, middle-class upbringing and single-offense rap sheet, was one of the "better people"—eloquent prison vernacular for the more accomplished inmates—Suki was not about to go into a closed room with a convicted murderer. Complacency could be lethal. Watching your back at all times was a requirement of the job. "I'd prefer a room with a desk and a panic button," Suki told the officer. "Is there one available?"

The man shrugged and led her further down the hall. He opened another door and bowed sarcastically. "The button's at the end there, *Doctor*," he said, then turned and left her alone.

Suki found the panic button under the edge of the old wooden table. After assuring herself the button was in easy reach, she flipped the catch on the window to open it. Only then did she sit down and begin pulling papers from her briefcase. She had hoped to squeeze in a few hours to review the Kern files earlier in the day, but between Alexa's insomnia the previous night and a suicidal patient first thing this morning, the time had just not materialized. Initial interviews were both difficult and intriguing: part psych intake, part legal assessment, part therapy session, part dancing lesson.

After fifteen years of working in the forensic trenches at Roxbury District Court, assessing the competency, sanity and criminal responsibility of Boston's hardest core, Suki left public service to set up a practice in forensic consulting and posttraumatic stress therapy—a combination more compatible than might appear at first glance. It was hard work with no regular paycheck, but Suki loved the entrepreneurial freedom and excitement, and she was beginning to develop a reputation for impartiality in the courtroom and sensitivity in the office that permitted her to pay most of her bills. The call from Mike Dannow was a sign that the envelopes with PAST DUE stamped across their faces might soon be a thing of the past.

Mike wanted her to develop an opinion as to Lindsey Kern's state of mind at the time of Richard Stoddard's death. This opinion was to be rendered in a multisection report called a forensic evaluation, followed, if Mike found her conclusion appropriate to his defense, by court testimony. So Suki had less than three weeks to determine whether Lindsey was legally sane or insane at the time of the alleged crime, a determination that came down to answering two questions: Could Lindsey understand that killing Richard was wrong? Could Lindsey stop herself from doing it? It was that simple—and that difficult.

Suki retrieved a blank evaluation form from her briefcase; she had developed this twelve-page forensic questionnaire about ten years ago. She began filling in the top portion with the little bit of information she knew from Mike's materials: name, date of birth, attorney, charges, correctional facility, date of the alleged offense(s).

She had only been able to skim Lindsey's files, but still, it appeared to Suki that Mike's case was weak. Based on the testimony of Edgar Price, an eyewitness who claimed he saw Lindsey push her boyfriend, Richard Stoddard, down the stairs, Lindsey had been convicted of second-degree murder. But Mike had petitioned the court for a retrial after he unearthed a statement of Price's that had not been shared with the defense during the discovery process, as was the law. The statement acknowledged that previous to Stoddard's death, Lindsey had told Price she was seeing ghosts, an incident Price never mentioned at the first trial, an incident he refused to discuss when Mike visited him at his office.

Mike's strategy was to convince the jury that Lindsey's belief that a ghost killed Richard was proof that at the moment of the crime, she had been unable to form the requisite intent to commit murder, to tell fact from fiction: not guilty by reason of insanity. If, as was so often the case, this defense failed—NGRI was rarely used and even more rarely effective—Mike would exploit Price's previous lack of full disclosure to undermine his credibility as an eyewitness, thereby raising the question of whether Stoddard's death had been murder or accident and establishing reasonable doubt as to Lindsey's guilt. As he had failed with the accident argument during the original trial, Mike's tactic this time around was to go the insanity route first.

Suki was impressed with Mike's daring, though far from convinced it would lead to success. Presumably, her verification of Lindsey's current ESP fantasies would add credence to his insanity claim. Although Suki was painfully aware that belief in one's clairvoyance was associated with mental illness, she reminded herself that this was professional, not personal.

Just as Suki was zipping her briefcase, a tall woman in a faded orange work shirt and matching pants was led in. She was handsome in an unusual way, her deep-set gray eyes wide and haunting, her large nose and mouth keeping her from classical beauty.

"I'll be right outside the door," the officer said.

Suki nodded and the officer closed the door behind Lindsey, leaving them alone in the tiny room.

"So I hear Nathan's deserted me for some big-time conference," Lindsey said when Suki rose to shake her hand.

Suki smiled and returned to her seat. "About as big-time as they come."

Lindsey sat down across from her. "Nathan and Mike say you'll be able to do as good a job for me as he would—what do you think?"

Suki liked Lindsey's directness. "I don't know Nathan, but Mike's got good instincts."

"Do you think sane people can see ghosts?" Lindsey asked without preamble.

Suki regarded Lindsey closely. As much as she wanted to delve into Lindsey's story—and even more, Lindsey's explanation for that story—time was tight, and if she was going to collect all the data she needed, a lengthy metaphysical debate was not an option. She hoped to complete her questionnaire in three or four interviews. Anything more than that and she wouldn't be able to meet Mike's deadline. Yet, she felt the irresistible tug of Lindsey's challenge. "Do you?"

"The shrink's classic trick: When in doubt, answer a question with a question." Lindsey's voice was colored with wry amusement. She crossed her arms and leaned back in her chair. "Do me a favor and level with me. What do you really think?"

Although Suki's counseling style was to mix and match all sorts of theories and models, honesty was one of her consistent principles. She chose her words carefully. "I guess I'd have to call myself agnostic on the subject: I haven't seen any evidence to conclusively convince me either way."

"That sounds good. . . ." Lindsey looked at her with a probing gaze. "But I sense some confusion, maybe even a bit of fear, beneath your carefully chosen words."

"This isn't about what *I* think, it's about what I'm going to learn."

"I hope so. I really do—more for your sake than for mine."

"Lindsey," Suki said, shifting the interview back on track, "you do understand that although I'm a psychologist, I'm not actually your therapist? That I've been hired by your lawyer?"

Lindsey stared over Suki's shoulder.

"It's important that this is really clear," Suki said. "What we discuss here *is* confidential, unless Mike decides it furthers his case, then it might be used as evidence."

"Whatever." Lindsey shrugged.

One of Suki's professors had speculated that communication was ten percent words and ninety percent "other." Today Suki hoped to complete the clinical observation segment of the evaluation: emotional tone, mental status, cognitive state, ability to concentrate. What was Lindsey saying with her "other"? Suki waited, and watched.

Lindsey shifted in her seat. "This whole retrial thing was Mike's idea. And my mother's—she hates me being in here. I told her not to, but she sold all her stocks to foot the bill. I've tried to convince her that I've gotten used to the place. I work in the library. Mostly get left alone. With some luck, I'll be out in five to fifteen. . . ."

"But you're willing to go along with the retrial?"

"I guess." Lindsey shrugged. "To tell you the truth, in some ways I'm more afraid of going to Bridgeriver with an indefinite sentence than staying in here."

Suki nodded. Quite often, inmates preferred a limited prison term to open-ended hospitalization. But as long as Lindsey was willing to cooperate, her preferences were not Suki's business, evaluating her mental state was. "How about we get started?" Suki asked, pointing to the questionnaire.

"I never used to believe in ghosts," Lindsey began. "I used to think I could control it all. That everything made sense. That science was king. Then I met Isabel."

Suki looked up from the questionnaire. "Isabel is the ghost you think killed Richard Stoddard?" she asked.

"The one I *know* killed Richard."

"Do you still see her?"

Lindsey shook her head. "That's been one of the strange parts of this whole experience, of my opening up. I've grown so much, come so far, learned incredible things. . . . But Isabel's never come back. Despite everything, I'd like to see her again."

As Suki listened to Lindsey, she continued to watch for signs of what wasn't being said. Malingering—faking—was not uncommon in cases of this type. Lindsey's claim that she wanted to remain at Watkins could be part of her scheme to get released. Yet, Suki's gut impression was that Lindsey really did believe in her ghost. "Why don't we put Isabel aside for the moment?" Suki suggested as she picked up her pen. "I'd like you to remember four items. I'll tell them to you now, and then ask you to repeat them in about five minutes: microscope, red, baseball and love."

"Serial sevens backward from fifty-one," Lindsey countered. "Fifty-one, forty-four, thirty-seven, thirty, twenty-three, sixteen, nine, two. There are twelve items in a dozen. Athens is the capital of Greece. The pope lives in Rome."

"You've been through this before?" Suki suppressed a smile, but when she glanced down at her questions—questions she had developed herself from a virtually limitless set of items—she saw that Lindsey's responses answered what she was preparing to ask. What had made Lindsey think of sevens, instead of eights or nines? Why Greece instead of England or France?

"Concentration and mental acuity," Lindsey said.

"Orientation to person, time and place. It's Thursday, the twentieth of April. Apples and oranges are both fruits. A clarinet and a guitar are both instruments. The proverb about crying over spilt milk means you can't do anything about what's already happened."

Suki put her pen down. This woman's concentration and mental acuity were just fine—as was her ability to guess what Suki was going to ask next. Suki cleared her throat. Maybe she had more time than she thought. "You wanted to tell me about ESP?"

Lindsey smiled in triumph. "Ten years ago I would've told you there wasn't a chance in hell I'd ever be into this stuff. But after Isabel—after being in prison—everything changed. I changed. And I guess, using the half-full optimist model of the world, it's been one of the few good things—perhaps the *only* good thing—to come out of the whole mess."

"How so?"

"I'm taking correspondence courses in parapsychology at the University of Edinburgh. Graduate courses toward a master's degree. I've been communicating with other psychics, learning how to expand my powers of precognition and clairvoyance. Increase my sensitivity to both people and events."

"Expand your powers?" Suki prompted.

"Through dreamwork," Lindsey explained. "And astral projection. The ability to remove oneself from the confines of the physical body is a powerful enhancer of both. Not to mention, it gets me out of prison."

Suki laughed out loud.

Lindsey grinned wickedly. "You think I'm nuts, don't you?"

Suki appraised Lindsey, trying to assess the seriousness of her question. "This isn't about snap judgments," she said. "I've lots more work to do before I start making determinations of mental competency." If she decided to take the case, Suki added to herself. Despite the fact that she was drawn to Lindsey, and to her story, there was much here she found disturbing.

"Studying parapsychology—the paranormal, ESP, whatever—is all about *expanding* mental competency, expanding one's vision. One's ability to believe and to know." Lindsey leaned her elbows on the table, pressing herself toward Suki. "You think what you see is all there is, but there's so much happening beyond your field of vision, so much you just don't let yourself believe. . . ." She paused and pointed to Suki's hand resting on the table. "May I?" Before Suki could respond, Lindsey pressed Suki's fingers between her own. She stared into Suki's eyes; Suki stared back. After a long moment, Lindsey abruptly let go.

Suki put her hand in her lap, uncomfortable with the memories Lindsey's behavior was stirring: her mother pressing her fingers to Suki's right temple, her mother staring for hours into a shiny piece of black obsidian, her mother curled into a fetal position behind the dining room credenza. "What did you learn from holding my hand?" Suki asked.

"More than I wanted to know," Lindsey said softly. "Much more."

"And what you just found out," Suki asked, "you believe is true?"

Lindsey nodded. "I've learned this the hard way—the hardest way there is. Reality is at the edges of your awareness, you just need to let yourself turn sideways a bit to see it." She leaned back in her chair and watched Suki watching her.

In her eighteen years of clinical practice, Suki had heard many strange declarations, declarations far stranger than Lindsey's, but this woman unnerved and intrigued her in ways that probably weren't good for either of them; it was growing clear that Lindsey would be better served by someone without Suki's personal baggage.

Still, not quite ready to let go, Suki waited for Lindsey to continue. Silence was a psychologist's greatest ally. But Lindsey didn't say any more, she just stared past Suki's shoulder, a sense of expectancy, of calm anticipation, to her muteness.

Just as Suki was about to speak, the pager hooked to the strap of her purse beeped. She glared at the offending little box. There must have been a shift change at her service. "Sorry," she said to Lindsey as she reached down to read the message.

Lindsey nodded as if she had expected the interruption.

DETECTIVE PENDERGAST WITTON POLICE CALL IMMEDIATELY, the message read. It was followed by a phone number.

Suki pressed the memory button and, as the message disappeared, she wondered which one of her patients had gotten into trouble with the Witton police. It was strange, though. She knew she didn't have any patients who lived in Witton. She was certain of this because that was where she lived.

When Suki looked up, Lindsey was watching her. "Trouble with one of your children?" she asked.

Suki shook her head. "What makes you say that?"

Lindsey didn't answer, she just stared, unblinking, at Suki. "Did you want to talk some more about enhancing clairvoyance through astral projection?" she finally asked.

Although Suki nodded and continued to record her clinical observations, it was at that moment that she decided she would call Mike and turn down the Kern case. It was far too loaded for both of them.

When Suki reached her car, there was a neon-orange citation for her expired inspection sticker fluttering under the windshield wiper. She mentally added another item to her endless to-do list and pulled the citation from under the wiper. She stuffed it into her purse and unlocked the car. All the phones in the prison lobby had been in use, so she now removed her cellular phone from its housing and punched in the number for the Witton police. She ran her finger along the dusty dashboard of her ten-year-old Celica as she waited to be put through to Detective Pendergast, hoping this had nothing to do with her suicidal patient of this morning.

"Not to worry, Mrs. Jacobs," Detective Pendergast said as soon as she had identified herself. "But we have Alexa down here—"

Suki jerked up in the seat; Alexa was her seventeen-year-old daughter. "Is she all right? Is she hurt?"

"She appears to be much better now," the detective said in a soothing voice. "She's right here in my office, I'll let you speak to her in a—"

"What happened?" Suki interrupted again. "Has there been an accident? Did someone hurt her?"

"No, no," he said quickly. "No one's hurt her and no laws have been broken. I, ah, I just found her wandering along River Road. She was upset. A bit disoriented . . ."

Wandering . . . disoriented . . . Suki sucked in her breath.

"She thought she saw a murder."

"A murder?" Suki was incredulous. "Someone was murdered in Witton?"

"Well," the detective said, obviously choosing his words carefully, "that doesn't quite appear to be the case. . . ."

"There wasn't a murder?"

"I had a few of the guys check the area Alexa indicated, and there's no sign of any body or any blood or anything amiss in any way."

The car grew very warm and an uneasiness reminiscent of childhood gripped Suki's stomach; for a fleeting moment she thought she smelled Chanel No. 5. "Can I speak to Alexa, please?" Suki asked with a calmness she didn't feel.

"Mom?"

"Alexa, honey, are you okay? What happened?"

"It's, it's Jonah. Jonah, he's . . . he's . . ." Alexa's words trailed off and she began to sob.

"What about Jonah?" Suki asked. Jonah Ward had been Alexa's boyfriend sophomore year. He had broken up with her this past fall, and Alexa had taken it quite hard. She hadn't recovered until she started dating Brendan—and even now, Suki wondered if the recovery was complete. "What about him?"

"He's dead."

"Alexa—"

"I saw him," Alexa cried, her voice rising with each word. "In the woods. He was shot. It was awful. There was blood everywhere. All over the leaves."

"Alexa, honey, you've got to calm down," Suki pleaded. "The detective said the police didn't find anything. Did anyone call Jonah's house?"

"Mrs. Ward says Jonah's at a basketball game, but I know that he's not. I know, I know . . ."

"I'm on my way," Suki said. "I'll be there in about—"

"I want to go home," Alexa wailed. "I don't want to be here."

Detective Pendergast came on the line. "Why don't I take Alexa to your house?" he suggested. "I'll stay with her until you get there."

"I'll meet you in twenty minutes. Maybe less."

"The boy's mother is going over to the high school. She promised to call as soon as she gets there," he said. "But, as we've no reason to believe he's anywhere but on the basketball court . . ." He cleared his throat and Suki waited for him to continue, but he didn't say any more.

"I'm a psychologist, Detective," Suki finally said into the awkward silence.

"Oh, good." The relief in Pendergast's voice was obvious.

As Suki hung up the phone, she glanced up at the prison, at the rows of barred windows marching down the long concrete facade. She thought of her mother, of her mother as she had last seen her, almost fifteen years ago, her eyes blazing with the same wild intensity she had heard in Alexa's voice on the phone. Blazing with insanity.

CHAPTER TWO

Suki and Stan had bought the house on Lawler Road when Suki was pregnant with Kyle. They were living in an apartment in Boston, but decided it was far too small for a family of four—the truth was, it was far too small for a family of two. Although they agreed that a quality school system was their top priority, Suki wanted to stay close to the city, while Stan wanted trees. Suki wanted Victorian, Stan wanted contemporary. Suki wanted to underbuy, Stan didn't mind being house-poor. They ended up twenty-five miles from Boston, in Stan's hometown, the proud owners of a modern home on a wooded lot, with a mortgage well beyond their means. And now, except for the mortgage, Suki wouldn't have it any other way. She loved the open floor plan, the multiple levels, the huge windows that brought the outside in— although she could have lived without the too-small rooms, the shoddy plumbing and the leaky kitchen roof. And she adored Witton: the safety, the small-town friendliness, the quiet, the trees.

When Suki got home from the prison, Alexa was curled up on the couch in the family room, alone. "Detective Pendergast got beeped a couple of minutes ago," Alexa explained. "He didn't want to leave, but I told him it was all right."

Suki sat down next to Alexa. "Are you okay?"

Alexa nodded, but kept her eyes cast downward.

"Alexa." Suki gently raised Alexa's chin with her forefinger. "What happened?"

"I saw Jonah and he was dead."

Suki stared into Alexa's eyes, dark and swimming with tears. Her mother's eyes. "Did you stop along River Road on your way home from school?" Suki asked calmly. "Rest for a bit, maybe? Could you have fallen asleep? Had a dream?"

"I was awake."

"An hallucination, then. Because of the insomnia." Suki reached out and smoothed back the hair on Alexa's forehead. "One of your waking nightmares? We've talked about how fuzzy that line between wake and sleep can be."

"No!" Alexa jerked away, her eyes aflame. Suki had seen that look before, and the memory cut deep. "It was no hallucination," Alexa said more softly.

For a moment, Suki's years of training deserted her, her doctorate in clinical psychology as useless as if it had been a degree in Sanskrit. "Honey," she tried again. "You know what sleeplessness can do. We've been through this before."

"No!" Alexa collapsed back into the couch and covered her face with trembling fingers.

Suki squatted down and gently pulled Alexa's hands from her cheeks; the fingers were damp with tears. "Why don't you go take a little nap?" Suki suggested. "We'll talk about it when you get up."

Before Alexa could answer, the phone rang. It was Detective Pendergast. He apologized for leaving before Suki arrived home and then told her he just received a call from Darcy Ward. "Jonah's not only alive," Pendergast said, "he's already scored twenty-two points against Acton-Boxborough. We're leading by fourteen."

Alexa went to bed before dinner and didn't wake until morning. Suki was reluctant to send her to school, but Alexa insisted, claiming she felt fine and had a calculus quiz that was crucial to her final grade. "Mrs. McArthur takes off ten points if you miss a test unless you have a doctor's note," she explained. When Suki offered to call the doctor, Alexa gave her an exasperated look and headed out the door. Suki rearranged two meetings so she could be home when school let out.

She called Mike Dannow while she waited at the kitchen table with a cup of tea. "The timing's just too tight on Kern," she told him. "And it's not really my kind of case."

"Oh?" His voice was skeptical. "I would've thought otherwise. Interesting. Challenging. Not your typical forensic eval."

"Look," she said, "it's personal. Loaded with all kinds of baggage you don't want to know about."

"You're a pro, Suki." Mike was so smooth, buttering her up for the kill. "The best. I'm sure you can see your way through any baggage."

"Can you do me a favor and try and find someone else?"

"And if I can't?" he asked.

"Then we'll talk."

"Great," Mike said. "Let's talk on Monday."

As Suki hung up the phone, the back door slammed. "How are you doing, honey?" she called down the stairs. "Feeling better?"

Alexa came into the kitchen and dropped her backpack on the floor. She headed for the refrigerator. "I told you this morning, Mom. I'm perfectly fine." Annoyance was crisp in her voice.

"You are?" Suki was almost relieved at the return of Alexa's irritating mood swings. She had discussed Alexa's seesawing emotional states with her office mate and friend, Jen Kreischer, who specialized in adolescent psychology—a more frustrating specialization Suki could not imagine—and Jen had assured her it was all extremely normal. "Especially girls and their mothers," Jen said. "As soon as she sees you, she goes into a state of frenzy. She loves you and wants to be with you, yet desperately needs to be free of you, and everything you represent. This sends her into a rage which she, on some level, recognizes is irrational, yet is powerless to control. The fact is," Jen had added in her distinctive professional manner, "they just can't help being assholes—it's their job."

"Today's today, yesterday's gone," Alexa declared with all the philosophical depth of her seventeen years. She spun in a jerky circle, started to lose her balance and righted herself by grabbing the refrigerator door. Her laughter peeled across the room.

"Still . . ." Suki said. It had only been twenty-four hours since Pendergast had found Alexa on River Road, and Suki wasn't sure denial was the best defense mechanism.

"Jonah's an idiot," Alexa continued, her head in

the refrigerator. Last year, Alexa's life had revolved around Jonah, a fresh-faced gangly basketball star; now she couldn't stand the sight of him. Suki knew all too well how hurtful abandonment could be, and she empathized with Alexa's pain. Alexa turned, holding a diet Coke in her hand, her eyes filled with loathing. "I don't even care if he dies," she added. "It'd be the best thing that could happen."

"I wish you wouldn't talk like that," Suki said.

Alexa lifted her chin, but didn't say anything, and Suki could see from her expression that no purpose would be served by arguing the point.

"Then how about eating something?" Suki asked, another point she knew was senseless to discuss. But she was unable to help herself: If Alexa weighed ninety pounds it was a lot, and even at barely five feet, that wasn't nearly enough. She *did* need to eat something.

"I had *something* for lunch, Mother." Alexa closed the refrigerator door with her hip and raised the soda can. "Want to split it?"

When Suki pointed to her teacup, Alexa began digging through her backpack. She waved a report and placed it triumphantly on the table. It was titled, "Before Their Time: Kate Chopin and Edith Wharton, Nineteenth Century Feminists." A large A+ was scrawled beneath the title. "I analyzed *The House of Mirth* and *The Awakening*," Alexa said. "Mrs. Eisner said it's as good as anything she'd expect from someone in college."

Suki gave her daughter a hug. "That's fabulous, honey," she said. "Just fabulous. Princeton will be lucky to get you." There is no pride like parental pride, Suki thought, at once your own and yet better than your own. And no anxiety like parental anxiety.

Alexa laughed happily, a completely different girl from the one who had sobbed in her arms yesterday. "What's that old Jewish proverb Grandpa's always saying about lips and God's ears?" Before Suki could answer, Alexa leaned toward her mother. "I did real well on my calculus quiz, too. Do you think I could take the car to go to the movies with Brendan tonight?" she asked with a fetching smile. "Please? I promise we'll be home early. We haven't had much time to see each other this week. What with studying and all." She raised her A+ paper hopefully.

Suki sighed. This year, Brendan had replaced Jonah as the center of Alexa's universe, and although Suki preferred Jonah, she had to admit that Brendan was one very smart kid. Since Alexa had begun dating him, her grades had improved almost to the level of Brendan's and she was spending much less time moping around the house—although the rapidity of her mood swings had increased to a dizzying pace. "Oh, Alexa," Suki finally said, "I don't think so. Not after what happened yesterday. I think you should just stay home and relax. Go to bed early. Sleep in tomorrow."

"But, Mom," Alexa cajoled, "I told you, I'm fine. You were right, I must've just fallen asleep and had a weird dream. I don't even know why I was so freaked out."

Suki scrutinized her daughter. "You were freaked out because you were exhausted—*are* exhausted," she finally said. "You need a good night's rest."

"I'm not exhausted—I'm wide awake." Alexa

jumped up and stood in front of her mother. "Do I look exhausted?"

Suki had to admit that Alexa didn't; she looked bright and young and healthy, albeit a bit too skinny. "Well . . ."

"Thanks," Alexa said, giving Suki a big hug. "You're the best."

Against a background of human screams and ear-piercing sirens, a swarm of militia men, dressed in full jungle livery and clutching enough semiautomatic weaponry to destroy a small country, barreled through the wide door of the Senate Ways and Means Committee conference room. Within moments, the entire committee was taken hostage.

"You see that, Mom?" Kyle demanded. "Pretty cool, huh?"

"Cool," Suki concurred, although without much enthusiasm. This was Kyle's week to choose a movie, and fourteen-year-old boys are not known for their sophisticated taste in cinema. She'd get him back next Friday night.

Suki and Kyle were indulging in their favorite activity: watching a video and eating popcorn in the family room. The upside of Suki's decision to let Alexa take the car was that she and Kyle were now free to enjoy the movie without Alexa's caustic commentary. The two of them were much more willing to suspend disbelief than Alexa, who needed every plot sequence and every bit of backstory to make what she referred to as "minimal sense." According to Jen, Alexa's demand for perfection in everything from movies to her mother was a "normal teenage response"—an oxymoron if there ever was one—and Suki couldn't help wondering how Brendan, with his ripped jeans and buzz cut, fit into this scheme.

Kyle sat on the beat-up leather chair across from Suki, his eyes riveted to the television screen, his left arm rhythmically pecking into the popcorn bowl with uncanny blind precision. It used to be the four of them on Friday nights, going out for Chinese food and stopping at the video store for Alexa and Kyle's inevitable argument over which movie to rent. That was before Stan decided he had made a mistake, that he just wasn't cut out to be a stockbroker and live the "straight suburban life."

Suki suddenly remembered a bright summer day when Alexa was about six. They were climbing the craggy boulders that lined Rockport harbor, a favorite family outing, when Alexa cried out. Fearing Alexa had hurt herself, Suki hurried over. But the little girl wasn't hurt. "Daddy's gone, Mommy," she cried. "He's gone." Suki pointed to where Stan was standing, atop a tall rock, but Alexa would not be consoled. "No, no!" she had screamed hysterically. "Not today! In the future. In the future!" And, of course, now Stan *was* gone.

Alexa. Her inexplicable firstborn. So like her own mother with her petite prettiness and wild blond curls, so unlike herself. Could a physical resemblance presage other resemblances? Suki wondered. It was a well-established fact that talents and mental illnesses ran in families. Had her mother passed on more to her granddaughter than good looks?

Suki stared, unseeing, at the TV screen. Maybe taking the Kern case would be a way to find the answer. Instead of running from her questions and her guilt, she could face them, challenge them. It wouldn't be the first time a psychologist had taken on a patient because the puzzle he or she presented had personal resonance. Suki decided she would call Mike first thing Monday morning and tell him she had changed her mind. The sound of a car in the driveway interrupted her reverie. Rapid footsteps hurried along the side of the house.

"Alexa's gonna wreck everything," Kyle muttered.

Suki reached for the remote control and stopped the video with a quick punch at the button. Alexa never came home before curfew.

Kyle crossed his arms and glared at the PBS special that had replaced his movie. "Oh great," he muttered. "Aphids."

The back door slammed open, and Alexa appeared in the doorway. Her face was gray and her blouse had worked its way from the waist of her jeans. One of her earrings was missing. She covered her face with her hands. "Oh, Mom," she wailed.

Suki jumped up.

"It . . . it's so horrible," Alexa said as Suki crossed the room toward her.

"What?" Suki's voice shot up an octave. "Did Brendan hurt you?" If that boy had done anything to Alexa, she would tear him in two.

"There . . . there was a shooting," Alexa stammered.

"Are you okay?" Suki's eyes scoured her daughter's face and clothes for blood, while her fingers felt for broken bones. Alexa felt like a hummingbird, trembling within her tiny frame. Suki had to be careful not to press too hard. Alexa might break.

"I'm okay," Alexa whispered.

Satisfied Alexa was indeed unhurt, Suki pushed her to arm's length. "A shooting," she said. "You say there was a shooting?"

"Yes." Alexa twisted the end of her blouse. "A shooting." She was confused, clearly disoriented, most likely in shock.

Wandering . . . disoriented . . . Suki heard Detective Pendergast's voice in her head. She held her breath.

Alexa seemed to come back to herself. "It . . . it was like I said. Like I saw . . ." She broke into hiccuping sobs. "It was awful."

Suki tried to wrap her arms around her, but Alexa stiffened and leaned away. Suki persisted and finally Alexa allowed herself to be led, zombielike, to the couch. She sat huddled into herself, her body shaking violently as she cried. Suki looked at Kyle. He started to say something, but Suki shook her head.

"Devin . . . Devin . . ." Alexa began, then dissolved into tears again. Devin McKinna was Brendan's best friend, and although he too made high honors, rumors were constantly circulating that linked Devin with fast driving, wild parties and just about everything negative with which a teenager could be involved.

"Devin . . ." Suki prompted.

"Devin shot Jonah," Alexa whispered so low Suki could barely catch the words. "It was just like I told the policeman."

Suki closed her eyes. Was this a rerun of yesterday? Was Alexa hallucinating, confusing fact with her own mental fiction? Suki opened her eyes and gently raised Alexa's chin so she could see her face more clearly. She pressed a hand to each cheek to orient Alexa in reality and asked softly, "Alexa, honey, do you know where you are?"

Alexa's eyes had the shell-shocked sheen Suki so often saw in her trauma patients, but they were also wide open and met Suki's straight-on. "Mom," she said slowly, but distinctly, "I know exactly where I am."

Suki took in Alexa's clear gaze, her unequivocal tone, her disheveled clothing, and she was filled with a dread like none she had ever known.

Alexa was telling the truth.

CHAPTER THREE

Kyle jumped up and stood in front of his sister. "Jonah's dead?" he demanded.

Alexa buried her head in her hands. "I don't know," she wailed.

He's not dead, Suki thought, hope rising in her chest. "Do you think he's all right?"

"I saw him fall when we drove away," Alexa mumbled.

In her mind's eye Suki saw Jonah gliding effortlessly across the basketball court. Darcy Ward raised her arms and a wide grin split her face as she watched her son score the winning basket against Lincoln-Sudbury. As Suki's fear for Jonah cut through her fear for Alexa, Alexa's words slowly took on meaning. Suki grabbed Alexa by the shoulders. "What do you mean, 'when *we* drove away'?"

Alexa's head jerked back from the roughness of Suki's grasp, but she didn't say anything.

"Did you leave Jonah by himself in the road?" Suki was appalled. "Were you driving?"

Alexa nodded mutely in answer to both questions.

Suki let go of her and reached for the telephone. "We have to call the police."

After she hung up, Suki turned to Alexa. "They want us to come down to the station," she said, although she knew Alexa understood this from hearing her end of the conversation. "I told them we'd be there in half an hour."

The girl stared at Suki but said nothing. Tears streamed silently down her face.

"I know this is upsetting," Suki said, well aware she was understating the obvious, "but you've got to pull yourself together. You've got to tell me everything that happened tonight. Then you've got to tell the police."

Alexa's face paled from gray to white and she started to sway. Suki grabbed her. "I'm with you, honey," she just about shouted. "I love you. I'll help you. We'll get through this together."

We'll get through this together. Suki heard the echo of Alexa's voice from four years before. It was about a month after Stan left, a month in which fury had overwhelmed any other emotion Suki might have felt. Then, as that first burst of rage burned itself out, Suki found herself sucked into a vortex of sadness. She cried for three days, sitting at the kitchen table surrounded by used tissues and half-drunk cups of tea. On the afternoon of the third day, thirteen-year-old Alexa came home and laid her head on her mother's lap. She wrapped her arms around Suki's waist and said, "It's going to be okay, Mom. I'll help you. We'll get through this together." And they had.

Suki kissed her daughter's forehead. "We'll get through this together," she repeated, although she had no idea what *this* might be.

Suki's words seemed to have an effect. Alexa blinked and raised her chin. "We, we didn't go to the movies," she said softly. "There was a party at Devin's . . ."

Suki stood and began to pace the small room. Alexa knew she neither liked nor trusted Devin McKinna—an antipathy now more than justified—and she also knew Suki would not have allowed her to take her car to a party at Devin's house. Alexa had lied.

Suki turned from Alexa and looked out the window. The irate face reflected in the dark glass scared her. Whirling away from her anger, Suki sat down beside Alexa. "Okay," she said. "Then what happened?"

Alexa had three rings on her left hand. She twisted two of them before speaking. "The party was a bust so we left and went driving around."

"In my car," Suki said before she could stop herself.

Alexa stared at the ring on her thumb as if she had never seen it before. Her remorse-colored bewilderment reminded Suki of Alexa as an eight-year-old, when she had found the scrambled eggs Alexa hadn't wanted to eat for breakfast at the bottom of the basement steps. "I don't know why I threw them down there," Alexa had said through her tears. "It kind of just happened before I could stop it."

Now, as then, Suki wrapped Alexa in her arms and pressed her to her chest. "It's okay, baby," she said. "Just tell me what happened."

"I . . . I was driving," Alexa said haltingly. "Just like I promised."

Suki nodded. That Alexa never let anyone else drive was a stipulation to her taking the car. It was only insured for the two of them. Of course, there had been that one time last year when Jen had seen Jonah at the wheel of Suki's Celica cruising through Witton Center. . . . But after being grounded without a car for a month, Alexa appeared to have learned her lesson.

"Brendan," Alexa was saying. She stopped and swallowed hard. "Brendan was in front with me. Devin and Sam were in back." She stood up and began to pace, outlining the same small square Suki had just walked.

Suki noticed the shoelace of Alexa's right sneaker slapping around her foot and she had a powerful urge to tell her to tie it. She caught her lower lip in her teeth.

"We were on our way to the center," Alexa continued. "You know, to cruise through the parking lot. See who was hanging out . . ."

Suki wanted to question her, to press her: "Was this what you saw yesterday? Was there blood all over the leaves?" Instead she took a deep breath. Alexa needed the space to tell the story her own way.

Alexa stared silently into the dark glass, just as Suki had done, her back to the room. When she turned, her eyes were clearer, her face set and determined. "Jonah was walking along the side of the road and Devin told me to pull over so he could talk to him."

"I didn't know Jonah and Devin were friends." Jonah was a junior at Witton High, as were all the others, but he hung with a very different crowd. Devin and Brendan were faster and flashier, strutting their intellect and daring. Jonah, an athlete, hung out at the boathouse and didn't waste his time on schoolwork. Suki had known all of them since they were in kindergarten together.

"They're not," Alexa said. "Brendan . . . Devin . . ." She looked as if she wanted to say more, but checked herself.

"So you pulled the car over . . ." Suki prompted, suddenly afraid if they didn't get to the police station at the time she'd promised, the police might come get them. Even as she thought this, she knew it was ridiculous. Things didn't work that way in Witton.

Avoiding her mother's eye, Alexa pushed the toe of her sneaker into the carpet. "Before I even got the car to the side of the road, Devin was leaning over the front seat, screaming at Brendan to roll down his window." She glanced quickly at Suki and then averted her eyes again. "You know how the back window on that side of the car's broken? How it doesn't open?"

"Please, Alexa," Suki begged, all too familiar with the many failings of her ancient Toyota. "We need to get going. Just tell me what happened."

"I'm trying," she wailed. "I'm trying."

"Okay," Suki said quickly. "Okay."

Alexa took a deep shuddering breath. "So Brendan rolled down his window and Devin stuck his head out." She covered her face with her hands. "They were all yelling at once. I couldn't see what was going on. They were all blocking my view. I don't know what they were saying. But it got angrier and angrier and I got more and more scared. I kept begging Brendan to let me leave. But he wasn't listening to me. He was yelling at Jonah, too." She dropped her hands and looked at Suki, her wide gray eyes full of terror.

Leaning into the wall for support, Alexa continued. "So I decided to just go. At first I was scared Devin might fall out of the car. Then I didn't care. But I was so nervous when I put the car into gear, I stalled out. Then, when I looked up, I saw there was a gun in Devin's hand. I think I screamed, and I think Brendan told Devin to put the gun down and then told me to get going. Somehow I managed to get the car started, but as we drove away, Brendan and Devin, they, they were both leaning way far out the window. Then someone, Devin . . . then Devin shot Jonah."

"Holy shit," Kyle said.

"Watch your language," Suki corrected instinctively.

"Like it really matters compared to this," he retorted.

Without acknowledging the truth of Kyle's comment, Suki turned back to Alexa.

"Then he fell down. I saw him in the rearview mirror. He looked so, so surprised." Alexa covered her face again. "It was just the way I saw it yesterday. How he was lying. All the blood . . . all over the leaves . . ." She burst into tears and dropped to the couch next to Suki. "I didn't mean it when I said I wished he was dead," she wailed. "I didn't mean it."

"Where are the boys now?" Suki asked, trying to get a grip on the situation. "Where's the gun?"

"They were going to throw it in the river," Alexa mumbled. "I dropped them off at Devin's house. Then I came straight home."

Suki wrapped Alexa in her arms and held her

tight as the enormity of the disaster flooded over her. A drive-by shooting. In Witton. In her car. A hurt child. Maybe a dead one.

And Alexa saw it all happen twenty-four hours before it had occurred.

They needed a lawyer, Suki thought as she drove the narrow river road that led to Witton Center, imagining she could smell gunpowder in the car. She had spent enough time in courtrooms to know that only the stupidest people talked to the police without a lawyer.

"Do you think I need a lawyer?" Alexa asked as Suki took the tight turns faster than she knew she should. The Concord River was high and swift, swollen by winter melt and recent rains. For a moment Suki imagined she saw something small and shiny skimming the tops of the waves, but when she looked again, there was nothing.

"I'm sure a lawyer won't be necessary," Suki said, trying to keep her voice light, her mind focused on things that could be explained, away from things that could not. "You're a good kid who got a bad break. The police will see that right away. You've never been in any kind of trouble before—you got over fourteen hundred on your SATs and you're going to be applying to Princeton early decision, for God's sake." She recognized the foolishness of her words as soon as she spoke them.

"But I left Jonah there all alone." Alexa paused. "What if he's . . . what if I could have saved him?"

Suki reached over and squeezed her knee reassuringly. "Let's take this one thing at a time," she said. One thing at a time, she repeated to herself. Shootings before the paranormal. Things for which there might be answers before things for which there were none.

When they got to the squat brick building that housed Witton's police station, town offices and school department, the place was in an uproar. A vaguely familiar-looking woman was shoving a microphone at Charlie Gasperini, the chief of police. Channel 5's *News at Six* anchor stood under a flood of lights and spoke into a camera with a self-important expression on his face. More uniformed police than Suki thought Witton employed raced in and out of the front door.

She gripped Alexa's arm tightly and they marched up the steps. They found themselves in an anteroom so small that even its two glass walls didn't mitigate the claustrophobia; it smelled like men. A uniformed officer with a sour expression on his face sat behind a half-open window. Rubbing her palms on her jeans, Suki shot Alexa what she hoped was an encouraging smile, then approached him. When she gave him her name, he buzzed them into the station. Before they'd cleared the doorway, a tall, lanky man with a bushy red beard and even redder hair, was upon them. He reached out a large hand to Suki.

"I'm Detective Kenneth Pendergast," he said with a gracious smile. "Sorry I missed you yesterday."

Yesterday. He knew all about yesterday. Suki had forgotten.

Unperturbed by her silence, the detective covered Suki's hand with his for a second, then released it. "You have a son Kyle who plays soccer, right?" he asked. At her nod, he explained, "I sometimes help the coach out at the middle school. I remember Kyle—he's a tough competitor. Good kid."

"And so is Alexa," Suki said, her voice returning. She placed her hand on Alexa's shoulder.

"Thanks so much for coming," he said to Alexa. "I know this couldn't have been easy for you."

Especially after yesterday, Suki couldn't help finishing his sentence in her head, but she said nothing. Neither did Alexa.

He led them into a small room with a beat-up metal desk and a half dozen chairs that had seen better days. Prints of colonial Witton hung on three walls. The fourth was covered with children's crayon drawings of the police station. After motioning them to be seated, he walked behind the desk, but he didn't sit. Instead he leaned toward them and, looking at Alexa, said, "Jonah's dead."

Alexa moaned softly in the back of her throat and began to cry.

Suki gripped the arms of her chair and bit the inside of her mouth, remembering the certainty with which Alexa had spoken those exact same words yesterday. *"Jonah's dead . . . I know he is."*

Suki thought of Jonah as he had been on the field trip to the Science Museum she'd chaperoned last fall, joking and goofing off, charming all the girls. She thought of Darcy Ward, Jonah's mother, who was assistant manager at the Witton Savings Bank and always had a smile and a friendly word to say whether you were opening an account or had bounced a check. What kind of hell was Darcy going through now?

Suki blinked and glanced over at Alexa. She thought of all the wild predictions her mother had made in the grip of her psychosis. How every once in a while, one of them came true. How could Alexa have known? Suki reached into her purse and handed Alexa a wad of tissues. Then she patted her daughter's hand in what she hoped was an encouraging manner and turned her attention back to Pendergast.

He was watching her. When their eyes met, he nodded and sat down behind the desk. Two more men entered the room and took seats on either side of them. One was the chief of police, Charlie Gasperini, who had been a fishing buddy of Stan's—and Alexa's. From the time Alexa was a little girl until she was about twelve, she and Stan and Charlie used to go fishing together on Saturday mornings. Charlie and Suki were both on the Friends of the Library advisory board. Pendergast introduced the other policeman as a state cop from the DA's office who specialized in homicide. Suki didn't catch his name. Had the detective told Charlie Alexa had been here yesterday telling a wild story that had inexplicably come true?

The room was suddenly very warm. And very full. Suki felt smothered by all the maleness around her. They were so big and so many. She and Alexa were so small and so few.

"Alexa wants to tell you what happened," Suki said, deciding it was better to offer the information than to be asked. "She wants to help in any way she can."

Charlie smiled warmly. "Would either of you like something to drink? Coffee? Soda?" When they both shook their heads, he turned to Alexa. "Are you seventeen yet?" he asked.

Alexa tried to speak, but only a high squeak came out of her mouth. She swallowed hard and her voice quivered when she finally answered, "I turned seventeen in January."

"Your mother is, of course, welcome to stay," Charlie explained, "but at seventeen you're considered an adult under the law. If you'd be more comfortable speaking to us alone, that would be fine, too."

Alexa lunged for Suki as Suki lunged for her. "No," she said at the same time Suki did. "No," she repeated more loudly. "I want her to be here."

Kenneth Pendergast took over the interview. "Fine," the detective said. "Why don't you just start from the beginning, Alexa? Take it slowly and tell us exactly what happened tonight." His use of the word "tonight" gave Suki hope that he had not told his colleagues about Alexa's prediction. Yet.

"I'd like to call a lawyer," Suki said, before Alexa could speak.

Alexa looked at her in horror, as if she had somehow let her down, and Pendergast and Charlie Gasperini exchanged a quick glance.

"You're of course welcome to call your attorney, Mrs. Jacobs," Pendergast said. "But at this point, Alexa is just a friendly witness. She came to us of her own volition. As a good citizen."

"*Dr.* Jacobs," Charlie corrected the detective, then leaned forward and touched Suki's knee. "We're very appreciative that you've come, Suki. A serious crime has been committed and we want to catch whoever did this as quickly as possible." He gave Alexa a sad smile. "I'm sure the Wards appreciate it, too."

Alexa threw a scared glance in Suki's direction, then sank more deeply into her chair. She began twisting her rings.

Suki looked at the two Witton policemen and the silent state cop; all were sitting stiffly in their chairs, looking steadily back at her. She wanted to believe them. To believe they perceived Alexa to be a friendly witness. To believe they thought Alexa had done nothing wrong. That she was, in fact, doing the right thing.

"Time is important here, Suki," Charlie said.

She could call Mike Dannow. He was a well-known nice guy, unable to turn down pro bono cases, doggedly working unchargeable hours, ready to help any friend—or any passing acquaintance—in need. But it was almost eleven o'clock on a Friday night, and she had no idea where he lived. Although there probably was an emergency number on the answering machine at his office—

"Please help us get to the bottom of this as quickly as possible, Suki," Charlie pressed. "A child has been murdered."

Alexa whimpered.

Suki turned and took one of Alexa's ice cold hands in both of hers. "Okay, honey," she said. "Why don't you just tell them what you told me?"

The three men visibly relaxed at her words. Pendergast and the state cop each took out a pen and small notebook. Charlie smiled.

As Alexa told her story Suki was too concerned with the policemen's responses to concentrate on her daughter's words. She watched each of their faces in turn. Did Charlie's frown connote disbelief? Did Pendergast's nod mean he thought Alexa was telling the truth? That he believed Jonah's death had nothing to do with what had happened yesterday? Was the state cop incapable of speech? She felt as if they, or she, were underwater, for only snippets of their conversation reached her.

"Had no idea he had a gun . . ."

"You were the driver?" Pendergast's voice was very loud, then it grew soft, and then loud again. ". . . three others?"

". . . two-door Toyota Celica . . ."

". . . he leaned over the front seat . . ."

". . . just one shot . . ."

Suki's eyes scoured the policemen's inscrutable faces, trying to read their thoughts. What did Jonah's death mean for Alexa? she couldn't help wondering, even as her heart ached for the dead boy's mother. Alexa had taken Devin home, knowing he had committed a crime. . . . She had left Jonah hurt and dying, alone on the road. . . . She had seen him motionless, covered with blood, twenty-four hours before he had fallen.

"I think I remember headlights," Alexa was saying. "Maybe a car even passed us."

Suki jerked to attention.

"Did you see who it was?" Pendergast asked. "What kind of car?"

Alexa played with her rings. "Something dark," she said. "Something big. Blue, I think. American."

The detective looked at his boss. "Our anonymous caller—sounds like he might have seen something."

Charlie stood. Without meeting Suki's eye, he thanked Alexa and, mumbling something about an APB, quickly left the room.

Pendergast rubbed his beard with an absent gesture. "Where's the gun?" he asked.

"Devin was going to throw it in the river," Alexa said. "He took it with him."

"People have no idea how sophisticated our forensics are now." Pendergast's voice was nonchalant, as if he were carrying on a casual conversation at a dinner party. "Do you know we can get a good print off a gun that's been underwater for years?" he asked Alexa. When she didn't respond he resumed his detective-questioning-a-witness tone. "Do you know where Devin got the gun?"

Alexa raised her eyes. "His father?" Her answer was a question.

The detective nodded. "How are your grades?"

Startled, Alexa shrugged. "Good," she said.

"Excellent," Suki corrected. "Alexa's planning to apply to almost all the top schools in the fall—early admission to Princeton." She could hear that the pride with which she usually dispensed this information was missing from her voice. She curled her hands into fists.

"I know you've never been in any trouble with the police, Alexa," Pendergast said, "I assume it's the same at school?"

"No trouble," Suki answered for Alexa, her nails cutting into her palms. "Never any trouble at all."

The detective looked at her with a gentle smile. "Please let Alexa answer the question."

"A few detentions," Alexa said, keeping her eyes averted from her mother's. "Skipping class, talking." She shrugged. "You know, the usual stuff."

Suki stared at her in surprise. This was the second time this evening she had caught Alexa in a lie. She's a teenager, Suki reminded herself. Jen said all teenagers lied, that it was an occupational hazard of adolescence. She, herself, had lied to her own mother when she was Alexa's age. More than once.

"And the boys?" Pendergast flipped through his notebook. "Devin McKinna, Brendan Ricker, Sam Cooperstein? Are they all boy scouts?"

A ghost of a smile crossed Alexa's face. "Not exactly boy scouts," she said. "But they've pretty much managed to keep out of real trouble."

"Cooperstein . . . Sam Cooperstein . . ." He frowned. "Not Ned Hunt's new stepson?"

Suki nodded. Ned Hunt was a sergeant on the Witton police force. He and Nancy Cooperstein had had a New Year's Eve wedding.

The detective's frown deepened.

A uniformed officer stuck her head in the door and told the state cop someone from the medical examiner's office was on the phone for him. Still without uttering a word, he stood and left the room.

Pendergast leaned forward in his chair. "I can't thank you enough for coming in," he said to Alexa. "Your information has been a terrific help."

"So we're free to go?" Suki jumped from her chair.

"Of course," he said. "You were always free to go—you came to us, remember?"

"Right." Suki unclenched her fists and stretched out her aching fingers. They had come. They were free to go. He understood Alexa was a good kid who had gotten a bad break. He realized that yesterday had been some kind of bizarre coincidence. It was going to be okay.

Suki turned to Alexa, but Alexa appeared not to have heard the detective. Her eyes were unfocused and her body hung limp in the chair. Suki knelt in front of her. "We're going home, honey," she said softly, pushing Alexa's hair behind her ear. "It's time to go home."

Alexa nodded and stood, but her movements were stiff, uncoordinated.

Suki put her arm across Alexa's shoulders to steady her and led her to the door. "You'll want to talk to us again?" she asked the detective.

"We're going to need an official statement, and I'm sure we'll have more questions after we've talked to the boys. But why don't you just go on home now and try to get some rest?" he said. "There's nothing that can't wait till morning. I'll call you then with an update."

When they got home Suki gave Alexa a Valium and told her she'd stay with her until she fell asleep. "Do you want to talk?" she asked. "About anything? About yesterday?"

"No," Alexa said, curling her body away.

"I think we need to at least discuss what happened—"

"Nothing happened yesterday!" Alexa cried,

whipping herself around to face Suki. "It was like you said, I fell asleep. Had a nightmare."

"But it was a nightmare that came true," Suki said gently. "That's some kind of a nightmare."

"You're the hotshot psychologist." Alexa sat up and glared at her mother. "You figure it out. My subconscious mind guessed what would happen? I was worried because Brendan was mad at Jonah, so I turned it into a dream? I don't know—you tell me."

"Did you know Brendan was mad at Jonah?" Suki asked quickly. If Alexa had been aware the boys were feuding, her psychological reading of the events was quite plausible.

Alexa set her lips in a tight line and nodded.

Suki could see she was holding something back. "So you *did* know Brendan was mad at Jonah?"

Alexa's head fell forward. "Yeah," she whispered, her anger dissipated. "I knew."

"Let's leave it there, then." Suki knew it was far from that simple—and recognized that Alexa wasn't telling the whole story—but she also knew they needed to put the issue to rest for the moment. She reached out to take Alexa in her arms, but Alexa threw herself back down on the bed and turned her face to the wall.

"You don't have to stay," she mumbled.

Suki didn't answer and she didn't leave. She sat on the edge of her bed until Alexa's breathing became deep and even. Then she took two Valiums.

Still, even with the pills, Suki couldn't sleep. She paced the house, thunderstruck by what had happened. By what might yet be to come. She thought of Alexa, of her mother, of Lindsey Kern. She paced some more.

Kenneth Pendergast's call came at seven the following morning. Suki was in the kitchen, waiting, and picked up the phone on the first ring.

"We haven't been able to find either the gun or the witness." Pendergast's voice was weary.

The line hung with heavy silence. "Is there something else?"

His sigh was audible over the phone wires. "A complication has arisen."

Suki said nothing. The blue-and-white kitchen, a room as familiar to her as her own body, suddenly looked foreign, as if it belonged to another woman. A whooshing sound filled her ears, and the doorway to the dining room elongated, as if it were being pulled into the distance on a railroad track. She gripped the edge of the counter for support and closed her eyes against the illusion. "What kind of complication?"

"The boys say they weren't with Alexa."

"That's impossible," she sputtered. "They're lying."

"You may be right, Dr. Jacobs," he acknowledged, "but we need you and Alexa to come back down to the station. At the moment it appears all three have an alibi."

CHAPTER FOUR

"Wish you'd got me involved earlier." Mike Dannow tapped the back of his pen on the legal pad in his lap and gazed at Suki over the rims of his reading glasses. He looked like a teacher disappointed with the performance of his favorite student. "Why didn't you call me Friday night? You knew I'd come."

Suki shrugged. "I guess I was in denial."

Mike nodded, his eyes full of compassion; most likely, he'd seen his fair share of denial. "It's just that some of the things Alexa told the police yesterday aren't good for us." Tap. Tap. Tap. "Not good at all."

Suki watched him silently. Alexa stared at the floor. Suki too wished she'd involved Mike earlier. As she had guessed, there was an emergency number on his office machine; she had reached him at home right after her conversation with Kenneth Pendergast.

Mike had been more than gracious, assuring her that working on the Kern case was not a prerequisite to obtaining his help. Suki hesitated for a moment, wondering if perhaps now wasn't the best time to be taking on a high-pressure job, but she reassured herself that this whole mess was sure to be straightened out quickly and explained to Mike that she had decided to take the case before Jonah was killed;

Mike quickly accepted her offer. They agreed that Suki would go to Watkins on Sunday, and that Mike would meet them at the police station as soon as he got dressed. Mike had ended up driving them home after a two hour conference with Pendergast, Charlie Gasperini and a young assistant DA. They needed the ride because, after both Alexa and Suki had been fingerprinted, the police had impounded Suki's car.

Mike looked like a bantamweight prizefighter, sitting across from Suki in Stan's beat-up leather chair. Shorter than Suki—who was five foot eight—and probably less than one hundred and forty pounds, he tapped his yellow pad as if it were his pre-fight workout, emanating a fierce "don't tread on me" energy. He had already gone ten rounds at the police station, halting Pendergast in midquestion and trading punches with Charlie over the legal definitions of joint enterprise and obstruction of justice. But even the great Michael Dannow had been struck speechless when Kenneth Pendergast explained how Alexa had described the exact location and condition of Jonah's bloody body a day before he was killed.

Now Mike studied Alexa, who leaned stiffly against the family room wall. "This prophecy thing has got me a bit stymied." He shook his head. "We're on murky legal ground here. Very murky."

"Can we just put it aside for the moment?" Suki asked. "Assume it was a coincidence?"

"We're going to have to," he agreed. "Can't begin to factor it into the equation yet. Need to think. Call a few people. Check a few precedents." Mike tapped his pen double-time. "Our big problem at the moment is that Alexa admitted to dropping Devin off at his house. Knowing he was planning on getting rid of the gun. If only she hadn't—"

"She just told the police what happened," Suki interrupted. "A boy was dead, for God's sake. She did the right thing."

But Mike was concentrating on the legal, not the moral, aspects of the situation. "Which makes Alexa an accessory after the fact. . . ." He scribbled on his pad. "Seven-year felony. Charged and convicted . . ."

"But how can they even think about charging Alexa when Devin McKinna claims he wasn't with her?" Suki argued. "How can she be an accessory after the fact if the person who's supposed to have done the fact says he didn't see her all evening?" As furious as Suki was with Devin, it was her anger at Brendan that had gnawed at her all day. This was the boy who was supposed to care about Alexa, the one who had climbed their kitchen roof to shovel the snow before it had a chance to leak through the ceiling, the one who played Ping-Pong with Kyle for hours on end. Brendan had obviously chosen Devin over Alexa. How could he abandon her like that? How could Alexa stand another abandonment?

"Alexa placed herself at the scene and accurately described the crime." Mike was saying. "It's enough." From the expression on Mike's face Suki knew he was thinking that Alexa had done all this both *before* and after the murder had occurred. He didn't verbalize this observation, and neither did she.

"But where would Alexa get a gun?" Suki asked. "She doesn't even know how to shoot. And why would she want to shoot Jonah, anyway?" She leaned closer to Mike, her voice rising with excitement as an idea came to her. "It's not possible for her to have done it! How could she drive and shoot at the same time? The logistics are unworkable." Suki sat back in triumph. "Once they think this through they'll see it makes no sense, no sense at all. Then they'll move on to the boys. Right? I'm right, aren't I?"

"I'm sorry, Suki," Mike put down his pen and stared out the window, "but all that matters a lot less than you might think—and I guess someone could make the argument that if the car was stopped, one *could* actually be both driver and shooter."

"But that's completely nonsensical." Suki was just about spitting.

"The point is that Alexa admitted to the police that she left the scene with the murder weapon." Mike slowly turned his eyes back to Suki. "We'll just have to sit tight and wait until the tests on your car have been completed—maybe something good'll turn up for us there."

"And if it doesn't?"

He shrugged. "My guess is then the police'll push for an arrest."

"But it makes no sense." Suki slumped into the couch. "And the boys are *lying*."

According to the police, after Suki and Alexa left the station, an APB had been put out on Devin, Brendan and Sam. The three had been found in the gym at the rec center helping Devin's father, Ellery McKinna, decorate for a teen dance scheduled for tonight. Ellery claimed they had been with him all evening. Finlay Thompson, the custodian, concurred, as did the secretary, although she admitted to being "in and out." Still, based on Alexa's statement, the boys were questioned separately and their houses searched. All three stories matched. The search for the gun and the possible witness were still ongoing, but so far, neither had been found.

"They're lying," Suki repeated.

"Both good news and bad," Mike said.

Suki looked at him questioningly.

"As you've pointed out," Mike explained, slowing down enough to frame his argument in complete sentences, "we can contend there's no corroboration for Alexa's statement. If the boys insist they weren't with her, I can make the logical argument that she couldn't have dropped them off, and therefore, couldn't have been an accessory after the fact. If this doesn't go over with the police, it'll at least raise a few eyebrows in the press."

The press, Suki thought, glancing toward the front of the house. She had found a band of reporters camped out in the driveway this morning, their vans and cameras and wires littering the street. There had been twice as many by the time they returned from the police station.

Mike had helped them maneuver through the noisy, demanding throng, yelling "no comment" and keeping one arm around Suki and one around Alexa. When they got inside the house, Kyle reported that the phone had been ringing nonstop all morning. He excitedly informed them that the *Boston Globe* and *Boston Herald*, as well as the *New York Times*, had left messages. But when his eyes connected with his sister's, he sobered and offered to station himself in the kitchen to screen calls through the answering machine. Suki had been more than glad to let him.

Suki turned back to Mike. "So you're saying that the one thing we've got going for us is that the lying little bastards are hanging Alexa out to dry?"

"Oh, we've got lots more than that," Mike corrected her. "Presuming no evidence shows up at the crime scene that implicates Alexa beyond what she's already said, we have a highly credible girl, with no history of trouble, who came forward voluntarily to help the police. There's no malice aforethought." Mike began to tick off items on her fingers. "No reckless driving. No alcohol involved." Mike looked up at Alexa, who nodded almost imperceptibly.

"So she won't be arrested," Suki said, beginning to warm toward Mike's take on the situation.

"That's the plan." The lawyer flashed her an encouraging smile, then turned to Alexa. "Anything happen recently that could be construed as motive? Did you two have a fight? Any kind of disagreement?"

"They broke up ages ago," Suki answered for Alexa. "Six or seven months, at least. Before Thanksgiving. Too long for any hard feelings to be left." She tried to smile at Mike. "And anyway, Alexa has a new boy—" Suki stopped herself. Some boyfriend. "Alexa never even saw Jonah out of school anymore."

Mike began tapping again. "That'll probably work as long as the police don't start focusing on the prediction angle. Figure that the only way Alexa could have known Jonah would die was if she was planning to kill him."

Alexa let out a soft moan and slumped further into the wall.

"That's ridiculous," Suki said, although she had had the same thought, wandering the house in the darkness of early morning, doubt creeping with the shadows. "No one could possibly believe Alexa's a murderer. And anyway, didn't you just say we were going to put that aside for the moment?"

"Even so," Mike said, "there're a few problems. You've got to keep in mind that Alexa *did* admit to helping Devin get rid of the gun when she knew a crime had been committed with it."

"But Devin claims he never *had* a gun," Suki argued.

"Then who killed Jonah Ward?"

Kyle came hesitantly down the stairs and into the family room before anyone could answer Mike's question. "Mom?" he asked tentatively. "Can I talk to you for a sec?"

Suki ran her fingers through her hair. "What is it, honey?"

"It's Grandpa," he said. "On the phone."

Icy fingers gripped her stomach. "Does he know?"

Kyle shook his head. "I don't think so. He made a batch of lasagna. He wants us to come over for dinner."

Suki knew this was going to devastate her father, who was in his late seventies. She thought of Seymour's slowing gait and failing hearing, of the sweet, blind way he had always referred to his wife's depressions—Harriet had called them her "melancholies"—as headaches, despite the fact that they often lasted for months. Suki had planned to call him. She knew the news would be easier to take from her than someone at the senior center, but she hadn't had the time between Pendergast's phone call and their second trip to the police station.

She had barely had the time for the calls she had made. The first was to Stan, but it had been fruitless—as was so much with Stan. Her oh-so-reliable ex-husband was off somewhere in the outback of New Zealand and no one seemed to know where. She wanted to call her sister Julie in California, but it was 4:00 A.M. on the West Coast, and Suki knew Julie had more than enough trouble with her own daughter—and no money to fly out anyway. So Suki called Jen and Phyllis, her two closest friends. Phyllis was her buddy from day-care days, friends since their children had met at the Witton Children's Center, but the machine answered the phone and Suki didn't want to leave such news on a recording. Jen had come over and stayed with Suki until they left for the police station. Suki had been planning to call her father next, but her time had run out.

"Mom?" Kyle asked, his voice nervous. "What should I do?"

Suki blinked. "Tell Grandpa tonight's not good. Tell him I'm tied up right now, but I'll call back later this afternoon."

Kyle nodded and shot a glance at Alexa. She was staring at the carpet, and Suki watched a tear fall from her cheek to her sweatshirt. Most likely she was thinking of her grandfather, who she adored, and how this news might affect him.

As Kyle left the room, Suki continued to watch Alexa. Her vibrant daughter had been transformed into a lifeless waif in less than twenty-four hours. Alexa looked as if she'd lost ten pounds and a week's sleep since yesterday, and she had been growing more distant and silent with each passing hour. She was both painfully familiar and frighteningly unknown. Suki again recognized the haunted expression in Alexa's unfocused eyes. Seymour would recognize it, too.

"Ellery McKinna." Mike cleared his throat. "Devin's father. Got the feeling at the station that he was 'big man on campus.' Then someone said he was just the recreation commissioner. What's the deal? Does he hold town office? Have a lot of money?"

Suki was relieved to focus on Mike's question. "In this town, being recreation commissioner is about as big a deal as you can get."

"You're kidding, right?"

Suki looked over at Alexa for corroboration, but Alexa was still staring at her feet. As it had been last night, one of her shoelaces was untied, and Suki had the absurd image of her sleeping in her sneakers. She turned back to Mike. "A big chunk of Witton's budget goes to recreation," she told him. "Sports are huge. And Ellery's very well liked, almost revered."

Mike took down the information. "And I suppose this upstanding citizen is beyond reproach?"

"He's been commissioner forever. Brings in big contributions, federal grants. He's the reason we got the new skating rink—and he plays poker with the chief of police every Friday night."

Mike raised an eyebrow.

"Witton can be a pretty incestuous place," Suki said. "Did I tell you Sam Cooperstein's stepfather is a cop?"

"Not good news," Mike said, as if, after years of being caught in a miserable marriage, Nancy Cooperstein's newfound happiness was his own personal tragedy. "Not good at all."

"It's a small town—" Suki stopped as a new take on the situation occurred to her. "But that's not necessarily a bad thing," she said slowly.

"How so?" Mike asked.

"Everyone knows everyone—or just about. And they know Alexa would never shoot anyone," she explained. "Could never shoot anyone. They also know Devin McKinna's not Mr. Clean—despite what his father might like everyone to believe."

Alexa perked up a bit at Suki's words, although Mike appeared unimpressed. He listened politely but didn't write anything down, just tapped his pen on his pad.

"Even if Charlie Gasperini plays poker with Ellery, he still knows what kind of kid Devin is," Suki said. "And what kind of a kid Alexa is. At least this is Witton—we've got that going for us."

Mike motioned for Alexa to sit next to Suki on the couch. "Let's review this alibi business."

With stiff, wooden motions, Alexa complied. When she sat, Suki took Alexa's hand in hers, looking for solace as much as seeking to give it. Alexa didn't pull away as Suki feared she might, but allowed her fingers to lay motionless in her mother's. They felt like death.

Out of nowhere, a loud noise broke the silence. Alexa screamed and bolted across the room.

"What the hell—" Suki said as she turned to the large window that overlooked the backyard. There, framed within one of the panels of glass, was a man bumping the lens of a video camera against the pane. He was filming them.

"Stop it!" Suki yelled at him as Alexa slid down the wall and slumped into the corner. "Stop it right this minute!"

It was Mike who walked over and calmly pulled the drapes.

After Mike left, Suki called her father. She considered driving to his apartment in Arlington, about half an hour away, but didn't want to leave Alexa. She also didn't know if she could bear to see the pain in his eyes when he heard the news. He'd never fully recovered from her mother's death almost fifteen years ago, and she worried about his ability to handle the stress.

"I need you to sit down," Suki told him as soon as he answered, torn by contradictory emotions demanding she tell him as quickly as possible and ordering her not to tell him at all. "There's something I need to talk to you about." She explained, as quickly and simply as she could, what had happened, but didn't mention Alexa's prediction. There would be time for that later. When she finished, there was total silence. Suki held her breath.

"I'm on my way," Seymour said calmly. Suki tried to dissuade him, but he would have none of it.

"This is when you need your family," he told her in his I'll-brook-no-nonsense tone. "This is what family is all about."

He arrived within the hour prepared to stay for the duration, armed with suitcases and food and videotapes. "One thing you learn when you've lived as long as I have," he said, hugging her to him, "is that nothing is as bad—or as important—as it seems at the moment it's happening."

Suki pressed herself tight within the comfort of her father's arms. She wanted more than anything to believe him.

The air in the interrogation room was close, stale: it smelled of anxiety and the last inmate's heavy hand with perfume. It was the same room in which Suki had met Lindsey last Thursday, and she was anxious to talk to her again. Suki's typical interviewee was a man with a long rap sheet and bad hygiene, in desperate need of a dentist; in comparison, Lindsey Kern was a delight. But Suki knew Lindsey's even, white teeth were not the source of her anticipation.

Suki skimmed the evaluation form she had started to fill out last week. There were many holes to be plugged, and Mike had promised to get her Lindsey's records and the trial transcripts as soon as possible. She stared through the open doorway into the hallway beyond. The cinder blocks were painted a sickly brown. The brown was of the same color family as the pea green that covered the walls of the interrogation room. Puke colors, Kyle would call them. Why couldn't they pick something cheerier?

Suki wondered. Wasn't being in prison punishment enough?

Lindsey appeared in the doorway, gave the officer a little wave, and sat down across from Suki. "Hi," she said as the door clicked shut behind her. "I didn't expect to see you again."

Suki watched the door close and realized that despite this woman's murder conviction, she felt no sense of personal danger. She reminded herself that although this might be accurate, it was not very smart, and realigned her chair so the panic button was within easy reach. "Why not?" she asked.

"I just had a feeling, when you left here last week, that you weren't planning on coming back." Lindsey shrugged. "Sometimes my feelings are right on, and as you can see, sometimes they're not."

Suki glanced from her watch to the partially completed evaluation form in front of her. She needed to get home as soon as possible. She had left Alexa with her father, and she didn't want to give the two of them too much time alone; Seymour's heart might not be able to handle the fact that once again, someone he loved was able to predict disaster. Yet she found Lindsey's statement irresistible. "Could you tell me about some of these 'feelings'?" she asked, although this was not one of the items on her form. "Have you always believed you were clairvoyant?"

Lindsey tilted in her chair, resting the back against the wall and raising the front legs off the floor. She placed her hands behind her neck, looking for all the world like a professor expounding to a group of attentive graduate students. "I would've told you I never thought I was clairvoyant until just recently—and I know this sounds crazy—but once I started noticing, and remembering, I realized I'd had lots of these experiences, all my life. I just didn't recognize them."

Suki ignored the clock ticking in her head. "Can you tell me a couple?"

"Oh," Lindsey said airily, "you know, lots of small stuff, like answering the phone before it rang and being able to tell who was going to win the next election. I remember, once, I told my friend Wendy her father would be in a car crash." The legs of Lindsey's chair cracked to the floor and she laughed sharply. "Wendy was really pissed off when I told her father not to drive into Hartford to pick up her new dress, but boy, was she pissed after the accident. It was as if she believed I had *made* his brakes fail."

A brittle shiver scurried up Suki's spine, the kind the kids used to say meant someone was walking on your grave. Her mother had once predicted a similar event, with a similar outcome: her friend Florence had stopped speaking to her after her husband was killed on a bus trip to the Grand Canyon Harriet had told them not to take. "Did Wendy's father die?" Suki asked.

"Oh, no," Lindsey assured her. "Just a broken wrist. The car was totaled, though. Just like I told Wendy it would be."

"Exactly how did you know? About the car, I mean. Did you see it? Hear it?"

Lindsey was silent for a moment. "I guess it's mostly a visual thing. But also a sort of overwhelming sense of knowledge. More like a memory than anything else."

Suki reminded herself that there were many rational explanations for what Lindsey was describing, including both coincidence and deceit. Many types of psychosis caused hallucinations and delusions, most notably schizophrenia and dissociative disorders; one could even argue that the definition of psychosis was a false observation that was then used as the basis for a false conclusion about the world. Still, Suki didn't see Lindsey as psychotic.

Lindsey's explanation for what she believed was so reasoned; most psychotics didn't think their delusions needed explanation—they seemed to be missing the piece of ego necessary to stand back and observe. Yet, Suki knew psychologists far more experienced than she had been fooled before, and that a complete psych history was in order. "So you think this knowledge, this memory, comes to you through some kind of psychic mechanism?" Suki asked.

"I still have days when I wonder what's happening to me," Lindsey admitted. "How it can be happening to me. But yes, I do think it's psychic."

Suki rubbed the bridge of her nose. Definitely not a psychotic response. But hallucinations could also be caused by alcohol psychosis and drug abuse—the often cited, but rarely seen, LSD flashback, for example—and there were all kinds of toxic drug interactions. Lindsey was about the right age to have dabbled in LSD, and it was a well-known fact that prisons were rampant with drugs; Suki had once had a patient who kept getting arrested so he could return to prison and its easy access to high-quality heroin. Who knew what Lindsey might be taking to keep herself occupied? She might even be high right now. Suki looked into Lindsey's eyes, which were clear and not the least bit dilated.

Lindsey smiled. "I heard Wendy became a drug abuse counselor," she said with a wink.

"Do you ever get these memories any other way beside seeing them?" Suki asked. Visual hallucinations were actually quite unusual; auditory were the most common.

"Sometimes I smell them."

Suki looked down at her form. Olfactory hallucinations were reported even less, and often indicated a diagnosis of temporal lobe epilepsy. But they could also signal a brain tumor. Or Lindsey's symptoms could be metabolic, an abnormality of her limbic system or a pituitary imbalance. Migraines, and even severe sexual abuse, had been known to cause hallucinations.

It occurred to Suki that this evaluation might take longer than she had initially estimated. But instead of probing for Lindsey's medical, psychiatric, or drug history, she asked, "So you didn't think it was weird when it happened? When your predictions came true?"

"Well," Lindsey said, "most of them didn't come true. And the others, I don't know." She shrugged. "I guess I just assumed they were coincidences. There didn't seem to be any other explanation."

Suki put down her pen along with all pretense of filling out the form. "So what was it that made you decide they were more than just coincidence?"

"Isabel."

"But aren't they different things? Predicting the future and believing in ghosts?"

"Yes," Lindsey said, giving Suki an appreciative nod. "And no. It's actually a big controversy in the field—purists say that ghosts have no place in parapsychology, that ghosts and poltergeists are the realm of fairy tale and religion. The conservative wing thinks only actual psychic ability—clairvoyance, telepathy, psychokinesis, things like that—are worthy of scientific study."

Despite Lindsey's oxymoronic pairing of conservative and parapsychologist, Suki was fascinated. "But you don't agree?"

"I think it's all part of a bigger issue. Like I told you last week, this is about opening up your mind so you can see more, understand more. It's not about closing it to only what's convenient to study." Lindsey grabbed Suki's pen from the table. "I'll show you what I mean." She turned the evaluation form over and made a dot on the back. "My friend Babs does this with an apple, but this'll have to do." She licked the top of the pen and pressed it to the paper, leaving a small damp circle in the corner. Then she put the pen down. "What do this dot, this spot of spit, and this pen, all have in common?"

"They're all ways for you to avoid answering my questions?"

"They are that," Lindsey acknowledged. "But they're also something more—and something less." When Suki didn't answer, Lindsey smiled broadly. "They're all the pen."

Suki raised an eyebrow. "How do you mean?"

"A pen in one dimension is a dot, in two dimensions it's a circle, and in three dimensions, it's a pen!" Lindsey handed it back to Suki. "When you limit what you let yourself see," she explained, "you limit what you let yourself understand."

Suki turned the pen between her fingers, watching it as if it held all the answers within its shiny black surface. Life was already so chaotic, did she really need to see any more? She flipped the evaluation form face-up. "Were there many drugs around when you were in college?" she asked.

CHAPTER FIVE

On Monday, they closed the schools for Jonah Ward's funeral.

An hour before the service was scheduled to begin, Alexa still couldn't decide what to do. "I need to go," she said to Suki over a glass of orange juice she wasn't drinking. "Everyone'll be there."

"Then we'll go together." Suki nibbled at her dry toast. "As a family. Grandpa and Kyle will come, too."

"But what if Brendan's there? Or Devin? What will I say to them?"

Suki reached to take her daughter's hand, but Alexa yanked it away and stared at Suki as if it were her fault this was happening. Suki tried to think of how she would advise a patient to handle a similar situation, but as was so often true when she tried to apply her training to her personal life, she drew a blank. "No one will blame you for staying home," she finally said.

"And Mrs. Ward," Alexa said as if Suki hadn't spoken. "What if I have to talk to Mrs. Ward?"

"You won't have to talk to anyone," Suki tried again. "We'll go late and leave early."

Without a word, Alexa stood and left the room.

Suki called Phyllis, hoping they could go to the funeral together, but Phyllis had a meeting downtown—she was a deputy commissioner for the department of motor vehicles and all the state's deputies met to one-up each other on the last Monday of every month. Phyllis offered to skip the meeting, but Phyllis was in line for commissioner and Suki would have no part of it. When she called Jen, Jen was already with a patient. Suki wished she had the money to fly Julie in from California. There were others she could call, but she didn't. Instead, she dressed and went in to see what Alexa had decided. Alexa was seated on her bed in a dirty T-shirt. Suki went to the funeral alone.

Driving her father's car to the church, she couldn't stop thinking of Darcy Ward, and allowed herself the tears she knew she could not cry at the funeral. Suki understood her position to be awkward, that she couldn't squeeze Darcy's hand and dab at her eyes as she might have done if Alexa had stayed home Friday night. But she wanted Darcy to know that she, too, was grieving for her. That she understood there was no pain greater than Darcy's.

Suki slipped into the church just as the organ began to play. The small chapel was packed, and as she settled into the dimness of a back pew she felt, rather than saw, a wave of restless motion. She looked up to see a swell of faces twisting toward her. She nodded to Andrea and Marcy from her book group, to Louise and Arthur from the Friends of the Library, to Mr. Quinn, who managed the Stop and Shop. She tried to smile at Pat Hosansky, who headed up the education and technology commission she'd been a member of for years, but it felt like a grimace. Pat and Andrea smiled sadly at her and Louise fluttered her fingers in a small wave, then they turned quickly to the front of the church. The others did the same.

Suki's eyes followed theirs to the casket. It stood before the altar, raised above the mourners in the first row, open. Jonah's shoulders rested against creamy satin and even from where she sat, she could see that his face was waxy and overly made-up. In direct antithesis to the cliché, he neither looked asleep nor at peace. He looked dead.

Suki closed her eyes against the sight, against the reality it proclaimed. She knew Jonah was dead. She would have thought no single fact could be clearer to her. But she was acutely aware that up to this moment, she had only understood his death on an abstract level. The horror of it, the truth of it, now lay in that copper box.

She searched the crowd for Ellery McKinna, knowing that he, too, would be compelled to come, wondering what he must be feeling as he tried to reconcile his lies with the reality of Jonah's lifeless body, the false defense of his son with Darcy's grief. Ellery was prominently seated on an aisle close to the front of the church. His wife Carol was beside him, Devin beside her. She didn't see Brendan or Sam.

Ellery had composed his face in an appropriate expression of solemnity and sadness, and he held his head high, making eye contact and nodding with the agility of a seasoned politician. Devin stared straight ahead, but he too kept his chin forward. Suki thought for a moment she might be sick and turned her attention to the priest.

Father Francis was not a young man, and his gravelly voice cracked as he spoke of Jonah. About what a terrific athlete he had been. A fine boy. A promising future. When he told of a prank Jonah had pulled as an altar boy with his friends Nicholas and Maxwell, he reached his arms out to where Nick and Max sat with their families, as if offering his story to them as consolation. "Jonah possessed a happy soul," he said. "Jubilant and rich with life. That we were allowed to share in his few short years on this earth was a gift from God." Amidst the sniffles, a full sob broke out from a woman Suki didn't recognize.

Suki bowed her head and did not look up again until Warren Blanchard, Jonah's uncle, had replaced Father Francis at the pulpit. Although he was close to her age, Warren was a graduate student at MIT and lived with his sister and her family. He had been the high school gym teacher for years, but quit suddenly, deciding he needed a change. He still continued as the boys' soccer coach, and, as Kyle had been playing since first grade, Suki knew him fairly well.

Warren ran his finger around the edge of his collar and played with the cuff of his jacket. She was more accustomed to seeing him in a sweat suit on the playing field, or in shorts and a T-shirt when their paths crossed on their early morning jogs, and was surprised at how different he looked: somehow younger, more handsome, and heartbreakingly vulnerable. As he continued to pull at his clothes, it was obvious that he, too, was unaccustomed to himself in a suit.

Warren Blanchard was a real iconoclast, a sixties throwback with his longish hair, liberal notions and acute sense of morality. He had angered many football parents at the high school when he reallocated football program money into the soccer budget, declaring it a far less violent, and therefore more worthy, sport. Then, to keep things fair, he angered the soccer parents by refusing to accept the Middlesex Tournament trophy, claiming the final game had been won on a bad call against the opposing team. But no one was angry with Warren Blanchard today.

He cleared his throat. "I, ah, I don't think I'm going to be able to last up here for too long," Warren began, his deep voice shaking with emotion. "I . . . I know I can't talk about Jonah, or what this means to me, or to my sister, or to our . . ." His voice trailed off into a whisper as he struggled to regain his composure. He had lost his wife to breast cancer just a few years ago. And now this. Warren raised his hands in a gesture of helplessness. "I just wanted to thank you all for caring," he said, then stumbled back to his seat.

Suki closed her eyes against Warren's pain, against Darcy's, and against her own, but they flew open when she recognized the voice of Ellery McKinna. The man had no shame. He stood at the pulpit, his gold watch chain smiling tightly across his taut stomach, the flat planes of his face accentuated by the light from the side window. She could almost feel the crowd responding to him: their guy, Mr. Rec Center, Mr. Skating Rink. Speaking from the heart. For all of them.

McKinna did not twitch or pull at his clothes as Warren had. He placed his hand under his jacket, over his heart, in an Napoleonic gesture, and began to speak. After a short opening of appropriate platitudes, he turned to the issues of violence and divisiveness and the crumbling of family and community ties. Of how everyone had failed Jonah and God and each other. Of how Witton needed to take this opportunity to grow closer, to strengthen its bonds.

"Now is not the time for anger and vengeance and violence," McKinna said. "We have had more than enough of that. Now is the time to turn to each other with love. To offer support and comfort to everyone who's suffering. Now is the time to heal." He looked out over the church, and his eyes met Suki's. "For everyone—everyone—needs to be healed."

The heat roared up Suki's cheeks as an undulating rumble swept through the church. No one turned, and no one looked at her, but Suki felt the power of their effort. Father Francis stood and quickly thanked Ellery, who stepped down. The rest of the service passed by in a blur. There were more prayers and talk of children and lambs, followed by the sprinkling of water. A few other people spoke, but Suki couldn't say who. As the pallbearers wheeled Jonah's casket down the aisle, Suki sat motionless, staring down at her hands.

When she finally stood, she was caught in the press of mourners streaming from the church. She nodded politely to those she could not avoid, but kept her eyes downcast and followed the shoes ahead of her toward the door. Someone grasped her hand and she looked up in surprise. Warren Blanchard stood before her, apparently as startled at the sight of her as she was at him. Somehow she had gotten into a makeshift receiving line. Darcy was standing next to Warren, but fortunately her back was to Suki. Suki wondered what she could say to them: their pain was so great, her part in it so uncertain.

"Suki," Warren said, his eyes shifting between her face and some place beyond her left shoulder. "Suki."

"Sorry," she whispered, pulling her hand from his. "I'm so sorry." She turned quickly and pushed back into the crowd, trying to lose herself amidst the pressing bodies. The going wasn't easy as the crowd strained toward Darcy and Warren while she, in opposition, strained toward the door.

Just as she broke from the throng and into the sunlight, Suki felt a sharp tap on her shoulder. She jumped, but relaxed when she recognized, from the air of professional detachment surrounding him, that the man who had intercepted her was associated with the funeral parlor.

"The family has requested that guests not go to the cemetery, ma'am," he said in a solemn voice. "The interment is to be private. Family only."

Suki nodded her understanding and headed down the stairs. As she made her way toward the block where she had parked, she was surprised by the number of cars queuing up in the church lot with their headlamps lit. She hadn't known the Ward family was so large.

When Suki got home from the funeral she was wound tight, restless with a nervous energy she couldn't shed. Alexa didn't respond to her knock, so she opened the door a crack and peered in. Alexa was just as Suki had left her, seated on her bed, staring at a poster of the CD cover of Bush's *Razor Blade Suitcase* on the wall across from her.

Alexa's room was in its usual state of complete disarray—yet another example of what Jen called "hormonally induced obnoxiousness," something Jen counseled Suki to ignore—overflowing with Alexa's many collections: stuffed animals, incense, nail polish, candles, baseball hats, CDs. Alexa's mismatched accumulations always struck Suki as an interesting comment on her many personas: child, teenager, adult, female, male. Piles of magazines rose from the floor and the mirror was plastered with so many photos and postcards that it was impossible to see a reflected image. The desk and bureau were no better. Maybe worse.

Without moving her head, Alexa slowly turned her eyes toward her mother. It took a moment for Suki's presence to register. "Not now, Mom." Her voice was thick, as if she had just awoken. "Not now," she repeated and returned her gaze to *Razor Blade Suitcase*.

"*Not now, Suzanne,*" Suki's mother used to say when Suki came upon her in the darkened living room. "*Not now.*" Suki knew from experience that there was no intruding on this lethargy. She closed the door and prowled the house, her restlessness increasing as her mind jumped from one worry to the next. Kyle and her father cooked in the kitchen. They didn't ask how the funeral had gone, nor how she was doing, and for this she was tremendously grateful.

Suki stood over the desk in her study, a tiny space tucked off the side of the family room; it was half-buried, two casement windows at dirt level bringing in thin rectangles of light. The Kern file jutted from her open briefcase, and she longed to escape into it, into an all-absorbing quest for a solution to an academic puzzle—even if this case promised to be more than just academic.

A general text on posttraumatic stress disorder lay on her desk, and she turned to the section on sexual abuse. As she had thought, it was not uncommon for extremely severe childhood abuse to cause dissociation and hallucinations in adulthood—she had once had a patient whose violation had been so horrific a PET scan indicated that the abuse had actually altered her brain structure. It was possible Lindsey had been mistreated as a child. Although Suki had only met the woman twice, and hadn't received the medical and psychiatric history from Mike yet, she was pretty confident Lindsey did not fit the profile: the dissociative amnesia, the numbing, the depersonalization, the recurrent images and flashback episodes.

Suki put the book down and looked at the collage of photos she'd tacked to a few squares of pegboard: Alexa and Kyle at ages six and three, riding a pony at her cousin Tracy's wedding; her high school clique at their twenty-fifth reunion; Stan and two buddies dressed as the three amigos on a trip to Mexico they'd made decades ago; Alexa and Jonah at the tenth grade Star Ball. In the bottom corner of the board was a picture of her mother and Alexa; even though Alexa was only two, the same smile shone out of both faces. Suki turned and walked from the study.

After another hour of aimless wandering, her jittery energy was finally exhausted, and Suki found herself standing at the living room window, staring out at nothing. That's when the cars began driving by. She moved behind the pulled bundle of drape, so that she could see but not be seen, and watched the procession make its way slowly down Lawler Road. Suki knew the funeral had to be over, that Jonah's body must have been buried for at least an hour now, and yet a string of cars, their headlamps lit, was streaming past her house.

Her father came up behind her and touched her arm. "The lentil soup's ready," he said as if nothing out of the ordinary was occurring, as if she had been eating three hearty meals a day instead of choking down a fraction of what he placed before her. "Come. Have a bowl with us."

She shook her head without turning around, her eyes glued to the grim parade in the road.

He gave her shoulders a squeeze. "I'll keep the soup warm for when you change your mind."

Suki listened to his steps return to the kitchen. Since Saturday, he had made noodle pudding, manicotti, vegetable stew and now lentil soup. Comfort foods.

As she watched the cars, Suki wondered if her father could possibly be right about troubles passing, about everything being enlarged under the electron microscope of the present; he had always been so wise about so many things. Just as she was allowing herself to warm to the notion, as she was thinking she might be able to swallow a bit of lentil soup, she caught her breath. Something was happening outside the window. Something more than a few cars cruising by.

A pattern was emerging. That green Camry had been by before, as had the white station wagon and the mud-covered van. Somewhere beyond her vision, the cars were turning around. Circling back.

How long she stood there Suki could not say, but it felt both like forever and like only the quickest flash of a second before she understood what was unfolding before her. More cars came. The circle slowed to a sluggish creep, but it kept moving. And growing. Although no one honked or threw tomatoes, and no one yelled obscenities, there was a tangible sense of the ominous in the relentless circling. Suki looked into the cars, saw the faces of their occupants. She recognized many. Jan and Carl Richardson. Becky Alley. Carol and Ellery McKinna.

Suki jumped when she felt her father's arms around her, then turned into the familiar comfort of his chest. He didn't say anything, just held her and brushed her hair off her forehead with the same gesture he'd been using since she was a little girl. Finally, she pulled away. "Alexa saw Jonah's body laying in the woods," she said.

He blinked and looked at her through his thick glasses. "Yes," he said slowly. "I assumed that she had."

"No," Suki said. "You don't understand. She saw him *before* it happened. Like Mom."

He blinked again. "What are you saying?"

"I don't know what I'm saying, I'm just telling you what happened."

"Do you think Alexa can see into the future? That your mother could?" He took her hand and led her to the couch. "Sit."

Suki sat. "Remember the time Mom wouldn't let us get on that plane in Chicago?" she asked.

There was no need for her father to answer what was so clearly a rhetorical question, and he didn't. They both knew all too well that the plane had crashed, killing all 263 people aboard. It should have been 267. Instead, he asked questions of his own: "What about when she wouldn't let us fly and nothing happened? When she refused to allow Julie to take the train to Philadelphia—or let you baby-sit for the Lubins, those perfectly nice people who lived down the street?"

"But this was just the way Alexa said it would be. The same spot. Jonah. Blood on the leaves . . ."

He touched her chin and turned her face toward him. "We'll probably never know exactly what happened the other night, Suzanne—or why. Maybe Alexa had a clue the boys were itching for a fight, maybe it was some bizarre coincidence. Maybe there are just some things we're not supposed to understand."

"I have a patient who believes she's clairvoyant. Sees into the future, predicts things. She's quite convincing."

"Suki, don't you see what you're saying?" Seymour asked. "You're talking about a patient—a mental patient. Is she in the hospital?"

"A prison."

"Enough said."

"But what if she's right, Dad? What if there *is* another sense that only some people have? What if Lindsey suffers from nothing worse than being misunderstood? If Mom wasn't sick at all?"

"As Kyle would say: 'Been there, done that.'" Seymour smiled at her gently. "I gave it a try for a while. I went with your mother to mediums and explored my previous lives. I talked to people who claimed they'd lived with ghosts, and I've had my palm and Tarot cards read more times than I can count." He shook his head. "One woman told me I'd make a killing on the stock market in 1988 and another said your mother and I were going to celebrate our sixtieth wedding anniversary on the left bank of the Seine."

"But—"

"Do you really think I could've been Julius Caesar?" The sadness burrowed deep within the creases of his face. "I wanted to be convinced, I tried, I really did. But there's nothing to it, darling, I promise you. It's a lot of charlatans taking advantage of people who want, who need, to believe."

Suki swallowed around the lump in her throat. "I worry about what I did to Mom."

"You did the right thing for your mother," he assured her. "Don't ever think for a second that you didn't. You can't blame yourself for what happened." His eyes sparkled with unshed tears. "You did what you could, given the reality of the situation."

Suki kissed her father's papery cheek and snuggled into his arms, but she kept hearing Lindsey Kern's voice: *"Reality is at the edges of your awareness. You just need to let yourself turn sideways a bit to see it."*

CHAPTER SIX

The morning after Jonah's funeral, Suki got up at 5:00 A.M. to walk her four miles before getting ready for work. She did her stretches in the sharp circle of light her reading lamp carved in the predawn darkness, strapped on her waist pack and slipped out into the silent street as if all were as it always had been.

As the sun rose behind her, she quickly left the small contemporaries and modest ranches of her neighborhood for the more expansive houses and acreage that dominated Witton. She turned onto Country Club Lane and picked up speed, hiking past huge colonials and turreted Victorians that would soon disappear behind the foliage hiding within the fuzzy red buds of the trees. The forsythias were shooting fingers of yellow into the brightening sky, and the lawns were beginning to green. After a long hiatus, life was returning to the patient earth—just as Suki knew her own life, and the life of her family, would return to them when the present darkness passed.

Yet, as she took the wide turn at Roaring Brook, she was haunted by the image of Alexa, barely able to speak, not even calling her best friend Kendra, staring at the wall across from her bed where she sat cross-legged, hour after hour, in an oversize T-shirt. Suki pushed the image from her mind. Although Alexa had indeed made a drastic mistake, which had had profound consequences, she hadn't hurt anyone. Devin was the guilty party. Devin had killed Jonah, not Alexa. And although he and Brendan and Sam and that self-serving Ellery McKinna were still sticking to their story, Suki knew the lie would be found out, for their fabrication made no more sense today that it had on Friday. Perhaps even less.

"The truth has a way of climbing out of the lies, Suki," Kenneth Pendergast had told her over the phone after the funeral. "You've just got to give it the time it needs."

Suki forced air deep into her lungs as she marched around the corner. Murder was not an easy crime to get away with in these days of high-tech forensics. The truth would come out when the car was dusted for fingerprints, when the tread marks and entry wounds and powder burns were analyzed. The truth would come out. She timed her steps to her new mantra. The truth would come out. She lengthened her stride and punched her arms higher in front of her. The truth would come out. But what about Alexa's prediction? she wondered. Would the truth behind that come out, too? And, if it did, what would it be?

Suki was so lost in thought that she almost punched the runner coming toward her. It was Warren Blanchard, Jonah's uncle. They both stopped. Kyle had heard from a friend that the Wards were furious that Alexa hadn't been arrested, but Suki couldn't believe Darcy and Warren wanted

Alexa behind bars. She scoured his eyes to see what they held. All she could see was desolation.

"Suki," he said, his voice scratchy. He cleared his throat and tried again, but no words came out. He threw up his hands in frustration. "It's awful for everyone," he finally croaked. "We know we've got no corner on pain."

"But you, you and Darcy . . ." Suki stuttered. "She's the one who's got it the worst—the worst pain there is."

"Perhaps." His smile was sad. "But in this kind of contest, the winners and the losers all lose."

Suki tried to return his smile, but couldn't.

"People need someone to blame when something like this happens—to try and make some sense of it all." Warren ran his fingers through his damp hair. "The town council. The DA's office. The media. Maybe even Darcy. But the truth is, it was nobody's fault—and it was everybody's fault." He awkwardly patted her shoulder and took off at a slow jog.

Suki watched him disappear around the corner of Shirley and Si Poverman's house. Kenneth Pendergast had mentioned something about both the town council and the DA's office yesterday, but she had been too distracted to hear what he said. Suki saw the cars circling past her house after the funeral. They needed someone to blame. And Ellery McKinna was going to make sure that someone was Alexa.

Suki started to walk. She could not live within this negativity and fear. She would not. Ellery would fail, and the boys would be forced to admit their crime. Then the DA and the town council and the media would turn their misplaced glare from Alexa, and this time in her family's life would fade into a sad, sepia-toned memory, would become "that awful spring when Jonah Ward died" and nothing more. Perhaps it was already beginning. Kenneth had said the autopsy results and some of the crime scene evidence would be available this afternoon. By now the media might even have found a new story to beat to a pulp.

Suki headed toward the Stone Store—actually the Concord Hill Market, but nobody ever called it anything but the Stone Store, after the huge field stones that formed its walls, the same stones the colonial farmers had cleared from their land and used to mark the boundaries of their acreage. It was a tiny throwback of a store, smelling of sawdust, floored in boards of wide pine, overseen by an elderly proprietor named Jake with eyeglasses so smudged she wondered how he could read the ancient cash register. They needed milk and Jake always opened promptly at 6:00 A.M.

When Suki rounded the corner she saw that the interior of the store was still dark. Stopping to check her watch, she noticed a bundle of newspapers sitting next to the front step.

Fat black letters filled the entire space above the fold on the front page of the *Boston Herald*. MURDER AND GANG VIOLENCE IN YOUR HOME TOWN, it read. But it was the more subdued headline of the *Globe* that made Suki's heart sink. AGGRESSIVE SEARCH ONGOING FOR WITTON MURDERER.

● ● ●

When Suki got home, her father was waiting for her in the kitchen. He poured her a cup of coffee and motioned for her to sit at the table. "Alexa was up all night playing video games in the basement," he said as soon as she was seated.

Suki stared into her coffee mug. Her father never slept much, so she wasn't surprised he knew of Alexa's nocturnal activities. Although she was well aware that a lot of what was written in newspapers was pure fabrication, the words of the *Globe* headline were seared into her brain: Witton Murderer.

"Do you want to talk about it?" her father asked in his wise, lightly probing, way.

Suki nodded but didn't meet his eye.

Seymour reached over and touched her hand. "What do you think, Suke? What do you want to do?"

"Go back to last week. Go back to our old lives."

He chuckled softly, sadly. "If only that were possible."

"Then we'll pretend," Suki said with as much conviction as she could muster. "I'll go to work. The kids'll go to school, and you'll go home. We'll act normal and that way we'll *be* normal. Except . . ." Her voice trailed off as she stared out the large plate-glass window.

"Except?"

"Except how can Alexa go back to school?" Suki asked the massive oak tree that dominated the backyard. "How can I let her walk into that place? That's where those boys are. And all the lies. The whispering, the finger-pointing." Once again, the *Globe* headline rose before her eyes. "Maybe I could hire a tutor. She can finish out the year at home. Maybe go to a private school in the fall?"

Her father said nothing.

"I can't let her go back," Suki said. "She'll be too scared."

"Is it you or Alexa who's scared?"

Suki sipped her coffee and thought over the question. It was always her father who, in his own mild fashion, urged her to see things as they were. Suki stood and leaned over to kiss his forehead. "Guess I should go find out."

Seymour patted her arm as she passed. "Give her some elbow room."

Suki was surprised to find Alexa both awake and wearing a different T-shirt than the one she had had on the previous night. Although still seated on her bed, without pants, her hair matted on the right side of her head, her feet were planted on the floor and she seemed more like her old self. But she was startled when Suki entered the room, as if she hadn't heard the knock or called for her to come in.

"How's it going?" Suki asked from the doorway.

"You look tired, Mom," Alexa answered.

Suki dropped to the bed next to her daughter. "I guess I am."

Alexa twirled the ring on her thumb. "Please don't worry about me so much."

"I think we need to talk."

"About how long I plan to spend in my bedroom?"

"That and figure out what you want to do next."

Alexa pushed herself up against the wall and

watched the circles she was making in the air with her right foot. "You haven't heard from Daddy yet?"

Suki shook her head. "I'm sure he'll be in touch soon," she said. "But for right now we're going to have to figure this out for ourselves." As if, she wanted to add, they didn't always have to solve their problems themselves.

"Kendra and I already figured it out," Alexa said, her eyes bright. "We decided I should go to school today. To show everyone I didn't do it. That Brendan and Devin are lying ass—, are lying. Kendra's going to get a bunch of kids to hang out with us all day."

Suki was stunned by the change in Alexa, yet part of her knew she shouldn't be: despite all that had happened, Alexa was still Alexa. "That's not a bad idea, honey. But, you know, it could be kind of difficult."

"I can handle it." Alexa raised her chin and looked at Suki defiantly.

"It's not just about Jonah," Suki said, the bravado in Alexa's eyes reminding her so much of her own mother that she winced. "It's about all the other things, too. I was thinking it might be a good idea to go see a therapist—to get some help finding out what's happening here."

"Just because I look like Grandma, that doesn't mean I'm going to do what she did," Alexa said.

Suki flinched. Alexa's words brought it all back. For despite what her father had said—and what she knew on an intellectual level to be true—Suki would always feel partially responsible, always feel at fault. It was she, after all, who had arranged for her mother to be committed to Outland State. She, the new

Ph.D., who was so sure Harriet's symptoms—the delirium, the wanderings, the claims of being able to see into the future—were those of psychotic depression. She who had had to identify her mother's body when, exactly one month to the day of her commitment, Harriet had thrown herself down an elevator shaft.

"I know all about the airplane that crashed, too," Alexa said.

"What?" Although Suki had been fairly open with Alexa about her grandmother's illness, she had tried to protect her from some of the more inexplicable details.

"Daddy told me."

Suki nodded. Good going, Stan.

"Maybe Grandma wasn't as crazy as you thought she was," Alexa said, the familiar baiting tone to her voice. "And maybe I'm not either."

Suki stood up and began to pace Alexa's small room. Don't let her get to you, she reminded herself for the hundredth time since Alexa had hit her teenage years. Don't let her do it. "Just because I want you to see a therapist doesn't mean I think you're crazy," she said calmly. "But your grandmother *was* sick, she had been for many years—I know, I was there."

"You've been wrong before." Alexa began to draw air circles with her left foot.

"Not about this, honey. Not about this," Suki said, the conviction in her voice surprising her; the discussion with her father had obviously had an impact. "And anyway, we're talking about you, not Grandma, and what you're going to do today." She came and stood before Alexa. "If you feel like you want to go to school, well then, why don't you go? Go take a shower and get dressed, and I'll make another pot of coffee. How does that sound?"

"Why is it always your agenda?" Alexa mumbled.

The telephone rang and Suki was glad for a reason to break off the argument she knew could have no winner. She went into her bedroom to get the phone.

It was Kenneth Pendergast. "Sorry to call so early," he apologized. "But I've got a couple of pieces of news I thought you'd want to hear—one's good and the other not so good."

Suki sat down hard on the bed.

"The good news is that they're finished with your car," Kenneth said before Suki could tell him which news she wanted to hear first. "If you can give me a ride back to the station, I can run it over for you now. That'll save you having to get someone to drive you down here."

Suki was surprised and relieved that they were returning the car so quickly; she couldn't afford the rental she thought she was going to need when her father went home. "That would be great," she said. "Really thoughtful." She took a deep breath. "What did they find?"

"Don't know," he said quickly. "The report should be out this afternoon."

Suki had the feeling he knew all too well, but she didn't press him. "There was something else?"

"Yesterday we got statements from two girls who claim they heard Alexa say she wanted to kill Jonah."

"Two girls . . ." Suki repeated. "What girls?"

"It doesn't matter much who they are," Kenneth said. "They know Alexa from school and claim that a couple of weeks ago, in the girls' room, Alexa was fuming mad. Talking about wishing Jonah was dead."

"But that doesn't mean anything," Suki argued. "Alexa says the same thing about me. She says it about her brother all the time."

"It's the context that makes it tough, Suki."

"But it's just a figure of speech. Kids are always—"

"The DA's hot to make a move. He's getting pressure from above. And from the media."

"Why don't you guys go after Ellery and the boys? Try to get them to change their story? Has anyone talked to Finlay again, the custodian? Has anyone asked Ellery where his gun is?"

Kenneth was silent for a long moment. "People here aren't putting a lot of effort into those avenues, Suki," he said carefully.

"What are you trying to say?"

"I'm not trying to say anything. I'm just telling you that with these girls' statements, the boys' alibi and the prediction thing . . . Well, it's just starting to look bad."

"The 'prediction thing,' as you call it, was just a coincidence," Suki said. "Or maybe a nightmare because Alexa knew Devin was out to get Jonah. Whatever. They can't make anything out of this. It's too far-fetched. They just can't."

"I'm real sorry, Suki," Kenneth replied. "But unless you can come up with some other explanation for how Alexa knew Jonah was going to be killed—as well as exactly how and where—I think we're looking at an arrest here. Maybe soon."

CHAPTER SEVEN

Suki shared an office with three other psychologists in a rambling farmhouse on the edge of Hayden Park. When Clara Hayden, the last of *the* Haydens, died in 1985, she left the family farm to the town of Witton, but stipulated that the land must remain undeveloped. The wording of her will was very specific, indicating which pond could be used for ice skating, how many tennis courts could be built in the east pasture, and that the park be named for her grandfather. Her lawyer had not been quite as clear about the buildings, and the town discovered a loophole that allowed it to convert the century-old wood-frame house into a dozen office suites, providing Witton with a continuous stream of badly needed revenue.

It was perfect for Suki and her partners: private, isolated and very quiet. It was also beautiful, giving both therapist and patient a sense of connection with the outdoors, with the land, with the past. Suki wished she had more access to the farmhouse, so she could work here more often, but as the four doctors rotated through the two offices in the suite, she couldn't use her office whenever she pleased. Like today. On her way out to Watkins, Suki had stopped at the farmhouse to get the Kern files Mike had messengered over, but as Jen was with a patient, Suki had to sit at the receptionist's desk—a desk that was always available, as they had no receptionist, just an answering machine.

Suki skimmed the results of Lindsey's EEG and MRI, and although both tests were inconclusive, her heart quickened. *"Slight abnormal slowing in nonfocal area of brain." "Increased tissue density in right temporal lobe." "Mild atrophy in drainage areas."* Nothing that one could say conclusively indicated the presence of neurological disease, and yet . . .

She searched through the stack for possible explanations of Lindsey's behavior. The sheer volume of paper was daunting: police reports on Richard Stoddard's death, transcripts of Lindsey's first trial, Lindsey's medical and psychiatric records, Mike's interview notes, miscellaneous letters and scribbles. Suki focused on the medical and psychiatric.

As she had guessed, no indications of childhood sexual abuse or symptoms related to posttraumatic stress disorder. There didn't appear to be any history of migraine headaches or abuse of either alcohol or drugs—although Lindsey *had* told her at their last visit that she tried both LSD and mescaline in college. But these neurological reports . . . Lindsey reported olfactory hallucinations, and the test results were consistent with temporal lobe epilepsy.

TLE could be very good news for Mike—and for Suki, as she was under tremendous pressure to formulate her opinion as soon as possible. Beyond reading and synthesizing the materials before her, Suki had interviews to conduct, tests to administer and research materials to examine and digest. But, more

importantly, Mike had agreed to pay her in incre-
ments: a portion of her fee for each section of the
evaluation.

If she could get the first section—which
included a complete summary of Lindsey's personal,
medical, psychiatric and legal histories—finished by
the end of the week, she could add that check to the
small down payment she had given Mike against
the hours he had already put in on Alexa's case. The
whole thing felt vaguely incestuous, even though
they had decided to keep their professional services
separate rather than having a barter arrangement.
Barter might not have worked anyway, for, unless
they got this mess with Alexa straightened out very
soon, Mike's services to her were going to far exceed
hers to him. But despite Kenneth's warning about
the imminence of Alexa's arrest, Suki couldn't
believe it was going to come to that.

She glanced at her watch and turned back to the
files, hoping to lose herself within the complexities
of the Kern case. But the words swam meaninglessly
across the pages, and she found herself wondering
how so much could have changed in the five short
days since she had first met Lindsey Kern. If someone had told her last Thursday that Jonah Ward
would be dead and Alexa the prime suspect in his
murder, she would have denied the possibility.
Simply impossible, she would have said. And yet,
now, simply so.

The door behind Suki opened and Jen's patient,
a painfully handsome boy around sixteen, walked
out. He looked at Suki, blushed, then rushed from
the office.

"Be out of here in a flash." Jen poked her head through the open doorway, then retreated back into the office. "How's it going?" she called.

"Good," Suki said automatically.

"For real?" Jen yelled. Suki wished Jen would lower her voice, but no one had ever accused Jen of being soft-spoken. "Are the police finally coming to their senses?" Jen demanded, throwing her tall, lean body through the door and into the waiting room. The woman was a study in frenetic angles: elbows, knees, knuckles, chin, everything pointed and everything in constant motion.

"No," Suki said with a weak smile. "I was just being polite."

Jen's whole body sagged under the weight of her disappointment, and she rested her hip against the edge of the desk. "I hate polite," she said. "Except for Miss Manners—she does polite with an attitude."

Suki didn't say anything.

"It's just Ellery McKinna hatching his nasty plans over a bad poker hand." Jen also lived in Witton. "Don't listen to what those gossip mongers are saying—it's a bunch of bunk." Jen was always saying things like "a bunch of bunk," but somehow she could get away with it.

"What's a bunch of bunk?" Suki demanded.

It was clear from Jen's startled expression that she realized a beat too late that she had said more than she should have—a rather common event in Jen's daily life. "They've got nothing solid on Alexa," she said, recovering quickly. "And McKinna's not going to be able to keep the police away from Devin forever."

"Do you know something I don't?"

Jen shook her head furiously, too furiously, Suki thought. "All I know is Devin McKinna's a bad seed—and that everyone in Witton knows it, too."

Suki sighed. "I wish I could be so sure. Ellery and Charlie Gasperini are a powerful team. They can twist a lot of arms—and a lot of minds."

Jen leaned over and wrapped herself around Suki; she gave a hard squeeze. "Look at the bright side," she said, sitting up. "If McKinna and Gasperini drive the whole town nuts, it'll create a lot more business for us!"

"That kind of business I don't need," Suki muttered.

Jen's eyes narrowed in concern. "You want to talk?"

Suki didn't want to tell Jen what Kenneth had said; repeating his words would give them more power, maybe even make them true—and anyway, it appeared quite likely Jen already knew. "Can't," Suki said crisply, flipping open a file. "I've got to get through all this paper and then get my butt over to Watkins. Mike Dannow's time is mounting up, and I've got hours to bill."

"You sure?"

Suki pulled out Mike's letter of authorization and waved it at Jen. "Maybe some other time," she said, knowing that at the moment, work was the only thing standing between herself and a major meltdown. "I'm really jammed."

Jen looked skeptical, but she nodded. Jen might be out there, but the woman's antenna was always right on. She gave Suki another quick hug, jammed a wide-brimmed hat down on her head and walked out the door. "You've got my number," she called over her shoulder. "No charge for the first hour."

Suki turned to Mike's letter. The first time through, it made little sense, but she forced herself to concentrate and read it again. Not guilty by reason of insanity. Even Mike Dannow was going to have a tough time pulling off an NGRI. Lindsey was highly functional, highly intelligent and had no history of serious mental illness—and Suki's clinical observations of Lindsey's present cognitive functioning only contributed to this picture of mental health. The trial transcripts appeared even more damning to Mike's case: a cut-and-dried murder, complete with motive (Lindsey and Richard were apparently in the middle of a screaming match moments before he fell), opportunity (Lindsey was standing at the top of the stairs, right next to him) and a credible eyewitness (Edgar Price was a well-respected literary critic who claimed he heard and saw it all).

But these neurological results could be the evidence Mike was seeking. Right before Richard's death Lindsey had been screened for temporal lobe epilepsy, a not uncommon neurological disorder characterized by hallucinations—one of the few diseases that produced olfactory ones—and occasionally, outbursts of violence. The timing was right; unfortunately, the test results alone would probably not be strong enough to convince a jury.

But if Suki could get some specifics from Lindsey on her history and symptoms and get corroboration from the neurologist who had conducted the tests, she might be on her way. She could administer a personality assessment to rule out mental illness; although paper-and-pencil tests were never as good an indicator as spending time with a patient, time was something Suki just didn't have, and juries loved objective data. The Minnesota Multiphasic Personality Inventory, the MMPI, would work; it was the most commonly used test and therefore the easiest to defend under cross-examination. If Lindsey underwent another battery of neurological screens that came out similarly to the ones she had ten years ago, it would bolster the argument for organic disease.

Suki flipped back through the thick file. A psychiatrist Lindsey had seen as a child had speculated on the possibility of TLE as early as 1960. If Lindsey was found to have TLE, the presence of the disease could be used to explain both the ghost hallucination and the violent behavior. If she and Mike were very, very clever, it just might get Lindsey an NGRI.

As Suki waited for Lindsey in the now-familiar interrogation room, she read the graffiti scarred table. ASSHOLE. FUCK YOU. GIVE IT UP, CUNT. It was always the same witty scribbles. She stood and walked over to the grimy window, her power to lose herself in her work suddenly gone.

Unless you can come up with some other explanation for how Alexa knew Jonah was going to be killed . . . we're looking at an arrest here. . . . Kenneth Pendergast couldn't be silenced. *We're looking at an arrest. . . .*

Across the narrow alley, a row of barred windows stared back at her. The bars were so close she could see patterns in the rust streaking their sides: elongated Arabic letters, a pair of legs, tears. She turned away. Maybe the issue wasn't how Alexa had known Jonah would be killed, but how to prove she hadn't killed him. If, as Kenneth had also said, the police weren't going to question Ellery McKinna's story—not the chief's good pal—then it was upon her to expose the lies. To go to the rec center and question Ellery and the janitor, Finlay Thompson, and the secretary, whatever her name was. To insist that—

The door knob turned and Suki put on her "doctor face," but when she saw Lindsey, Suki's professional smile disappeared. Lindsey's right cheek was streaked with green and yellow bruises, her beautiful eye hidden by a swollen mass of discolored skin.

Suki stepped closer. "What happened?"

Lindsey's smile was lopsided and obviously painful. "People get mad when they're confronted with facts that contradict what they're so sure they know," she said with a shrug.

"Were they punished?"

Lindsey shrugged again and slid into her chair.

The corrections officer, a black woman whose huge bosom strained against the buttons of her uniform, clucked her tongue. "I'll be right outside if you need me," she told Suki. Then she patted Lindsey's shoulder and walked into the hallway, closing the door behind her. Suki got the impression the officer was speaking to Lindsey, not to her.

Suki sat down across from Lindsey. "Want to tell me about it?" she asked gently, wondering if Lindsey might decide Bridgeriver was preferable to Watkins.

Lindsey raised her hand to her cheek and Suki noticed her fingernails were bitten down to nubs. "It happens," Lindsey said, jutting out her chin. Again, the painful smile. "Life on the inside."

Suki nodded sympathetically and began to rummage through the papers for Lindsey's medical file. Then she stopped. *Life on the inside.* Suddenly, these words had new meaning. This wasn't just about a patient, about something that happened at work, something she could leave at the door like a wet coat or a pair of muddy boots. "Life on the inside" could be life for Alexa.

"I'm sorry about your troubles," Lindsey said.

Suki glanced at her, surprised.

"Even in here we get the paper. Watch the news."

"Oh, sure," Suki said. "Thanks."

"So that call you got when you were here last week *was* about your daughter."

"Trouble with one of your children?" Lindsey had asked when Suki's pager beeped. Suki had completely forgotten. "No," she said slowly, "the accident wasn't until the next day."

"Still," Lindsey pressed.

Suki smiled and raised a thick file with dog-eared pages sticking out from three sides. "We've got a lot of ground to cover in very little time," she said. "What do you say we get a move on?"

Lindsey nodded. "Microscope, red, baseball, love."

Suki laughed out loud. "Very good." She couldn't help being drawn to Lindsey; she was like a tough little kid, struggling to keep from crying, valiantly trying to pretend things weren't as they were. But it wasn't Suki's job to empathize with Lindsey, it was her job to evaluate her. Suki realized it was much easier to maintain clinical distance with someone who smelled bad and needed to see a dentist. "So, did Dr. Breman explain the issue of criminal responsibility to you?" Suki asked. "About what I'm trying to figure out, and how Mike's hoping to use the report I give him?"

"Mike wants you to say I was so nuts that night that I didn't know killing Richard was wrong." Lindsey began to quote solemnly, "'A person who is mentally ill has less freedom to make choices, and therefore has a diminished ability to conform to the law.'"

Suki watched Lindsey, who was calmly scrutinizing her fingers, an amused smile playing on the unbruised side of her lips. At this moment, the woman appeared completely lucid and in control—astonishingly sane. But Suki knew appearances could be deceiving. "Right," she said, "but that's only half of it: Mike could also try to prove you were incapable of stopping yourself from killing Richard."

Appreciate and conform. These two concepts were, in essence, the legal definition of sanity. Suki, and every forensic psychologist, knew the ALI—American Law Institute—rule by heart: "A defendant is excused from criminal responsibility if, because of a mental disease or defect, he lacks substantial capacity to appreciate the criminality of his conduct or is unable to conform his conduct to the requirements of the law." Massachusetts Penal Code, Section 4.01.

Lindsey raised her swollen face, and Suki could

see the raw pain in her open eye. "Except I didn't kill him—Isabel did."

She didn't do it, Suki thought, and then caught herself: jumping to conclusions this early in an evaluation was not a good idea.

"Isabel Lyman Jessel Davenport," Lindsey continued, and the pain on her face shifted into something else. "Born, August twenty-eighth, 1863. Died, never."

"Lindsey—"

"Do you know that there have been thousands, maybe millions, of people who have seen ghosts?" Lindsey interrupted. "There was a *Nova* show, on PBS, just the other night, that aired a tape that had been recorded in a haunted house in Maryland. They used some kind of special camera and you could clearly see the ghost—there was no question it was real." Lindsey raised her chin and Suki guessed that her black eye was the result of a debate on the ghost from Maryland.

"The show was hosted by this professor from Brown," Lindsey continued. "He sure knew his stuff. Talked about the difference between a one-time ghost sighting and what he called 'recurrent localized apparitions'—a ghost who's seen by a bunch of different people, at different times, but in the same place."

"Did anyone else ever see Isabel?"

"Edgar did."

"Edgar Price?" Suki asked. "The eyewitness?"

"He's a jerk." Lindsey dismissed Edgar with the wave of a hand. "But I want to tell you about this professor, I forget his name, who was talking about Isabel."

"Your Isabel?"

"Not exactly Isabel," Lindsey said impatiently. "What he was *saying* was about Isabel. He explained it so clearly. Perfectly. He said ghosts are the 'emotional memory' of a person caught between two states who can't adjust to either one. The ghost refuses to accept her death and holds onto the material surroundings she had when she was alive. Her feelings then become psychotic, and she believes whoever's living in her house is an intruder who must be kicked out—or destroyed." Lindsey leaned closer to Suki. " 'Discarnate-entity theory,' he called it. The soul is detained by some terrible event—a rape or a murder, something like that—and then impregnates the place where the event occurred, locking itself in. And that's what happened to Isabel."

"You think Isabel impregnated your condominium?" As soon as the words were out of her mouth, Suki wished she could take them back. There was something in her phrasing that implied a lack of sincerity, almost ridicule. Unfortunately, Lindsey thought so, too.

"I don't understand why we're wasting our time with this metaphysical discussion," Lindsey said, forgetting it was she who had raised the issue. "Isabel is as real as you and I, and it's Isabel who needs to be assessed for criminal responsibility—not me." Her voice grew louder and her diction more precise. "At Isabel's trial, I will gladly testify to the fact that Isabel Jessel Davenport did indeed know right from wrong the night she killed Richard Stoddard. She knew it then, and she knows it still." Lindsey threw her head back and then brought it quickly forward, wincing.

"Isabel still knows right from wrong?" Suki asked. Lindsey's mood swings reminded her of Alexa's. She pushed the thought away.

"Indeed she does."

"But I thought you said you hadn't seen Isabel since the night Richard was killed?" Suki asked. "Didn't you tell me you wished you could see her again?"

"I can see Isabel whenever I want. I can find people—living or dead. Anywhere they are," Lindsey declared. "Try me the next time you want to find someone."

Suki watched Lindsey in silence, annoyed with herself. She knew better than to contradict a patient as skittish as Lindsey. She pulled another pen from her case, hoping to give Lindsey time to save face.

Instead, Lindsey grew increasingly agitated by the silence. She squirmed in her seat. Beat her index finger against the table. Pulled at her earlobe.

Suki calmly scanned the files before her. She made a quick note.

"I never said I wanted to see her again."

"I must be mistaken, then," Suki said. "Sorry."

"I didn't."

"It doesn't matter, Lindsey. I'm sorry if I misunderstood you. It's my mistake. Right now, I need to talk to you about these neurological tests Dr. Smith-Holt conducted. Do you remember having an MRI?"

"A person doesn't forget an MRI." Lindsey gave Suki a withering look, stood and walked over to the door. She rapped loudly.

The door immediately swung inward, the

impressive heft of the officer filling the entire opening. Suki started to stand, but Darla motioned for her
to stay where she was. "You ready to go back, hon?"
she asked Lindsey.

"Yes," Lindsey said. "We're finished."

Darla glanced over at Suki, who nodded, then
placed her hand gently on Lindsey's arm and started
to escort her from the room.

Lindsey looked at Suki. "What you plan to do
won't solve your problems," she said. "Pan to fire."

"I don't understand—"

"What you need to know is written in a dead
boy's hand." Lindsey turned and walked out ahead
of Darla.

The Witton Recreation Center sits atop a wide
rolling hill on the western edge of town. Three ivy-
covered buildings flank the perimeter of a sweeping circular drive; one houses a skating rink, one
an indoor swimming pool, and the largest, the old-
est, the original building, contains two gyms as
well as a warren of exercise and game rooms. When
the gyms were built in the early forties, one had
been designated for girls and the other for boys;
this outdated configuration now afforded Witton
the luxury of dual programming. After school, the
high school girls could play basketball while fifth
graders climbed ropes in Adventure class; at mid-
morning, postpartum mothers could practice step
aerobics while preschoolers stumbled through
modern dance.

The campus spreads out behind the brick build-

ings: a series of playing fields—baseball, football, soccer—a dozen tennis courts and two swimming pools.
Real estate agents drive prospective buyers past the
center because it enhances sales. At the rec center,
Ellery McKinna is king.

As Suki turned onto the road leading to the center, she noticed a Witton police car behind her.
Looking more closely in her rearview mirror, she saw
the driver was Abe Fleming, a friend of Stan's—one
of the few she liked. Abe followed her to the
entrance, pulling directly behind her, his indicator,
in rhythm with hers, blinking his desire to turn into
the parking lot. Probably stopping in for his midday
bench press, Suki thought. She waved to him, but
apparently he didn't notice it was she in the car; he
didn't wave back.

Suki turned and began to hunt for a parking spot
in the lot crowded with lunch-hour exercisers. But
before she could find a place, Abe's siren began to
whoop, his blue lights to strobe. She looked for a
place to pull over, to let him by, but there was none.
So she headed toward the back of the lot as quickly
as she could, trying to get out of his way. But he
didn't want her out of his way. He wanted her.

When she finally found a spot, Abe pulled his
cruiser perpendicular to the back of her car, as if he
were blocking her escape route. He cut the siren, but
left the lights strobing.

"Hey Abe," Suki called, as she started to climb
from the car. "What's up?" She glanced at her watch,
anxious to find Ellery and Finlay before they left for
lunch. The digital numbers were difficult to read in
the flashing light.

"Stay in the car, please," Abe said, not looking at her face. "License and registration."

Suki shrugged and dropped back into the seat. She reached into the glove compartment. "As if you didn't know my name," she said, poking her head out of the car. "As if you hadn't ridden in this car dozens of times." She smiled up at Abe, but he wasn't smiling. His badge winked blue, then silver, then blue again.

"May I see your license and registration, please?"

Suki's palms began to sweat. Then her brain caught up with her senses. Abe was a regular in the Friday night poker game. Gasperini and McKinna's poker game. "What's this about?" she demanded, slapping both her license and the registration into his hand. She climbed from the car and stood with her hands on her hips.

Abe stared at the documents as if he were a state trooper who had stopped an out-of-state speeder. He grunted, then cleared his throat. "Gonna have to take you in," he said.

"Take me in?" Suki sputtered. "To the police station? Take me in for what?"

He pointed to the inspection sticker on her windshield. "You had forty-eight hours to get a new one. Been more than twice that since you got the ticket."

"I've been a bit distracted over the last few days—as if you didn't know."

"Law's the law."

"So you're going to *arrest* me?"

"It's the law," he said, avoiding eye contact.

"This isn't about the law," Suki corrected him.

"This is about Ellery McKinna pulling the strings to get his precious son off the hook. He's afraid to talk to me—he's afraid for me to talk to Finlay Thompson."

"If you look at your ticket, you'll see that it clearly states you have forty-eight hours to get the car inspected," Abe said to his shoes. "After that, it's the prerogative of the arresting officer to issue an additional ticket, at a greatly increased fine, or to arrest the perpetrator."

"The perpetrator?" Suki cried. "How the hell did you guys even know I got a ticket—" She stopped short.

Clumps of women were sprouting behind Abe: standing next to their vans, behind their station wagons, on the edge of the grass. Suki recognized Diane Tyler and Sue Silverstone and Becky Alley. Not a single one said a word, and not a single one bothered to pretend she wasn't gawking.

"Abe," Suki said softly. "This is me, Suki. Suki Jacobs. You know, the one who got your sister into the alcoholism program? Who got your mother to go to Al-Anon?" She touched his arm. "Look at me, Abe. Look at me."

Abe sighed and his eyes flickered to hers for a second. "Go to the gas station and get a new sticker right now," he said between clenched teeth. "Don't stop anywhere and forget I ever talked to you about it." Then he strode to his car, cut the flashing lights and quickly drove out of the parking lot.

CHAPTER EIGHT

Although she was furious with Abe, Suki knew she had to follow his instructions, so she went straight to the Shell station and got a new inspection sticker. Then she went to her office and saw two of her regular patients. Between sessions she put calls into Dr. Smith-Holt and Kenneth Pendergast. Smith-Holt was unavailable and Kenneth hesitated when she said she needed to talk to him, but then he acquiesced, suggesting they meet at the Pepperell Coffee Shoppe because it was on his way home and "made a mean cranberry muffin." Pepperell was a sleepy village about twenty miles northwest of Witton, and Suki had no doubt as to the real reason Kenneth had chosen such an out-of-the-way spot.

As Suki headed west on Route 2A, she checked the time and punched the SPEED DIAL button on her phone; Alexa was home from her first day at school since Jonah's death.

"It went fine," Alexa said in her mother-you-are-just-too-trying voice, as if Suki were inquiring about an ordinary day.

"What exactly went fine?" Suki persisted. "Did anyone bother you? Say anything to you? Kids? Teachers?"

"I told you already." Alexa's voice was tight and

thin. "There's nothing to get all bent out of shape over."

Under normal circumstances Suki would have let it go, but these circumstances were anything but normal. "Honey," she said gently, "there aren't too many people on your team at the moment, I wouldn't alienate one of the few you still have."

Alexa sighed through the phone's static. "Kendra got Robin and Steph to walk me to every class."

"And that worked out okay?"

"I guess." Alexa's shrug was almost audible over the phone.

"But?"

"But she didn't need to."

"Why not?" Suki pressed.

"Because no one bothered me," Alexa said in a small voice. "No one would even look at me."

Suki's heart ached. "Well, it's great that you've got your good friends to stand by you," she said. "That means a lot."

"I guess."

"Have you got much homework?" Suki asked, hoping that by acting normal she would make them both feel normal.

"Calculus, history, English. The usual."

"Well, why don't you get to it? I should be home around five-thirty. Maybe I'll pick up some McDonald's for dinner."

"Can I go now?" Alexa asked.

"Screen the calls through the machine before you answer the phone," Suki added. "And tell Kyle to do his homework, too."

"Later," Alexa said and hung up.

Suki pressed the END button on the phone, but she pushed too hard and the receiver fell from its housing onto the floor in front of the passenger seat. The phone stared up at her, its blank screen beseeching her to take action. Suki gripped the steering wheel and focused on the road.

The Pepperell Coffee Shoppe was just as she had imagined it, down to the frosted glass windows and plump, floury woman behind the counter. It was steamy and warm and homey. It smelled like raisins.

Kenneth's tall frame was folded into a booth toward the back. He waved her over. "Hi," he said with an awkward smile.

"Hi," she answered, sitting across from him. He continued to smile at her, and Suki realized he was far younger than she had thought upon first meeting him. His beard conferred the initial impression of age, but his brown eyes, a surprising color given his red hair, were only lightly webbed. The beard also hid the height of his cheekbones and the keen nobility of his lean, craggy face. "Off for the day?" she asked.

His smile disappeared. "Am I?"

"You tell me." After the woman had taken their order, Suki told him what had happened with Abe Fleming in the rec center parking lot.

Kenneth was silent as she added sweetener and a touch of cream to her coffee. He was silent as she bit into her cranberry muffin, which was as good as he had promised. He was silent for so long that Suki began to shift in her seat. She picked lint from her navy blue skirt.

Finally, he cleared his throat. "I didn't hear that story from you."

She watched him over the rim of her mug.

"I heard it somewhere else. A rumor. Tales of the street."

"Tales of the streets of Witton?" she asked, forcing a smile.

"If this whole thing doesn't show you that Witton has no protective magic, I don't know what will."

Suki blinked and sipped her coffee.

Kenneth reached out and touched her arm lightly. "I'll do what I can, Suki, but I doubt it'll come to much. These types of situations are tough—and I'm kind of odd-man-out down at the station."

Suki guessed that meant Kenneth didn't play poker with Charlie and Ellery on Friday nights.

"I left the NYPD because of this kind of thing," he continued. "Politics and self-interest." He stared out the steamy window into the past; through his thick beard, Suki could see his facial muscles tensing. "Not to mention drugs and a lot of bad blood. . . ."

Suki was curious about the story Kenneth wasn't telling, but she knew not to ask. Everyone had their secrets. "How long ago did you leave New York?"

"Two years in June." He gestured to the lime green buds outside the window, the tree branches rocking in the wind. "I moved out here to get some fresh air—both literally and figuratively."

"Guess it doesn't smell too great anywhere."

"Small towns have an odor all their own." He rubbed his beard with a gesture that, although she had only met him once before, Suki recognized as habitual.

"I'm going to go back to the rec center and make Ellery talk to me," she told him. "Finlay Thompson, too. But this time I'll take my father's car."

"We got the report on your car."

"And?" Suki asked, not encouraged by the expression on Kenneth's face.

"Mostly what you'd expect." He shrugged with exaggerated nonchalance. "Tread marks match the ones on River Road. Powder residue inside and out . . ."

"And the fingerprints?"

"Alexa's are all over the place. Yours, too," Kenneth said to his coffee cup. "Steering wheel, passenger window, back seat. Lots of others, but they're partials. Smudges."

"What about the boys?"

He raised his eyes and met hers. "No clear prints on any of them."

"None?" Suki was horrified. "But how can that be? They've all been in the car at one time or another. I've driven them myself."

"I'm sure you have," Kenneth said. "Good prints aren't as easy to get in the real world as they are in the movies. This happens more often than you'd think." He cleared his throat. "So, although this doesn't prove that the boys *weren't* in the car, it doesn't prove that they were, or when they were— and that's what Alexa needs right now."

Suki stared at her hands. They looked like her mother's hands, not hers. The veins were blue and raised, the skin looser than she remembered it. When had her hands gotten so old?

"I worked with a real psychic in New York," Kenneth said.

"What?" Suki raised her head, not sure she had heard correctly.

"On a bunch of different cases. Very impressive." He grinned. "Believe it or not, she's a Jewish grandmother from Great Neck."

"Is this a joke?"

Kenneth sobered. "No," he said. "I'm serious. Her name's Doris Sheketoff and we've become good friends. As a matter of fact, I was supposed to go to the seder at her house last Friday night."

"You're Jewish?" Suki asked, more willing to focus on the unlikelihood of a redheaded man named Pendergast being Jewish, than on last Friday night.

Kenneth reached into his shirt and pulled out a gold chain with the Hebrew word *chai* hanging from it; *chai* was the symbol for life. "A convert," he said.

Suki nodded. People were full of surprises. "Tell me about this woman."

"She found a kidnapper when no one else could. A lost child, too."

"And you think she did these things with psychic powers?"

"You tell me." Kenneth leaned back and crossed his arms over his chest. "There was a kid missing on the east side. Nice neighborhood. Nice little girl. Nice parents. And no trace of Heather. No ransom note, no nothing. The media's going nuts, and we've got almost the entire detective force working on the case. Time goes by and still nothing. Then I get a call from Doris. She tells me Heather's underwater."

"Did the little girl drown?"

Kenneth shook his head. "Doris said she had the sense Heather was still alive. So naturally, I had the sense the lady was loony tunes—we got lots of those in the city—and hung up. But she kept calling. And then she got the parents involved."

"So what happened?"

"To make a long story short, Doris ultimately led us to an underground bunker where this maniac was keeping the kid."

"She was all right?"

"As all right as a little girl can be who's been buried alive for a month."

"But what about the underwater part?"

Kenneth grinned. "The bunker was directly under a billboard advertising suntan lotion: it was a picture of a woman floating on a raft in a big swimming pool."

Suki stared at him incredulously. "What are you saying?"

"I don't know what I'm saying—anymore than I know how Doris can do what she does. It's just that I've learned things aren't always the way they seem to be." He leaned over the table. "Just because we can't explain it, does that mean it didn't happen?"

"Are you telling me you believe Alexa's psychic?"

"I'm only raising possibilities. But the truth is, if Alexa isn't psychic—or if no one believes that she possibly could be—then all the evidence is pointing in only one direction."

Suki played with the ceramic sugar bowl in front of her. She took the top off. She put it back on. She took it off again.

"The thing you need to—"

"Does anyone else on the Witton force know Doris?" Suki interrupted. "Does anyone else beside you believe psychics are possible?"

Kenneth shook his head. "My hands are pretty much tied. I probably shouldn't even be here, but this whole thing has gotten under my skin. There was a great show on ghosts on PBS the other night—full of facts and research, really credible stuff that was hard to dispute. And it all makes me wonder. About what's true and what isn't true, and about how someone like Alexa can get caught in it all."

"Can't you talk to Charlie? Tell him what you've just told me?"

"I doubt it would make much difference," Kenneth said. "Look, you seem like a nice woman, like a nice family, so when you called, when you sounded so upset, I figured, well, I just figured I should at least talk to you." He played with the crumbs of his muffin. "But I don't know what else I can do."

Suki exhaled slowly. Kenneth was a gift, a gift that could be yanked from her at any moment. She would take everything he had to give her while she had the opportunity. "Talk is good," she said with a small smile. "Talk to me about what's happening."

Kenneth gave her a look that clearly said: You don't want to know, but when Suki nodded, he began, "I can't go into the specifics, but let's just say that Charlie's getting a lot of pressure to make an arrest—pressure from pretty high up. And you can be sure the people turning the screws on him don't believe in psychics. The way the evidence is falling, the easiest thing for them is to pin it on Alexa. There's no point in looking for evidence, or bringing in the paranormal, when you've got such a strong suspect."

"But Alexa's *not* that strong a suspect," Suki argued. "The whole thing makes no sense. How could she drive the car and shoot Jonah at the same time? Where'd she get a gun? When did she learn to use it, and most importantly, why would she *want* to kill him?" Suki's voice rose with the last question and a man sitting at the counter turned to look at them. "There's opportunity and no motive," Suki added more softly. "How can she be a strong suspect when there's no reason why she would kill him?"

"They determined the car was stationary when the shot was fired. Alexa and Jonah were lov— boyfriend and girlfriend." Kenneth put his large hand over hers for a second. "It all depends on your vantage point," he said, quickly drawing his hand and eyes from hers. "It all depends on your agenda."

Kenneth had the kindness not to list all the evidence against Alexa, but Suki mentally ticked off each item as if he had: Alexa's prediction, Alexa's admission to being at the scene, tread marks that placed the car at the scene, the boys' alibi, the report of Alexa saying she wished Jonah were dead, Alexa's fingerprints in the car, none of the boys' fingerprints in the car. . . . "I'm going to break that damn alibi," Suki said. "This time, when I go to the rec center, I'll talk to Finlay first. Get him to admit Devin wasn't there that night. Then I can prove the boys are lying. Prove that Devin fired the gun."

"The divers have never found the gun in the river, you know."

"But the alibi's the key," Suki argued.

"Find the gun and you'll have the evidence you need to break the alibi." Kenneth leaned back in the booth and watched her carefully.

"You think maybe the gun isn't in the river?" Suki grabbed onto her coffee cup as hope surged through her.

"If it isn't, maybe Alexa knows where they stashed it."

The Community Boathouse is at the end of a long rutted road. Suki hadn't been out there since Stan had left, and as she drove up to the building, memories emerged from the shadows: Stan and her walking hand and hand in the early morning fog, a tangle of legs and tanned skin as they made love in the hull of Stan's boat, picnic baskets and pickles and the sweet sound of Alexa's little-girl giggle. Suki pulled to a stop in front of the tall, silent structure and wondered when she would finally be done with the pain.

"Do you think anyone's here?" Alexa asked.

There were no cars in sight. "It's a bit early in the season," Suki assured her. "And the weather's rotten." Which it was. Yesterday's warm promise of spring was obliterated by today's cold rain. It was the kind of damp that crawled into the bone marrow, chilling from the inside out.

Alexa pulled her sweater more tightly around her, but she didn't make any motion to leave the car. "It's not going to be there."

"We don't have the luxury of pessimism, Alexa," Suki reminded her.

"Sorry," Alexa said, looking down at her lap.

Suki leaned over and raised her chin. "We're going to beat this thing," she said. "We will. You and I."

Alexa nodded slightly and tried to smile; the corner of her mouth wobbled. "Sure, Mom," she said, clearly attempting to convince them both. "Sure we will."

"Then let's go do it." Suki slapped the steering wheel and jumped out of the car. Alexa followed more slowly.

Suki braced herself before entering the boathouse, knowing the familiar mingled odor of sawdust and gasoline and life vests would bring back the memories. She pulled the hood of her poncho further down on her head, breathing in the cotton-rubber smell of the fabric. Then she pushed the tall door open. It squeaked under her hand.

The boathouse is always open because it isn't really a boathouse, not the kind where boats are stored; it's a place where people who owned boats keep their gear. The boats are either tied to the docks or launched from the ramp on the left side of the building.

Suki peered into the murky interior. Birds fled to the rafters and mice scurried for cover, and she wondered if the owl who had kept the mouse population under control for so many years was still in residence. She scanned the dark corners of the tall ceiling, but didn't see the glint of his yellow eyes. She wiped the cobwebs away from her face.

"Over there, Mom," Alexa said, pointing to the bank of lockers that ran along the west wall.

Suki nodded and followed Alexa, remembering: the Sunfish, the motorboat, the canoe, the tiny island on the far side of Echo Lake.

Alexa walked across the open space as if she had been here yesterday, and Suki realized she might have been. Alexa had always loved boats, whether it was sailing or kayaking or fiddling with greasy engines. For years, she had fished with Stan and Charlie Gasperini on Saturday mornings, worked on Charlie's boat with him. And she and Jonah used to come out here all the time. Charlie and Jonah. How ironic.

As Suki watched Alexa expertly spin the combination on one of the small lockers, she wanted to ask exactly what the kids came up here for and why Alexa was so sure that, if the gun wasn't in the river, it was in this one particular locker. She didn't say anything.

"We leave notes and stuff." Alexa glanced quickly up at her mother and then down again. "Sometimes kids have parties."

Suki came and stood beside Alexa, but Alexa blocked her view with her body. Suki stepped back.

Alexa pulled open the lock and slipped it from the hook. Making sure Suki couldn't see into the locker, she quickly pulled the door toward her and looked inside. Her shoulders slumped.

"It's not there?" Suki asked.

"There's another one I can try," Alexa said, snapping the door shut. "But I doubt there'll be anything in it either." She walked along the bank of lockers and grabbed another lock, spinning it quickly. It pulled free of its housing and Alexa stuck her head into the locker.

"Nothing?" Suki came up behind her.

"Just a note." Alexa pulled out a square of folded lined paper. "It's for me," she said, backing away from her mother and into the shadows.

Suki turned from Alexa and looked into the empty locker. She stuck her hand inside and stretched her fingers toward the far wall. There was no gun, but there were a few items stuffed in the corner. She pulled them out: matches, cigarette rolling papers, an empty film canister. She knew what the paraphernalia was used for, but she felt surprisingly numb to its significance. There was no gun. That was all that mattered. She had known finding the gun was a long shot—a long, long shot. But she also knew that in order to win this gamble, a long shot was going to have to come in. Suki threw the things back into the locker and closed the door. Now she'd have to go to Finlay empty-handed, his sense of morality her only appeal.

Alexa let out a low moan.

Suki whirled around as Alexa slumped to the floor. The note fluttered open to the sawdust next to her. "What is it?" Suki crouched and took Alexa in her arms.

Alexa shook her head, clearly unable to speak.

"Are you hurt, honey?" Suki asked softly. "Are you okay?"

Alexa managed to nod, then she burst into tears. She sobbed as if her heart would break, as if it were broken.

Suki held on to her daughter, rocked her as she hadn't rocked her in many years. She crooned into Alexa's ear, then she rocked her some more. As they sat there in the still, shadowy boathouse, Suki looked down at the open note. She couldn't help but read it.

Alexa,

What happened isn't my problem. You have to stop bad mouthing me around school. It's over and it's time to grow up and let it go. I'll meet you here Monday at the usual time. We have to talk.

Jonah

Suki reread the note as Alexa cried. Jonah had been mad at Alexa and it sounded as if Alexa had been mad at him, too. And now Jonah was dead. Suki held Alexa tighter.

When Alexa finally quieted, Suki caressed her hair. "What does the note mean, honey?" she asked gently. "What wasn't Jonah's problem? What did he want you to let go of?"

Alexa pulled away and looked up at Suki, her eyes huge and miserable. "He lied to me, Mom," she whispered. "He . . . he told me he loved me. That he wanted us to get back together. And then . . ."

"And then what, sweetie?" Suki asked although she was pretty sure she didn't want to know. "And then what?"

Alexa shook her head.

"I think you need to tell me."

"W-we," Alexa stuttered, "we did it. And then,

after . . . afterward he went back to Dara! He told me he didn't love me, he only wanted to make her jealous." Alexa hid her face in Suki's sweatshirt.

Suki withdrew her arms and pressed them to her sides. Alexa had lied again. Pretending to be who she wasn't, lying and running off to her parties and having sex and doing who knew what else. And now it was all coming due, perhaps deservedly so. But Suki also recognized that she was not without blame. This had all happened, while she, a trained psychologist, was going about life as usual: seeing clients, writing reports, buying milk and orange juice. It had been all too easy for her to believe Alexa's lies. She put her arms back around her daughter. "Sounds like he deserved being bad-mouthed," she said.

Alexa shook her head against Suki's chest. "That's not why," she mumbled.

Suki held her breath.

"There's more." Alexa pressed her lips tightly together. "I . . . I got pregnant," she said, her words tumbling out. "But Jonah said it wasn't his—that it wasn't his responsibility and that he wouldn't help me. He said that I . . . that I slept around. That I was a slut. He told *everybody*." She met Suki's eyes straight on, and Suki knew her daughter well enough to know that what she was going to say next was the truth. "But I'm not, Mom," Alexa told her, her voice ringing with conviction. "I don't sleep around. I never had sex with anyone but Jonah. Not even Brendan."

Alexa had had sex with Jonah. Alexa had had sexual intercourse, had made love, had screwed. Had been screwed. Jonah had screwed her, lied to her, humiliated her. And she had gotten pregnant. Suki took a deep breath. "You're pregnant?"

"Not any more."

"You had an abortion?" Suki asked sharply.

"What else did you expect me to do?" Alexa's voice rose to meet Suki's. "Somehow I couldn't picture you with an unwed teenage daughter instead of a Princeton freshman in your family," she spat.

"Don't turn this around at—"

"Brendan took me to the clinic," Alexa interrupted. "A few weeks ago. That's why he was so mad at Jonah. That's why we were out looking for him that night."

The birds and the mice were quiet, the sound of the lapping water muffled by the walls of the boathouse. Suki listened to Alexa's ragged breathing and clenched her fists. Then she heard a roaring in her ears. She looked around, surprised, before she realized it was the roar of her own anger.

How dare he? How dare Jonah manipulate, then violate, then abandon Alexa? How dare he hurt and humiliate her like that? Alexa's only crime was that she had loved him, believed his lies. If Jonah weren't dead, Suki would kill him. Kill him with her own hands. She pictured her fingers around Jonah's neck, thought of the satisfaction she would feel as she watched his eyes fill with panic. Suki gasped.

If she wanted to kill Jonah, then so did Alexa.

CHAPTER NINE

Suki didn't get back to the rec center until late the next day. Upset as she was by Alexa's revelations, she still had to see patients, work on the first section of the Kern report, drive Kyle to his drum lesson and go food shopping. She found it amazing, and even slightly amusing, that even though her world was being torn asunder, she still needed to buy toilet paper.

She walked across the boys' gym, looking around for Finlay, but was unperturbed when she didn't see him. Finlay was always about, as present within the rec center as the gym was, fixing a leak or pushing a barrel of garbage or helping a crying child find her mother. He'd be easy enough to spot. She poked her head outside.

A soccer practice was in progress. Boys, sixth or seventh graders by the size of them, were sliding on the long unmowed grass and falling into mud puddles left by yesterday's rain, overseen by a coach who stood with his hands on his hips, a stance that even from this distance was clearly one of mock irritation. Laughter rang out as the boys pushed and jousted with shoulders and chests and hips, their hands clasped behind their backs. The coach shouted and they fell out into two ragged lines, still without the use of their hands, still butting each other with every available appendage. When he removed his hat, Suki saw the coach was Warren Blanchard.

Between the gym and the rear stairwell was a odd-shaped room that everyone called Finlay's place. It would have been called his office if there was any space in it for a desk. Amidst the buckets and tools and broken sports equipment was a beat-up chair and a wall phone, but that was the sum total of the office equipment. Finlay Thompson was not an office type of guy. He was an energetic, wiry man in his late sixties who equated sitting with old age and death. He was hardly ever in his "place," but Suki stuck her head in just in case. As she had expected, the room was devoid of human presence, but overflowing with all manner of junk.

Suki cast one more lingering glance at the soccer practice. Now the boys' hands were held to the tops of their heads as Warren put them through some kind of running drill.

"What you need to know is written in a dead boy's hand," Lindsey Kern's voice came at her as if, instead of having spoken the words two days before, Lindsey were speaking them now. Suki dropped to a seat on the bottom row of a set of bleachers pulled halfway out from the wall. She stared at the basketball hoop at the end of the gym, imagining she saw Jonah leap in front of it, slam-dunk the ball, and land on the floor, his arms raised in triumph. The crowd roared.

But the gym was silent. Jonah was dead. Jonah who had violated and abandoned Alexa, who had written Alexa a note, that if found, would destroy her life. Lindsey Kern was wrong: what Suki *didn't* need to know was written in a dead boy's hand.

What no one else needed to know. The note was gone. Burned in her kitchen sink yesterday, its ashes washed down the drain by the rushing water. Suki was well aware that she was destroying evidence, a significant crime, but she didn't care. She had more doubts about not telling Mike; he should know, but he was already freaked out by Alexa's prediction, and despite what defense lawyers claimed, Suki knew they always did a better job if they believed their client was innocent. Alexa had silently watched the flaming note curl into blackness, then without a word, had turned and gone to her room. She hadn't come down for dinner and had feigned sleep when Suki came up to kiss her good night. What no one needed to know.

Suki launched herself up from the bleachers and headed out to find Finlay. She walked down the narrow corridor that separated the two gyms, then meandered the labyrinth of hallways off of which opened game rooms and sewing rooms and kitchens and art studios. She searched both levels of the main building, then worked her way through the two smaller ones.

Children were everywhere, as were their mothers, who gossiped or read or just enjoyed a few moments in which nothing was expected of them. Suki recognized many, nodded to a few, smiled at even fewer. No one tried to engage her in conversation, and although such a thing would never have happened two weeks ago, Suki was just as glad. She wasn't in the mood for arch questions or oversolicitous condescension; she just wanted to find Finlay.

But Finlay, the man who was usually everywhere, didn't appear to be anywhere. Suki stood in front of the main building, kicking at the gravel at the edge of the sidewalk, eyeing the office windows. She had wanted to confront McKinna with Finlay's admission in hand, but it was obviously time for Plan B.

She walked into the building. Ellery's office opened to the right of the secretary's desk, which sat in the middle of a large airy room; Ellery's door was closed. Suki smiled as she approached the secretary. Alice was her name. Alice something-that-started-with-C. She was the one who claimed to have seen the boys in the rec center the night of Jonah's murder, but Alice's story hadn't stirred much interest in either the police or the press, because she had added that she hadn't been there for the entire evening.

"Hi," Suki said. "I'm looking for Finlay. Do you think you could page him for me, please?"

"Finlay Thompson?" Alice asked, as if there could be any other. Her eyes darted to Ellery's door.

"Yes," Suki said patiently. "That would be great."

Alice fiddled with the buttons on her phone, but didn't press any.

"I'd really appreciate it."

The door to Suki's right opened, and Ellery McKinna walked out. He was dressed in khakis and a short-sleeved shirt that displayed his muscular build far more than the suit he had worn to the funeral; dark hair curled above the shirt's open neck, contrasting with the ice blue of his eyes. There was no arguing that he was a seriously attractive man. A dangerous and powerful, seriously attractive man. Ellery pressed his hands together, then reached his right one toward her. "How you doing, Suki?" he asked as though she were an ordinary acquaintance. The slight hesitation in his voice could be interpreted as curiosity, as if she had just returned from a long trip.

Reflexively, Suki shook his outstretched hand. "I'm trying to find Finlay," she told him. "Alice was just paging him for me." Miss Manners would be proud of her deportment. Civility was a powerful force.

Ellery glanced at Alice, who shrugged. "I'm, ah, sorry," he said. "Finlay doesn't work here anymore."

Suki was stunned. "Doesn't work here anymore?"

"You just never know with people, do you?" Ellery turned his palms to the ceiling. "Man works for you for years and years, and suddenly he wants something else. Another job, Finlay said. Something easier. Less stressful."

Suki looked from Ellery to Alice. "Are you kidding?"

"I'm afraid not." Ellery appeared honestly saddened.

Alice gave Suki a thin smile, exposing a row of tiny white teeth. There was a spot of red lipstick on one.

Suki wondered what Miss Manners would suggest now. Continue the polite discourse, or confront Ellery with what she knew? There was no doubt in Suki's mind that Finlay's disappearance was Ellery's doing, and she felt a beat of encouragement at the desperation the move displayed. Then she thought about what other acts that kind of desperation might engender. Suki watched Ellery in silence—a psychologist's, rather than an etiquette maven's, trick.

"Look, Suki," he said, shoving his hands deep into the pockets of his pants, "I had no idea this was coming. No idea at all. Let me tell you, it's about the last thing I need right now." His gaze was level, and if Suki hadn't known better, she would have believed he was sincere. "The place is in a shambles," he added.

"Do you think you could tell me where he's gone?" Suki asked. Polite discourse appeared to be the game.

"I wish I could," Ellery said, his eyes still locked on hers. "But personnel rules, you know. Confidentiality and all that." He touched his hand to his forehead, as if he were wearing a cap, and flashed her a quick smile. "Sorry I couldn't be of more help." Then he turned and went into his office, shutting the door firmly behind him.

Speechless, Suki stared at the closed door. Ellery McKinna was even more dangerous and powerful than she had thought. For not only was he able to manipulate others' lives to a degree she wouldn't have thought possible, but even worse, he had the ability to convince himself that his lies were truth. And it was within this ability that Alexa's true peril lay.

Suki stopped at a phone booth and looked up Finlay's address. She drove to his house. No one was home. As she walked around the small cape, she noted the drapes were drawn against the living and dining room windows, and the yellow light above the front door was lit. Glancing over her shoulder to see if anyone had noticed her prowling, Suki pressed her nose to an undraped kitchen window. The counters were spotless and two chairs were neatly pushed under a tiny wooden table. It was extraordinarily tidy, too tidy, no pile of mail or open newspaper, no shirt thrown over the back of a chair, as if those who lived here planned to be absent for quite some time.

When Suki got home, Alexa was in her room working on an English project with Kendra, Robin, and Steph. The girls stayed through dinner, heating up a couple of frozen pizzas, and Alexa went to bed as soon as they left, deftly sidestepping her mother. Suki decided not to push the issue.

Instead, she helped Kyle with his homework, then went into her study to work on the Kern evaluation. As she sat down at the desk, she couldn't help but notice the unpaid bills stuffing the cubby next to the phone. The first section of the report had to be finished by tomorrow, and she was behind schedule. She needed that check.

Suki bent over Lindsey's medical file. She was surprised to see that Lindsey had had a fleeting flirtation with a psychotic diagnosis—by the same psychiatrist who had hypothesized TLE. At age nine, Lindsey's parents had taken her to see a Dr. Eugene Stieglitz; her presenting problem was chronic nightmares. Dr. Stieglitz had postulated either TLE or schizotypal personality structure as a diagnosis, but apparently the Kerns hadn't agreed with him, for no follow-up was recorded.

And it looked like the Kerns had been right. Except for a couple of visits to the university health center to get help with a "mild sleep disorder," Lindsey hadn't sought out any type of mental health professional until she went to a Boston psychologist, a Naomi Braverman, a few months before Richard Stoddard died. A single psychotic episode was an extremely unlikely occurrence.

But Dr. Stieglitz's suggestion of TLE so early in Lindsey's life could be used to further Mike's argument. Unfortunately, Lindsey's apparent mental health for the next twenty years could not. Suki recorded the facts on the graph paper she used to rough out chronologies and then flipped to Dr. Braverman's notes.

No definitive diagnosis had resulted from the neurological and psychological batteries done at the time. Beside the MRI and EEG, Lindsey had also taken Rorsharch, TAT, IQ and Wechsler tests. The first two tests provided information on the brain, the next two on psychopathology, and the last two on intelligence. The TAT and Rorsharch suggested an absence of psychosis and the other two indicated high intelligence. Bad news for Mike. Suki scrutinized the handwritten note at the bottom of the Rorsharch report. "Within normal range but pushing boundaries," Dr. Braverman had scribbled. Better news for Mike, and interestingly, a similar assessment to the one that could be made for the results of Lindsey's neurological tests. Suki wondered if anyone had ever attempted to correlate claims of paranormal abilities with scores on standard psychological and neurological tests. She rather doubted it.

Suki hunted for medication notations and found that Tegretol, a drug commonly used to treat temporal lobe epilepsy, had been prescribed. As she graphed the prescription date, Suki chalked up another point for Mike. But when she checked to see how long Lindsey had taken the medication, she saw that only one prescription had been written. "Apparently ineffective," Naomi Braverman had noted. Take Mike's point away.

Suki hit the pad of graph paper with the back of her pencil. This was doubly difficult because of the time lag. She was charged with assessing Lindsey's competence at the time of the crime—over nine years ago—and reconstructing a long past event was like trying to recapture a dream: confusing, elusive, almost impossible. But, as one of her law professors was fond of pointing out, American law was always about reconstructing a past event: Actus Mens.

Lindsey Kern was hard enough to comprehend in the present: her self-deprecating humor, her clear and lucid understanding of the legal concept of insanity, her mood swings and strange mutterings. Suki glanced at the pile of books at her feet. She had cleaned out the Witton library's paranormal section: books on ghosts, psychokinesis, precognition, clairvoyance, and psychical research lay at her feet. As the complexities and ambiguities in this case grew, so did her fascination.

"Try me the next time you want to find someone," Lindsey had bragged when Suki saw her last. "I can find people. Anywhere they are. Try me." Maybe Lindsey could help her find Finlay. The stack of books rose a couple of feet from the floor, and the card catalogue claimed the library's paranormal collection was even larger. Maybe finding lost people from a prison cell wasn't as far fetched as it seemed.

"Mom?" Kyle poked his head in the doorway.

Suki stared at him blankly.

He put his hands on his hips, his expression impatient. "It's me, Kyle. Remember? Your son?"

Suki tilted her head a bit and narrowed her eyes. "Oh yeah," she said. "Your face does look familiar. . . ." He looked just like his father. Suki could go for days without thinking of Stan, and then, suddenly, out of nowhere, she would feel his loss, like a punch in the stomach. "Last name is Jacobs, right?"

"Glad to see you still have a bit of your sense of humor left." Kyle walked into the room and casually dropped his hand to her shoulder. He patted her awkwardly and then retreated to the doorway; fourteen-year-old boys didn't go around touching their mothers. "Scott's mom said she'd pick me and Jeremiah up after soccer practice tomorrow and take us all to Papa Gino's."

"Jeremiah and me," Suki corrected.

"Whatever." Kyle made the "W" sign with his fingers and rolled his eyes. "Can I go? Scott's on the phone. He needs to know now."

Suki tried to imagine tomorrow, but drew a complete blank. For a moment, she couldn't remember what day today was.

"Come on, Mom," Kyle said, jamming his hand in and out of the pocket of his jeans. "It's Papa Gino's, not Bosnia."

"Sure, I guess, sure. How will you get home?"

"Mrs. Fleishman'll drive me or I'll call you," Kyle

said as he turned toward the hallway. He stopped his forward motion by grabbing the doorjamb and swinging himself back in. "Oh, I forgot to tell you, Coach Blanchard said I need to get new soccer shoes. Cleats are all shot." Then he disappeared.

Toilet paper and Papa Gino's and new soccer shoes. Suki started to pull the graph paper toward her, then stopped. She didn't need Lindsey, she could ask Warren Blanchard; he would be able to find out where Finlay Thompson had gone. But would Warren be willing to help her? The enemy? The mother of the prime suspect in his nephew's murder? Then she remembered the compassion in his eyes the last time they had met, his hatred of bureaucracy, his love of the underdog. It was worth a shot.

Suki got back to work and within an hour had completed graphing Lindsey Kern's life as a patient. She put her pencil down and stretched her hands over her head. How sane was Lindsey? How sane was anybody? She thought of Lindsey's mumblings about the dead boy's hand. She *had* found important information written in a dead boy's hand the very next day. Alexa *had* predicted Jonah's death. Her mother *had* predicted a plane crash. And then there was Kenneth's story about Doris Sheketoff.

Suki leaned down and picked up one of the library books. It was a general parapsychology textbook, and as she flipped through the first chapter describing the history of the discipline, she couldn't help but be impressed by the names: J. B. Rhine's lab at Duke University, Division of Parapsychology at the University of Virginia Medical School, Parapsychology Department at the University of Edinburgh, PSI Research Program at Princeton.

She turned to the chapter on precognition and was soon lost in a complex, but tantalizing, discussion of physics and unified field theory. She read about symmetry and parity and optical isomers, about how the discovery that parity doesn't always hold true for subatomic particles implied that time flowed both backward and forward—some physicist had apparently discovered the "footprint" of a "left-handed" particle that existed before the particle did. According to the book, that meant that the idea that time moved from the past into the present was a human one, invented to allow us to function in a world where all our ideas about space and time and the transmission of energy are wrong.

The argument reminded Suki of Voltaire's obervation that "if God did not exist, it would be necessary to invent him." She was filled with wonder. Was it possible? Could all times—past, present and future—always be here? Could one somehow cross over and tap into those other times?

A scream cut through the silence of the house. Suki was up the stairs so fast that she was standing in Alexa's doorway before she realized she had left her chair. Alexa was sitting straight up in bed, the blanket and sheets puddled at her waist. Her eyes were wide open, but focused on something Suki couldn't see.

"Alexa. Sweetheart," Suki said softly, not wanting to startle her. Alexa didn't move. "Alexa," she tried again, a bit louder. Suki stepped closer.

Alexa blinked but didn't say anything.

Suki sat down on the edge of the bed and cautiously reached out to touch Alexa's hand. When Alexa didn't stir, she gently pressed her toward the pillow. "Why don't you just lie back down, now?" she suggested. "Get some rest."

Alexa remained immobile, as if frozen into a seated position, paralyzed by her dream state.

"Sleep," Suki murmured. "Sleep."

Slowly, as if each movement was tied to a separate muscle, Alexa turned her head toward Suki, her eyes unseeing. "Mom," she said, drawing out the syllable. The low, slow disembodied voice seemed to emanate from somewhere behind the bed. Alexa was still asleep.

"Yes, honey, it's me. I'm right here—"

"No!" Alexa jerked up and went rigid again. Then, just as suddenly, she drooped and covered her face with her hands. She began to sob uncontrollably. Her whole body trembled.

Suki held onto her tightly. "Hush, honey," she said. "You're having another nightmare."

Alexa pulled away. "I saw you," she said, her voice more her own, but her eyes still distant. "You were at the bottom of a long tunnel, a mine shaft or something, with lots of pulleys and wires and things. I was at the top. Far, far away. It was dark. But I could see you. Clearly. Real clearly. You were all twisted and broken and I was trying to get you up, but you wouldn't move and I couldn't get down to you. I kept trying and trying but it was too far."

"It's just a dream—"

"Your hair was all white and curly and strange, but I knew it was you. And I couldn't get to you. I couldn't help you."

Suki didn't move.

"And somehow I knew it was all my fault. That it was because of me that you were down in that mine shaft—because I wouldn't believe something you were trying to tell me. It was my fault, my fault, you were . . . were . . ." Alexa covered her face with her hands again. "You were dead."

Suki just stared at Alexa. Alexa had never been told the exact circumstances of her grandmother's death. She knew it was suicide, but that was about all she knew.

"I don't want you to die, Mom," Alexa wailed. "I don't want you to die."

"I'm not going to die," Suki assured her. "At least not in the immediate future," she added, knowing there was no way she or Alexa could be sure.

Alexa stared at her mother and nodded slowly, apparently soothed by Suki's words. Then she closed her eyes and slumped back into the pillow, her arms flopping to her sides. Within minutes, her breathing subsided into deep measured sighs and Suki wondered if Alexa had ever been awake.

Suki pulled up the sheet and blanket. "Go to sleep, baby," she whispered. "Go to sleep." She kissed Alexa, then tiptoed down to the study.

She dropped into the chair at her desk. What was that all about? she wondered as she looked down at the parapsychology book open in front of her. Clairvoyance and precognition and time going forward and backward. Parity and optical isomers. Dead mothers and elevator shafts.

CHAPTER TEN

As Country Club Lane turns eastward, it becomes Roaring Brook and rises to a small bluff overlooking a snake of a stream that even in early spring could never be mistaken for a roaring brook. Suki stood knee-deep in the winter yellow grass that grew along the edge of the road, throwing pebbles into the water. Although the first streaks of morning sun had shaded the black sky to cloudy gray, it was an opaque light, hard and distant, holding no warmth. She shivered in her sweatshirt and threw another stone as she waited for Warren Blanchard. She missed the brook and her rock landed on the steep slope that marked the beginning of Judi Zvi's backyard. She had no idea whose property she was standing on.

She was tired, having stayed up until almost two o'clock in the morning working on the Kern report, although, she had to admit, she had been distracted by thoughts of Alexa. About Alexa's dream. About the prediction, the alibi, the abortion, the motive, the impending arrest. There was so much to worry about that her head was spinning. So much, in fact, that even a champion-caliber worrier such as she was having trouble keeping on track. Suki smiled wryly and kicked a good-sized rock over the edge of the bluff.

Last night, when reading Naomi Braverman's treatment notes, Suki had been struck by what Lindsey had called her "daymares," visions or hallucinations she experienced while awake. Lindsey had also complained of nightmares and headaches and blackouts and violent mood swings. Could Alexa suffer from temporal lobe epilepsy? Although TLE might explain Alexa's hallucination of Jonah's death and her nightmares, it didn't explain the uncanny accuracy with which her visions mirrored actual events.

Suki hoped to talk to both Naomi and Dr. Smith-Holt, the neurologist who had tested Lindsey at Mass General, this morning—she *had* to talk to them both if she was going to get the first section of the report to Mike by the end of the day. She could ask about Alexa's symptoms. Schedule tests. She threw another rock into the stream. If it turned out that Alexa did indeed have TLE, would this be good or bad news?

Suki heard pounding behind her. She quickly dropped one knee to the pavement and pretended to be tying her shoe. Warren Blanchard was rounding the bend of Country Club Lane. She felt a bit duplicitous about staging this meeting, but figured the morality, or more precisely, the immorality, of the encounter was the least of her worries. She stood up and turned toward him. He nodded and kept running.

"Warren?" she called, as if she had just had the idea to speak to him.

He turned and ran back to where she was standing. He looked at her expectantly as he ran in place, his ponytail slapping the back of his neck.

"Hi." Suki shifted from one foot to the other.

"Hi," Warren said and stopped running. He pulled a small towel from the back of his belt and wiped his face. He hiked up his left sock. "You, ah, you doing okay?"

"As well as can be expected, I suppose." She tried to smile but could feel from the downward tug of the corner of her mouth that she wasn't succeeding. "Better than I would have guessed."

"How 'bout Alexa?" he asked.

"Hard to tell." She shrugged. "Even under the best of circumstances, teenagers are usually far from okay."

Warren started jogging in place again. "I'm, ah, I'm kind of in a rush this morning. Early class. So I'm sorry, but I've got to get—"

"I only need a minute," Suki interrupted. "I know it's a lot to ask, and that given the circumstances, you'd have every right to turn me down, but Alexa didn't do it, and I think you know that, and you're the only one I can think of who can help me with this."

"I don't understand." He continued jogging.

"It's Finlay," she said in a rush. "Finlay Thompson. Ellery got him to quit his job and I don't know where he is."

"I don't see how I can help you." Warren had the look of a man extremely anxious to be on his way.

"You could find out where he is," Suki said quickly. "And I just thought, I just knew that you'd care about what really happened to Jonah, about who really killed him." She pulled out all the stops.

"If you don't want to do it for me, do it for your sister—for Jonah."

Warren stopped jogging. "You want to talk to Finlay about that night?"

Suki nodded.

"How about the police?"

"They're not interested in anything that might clear Alexa," Suki said. "They're only interested in making the easiest arrest—and apparently so is the town council."

Warren looked into the woods. "You think Ellery got Finlay to lie for him?" he asked.

"Don't you?" she countered.

Warren put his left heel on the pavement and leaned forward, chin jutting over his knee. He did the same to the right. "So I find out where Finlay is, and then you go there and get him to change his story?"

"That's the general plan."

"And Finlay's going to up and admit he lied to the police? To the newspapers?" Warren raised his eyebrows. "He's going to get himself in trouble, big trouble, just because you ask him to?"

"He's going to do it because it's the right thing to do," Suki said. "Because Finlay's a good person and this has got to be eating him up alive."

Warren stuffed his fists into the pockets of his running shorts then began to roll a large pebble beneath the sole of his sneaker. Back and forth. Back and forth against the asphalt. He watched the pebble as if fascinated by its movement, then kicked it across the stream. "I suppose it's possible," he finally said, eyeing Judi's rocky backyard. "If your underlying suppositions are correct."

"Oh, they're correct," she said, encouraged by his words, if not by his body language. "You don't really think Alexa was driving around alone that night, with a loaded gun on the seat, looking to kill Jonah, do you?"

Warren jerked his head up.

"Oh, I'm sorry, Warren." Suki reached out for his arm. "That was a stupid, horrid thing to say."

He dismissed her apologies with the shake of his head. "No," he said softly. "No, I don't suppose she was."

"Please," Suki continued, upset by the emotion that choked his voice. "You've got to excuse me, I'm not thinking clearly. I'm so wrapped up in my own—"

"Don't." Warren held up his hands to stop her words. "I hate it when those damn government agencies start pursuing their own agendas. When the little guy gets screwed. Sure," he said. "Sure, I'll be glad to try to help you. More than glad."

Suki smiled in relief. "Thanks," she said. "Thanks a lot."

"No need." Warren took a deep breath and began to jog in place again. "We're both after the same thing, aren't we?"

They discussed the details of how Warren might discover Finlay's location and when he would call her. He even offered to join her when she confronted Finlay, noting that two accusers might be more persuasive than one. Suki was so surprised by the offer that she agreed it might be good, although she was not at all certain it would be. As she watched Warren take off down Roaring

Brook, his legs covering the distance in his effort-
less yet powerful stride, she couldn't help but
notice how nicely defined the muscles of his body
were, how gracefully he moved. Then she checked
her watch and headed home.

Despite her abbreviated exercise, Suki felt surprisingly good as she power-walked the half mile
back to her house. If Jonah's uncle could be convinced Alexa was innocent, then other people could
be, too.

When Suki got home both Kyle and Alexa were
already at the kitchen table. From the empty box of
Multi-grain Cheerios on the counter—the one she
had just bought yesterday—Suki guessed Kyle was on
at least his third bowl of cereal. Alexa was drinking a
cup a black coffee. Occasionally she nibbled on a
Saltine.

"Good news, Alexa." Suki poured herself a glass
of orange juice and leaned against the sink. "Warren
Blanchard's going to help us break the boys' alibi."

"Coach," Kyle said, then turned his attention
back to his cereal.

"I don't understand." Alexa put down her coffee
cup. "How can he help?"

Suki explained why she wanted to talk to Finlay,
one of the many things she hadn't had the time to
discuss with Alexa, then described her visit to the rec
center.

Alexa's jaw tightened as she listened to what
Ellery had done. "Asshole," she muttered.

Suki let it go. She told Alexa and Kyle how she

had waited for Warren and asked him to help her find out where Finlay might have gone.

"Awesome." Kyle held his spoon in the air and looked at her approvingly. "Like a PI flick."

"This is no *PI flick*," Alexa snapped. "This is real life. My life. And we don't need Mr. Blanchard's help."

"Coach is cool," Kyle argued.

Alexa punched her brother in the arm. "Like you know what's cool."

He pushed her hands away as if he were swatting at a pesky mosquito. "Get out of my face."

Before Suki could admonish them, Alexa jumped from her seat. "I don't want you running around with Mr. Blanchard," she said.

Despite the seriousness of the situation, Suki smiled inwardly at Alexa's choice of words: as if she, rather than Suki, were the parent. "Warren Blanchard is one of the few people around here who seems willing to help—"

"I don't care what he's willing to do," Alexa interrupted. "He just wants to get into your pants—"

"Alexa!" Suki was stunned.

"Well it's the truth and you should know it. You never appreciated Daddy. That's why he left. You were too busy with everything else."

"You know that just isn't—"

"It is," Alexa interrupted, her voice rising. "You and Kyle were always too busy. With work, with your stupid library board, with Kyle's dumb soccer games. And neither of you miss Daddy now. You don't care that he's gone. You like it. I'm the only one who cares. The only one who misses him!" She slammed her chest with the flat of her hand. "Only me!" Then she burst into tears and ran out of the room.

Suki looked at Kyle.

"She's really gone over this time." He scooped up the last of his cereal, then raised his head from his bowl. "Think you could make me a couple English muffins?"

Suki opened the freezer and dropped a package of frozen muffins on the table. Kyle had the grace to look embarrassed. "Make them yourself," she said, then turned and followed Alexa to her bedroom.

Suki knocked with what she hoped was an upbeat tap. "Alexa?" she called. "Alexa, honey, let me in."

"It's open." Alexa's voice was empty of emotion. Barren. Dead. She was seated cross-legged on the bed. Her eyes were closed and she was massaging her temples.

Alexa had been such a beautiful baby, the kind people were always stopping to admire in malls and on the street. She and Stan used to complain that they couldn't get through a meal in a restaurant without someone interrupting them to fawn over the little girl. But of course, they loved every minute of it. So long ago, those days of jelly-covered fingers and tiny blue sneakers. "Headache?" Suki asked.

"It's like my forehead's being pounded from the inside out."

Suki sat down next to Alexa, who winced as the bed shifted, and pressed her lips to her daughter's forehead. It was clear Alexa needed more help than she was getting. "Honey," she said slowly, "you've been through so much the last couple of weeks. You can't handle this alone." Suki took Alexa's fingers in hers and rubbed them between her palms, trying to bring some warmth to the icy skin. "We need to talk. You need to tell me how you're feeling so I can help you. So we can figure out if we need to get you more help than I can—"

"I want Daddy!" Alexa threw herself at her mother and began sobbing again. "Daddy's all the help that I need."

"I tried to reach him again last night," Suki said. "I've left word everywhere I can think of. With everyone I can think of. I'm sure he'll call as soon as he can. As soon as he gets the message." As much as Stan's abandonment had hurt Suki, his abandonment of the children had hurt her more, but never as much as it did now, as Alexa sobbed in her arms for the father she didn't have. The father she would never have. Even if he walked through the door right this minute.

"Do you think he'll come home when he hears?" Alexa raised her tear-streaked face.

"I'm sure he will, honey," Suki said, although she was far from certain: Stan's selfishness knew no bounds. "I'm sure he will."

Alexa grabbed a tissue from the box on her end table. She blew her nose. "Remember when I had that dream?" she asked, then blew her nose again. "When I was a little girl?"

"Which one?"

"The one where the house was on fire." Alexa didn't need to elaborate because they both knew the end of the story. A month after Alexa's dream, a fire had started in the basement. Suki hadn't been home when it happened, but Stan, who was upstairs with Kyle, was alerted by a smoke detector. The fire was extinguished without too much damage to the house, or any to Alexa, who had been playing down there at the time. Stan had immediately purchased and installed another dozen smoke detectors. Even now, a puff of burning toast sent alarms blaring all over the house.

Suki wondered if she should tell Alexa about optical isomers and Doris Sheketoff, or if the fact that she was considering that precognition might be possible would upset Alexa even more, perhaps encourage more episodes. "And you think predicting the fire was the same as predicting Jonah's death?" Suki asked.

Alexa pressed her forehead into her palm.

"Alexa," Suki said softly. "Do you remember the dream you had last night? Do you remember calling out? Talking to me?"

Alexa shook her head and dropped back onto her pillow.

Suki looked at Alexa, at her almost skeletal cheekbones, at the hollows of her eye sockets deepened by dark smudges. She looked like the patients in the hospital where Suki had done her training. Like her own mother had looked right before her death.

Alexa opened her eyes. She stared over Suki's shoulder. "I don't want you to get involved with Warren Blanchard."

"I'm not *getting involved* with Warren Blanchard," Suki tried to explain it in a way Alexa could buy. "I'm getting him to help us prove the boys are lying—to break their alibi. This is something we need very badly and I don't think I can do it by myself."

"It's not worth it," Alexa argued.

"Sometimes I'm not sure you understand what's at stake here. I worry—"

"It's the wrong thing to do," Alexa interrupted. "Bad for you. Bad for us."

"It'll be worse if we don't get some help. That note from Jonah changes things—it gives you a motive. We're just lucky the police didn't find it, because if they had . . ." Suki caught herself. "It's just important that we break the boys' alibi as soon as possible."

"But I can see it," Alexa said. "I'm not making it up. It's wrong. Bad. I can see these things—you can't!"

"Are you telling me that you *see* that breaking the boys' alibi is bad the way you *saw* that Jonah was going to be shot?" Suki asked.

Alexa slumped against the wall. "You don't need Mr. Blanchard if Daddy's coming home."

CHAPTER ELEVEN

People who live in New England yearn for spring the way a convict yearns for early release, but New Englanders are inevitably disappointed, for the spring they dream of through the dark confinement of winter never comes to pass. Instead, winter melts into a series of raw, gray days, then it becomes hot as hell. Suki was a New Englander born and bred, and a lifetime of cold, wet springs had never managed to crowd out her hope that *this* April would be different.

As she stared through the raindrops streaking the windshield of Warren's car, Suki searched for the sun, for a brief glimmer of light, of hope, a sign that this trip wasn't just a futile attempt to convince herself that she had it within her power to help Alexa. It began to rain harder.

They were heading west on the Mass Pike, crossing the state to reach the little hamlet of Sunderland, where Finlay Thompson's daughter owned a fishing cabin on Okemo Lake. Warren had found Finlay so quickly that Suki was still having difficulty believing it had been this simple, that McKinna had gone to all the trouble of getting Finlay out of town, then made it so easy to find him. Ellery either thought her a fool or was so convinced by his own lies that he didn't think he needed to follow through on them. Both possibilities were encouraging.

Warren had simply walked into the rec center office and asked Alice where Finlay was. Alice told him Finlay was taking a short vacation at the lake before starting his new job. When Warren mentioned he might like to stop by for a visit, she gave him directions. Alice and Finlay's daughter, Donna, were good friends.

Suki smiled weakly at Warren, who smiled back, then they both quickly turned their eyes to the windshield. She lifted her coffee from the cup holder and took a sip. It burned her tongue. "So . . ." She cleared her throat. "Sure worked out well. You figuring out where Finlay was so fast. This being Saturday, and all."

"Yup," Warren said, flashing her a toothy grin. "Worked out well." In rhythm with the song on the oldies station, he tapped the dashboard with his right hand, but every once in a while he missed a beat—a dead giveaway that he was neither as calm nor as cheerful as he was acting. Either that or he had a very bad sense of rhythm. It crossed Suki's mind that Alexa might be right about Warren's romantic interest—he *had* always been very nice at Kyle's soccer games—but then she dismissed the idea. Given the circumstances, it was just too absurd.

Suki ran her fingers through her hair and stared out at the rain. Warren switched the wipers to the next highest speed. She took another sip of her coffee. It was still too hot. "Lovely weather," she said.

"Lovely," he agreed.

It had been like this since they left Witton, almost half an hour before. Stilted. Wary. The air in the car thick with their awkwardness. They didn't really know each other and now, suddenly, they were confined in a very small space. A space that felt ever smaller and more uncomfortably intimate as the sky lowered and darkened. Suki glanced at Warren. His hands on the steering wheel were large and capable, his chiseled profile intent, imperfectly handsome. She quickly returned her gaze to the rain.

Suki scoured her brain for something to talk about. Aside from being a Ph.D. student in biology and a soccer coach, Warren was also a science mentor at the high school. Ironically, Devin McKinna was one of the students with whom he regularly worked. But Devin McKinna didn't seem an appropriate topic, and she didn't know much about biology.

Warren ratcheted the wipers up another notch and began to whistle along with the radio, but had difficulty maintaining the sound; it came out like a lot of puffing and blowing. Suki found the sound endearing. As she watched the landscape rushing by, the rain-blackened trees, their forking branches growing more gaunt and crooked as they reached toward the sky, Suki wondered how she was going to convince Finlay to act against his own self-interest. She didn't need advanced degrees in psychology to know this was not a common motivation for human behavior.

Suki closed her eyes. The rain droning on the roof grew softer then louder then softer again. She drifted in and out. She was playing volleyball with her mother in the middle of a lake without shores. She was climbing rocks with Stan and six-year-old Alexa. She was at summer camp with Finlay, who grew uglier and uglier and laughed louder and louder, his tongue hanging from his mouth as he taunted her for her stupidity. She was at a prison visiting Alexa.

Suki's eyes flew open and she bolted upright. It was very warm in the car. She was sweating and her mouth was dry.

Warren turned onto the exit ramp. He pulled up to the toll gate, paid the fare and smiled at her. "Have a nice nap?" he asked.

Suki took a gulp of her now-tepid coffee. She leaned back against the headrest. "I don't know if it really was a nap. But it wasn't all that nice."

"You have those directions?"

Suki nodded, relieved Warren had no interest in the details of her emotional state. The route wasn't difficult, and within a few minutes they drove up to a small cabin perched at the end of a narrow finger of choppy, gray water. There was a dark midsize Buick in the gravel driveway. When Warren identified it as Finlay's, Suki swallowed hard.

"Ready?" Warren asked, pulling up the hood of his raincoat. It was still pouring.

"Ready," Suki answered, although she wasn't.

Warren raced to the cabin. There were no gutters or overhangs on the house, and the rain rolled down the roof onto Warren's hood. He banged on the door. When Suki saw the door swing inward, she followed.

"Warren," Finlay was saying, his lined face creased in a smile of welcome, his brow puckered with uncertainty. "Come in, come in! Come in out of the rain. What brings—" He stopped when he saw

Suki, and his face flushed a deep red. He squared his shoulders and straddled the threshold.

Suki stood on the walk letting the rain pour over her, her arms crossed over her chest as she silently watched Finlay.

"Let's get inside, Suki," Warren said as if Finlay weren't blocking their way. "It's raining out here, you know."

Finlay grunted and stepped aside, allowing them to enter.

The modest wood-paneled room smelled of dampness and decline; it contained far too much furniture. Light from a single lamp cut a cone of brightness through the gloom in one corner. A book lay open on an overstuffed chair. Sherlock Holmes. Finlay shifted from one foot to the other. He didn't take their coats or invite them to sit.

Suki took off her jacket and shook it over the mat at the front door, then she hung it on the back of a rocking chair and turned to Finlay.

Before she could say anything, Warren motioned toward the couch. "Why don't we all sit?" he suggested.

Neither Suki nor Finlay moved.

Warren touched Finlay's arm. "We have to talk."

"Now's not a good time," Finlay said. "Lil's not doing so well."

"What's wrong?" Suki asked, speaking for the first time. Lil was Finlay's wife. She had baby-sat for Stan when he was little and, although they didn't see much of her, she had remained in contact with the family, sending boxes of homemade Christmas cookies at the holidays and cards on the children's birthdays. "Stan'll be back with his tail between his legs," Lil told Suki about a month after Stan left. Stan always said Lil called them as she saw them—whether or not anyone asked her to. And this was true enough. "He's just a roamer," Lil continued. "Never satisfied, even as a little boy." Then she had pressed Suki to her huge bosom, immersing her in the smell of sugar cookies and toilet water. "But he'll tire of his adventure. They all do. God bless 'em." Of course, calling them as she saw them didn't mean Lil's vision was all that keen.

Finlay didn't acknowledge Suki's question. He looked at Warren. "She's in the kitchen."

"How's she doing?" Warren asked.

Finlay shrugged. "Good days and bad days. She goes in and out from minute to minute."

Suki tried to remember if she had heard anything about Lil Thompson's being sick, but came up empty. Yet clearly something was wrong. She looked into the kitchen.

Lil was there, seated at the Formica table, staring dreamily across the room at the stove, her head slightly bowed. She was wearing a housedress, the flowered cotton kind she had always favored. Her apron was on backward and her lipstick was drawn halfway across her left cheek. She had a large pink bow in her hair, the sort usually worn by five-year-old girls. Dementia, Suki thought. How awful.

When the old woman turned and saw Suki standing in the doorway, her face creased with joy. "Oh, my dear," she said, clapping her hands together. "I'm so glad you've come so early. I didn't expect you till dinnertime. I started to call, but when

I went to use the phone, I forgot how it worked."
Lil's matter-of-fact tone chilled Suki as much as her
words. "I wanted to ask you if Gary could look at
Dad's car. It's making an awful racket and I worry
that Dad's going to get stuck out on some deserted
road all alone one night. But I told your father that I
was sure Gary would know just what to do." Gary
was Lil's son-in-law. Impaired recognition, not a
good sign.

"Just tell her you'll ask him," Finlay said, coming
up behind Suki.

"Of course," Suki said smoothly. "I'm sure Gary
will be glad to take a look."

Lil smiled brightly, expectantly.

Finlay walked over to his wife and placed a hand
on her shoulder. "We're going to go into the living
room and talk for a bit, Lil. Will you be all right in
here by yourself?"

"You run along with the young folks, dear." Lil
patted Finlay's hand. "You know I can't talk to people anymore. I just forget what I'm saying and con-
fuse everyone."

Finlay leaned over and kissed her forehead, then
motioned Suki to follow him. They left Lil in the
kitchen, smiling vaguely in the direction of the living room.

"Oh, Finlay," Suki said, forgetting, for a moment,
the reason for their visit. "I'm so sorry. I had no idea.
Did they give you a specific diagnosis?"

"Doesn't much matter to me what fancy name
they call it." Finlay dropped into the rocking chair,
oblivious to Suki's wet coat. He cracked each of the
knuckles on his left hand.

"The reason it's important is because some types are treatable," Suki told him. "Depending on the cause. If the dementia's from heart disease or an endocrine disorder, even a vitamin deficiency—"

"Last week," Finlay interrupted, "instead of putting the newspapers in the closet, she put them in the oven and forgot they were there." He cracked each of the knuckles on his right hand. "Started a fire the next morning when she went to bake some bread."

Neither Suki nor Warren said anything.

"If Donna hadn't happened by at the time, who knows how bad it could've been." The shadows of the rivulets of rain cascading down the front window played across Finlay's creased face, dripping and crossing one another, flickering gloom and gloomier. "Lil was such a lively young thing," he said, his eyes focused on the past. "But now it's like she's just slowly fading away. . . ."

Suki turned from Finlay's pain. Lil was visible through the kitchen doorway. Gradual onset, Suki thought, progressive decline. "I'm sorry," she whispered, and she was—very, very sorry. Seeing Lil brought it all back. Her mother. How her mother had been. In and out. Missing. "My mother slowly disappeared, too," Suki said.

Finlay turned from the window and their eyes met for the first time. "My Lil comes and goes. And every time she goes, I wonder if it means she's not coming back. But the part of her that looks like her, whether she comes back or not, still needs to be taken care of."

Suki understood all too well what Finlay meant.

Her real mother, the mother who had read her stories and taught her to draw and passed on her love of historical novels and her empathy for the underdog, wasn't always within the woman who looked and smelled like her mother. But, somehow, that made Suki love that woman all the more.

"I love her just as much," Finlay was saying. "Maybe even more."

Suki nodded, knowing he was going to have to make the same tough decision she had made. Probably soon.

"I'm going to have to put Lil in a home soon. For her own safety." Finlay stared out the window again and the rain's shadows intermingled with his tears. He didn't sob or make any noise; the tears just flowed down his face: unimpeded, exposed, proud. "I'm sorry for your troubles," he said, "but I need my benefits. For Lil."

Suki pulled some tissues from her purse and offered one to Finlay, but he shook his head. "I understand," she said. "Really I do, but I still need to ask you to help me. I need you to come back to Witton with us. To talk to the police. To tell them the truth—to tell them the boys weren't at the rec center that night. To clear Alexa. Please," she pleaded, "I need you to help me save my daughter's life. She's just a child, a baby. She's only seventeen."

Finlay eyes still sparkled with tears. "I understand why you have to ask," he said. "And I know you'll understand when I tell you that there's nothing new I have to say to the police, nothing to change from my original statement. There just isn't anything I can do to help you."

It seemed to Suki that she had known Finlay's exact words before he formed them, as if she had heard each one in her mind a millisecond before he spoke it. Perhaps this was what Lindsey meant by clairvoyance. "But there is," Suki cried. "There's so much you can do. With a few simple words you can right a terrible wrong." She leaned over and grasped Finlay's hands in hers. "You've got to be feeling badly about this. I know that you must."

"Lil's my first priority." Finlay tried to pull his hands away, but Suki would not let go.

"Look," Suki said, "I know a lot of people in social services. I'm sure there's a way we can get you some coverage. Or help: a homemaker, transportation, day care." She squeezed his hands and then sat on the couch.

"Can you guarantee me that Lil will be in a nice place, that she'll be taken care of, not just thrown away?"

"There are no guarantees, but—"

"Can't take the chance," Finlay interrupted.

"Finlay?" Lil was standing in the kitchen doorway. Her apron was still on backward and her lipstick was still splayed across her face, but her eyes were alive. "Why didn't you tell me Warren and Suki were here?" she demanded. "Did you offer them some coffee or tea? Some cookies?" She turned to Suki and Warren. "I'm so glad to see you both. Let me go get you some of my fresh-baked cookies." She headed toward the kitchen then swung around. "Are you two an item?" she asked.

Suki smiled. The old Lil was back, speaking her mind. It was just as Finlay had said: in and out, minute by minute. "No," she said. "We just stopped by for a quick visit."

Lil narrowed her eyes suspiciously. "There's something funny going on here. . . ."

"Now, Lil," Finlay said, reaching up and placing a placating hand on her arm. "There's no need to bother your little head about—"

"I'm not a child," Lil snapped, whipping her arm out from under her husband's hand. The pink bow in her hair fell to the floor. "And my 'little head' *is* bothered. Why were you talking about Stan's girl, Alexa? Does this have something to do with your new job?"

Suki and Warren exchanged glances, but neither said a word. Suki felt hope flare through her and she grabbed Warren's hand.

"It's complicated, Lil," Finlay tried again. The crackling of his knuckles was sharp and loud.

Lil crossed her arms over her large breasts. "Right is right and wrong is wrong," she said, as if she had a much better grasp on the situation than Finlay had led them to believe.

"You know Ellery got me this new job. You know he'll jinx it for us and then we won't be able to make it."

"Pooh on Ellery McKinna," Lil said. "The Lord will provide."

"The Lord isn't going to pay the doctor bills," Finlay said, but Suki detected the beginning of resignation in his voice. She clutched Warren's hand more tightly and held her breath.

"Then the government will," Lil declared.

"Aw, Lil, that doesn't—"

Lil wagged her finger at him again. "Right is right and wrong is wrong, and it's very wrong not to offer our guests something to eat. I'm going to get those cookies I made this morning, and when I come back we'll continue our discussion."

"You didn't make any cookies this morning," Finlay said softly, but Lil didn't appear to hear him. She bustled toward the kitchen. When she got there, she sat back down at the table and resumed her dreamy gazing.

Finlay sighed and stood up. "'From the mouths of babes.'"

Suki paced the L-shaped corridor of the Witton police station. She had been up and down the hallway so many times she was beginning to imagine she could differentiate between the design of the brown-speckled tile at the entrance of the interrogation room and the design of the brown-speckled tile at the foot of the stairway. The station bustled with noise and activity, but no one paid her any mind. She couldn't imagine what was taking so long.

Although Kenneth had tried to convince her to go home, promising he would call as soon as the boys had completed their statements, Suki could not leave. Alexa was going to be cleared, and Suki wanted to be here. The second it happened. The moment it became fact. Even if it took all night.

The ride back from Sunderland had been even more uncomfortable than the ride out, if that was possible. Finlay had huddled in the back seat, silent and pale, cracking his knuckles until Suki was sure his fingers would fall off. Lil, who Finlay had decided could not be left alone, spent the ride reading every sign she saw. "Palmer Ware. Lee Lenox," she called out, as if she was reading men's names instead of passing towns. "Sturbridge Worcester."

Warren had been quiet, focused on seeing through the driving storm. Suki, too, said nothing as she stared out the window at the rain that continued unabated. She was edgy and jumpy and played silly games with herself such as if-I-see-three-Connecticut-licence-plates-in-three-minutes-it-means-Alexa-will-be-cleared and if-four-black-cars-pass-us-it-means-Finlay's-going-to-change-his-mind. By the time they reached the police station, Suki was a wreck.

But everything went smoothly. Kenneth was on duty and Finlay's daughter, who Finlay had called before they left Sunderland, was there waiting for them. With Donna at his elbow, Finlay stood tall and told the detective why he had come. As Kenneth disappeared into an interrogation room, he flashed Suki a "thumbs-up" sign. He looked like a happy, redheaded Abe Lincoln. Suki grinned at the closed door, finally allowing herself to believe that this really was happening.

Warren was having dinner with Darcy, so he had dropped Suki off at home. When he climbed out of the car, he had given her a hug and mumbled awkwardly about how glad he was things had turned out as they had. His voice shook slightly. Suki was touched by his concern and decided she would invite him to dinner when this was all over. But she quickly forgot Warren as she ran in to tell Alexa the news, then climbed into her own car and drove back to the station. She had been walking the halls ever since.

The boys had been brought in while she was gone and placed in separate interrogation rooms with their parents and a rotating group of police. Uniforms and detectives and the state cop from the night Jonah was killed all cycled through the rooms. The media had gotten wind that something was up. Reporters bumped into each other in the small lobby.

Suki was sorry that she had missed Ellery's arrival; she had been looking forward to greeting him, but consoled herself with the fact that she was sure to have another opportunity. Finlay and Lil were now long gone. They had left with Donna around five, both visibly exhausted. Suki hoped nothing would happen to Finlay. Given the situation, pressing charges seemed beyond cruel and unusual.

She continued her pacing, although she too was exhausted and, aside from coffee and a few packages of peanut butter crackers, hadn't eaten anything since breakfast. Her stomach growled and her head hurt; she decided a person couldn't eat too many peanut butter crackers. Climbing past two policemen talking on the stairway, she headed upstairs to the vending machine. As she reached down to remove the orange package from the drawer, a hand gripped her shoulder. She swung around. Kenneth's large frame filled the hallway. One look at his face and Suki froze.

"What?" she demanded.

"Come." Kenneth gently took her arm. "Come

on in here for a minute." He waved toward a shadowy room filled with rows of empty chairs facing a podium. "We need to talk."

"Finlay said the boys weren't at the rec center," Suki cried. "I heard him. He said Ellery got him to lie about it to save Devin's skin!"

"Suki," Kenneth begged, "it's not that simple."

Suki yanked her arm from Kenneth's grasp. "Yes, it is," she insisted, wishing that saying it would make it true, knowing that it did not. "It *is* that simple."

Kenneth steered her into the darkened room. He closed the door but didn't turn on the lights. A bank of windows lit the room with an eerie blue-white light from the parking lot below. The bustle and sounds of the station were muted; it all seemed very far away. Surreal.

"It's too early to know exactly what this is going to mean for—" Kenneth began.

"Do the boys deny being there?" Suki interrupted. "Does Ellery still claim they were with him?"

"No." Kenneth leaned against the back of one of the chairs and rubbed at his beard. "No, they admit they were in your car."

"So what's the problem?" Suki didn't like the sound of the words: *your car.*

Kenneth clasped Suki's shoulders and took a deep breath. "The boys all deny they had anything to do with the murder."

"Deny it?" Suki shook her head, as if this movement would help her make some sense of Kenneth's words. She felt as if she were floating, floating like Alice in a world where up was down and left was right. "But, but then how . . . ?"

Kenneth dropped into an empty chair and pulled Suki into the one next to him; he took her small hands in his big ones. "Brendan says he didn't see what happened, but both Devin and Sam claim it was Alexa who fired the gun."

Suki stared at Kenneth. The blue-white light from the parking lot made his cheekbones stand out. He was all shadows and angles. Not of this world. "No," Suki said from within a disquieting sense of déjà vu. "That can't be. It's impossible."

Kenneth pressed her hands between his own as if the human contact might ease her pain. "Impossibly so."

"It's the wrong thing to do," Alexa had said. *"Bad for you. Bad for us."*

CHAPTER TWELVE

It was first thing Monday morning, and Suki had a two-hour session with Lindsey to administer the Minnesota Multiphasic Personality Inventory. She would have preferred three hours, but she was overloaded with both work and schemes to expose Ellery McKinna's lies. She saw Ellery as a tiny, impotent figure, huddled behind a curtain like the Wizard of Oz, pulling the strings that kept tripping Alexa. And she saw herself ripping back that curtain and revealing him for the coward he was.

As she waited for Lindsey, Suki pulled two MMPI test booklets and a scoring sheet from her briefcase. For the first time since Saturday night, she had a chance to think about something beside Finlay Thompson and Ellery McKinna. She had chosen the MMPI because it was the best paper-and-pencil test for dividing people into one of two groups, sane or insane, and was equally good at assessing malingering (in the vernacular, faking); it was the simplest and most direct way to get a gross assessment of Lindsey's current mental status and, even more important, to rule out the chance that she was using her intelligence and manipulative skills to feign insanity.

Suki wondered if there was a paper-and-pencil test to assess precognitive ability. She knew quite a bit of research had been done in which subjects guessed the symbol on the back of so-called ESP cards, but somehow that seemed a qualitatively different thing from predicting the future. How would one even go about designing an experiment to measure precognition?

Suki flipped open one of the booklets. The MMPI consisted of over five hundred true-false questions such as "I worry about sexual matters," "I sometimes tease animals," and "I believe I'm being plotted against." Although the test contained scales measuring everything from depression to hypomania to schizophrenia, Suki was most interested in Validity Scales L and F which, when scored together, were strong indicators of malingering. She needed to know how much she could trust Lindsey.

The door opened, and Darla's large frame filled the doorway. Lindsey breezed into the room and wagged her finger playfully at Suki. "I told you I could've found that guy for you," she said. "You should've let me help when you had the chance. It would've been so much easier."

Suki said hello to Lindsey and nodded to Darla that she was free to leave.

Lindsey drummed the fingers of both hands on the table in a triumphant roll, then dropped into a chair. "I also warned you that you were on the wrong track—and I was right about that, too." She leaned forward eagerly. Her face looked much better, less swollen, the blackened skin around her eye had shifted toward yellow-green. "Tell me exactly what happened, and I'll tell you what I saw." She was almost bouncing in her seat.

Suki glanced from her watch to the booklets in front of her, and then back at Lindsey. "I'm sorry, Lindsey," she said, "but you know we can't do that."

Lindsey deflated into her chair, as if someone had pricked her with a pin and diffused all her energy. "More of that psychological mumbo-jumbo you shrinks like so much?" she grumbled.

"I want to give you what we call an objective personality assessment. It's a self-report paper-and-pencil test that measures—"

"I rest my case," Lindsey interrupted.

"Touché." Suki flashed a quick smile of appreciation. "Have you ever taken an MMPI before?"

"Those tests are absurd," Lindsey said. "How can you measure how crazy someone is by asking them if they like sex?"

Again, Suki had to appreciate Lindsey's point—and her range of knowledge about all manner of things. Although psychologists routinely used standardized assessment tests—as did human resource people screening job applicants and consultants running focus groups on car-buying behavior—to measure everything from self-esteem to IQ to proclivity to have an extramarital affair, the error factors *were* quite large. "I know it seems strange," Suki said, "and there're plenty of people who agree with you, but these tests can be pretty powerful in court."

"It's a lot of bullshit," Lindsey said without a hint of anger in her voice.

Suki watched Lindsey warily; these wide mood swings were not a good sign, nor was the contrast between Lindsey's affect and her words. Suki wondered again if Lindsey might be using drugs. She waited.

"You really believe some number's going to tell you anything about me?

"It's a piece of the picture."

Lindsey stuffed a tendril of hair back into her ponytail. "I'll make a deal with you," she offered. "You talk to me about what happened this weekend and I'll take your test."

Suki shook her head. "You don't have to take it if you don't want to."

"Did you know they have tests that measure precognitive ability?" Lindsey asked.

"You mean those ESP card experiments?"

Lindsey cleared her throat, assuming the demeanor of an instructor without much respect for her pupils. "They used to use those cards a lot—five symbols in a deck of twenty-five, five times five—especially J. B. Rhine and his cronies in the thirties and forties. But no one uses them any more. Now it's much more high tech: random-number generators, bio-PK, the ganzfeld technique."

Suki was hooked.

"And it's real science." Lindsey was grinning. "The random-number studies are a mind over matter thing. The subjects try to mentally 'change' how the numbers are distributed—you know, how with heads or tails, you'd expect a fifty-fifty split?—well, if the results aren't fifty-fifty, or whatever's expected, then the assumption is that there's a psychic effect going on."

"And they've done lots of these?" Suki asked. "With consistent results?"

Lindsey pulled at her earlobe. "I just wrote a

short paper on this for a research methods course," she said. "Let me see if I can remember. In 1989 a meta-analysis—that's where they combine the results of lots of the same kinds of studies—of over eight hundred random-number experiments was published, and although the effect wasn't huge, it was there—and it was consistent. Something like fifteen standard errors from the mean, which basically translates into the chance of it happening by chance being zero."

Suki was impressed. That kind of result was pretty meaningful. "But isn't that really a different thing than precognition?"

Lindsey became quite agitated, squirming in her seat and pulling again on her earlobe. "Kind of," she finally admitted. "But don't you see? It's related. Like bio-PK, where they study that 'feeling of being stared at' or the ganzfeld, where the subject is put into a meditative state to become a better receiver." She performed the same two-handed table drum roll she had executed earlier. "It's all about the fact that human consciousness is a much more powerful receiver and sender of sensory information than 'science' or 'biology' would suggest."

Suki thought about Alexa, her dreams of the past, her visions of the future. "Receiving information from the future?"

"Remember your pen?" Lindsey demanded, jumping up from her seat. "My friend Babs's apple? If time is the fourth dimension, then it's possible the future isn't happening in the future. It's happening now." She pressed her back into the wall and looked at Suki defiantly.

Suki was simultaneously attracted and repelled by the concept—in the same way she was attracted and repelled by Lindsey Kern.

"The interest in this is huge," Lindsey said, throwing her arms open wide; Suki could see the damp stain of sweat on the undersides of her sleeves. "Researchers did the same kind of a meta-analysis—but just on the precognition studies—and found that there had been something like fifty thousand subjects in almost two million trials. Two million trials! Can you believe they actually carried out two million trials? What a world!"

Suki casually waved for Lindsey to sit down. "But how do you do research on something that hasn't happened yet?"

Lindsey dropped back into her chair. "Forced-choice methods, mostly, like the ESP cards, except that the subject's guesses are recorded *before* the cards—or whatever the target—are chosen."

"And that works?"

"The results are weaker, but still there," Lindsey said. "They have the same problem in the lab that I do. Like I was telling you the other day. The vision, the image, whatever it is, just kind of comes. That's the way it is for me, and I guess for most people. Suddenly it's there and I know—or think I know—that X is going to happen." She shook her head sadly. "I've tried to make it happen, but it almost never works. I'm just not that good—I've no real talent—most of my images come in dreams." Then she perked up. "But if I've been meditating it seems to be easier."

One of the parapsychology books Suki had been reading mentioned that precognitive dreams were quite common. She thought she even remembered a discussion of some research. And something about meditation. She would have to check when she got home.

"And I have been meditating a lot." Lindsey closed her eyes and sat silently for a long moment.

Suki waited.

"I'm trying to find him," Lindsey said, her voice soft and dreamy. "Find him."

Suki glanced surreptitiously at her watch. Lindsey's eyes remained closed.

"Gray water," Lindsey said. "He's near gray water."

"Who?" Suki asked. "Who's near gray water?"

"The person you need to find. He's near water and trees."

Suki stared at Lindsey. Could she be talking about Finlay? Suki's pencil rolled off the table and onto the floor.

"West," Lindsey continued. "West of here, but not far."

Suki felt cold in the marrow of her bones. "I already found him," she said. "On Saturday."

"Damn it!" Lindsey's eyes flew open. "I told you I couldn't do it. I told you I was no good. No good at all!"

"Oh no," Suki assured her. "There's no need to be sorry. He *was* near gray water and he *was* west of here. Your time sequence was just off." The fourth dimension. Like Alexa's elevator shaft dream. Suki bent down to retrieve her pencil, and when she raised her eyes above the edge of the table, Lindsey's face was within inches of her own.

"You're going to need to find another missing person." Lindsey's breath was hot on Suki's cheek. "Let me help you next time." When Suki nodded, Lindsey smiled radiantly and pointed to the test booklet. "Shall we?" she asked.

The administration of psychological assessment tests is not usually a part of forensic training, and less often part of the job. But as a graduate student, Suki had worked for a professor who used the MMPI, the Rorschach and the Stanford-Binet as part of his research protocol, and she had become skilled at administering the tests.

Although the MMPI was sent out to be scored by an independent company, Suki was familiar enough with the test to take a to guess at Lindsey's scores. Despite Lindsey's unsettling mood swings during their interview, Suki was fairly certain she was going to register low on depression, hypomania and schizophrenia, midlevel on hypochondriasis and hysteria, and high on Scales L and F—the subtests used to detect deliberate misrepresentation. This combination was highly suggestive of the absence of mental illness and the presence of manipulation. In other words, there might be nothing wrong with Lindsey Kern that a little faking wouldn't explain.

As Suki climbed into her car she pondered the enigma that was Lindsey Kern. Was she faking? Was her lability an act, part of a preconceived plan? Were her claims of paranormal powers just a ruse to get out of prison? It had been done before—

usually not all that effectively—but Lindsey was a very smart woman, and Suki could imagine a scenario in which Lindsey's assertion that she didn't care if she stayed at Watkins furthered this plan. On the other hand, Lindsey seemed so sincere in her beliefs, so lucid in her explanations, and there was no denying that a number of the things she predicted had occurred. The fact that her prediction about Finlay was in the wrong time dimension somehow made it all even more believable.

The traffic on 128 stopped for no apparent reason, as it often did, and Suki strained to see how far ahead the jam stretched. It was useless. She couldn't see beyond the two vans in front of her, so she drummed her fingers on the steering wheel and wondered if perhaps Lindsey could help her find her daughter. Help her reclaim the Alexa who worried about pop quizzes and which sweater to wear to Robin's party. But Suki knew that that daughter was lost where no powers, no matter how potent or paranormal, could find her. Lost to sex, to betrayal, to guns and untimely death.

Suki flipped open her address book and punched Mike Dannow's number on the car phone. He was in court, but Betty, his secretary, promised he would return the call as soon as possible. She tried Kenneth, but her luck was no better. When the traffic finally broke, she rushed to her office, anxious to yield her own problems to those of her patients. And for a few hours it worked. Barry's fear of driving, Claire's depression and

Rebecca's nightmares, all posttraumatic stress responses, absorbed Suki. She didn't think about Alexa until she locked her office door behind her.

When she got home, Suki went straight to the answering machine in the kitchen, hoping to hear from Mike and Kenneth. She was relieved to see there were two messages, but the first was from Kyle. He explained that Mrs. Fleishman was going to take them to McDonald's on the way home from the soccer game. Suki sighed. Kyle was being a really terrific sport. She was going to owe him big—as well as Mrs. Fleishman, whom she had never met, but who was having dinner with her son more often than she. The second message was from Kenneth. He left his home number, and she finished dialing it before the tape had time to rewind.

"How you doing?" Kenneth asked as soon as he heard her voice.

"You tell me."

The line hung open and silent for what seemed an eternity. "Probably not so great," Kenneth finally said.

Suki stared at the row of canisters along the side of the sink. Blue, green, orange and yellow glazed pottery. Stan had bought them for her from a potter on Martha's Vineyard the summer before Alexa was born. It had been sunny that day. The woman had been very old. She must be dead at least a decade now. "They're going to believe the boys?" Suki asked.

"You didn't hear this from me."

Suki ran her finger along the edge of the blue glaze. Why was Kenneth doing this? Was he sticking his neck out because he believed Alexa was innocent? Or was there some other reason? She didn't really know anything about him, except that he believed in the paranormal and had converted to Judaism. Maybe Kenneth was part of a police plot to entrap her or Alexa into admitting something in-criminating. Maybe he *did* play poker with Ellery McKinna. Suki noticed the blue blob of glaze on the side of the largest canister was roughly the shape of a handcuff. Great, she thought, paranoia run amuck.

"You know who Teddy Sutterlund is?" Kenneth asked. When Suki didn't answer, he answered himself. "He's the Middlesex DA. The one whose office botched that big murder case last year? You've got to remember. It was a big trial in Waltham that the media covered to death. It had it all: drugs, guns, kids, gangs. I think the gang called themselves the Winter Hill Diamonds."

"Was that the one where they had to let the killer go because of some technicality?" Suki asked as it slowly came back. "Even though the guy had confessed or something?"

"And even though the technicality was an overeager cop's illegal search, Sutterlund took the fall with the press. He's running for reelection in November."

"What's this got to do with Alexa?" Suki demanded.

"Gangs. Kids killing kids."

Suki felt as if she had taken a blow to the solar

plexus. "But this isn't the same thing at all. This isn't about gangs or drugs or anything like that. There are no Winter Hill Diamonds here."

"Sutterlund wants an arrest ASAP," Kenneth said as if she hadn't spoken, or as if her argument was too hollow to warrant comment. "He needs it if he's going to win in November. He's pushing Gasperini. Hard. And when Teddy Sutterlund wants something, he usually gets it."

"So Charlie's going to forget that the boys lied? That Ellery lied?" Suki demanded. "Suddenly they're all going to become star witnesses? Good little boy scouts?"

"I don't know, Suki," Kenneth said softly. "I don't know what's going to finally come down—"

"Is this happening because Sam's mother is married to a Witton cop?" Suki interrupted. "Because Charlie and Ellery play poker together?"

"It's like I told you in Pepperell. This is happening because it's what's easiest for everyone."

Suki gripped the edge of the countertop. "I won't let my daughter's life be destroyed just because it's convenient for some cop—or worse, good for some DA's political career."

"Suki," Kenneth pleaded. "Please. Getting upset isn't going to help. Listen, I know your lawyer was on the phone with Charlie this afternoon. Have you talked to him today?"

"No." She slumped against the counter.

"Well, give him a call. See what he says. I'll do what I can at this end—which may not be much—and I'll be in touch."

Suki took a deep breath. "Thanks," she said.

"Thanks a lot." Kenneth wasn't the enemy, he wasn't involved in any police plot.

"Sure," he said. "Chin up."

Suki put the phone down and stared at the glazed canisters, at the odd shapes dripping and running into each other. *"Pan to fire,"* Lindsey had warned. *"Pan to fire."*

CHAPTER THIRTEEN

After hanging up with Kenneth, Suki dialed Mike's office, but he was still on the phone. Again, the promise he would return her call. Suki thought she detected a note of exasperation in Betty's voice. Yet more paranoia. When the phone rang almost immediately, she grabbed it.

It was Alexa. "I'm at Kendra's," she said. "And I'm going to stay for dinner."

"You'll do no such thing," Suki told her. "I want you home."

"But we have to work on an English project," Alexa whined. "And it's got to be good so I can get that recommendation."

"Work it out," Suki snapped. "And be home by five-thirty."

"Don't expect any heart-to-hearts," Alexa said.

"I'm growing to expect less and less," Suki said and hung up the phone. She leaned against the kitchen counter and stared into the living room.

Late afternoon sunlight spilled through the triangular clerestory window, throwing warmth and hope into the house. The hardwood floors gleamed, and lime green buds burst open in the backyard. Suki was cold. She sat down on the couch and wrapped an old afghan around her shoulders. The couch had been her mother's and was a deep red velvet. A decorating mistake that actually looked good, original and unusual, in this modern room. It had been awful in her mother's traditional parlor. Suki raised her eyes to the window, half expecting her mother to appear and tell her what to do. But there was nothing but the relentlessly cheerful sunlight.

Would they really arrest Alexa, so obviously innocent, just because it was convenient? Just because it suited the DA's career track? Suki was no fool, and she knew it could very well happen. But she also knew that if there was a trial, if it came to that, Mike would rip Gasperini's case to shreds. His witnesses were bogus, there was no opportunity, and, as far as anyone but she and Alexa knew, no motive. The afghan slipped from her shoulders and sweat pricked under her arms. Brendan knew. And probably Kendra and Robin and Steph. They had to be kept quiet. She retrieved the afghan. Keeping teenagers quiet was a near-impossible task.

But the abortion wasn't directly connected to the murder, she reminded herself. The linkage was just conjecture, a hypothetical supposition, a loosely braided web of logic that could easily be unwound. Mike was good at unwinding. It was purely circumstantial. Just like every piece of evidence against Alexa. Suki had studied enough law to know that the way to contradict a circumstantial case was with direct evidence. Like a witness.

The missing witness. Suki felt like a complete idiot. How had she forgotten? She had been so focused on the alibi and figuring out how to cut McKinna's strings, she had forgotten other avenues remained open. The witness might have seen the car full of kids, seen Alexa driving, seen Devin fire the gun. The witness's testimony could pulverize the circumstantial evidence into meaninglessness. Except that the witness had run from the scene of the crime, and anyone who was fearful enough to leave a boy on the road to die was not going to be easy to find.

Lindsey had said she could find missing people. Suki stood and paced the room. Except, if her guess about Lindsey's MMPI scores was correct, Lindsey was a fraud—she could not see into the future, she could not find a lost person, and her skills were in shrewdness and manipulation rather than in the paranormal. But reckoning final test scores based on responses to individual items was risky business. . . . Suki walked to the picture window that filled the west wall of the living room and stared into the greening trees. Maybe it was time to give Lindsey the chance to prove what she could do.

The *Boston Globe* was laying on the kitchen table, and had been since morning, unread and still held closed by an elastic band. Suki had been avoiding news, but now she pulled the band from the paper and opened it. As she feared, there was an article about the case on the front page. She sat down and read it through, even though she knew far more than it told, even though she saw all the mistakes: Jonah wasn't eighteen; Ellery hadn't worked at the rec center for only five years; Charlie Gasperini spelled his name with a *p*. They had all the details on Finlay right, though, accurately describing how he had come to the police station to change his story.

Finlay Thompson, a custodian at the Witton Recreational Center, retracted his previous statement that he had seen Devin McKinna, Brendan Ricker and Sam Cooperstein at the recreation center on the night of Jonah Ward's murder. Mr. Thompson, accompanied from his daughter's fishing lodge in Sunderland, MA, by Suzanne Jacobs, Alexa Jacobs's mother, arrived at the Witton police station late Saturday afternoon. . . .

She read the paragraph again, then checked the date on the top of the page. *"Even in here we get the paper,"* Lindsey had once told her. Suki started to laugh. Everything Lindsey had said about Finlay was printed in the newspaper, and the newspaper had been delivered to the prison hours before Suki had arrived.

Mike called two hours later and confirmed all Kenneth had told her about Teddy Sutterlund. "I'm not going to kid you," he said. "It doesn't look good for Alexa."

A vision of Lindsey's black eye rose before Suki. "When?"

"Hard to tell. It could come as early as next week. Could not happen at all."

Suki felt as if all the nerves in her body had been wired with neon. "But what if it does?" she cried. "What do we do?"

"Well, there's nothing we can do to stop the arrest, but there are a number of things that can soften it," Mike said slowly, thoughtfully, using full sentences. "If an arrest warrant is going to be issued, I can try to arrange for Alexa to go to the station voluntarily, first thing in the morning."

"First thing in the morning?" Suki couldn't believe he was actually telling her Alexa was going to be arrested. For murder. For killing Jonah Ward.

"That way we can get her arraigned the same day. Keep her from having to spend a night in a jail cell. If we play our cards right," Mike continued, "she'll stay in Witton. Low profile. I'll drive her in myself. Keep the media off balance. She'll be arraigned in Concord. We'll post bail and you can take her home right from the courthouse."

The Concord courthouse, a cold, hard, low-slung building, was not a place for Alexa. "Then what?" Suki asked, although she was probably almost as familiar with the procedure as Mike. But at the moment she wasn't Dr. Suzanne Jacobs; she was just Suki, a woman with a daughter in trouble.

Mike seemed to understand this. "Generally, a probable cause hearing," he said without a touch of impatience. "That's where we're going to prove that there isn't even close to enough evidence for this masquerade to go to trial."

"Do you think you can do that?"

"Good chance," he said. "Yeah, I think a really good chance. The witnesses are known liars, there's no murder weapon, no motive, no real opportunity if Alexa was driving the car—despite the logistical possibility argument they'll probably make." He hesitated. "But I'll need your okay to get going on the probable cause prep."

Suki could only imagine how much it was going

to cost. "Of course," she said quickly. "Sure. Do what you need to do."

"Took a quick look at your evaluation. Looks good. Very thorough."

For a moment Suki didn't know what he was talking about. "Oh, good. Great," she said. "I was there today. I gave Lindsey the MMPI."

"How'd she do?"

Now it was Suki's turn to hesitate. "We won't know until the test's scored. I put it in the mail this afternoon, so hopefully we'll have the answer soon."

"Interesting case, huh?"

"More than you know," Suki muttered.

"How do you mean?"

But Suki didn't want to talk about Lindsey. "Isn't there some way we can stop the arrest?" she asked. "There's got to be something we can do."

Mike sighed. "Teddy's turning the screws hard on Charlie Gasperini."

"What if we found new evidence? Something, someone, who would bolster Alexa's account?"

"The mysterious nine-one-one–dialing, fast-disappearing witness?"

A smile flitted across Suki's face for the first time in the conversation. "The very same."

"The police couldn't find him."

"The police didn't look very hard."

"And who's going to look harder?"

"Me."

"Not a job for you," Mike said. "If you want, I've got a private investigator I could put on it."

"I can't afford it."

"This stuff isn't for amateurs—despite what you

might see on TV," Mike warned her. "I don't want you doing this. Let me check around and see if I can come up with someone who'll do it on the cheap."

"That'd be great," Suki said. "I appreciate it. But I've got to at least make a stab while there's still time."

"I'm telling you, it's not a good idea."

"Neither is letting Alexa get arrested."

Mike was silent for a long moment. "I'll drop your check in the mail on my way home."

Suki had no idea how to find a person she knew nothing about. So she started with the only piece of information she did know: this person had been driving a car. That narrowed it down quite a bit.

When Alexa came home, Suki brought her into the family room and made her do what the police should have, but didn't. She had Alexa describe the car she had seen on River Road on the night Jonah was shot. At first, Alexa resisted. She didn't want to remember. She didn't want to go there again. The tears flowed, but Suki stood tough and finally Alexa acquiesced.

Suki had years of training and experience in memory retrieval, and she used every trick she had. Imagery. Relaxation. Evocation. Pulling the string. Zeroing in. Specifying. Soon, the dark, big American car was transformed into a black or navy midsize Chevrolet with Massachusetts plates that was about five years old. "I can see eyes," Alexa said, her face bright with excitement. "There were eyes. They were shining for a second, and then they were gone." The witness. Suki was very much encouraged.

River Road was a small, windy thoroughfare connecting Witton Center with Massbury, a town ten miles west with a population so small that by comparison, Witton was a major metropolis. Therefore, it made sense to assume that a person driving down the road on a Friday evening was a local. Or at least that was what Suki assumed. It was a start. As was the fact that Phyllis was a deputy commissioner for the Department of Motor Vehicles. Suki's sprits soared. This was something she could do. Something that just might work.

When she called Phyllis first thing the next morning, Phyllis was thrilled to be able to do something for Alexa and immediately offered to run a computer search. All midsize dark Chevrolets that had been registered to residents of the fifteen towns closest to Witton in the last eight years. They decided that was a wide enough, but not too wide, net. Suki was touched by Phyllis's kindness. Neither one mentioned the fact that this was clearly an illegal act.

After seeing two clients, meeting with a lawyer on a case she was finishing up and working for a couple of hours on the Kern evaluation, Suki was finally able to go to Watertown and pick up the printout. Her heart was pounding with anticipation as she drove into the parking lot behind Watertown Center. Maybe this would be her big break. Maybe her luck was about to change.

When she got to the DMV, Phyllis had left for the day, but a manila envelope was on her desk with Suki's name and a big smiley face printed on it. Phyllis knew Suki hated smiley faces; it was her attempt to bring a smile to Suki's face. But Suki didn't smile when she picked up the envelope. It was thick. Too thick. Her heart sank when she pulled out the printout. There were 357 late-model midsize dark Chevrolets registered in the fifteen towns. Three hundred and fifty-seven. Suki dropped into Phyllis's chair. She had 357 names, addresses and phone numbers. Now what the hell was she supposed to do?

She flipped through the pages of wide green bar; she hadn't seen a computer printout like this since graduate school. Leave it to the DMV to still be using twenty-year-old technology. The data had been sorted alphabetically, rather than by city—she hadn't thought to specify—making it difficult to separate out only Witton residents, or just those living in abutting towns. Suki stared at the picture of Phyllis and her family on a western ski trip: so colorful, so happy, so normal. She looked back down at the printout. It would take a year to screen all these people. And Mike had said Alexa could be arrested in less than a week.

When Suki got home, Alexa was in the kitchen making dinner. This was something she'd used to do all the time—she was a far better cook than Suki—and Suki's spirits lifted as she watched her daughter deftly season what she recognized from the smell to be Alexa's wonderful vegetable stew. Alexa had always been their star; she was just easily and simply good at everything. "OPK," Jen said whenever Suki told her of Alexa's latest accomplishment. OPK stood for "other people's kids," and was Jen's way of acknowledging Alexa's specialness while bemoaning this lack in her own children—a lack that existed only in Jen's mind.

Suki had to admit that Alexa was a tough act to be compared with: her schoolwork was superior, her social life full, she could fix a broken clock or get a stalled boat running, she could whip up a great dinner from whatever was in the refrigerator. Although, granted, she wasn't all that good at sports. Suki dropped the envelope on the kitchen table and sat down. "Hi, honey."

"There were a bunch of veggies going bad in the fridge," Alexa said without turning. She tapped her foot on the floor as she stirred.

"Great. Thanks. It's good to see you cooking again."

Alexa tasted the stew then reached for the coriander. She threw in a couple of bay leaves and lowered the heat.

"Kyle home yet?" Suki asked.

Alexa took a gulp of water from the glass next to the stove. "Soccer practice. He told me in school he'd be home about six-thirty." Alexa swept the stew debris from the counter into the sink. She still hadn't turned around, but Suki could see her set expression reflected in the large plate glass window over the sink. Alexa drained her water glass and refilled it.

Suki ran her fingers through her hair. "It's time we faced this."

Alexa shrugged and opened the dishwasher. She rinsed the dishes and placed them in their slots. She ran the garbage disposal and wiped the countertop. Then she stirred the stew.

"We need to talk about Jonah and the pregnancy and the abortion," Suki said to Alexa's reflection in the window. "These aren't things you should have to deal with yourself. And we need to think about what's happening now. About what might happen."

Alexa pulled the dish towel hanging over the handle of the oven, but when it came free, instead of wiping her hands, she twisted the towel between them. "Did Phyllis get you the car registrations?"

"All three hundred fifty-seven of them."

Alexa whirled around, still worrying the dish towel. "That many?"

Suki stood and took the towel. "Come," she said. "Sit."

Alexa sat.

"I got pregnant when I was seventeen." Suki hadn't known that this was what she was going to say, but now that it was said, she recognized the rightness of it.

Alexa's eye widened. "You never told me that."

"Didn't seem appropriate—until now."

"What happened?"

Suki smiled. "The usual."

"You know what I mean."

"It was just bad luck." Suki sighed. "Kind of like you. It was my boyfriend senior year. Only guy I had ever had sex with." She took Alexa's hand and kissed it. "Surprise."

Alexa allowed Suki to hold her hand. "What did you do?"

"Grandpa took me to Puerto Rico. It was 1969. Abortions weren't legal in this country."

"You had an illegal abortion?"

"It was terrible. Dirty. Slimy. We had to ask a cab driver where to go when we got off the plane. They gave me anesthesia without checking whether I had eaten anything." Suki could remember it all. Clearly. The blinding Puerto Rican sun. Herself, a terrified seventeen-year-old in a miniskirt. She could still feel the deep sorrow that gouged at her for what she was putting her father through, her guilt for letting him down. Suki suddenly understood that this must be just what Alexa was feeling.

"Oh, Mom." Alexa squeezed Suki's hand. "How horrible. How horrible for you."

"Horrible things happen," Suki said. "But Grandpa was great. He was there when I needed him. He was always there. Still is. And I want to be there for you the same way."

"You are, Mom," Alexa assured her. "You've been great. Are great."

"I love you, baby," Suki said softly. "No matter what."

"I'm so sorry—" Alexa was cut off by the sharp whack of glass against glass. A beer bottle exploded through the kitchen window.

Suki pushed Alexa behind her. Alexa began screaming, but Suki went dead calm. "Go up to my bedroom," she ordered. "Sit in the middle of the bed." Her bedroom was on the second floor and the windows were the farthest from the ground that sloped toward the backyard. Unfortunately, what she and Stan had always loved about this house were the huge expanses of glass in every room. She pushed Alexa toward the stairs. "Go." Alexa went.

Suki stomped to the kitchen window. She looked through the fractured edges of broken glass into her backyard. There was no one there. It looked peaceful and pleasant and safe in the early evening sunlight. Then there was a rustle in the trees at the west edge of the lawn. "Get out of here, you spineless punks!" she screamed through the gaping hole. "Get out!"

She bent down and picked up the beer bottle. Budweiser. MURDERER was scrawled across the label in red marker. Kids. Stupid, stupid kids. Although Ellery could easily have put them up to it, Suki thought. Or maybe the witness. The witness could have lots of reasons for wanting Alexa to keep quiet. Suki carefully placed the bottle on the table, word side to the wall, and dialed 911.

After talking with the police dispatcher, Suki went up to her bedroom. Alexa's hysteria had subsided into deep sobbing, and Suki held her while they waited for the police. They waited a long time.

It was almost an hour before a surly patrolman rang the doorbell. He was in and out in five minutes, asking few questions and writing down nothing. He took the bottle, walked the perimeter of the property and told her he would be in touch if they came up with anything. Suki knew he never would. She called both Mike and Kenneth, but didn't reach either.

Kyle came home and the two of them silently cleaned the kitchen. Alexa stayed in Suki's room, huddled in the middle of the bed. Glass had found its way into everything, and Alexa's vegetable stew had to be thrown out. No one was very hungry anyway. Suki called the few glass replacement outlets listed in the yellow pages, but everyone was closed for the day. She and Kyle found three pieces of poster board in the back of the basement and taped them inside the frame of the broken window. One was blue, one yellow and one hot pink.

When they were finished, Kyle disappeared into his room and Suki went to check on Alexa. She was stretched out on Suki's bed, her arm thrown over her eyes. She appeared to be sleeping.

Suki sat down and lightly kissed Alexa's forehead.

Alexa eyes flickered, but didn't open. Suki wasn't sure if she was awake or asleep.

"The police have come and gone," Suki told her anyway. "The coast is clear and Kyle and I cleaned up the kitchen."

"Sleep," Alexa muttered. Her breathing was deep and even. "Sleep."

"Yes," Suki said, "you sleep. You sleep here and I'll spend the night in your room." She flipped each side of the bedspread up and gently folded them around Alexa.

Alexa's eyes fluttered open. "Tell Lindsey I don't want to talk to her," she said, then her lids dropped and her breathing became slow and regular.

"Sure, baby, sure. Don't worry. You don't have to talk to Lindsey," Suki said, even though she couldn't remember Alexa ever mentioning a friend named Lindsey. She tiptoed out of the room.

Kyle's light was out, unusual this early in the evening, so Suki wandered downstairs. The sight of the garish colors in the kitchen window sent her down the other half flight to the family room. She tried watching television, but nothing could keep her attention, nothing could stop her from jumping at every sound, from bristling at every passing car. She would look into a security system tomorrow.

Suki switched from a hospital drama to an old Clint Eastwood movie, then to a political talk show where they were vehemently discussing campaign finance reform. She returned to Clint then switched it off. She got Phyllis's printout and spread it across her lap. There were so many names. When the phone at her elbow rang, she was glad for the distraction and picked up the receiver before the second ring.

"Collect call for Alexa Jacobs, please," a mechanical voice intoned. "From Lindsey Kern."

CHAPTER FOURTEEN

There were forty-two dark midsize late-model Chevrolets registered to residents of Witton. One belonged to Jake, the old man who owned the Stone Store, one belonged to Rick Rogers, the principal of the elementary school, and one belonged to Darcy Ward. Suki figured she was pretty safe eliminating those three. That left thirty-nine. She folded Phyllis's printout and poured the rest of her coffee down the sink. She'd have another cup at the office.

Alexa and Kyle had left for school together, not a usual occurrence, and although they both ate breakfast without mentioning the broken window, Suki noticed their shoulders were almost touching as they walked to the bus stop. She hadn't told Alexa about Lindsey's call.

Suki was amazed at the security breach at the prison. According to Massachusetts law, prisoners can make collect calls at designated times, but their phone use is restricted by computerized PIN cards embedded with a short list of approved numbers, usually only a lawyer and close family members. Suki could not imagine how the superintendent had allowed her home number to be added to Lindsey's list. As Suki had refused to accept the charges, she hadn't heard Lindsey's explanation, but she had put in a call to Rizzo's office.

"Tell Lindsey I don't want to talk to her," Alexa had said at least an hour before Lindsey had phoned.

Suki put Phyllis's printout in her briefcase along with the court transcripts and grand jury testimony she was going to need to work on the Kern evaluation this afternoon. She had three patients to see in the morning and a lunch meeting with a lawyer on a new case, but planned to spend the rest of the day focused on Lindsey. Somehow she had to squeeze in some time with the witness list—and figure out what she was going to do next. Suki was haunted by an unsettling vision of herself as the only thing standing between Alexa and an arrest warrant.

The doorbell rang, and Suki looked out Alexa's bedroom window to see who was there; she had learned not to answer the door or pick up the phone without knowing who wanted to speak to her. Kenneth Pendergast stood on the stoop, and an unmarked police car—which looked just like an unmarked police car—was parked in the driveway. She flew down the half flight of stairs and threw open the front door.

"Are you all right?" Kenneth demanded, looking her over closely. "Alexa? Kyle?" He was so serious, his warm brown eyes so intently focused, that Suki was touched.

"We're fine." Suki took him by the arm and gently pulled him into the house. "Come in. Please."

"I saw the bottle."

"I'm guessing it was kids—and I can also guess who put them up to it."

"You don't know that," Kenneth said, following her into the kitchen.

"Oh yes, I do."

Kenneth silently contemplated the garishly colored window. "How long did it take for Bob to show up last night?"

"Almost an hour."

"How long did he stay?"

"Five minutes. Maybe ten."

"Charlie," Kenneth muttered. "What a shit." Then he raised his eyebrows at Suki. "Sorry."

"I'm a lot more concerned about Charlie Gasperini than I am about your language." She attempted to smile, but her muscles responded to her real feelings, not her feigned ones, and she felt her mouth twist into a grimace. "I say a lot worse," she tried again for levity, "all the damn time."

Kenneth crossed his arms and strode through the kitchen, into the dining room, through the living room, back into the kitchen. "I saw the report," he said, inspecting the edge of the window. "Bob claimed there was no one around. No other damage. Is that true?"

Suki nodded again. "Kenneth," she said, "I've got to talk to you. I need your help, but I can't do it now." She glanced at the clock. "I've got a patient to see in twenty minutes. A full day of work. But I want to start looking for the witness. Actually, I *have* started looking for the witness. I think it's Alexa's only—"

"What do you mean, you've already started?" Kenneth interrupted.

Suki pulled the printout from her briefcase. "Three hundred and fifty-seven late-model dark Chevrolets registered here and in the fifteen surrounding towns—forty-two in Witton."

Kenneth flipped through the printout and whistled in appreciation. "Chevrolets?" he asked.

"Psychologists are trained to help people retrieve memories. I got Alexa to be more specific."

He handed the sheaf of papers back to her. "You should've been a cop."

Despite the situation, Suki felt a rush of pride. She shrugged.

"But you have to stop," Kenneth said. "We don't know why this person drove away. There's got to be a damn good reason for someone to leave a dying kid alone in the road—my bet is it's a dangerous one."

"Nothing's more dangerous than a police force that thinks my daughter's a murderer—and a police chief who's more intent on proving she's guilty than on finding the person who really did it." Suki shoved the witness list into her briefcase and grabbed her purse from the counter. "I'll do what I have to do." She nodded curtly. "I've got to go now."

Kenneth reluctantly allowed himself to be led to the front door. "It's not that I disagree with you, Suki. I don't. And I'd probably feel the same way if it were my kid. But people are angry." He gestured toward the kitchen window. "And there are lots of things more deadly than beer bottles."

Suki thought of all Kenneth had done since that first day he found Alexa confused and wandering down River Road. She was sorry she had been short. She touched the lapel of his jacket. "Kenneth, I appreciate your concern, I really do, but Mike Dannow told me the arrest could come as soon as a week." Suki turned her palms toward the ceiling. "She's my daughter."

"Can you give me a couple of days?" Kenneth pleaded. "Can you just lay off for two days? That's all I ask. Let me see what I can stir up down at the station. What I can find out."

Suki lifted her briefcase. "Are they going to let you follow up on this list? Look for the gun? Finger the person who's behind all of this?"

Kenneth was unfazed by her questions. "Can you copy that list for me?"

"Sure." Suki lowered the briefcase. "What are you going to do with it?"

"Run it through the MEAPS computer for matches. Felons, warrants, parole violations—that kind of thing."

Relief flooded through Suki. She wasn't the only person standing between Alexa and an arrest warrant. "That'd be great," she said. "Just great."

"I'll also see if I can get some action on the weapon angle," Kenneth said. "And I'm going to get protection on your house. Make sure a patrol car comes by here at least once an hour."

"I don't know how I can—"

"You can thank me by sitting still for a couple of days. By letting *me* be the cop." He opened the door and stepped out on the stoop. He turned. "Can you do that for me?"

Suki shrugged. "I'll try, but—"

Kenneth held up his hands. "No buts," he said. "I'll give you a ring tonight and let you know where I am."

"Thanks," Suki called. "Thanks for everything."

He waved off her thanks and climbed into his car. It was a dark midsize late-model Chevrolet.

Suki didn't do as Kenneth asked. Too much was at stake for her to sit still. After a full day of listening to other people's problems, pitching for a new case and preparing for her next interview with Lindsey, Suki took her witness list and a map of Witton and went cruising. She hadn't had time to plot out a logical route, so she looped up and down the listed streets in a haphazard, nonsensical manner. After she had driven by dozens of empty houses and seen five or six dark Chevys parked in driveways and along front yards, Suki realized she had no idea what she was doing. Where this was going. She drove home.

Alexa was bent over her homework at the kitchen table. As she hugged her daughter, Suki realized she was acting like a fool. There was no point in *her* looking at the cars. It was Alexa who needed to see them. Kenneth was wrong. She wouldn't have made a very good cop.

"Yo." Kyle wandered in and took a bag of cookies from the cabinet. He ripped the bag open, grabbed a large handful and stuffed them in his mouth faster than Suki would have believed possible. There is nothing more gluttonous than a fourteen-year-old boy. Except, Jen had warned her, a seventeen-year-old one.

"Do you happen to have any homework?" Suki asked him.

Kyle shrugged. "Did it in study hall."

"How come you manage to finish everything in

study hall and your sister always has lots of work to do at home?"

"Maybe I'm just smarter than she is." Kyle smiled his charming smile. Stan's smile.

Alexa reached out an arm and swatted him. "Yeah, I noticed your name on the honor roll."

"Don't hit me!" Kyle yelled, punching Alexa in the shoulder. "Watch your grubby hands."

"Jerk-off!" Alexa growled, grabbing his wrist and twisting it. "You're just too stupid to—"

Suki yanked Kyle free from Alexa's grip. "Stop it!" she shouted, much louder than she usually yelled. "Don't we have enough problems in this family already? Just stop it right now!"

They stopped it.

Suki dropped into the chair next to Alexa. "Kyle," she said. "I need to talk to your sister. Go do some homework."

"But I told you, I don't—"

"Then read a book."

Kyle conspicuously removed a book from his backpack and went into the living room. Suki heard him throw himself down on the couch. She was sure he wasn't going to turn a page.

Alexa watched her warily. "What?"

Suki explained about the Chevys, about what Kenneth was doing and what she was trying to do, about how Alexa needed to come with her to try to identify the car she had seen on River Road.

"You mean just kind of drive around and look?" Alexa asked. "Like in people's driveways and stuff?"

"Yes," Suki said. "I've got the addresses of all the Chevys in Witton."

"Seems kind of dumb."

"Do you have a better suggestion?"

"I don't think I'd be able to tell anyway," Alexa said sullenly. "It was dark."

"Well," Suki said, "you're just going to have to try."

"Now?" Alexa whined. "I've got a science test tomorrow. I need to study."

"I think this is more important."

"But I need this A in science," Alexa argued. "I just heard about a senior who didn't get into Princeton because her science grades were too low."

"If we don't get this mess straightened out," Suki said softly, "there may be no Princeton."

Alexa was startled into silence. She looked down at her book and played with her pen. "Sure," she finally whispered. "I guess I can give it a try."

Kyle came in and put his hands on Suki's shoulders. "I've got a better idea, Mom."

Suki raised her eyes to her son.

"It's the play at school tonight. *Bye Bye Birdie.* Remember?"

Suki remembered as if it had been another lifetime, someone else's lifetime. Last month she had bought four tickets from Kyle's friend Gil, who had a small part. The extra ticket was for Brendan.

"The cars, Mom," Kyle continued. "All the cars in town'll be there. It'll be a lot better than driving around all night looking in empty driveways."

"I'm not going to the play," Alexa said.

"Not to the play," he told his sister with exaggerated patience. "The parking lot. We go in the middle, when everyone's inside, and like, check out all the cars. You can see if you recognize any of them."

Alexa raised her right hand so that her thumb and forefinger formed an upper case L. Teenage sign language for "loser."

Suki turned to Kyle. "That's not a bad idea."

Alexa scowled at her brother.

"Well, I think we should take Kyle up on his idea." Suki jumped from her chair. "How about I whip up some pasta and then we go over and scout out the parking lot." She kissed the top of Alexa's head. "That'll give you time to study for your test."

Alexa shrugged and started scribbling in her notebook. "I'm not hungry," she said.

The grounds surrounding Witton High School are lush and wild and woodsy, but the building itself is unattractive, made of a nondescript beige brick, layered unimaginatively into a hill, blind on one side. The front door, painted a deep blue, is unimposing and has the appearance of a back door. The entrance is approached by a terrace of narrow steps and opens into a stairwell. Suki always wondered what the architects could have been thinking—or if they had been thinking at all.

As Kyle had predicted, the parking lot was full. Cars were parked on the edge of the bus turnaround and on the grass along both sides of the tennis courts. On first glance, there appeared to be a lot of dark Chevys. Suki had to park around the corner. The three of them climbed from the car as Kyle plotted out their course of action.

"I'll take the left side and Mom'll take the right," he ordered. "When we find one, we'll yell. Then

Alexa can come and look." He waved down the street toward the school. "When we get to the tennis courts, we'll, like, do the same thing. Same with the rows in the lot."

Suki nodded, both impressed and amused by how Kyle was taking control of the situation, by how much he was enjoying it. Just like his father. He loved to be in charge. She put the printout under her arm and pulled out a pen so that she could cross-check each car by license plate; she had highlighted the Witton cars in yellow. The play had started half an hour ago, and Suki figured it still had about an hour to run. She wanted to make sure they were long gone before the crowd broke.

"Want me to handle the list, Mom?" Kyle offered. "How about we cross off each car that Alexa says no to, and put a check at the ones she thinks are possible? That way, at the end, we'll know which cars we still have to find."

Suki handed him the pen and papers, more than glad to share any piece of the burden. Alexa hadn't said a word. She was lagging behind, leaning against a tree. Suki put her arm around her and gave her a squeeze. Alexa didn't respond. Suki let go, and they started down the line of cars.

It was quickly apparent their strategy was seriously flawed. Kyle had to devise a new category: the question mark. Almost every Chevy they saw got that designation, for when Alexa looked at each car, she shrugged and mumbled, "I can't tell."

When they crossed out Rick Rogers's and Darcy Ward's cars, on the assumption the two were completely implausible suspects, Kyle crowed with delight.

"Two down!" he cried. Suki didn't have the heart to tell him that she had already mentally eliminated both Rick and Darcy, but she did wonder what Darcy was doing here.

As they worked their way down the third row of the parking lot, Alexa grew more and more sluggish, if that was possible. "It's no use," she finally said. "This is stupid."

Suki was inclined to agree with her, but Kyle would have none of it. "What if we quit and the car's in the next row?" he argued. "What if we missed it just because you want to go home?"

"It's not in the next row," Alexa said. "And even if it was, I probably wouldn't be able to tell."

"How about we do two more rows?" Suki cajoled. "Kyle has a good point."

Alexa reluctantly followed her mother and brother. A dark Chevy was parked near the main entrance. Alexa walked over to it and shrugged. "I can't tell."

Suki noticed a police cruiser parked in the no-parking zone at the bottom of the front steps. CHIEF OF POLICE was printed under the driver's window. The car was empty. "Please, Alexa," she begged. "Please try."

"I *am* trying. They all look alike."

Suki had to admit that they did all look alike. She glanced over at Kyle. "I'm with Alexa. Let's go."

"One more row," he pleaded. "You promised we could do one more row."

Suki knew better than to renege on a promise. "Okay," she said, "but that's it."

They were standing no more than twenty feet

from the front entrance, facing it, when the door burst open and a boisterous, laughing group of kids poured down the steps. There were about a dozen of them. Intermission. Suki had completely forgotten about intermission.

At first the kids didn't notice them, they were too intent on looking cool as they lit their cigarettes and flirted with each other, and Suki thought they could slide away without an incident. But then a voice called out, "Hey, Alexa, what are you doing? Stealing a car?"

"Shut up, Parker," Alexa yelled back.

Suki was proud of Alexa for standing up for herself, but she felt sick to her stomach. Parker was Becky Alley's son. Parker and Alexa had gone to day care together. Played in Becky's backyard pool. She had driven four-year-old Parker and Becky to the hospital the day he shoved a pebble up his nose.

"What's grand theft auto to you?" Parker taunted. "Can't go to prison for more than one lifetime."

Kyle stepped in front of his sister. "Shut up, acne face."

"Owww," bellowed a squat, muscular boy standing with Parker, "that was a good one from the big ninth grader." He covered his face in mock terror. "I'm really scared now." More kids began to gather behind Parker and his friends. A few tittered, but most just watched in silence.

Suki grabbed Kyle's arm. "Let's go," she said.

But he yanked free of her grasp. "Not until he apologizes." He glared at Parker. "Apologize."

"I'm not apologizing for telling the truth," Parker

spat back. "Everyone knows Alexa did it. Everyone knows why."

Suki leaned close to Kyle's ear. "We've got to get out of here," she hissed. "We don't need any more trouble." She was chilled by Parker's words.

But, as always, Kyle was his father's son: not one to take orders. "Apologize, you asshole!" he yelled to Parker. "You don't know what really happened."

"We know!" someone behind Parker yelled out.

"Yeah! We know all right!"

"Yeah!"

Suki looked at the grumbling kids. This wasn't just a group of children, this was a crowd, the kind that could quickly ignite into a mob. The psychological literature was rife with examples of even the most reasonable people surrendering their personal identity to a moment of collective righteousness. And no one had ever accused teenagers of being reasonable. "Go back inside," Suki ordered as calmly as she could. "Just go back inside."

"Not till you go!" Parker said.

"Not till you apologize!" Kyle stood firm despite the fact that Suki was once again yanking on his arm.

"Go! Go! Go!" Parker began to chant.

"Go! Go! Go!" The kids picked up the dirge, but they began to close in, their bodies barring the way of their words.

"Get out of my way!" Suki shoved the two boys directly in front of her. "Get out of my face."

The boys dropped back, unsure how to respond to a grown-up, someone's mother, pushing them.

Into this moment of hesitancy, a whistle blew. Loud and authoritative. The kids fell silent in surprise. "Break it up!" ordered a voice used to command. "If you were my soccer team I'd have you all down doing a hundred push-ups. Maybe I will anyway." Warren Blanchard stood on the top step at the front of the school, his hands on his hips.

There was a smattering of uncomfortable laughter and the shifting of feet. Suki felt, rather than saw, the kids retreat, transform from a mob into individual children. They turned toward Warren.

"This is my family's tragedy," he said, speaking more softly, but still powerfully. "If we're not throwing stones, you shouldn't be either. You don't have the right."

The kids murmured and shuffled and began to disperse. They crushed out their cigarettes. Climbed the stairs. Went inside. No one looked back. Suddenly there was space and air and room to breathe.

Suki wrapped her arms around Alexa and Kyle, who were both trembling. Warren was sitting on the top step, his head in his hands. After a long hug, she untangled herself from her children and sat down next to Warren. She took his hand. He didn't raise his head. They sat without speaking, hand in hand, for a long time.

No one said anything on the ride home. There didn't seem to be anything to say. As soon as they got in the house, Alexa and Kyle climbed the stairs and went into their bedrooms. They closed their doors.

Suki looked at the blank, expressionless doors of her children's rooms and then at the lighthearted colors of the poster board filling the kitchen window. She took a bottle of wine from the rack in the living room. When she went into the kitchen for a glass, she noticed that the answering machine was blinking. There was one message. It was Superintendent Rizzo.

"I'm very sorry about this mix-up, Dr. Jacobs," Rizzo's stiff voice rose from the speaker. "But I checked my records and Lindsey Kern put you on her PIN in 1995 when the Inmate Interchange law was enacted. It says here that you're her therapist, and all the appropriate paperwork was signed by Lawrence Willard, who was superintendent at that time. Everything appears to be in order. I'm sorry if this has been an inconvenience for you. Call me tomorrow if you want your number removed from her list."

Suki stared at the machine as it whirled and clicked and reset itself. In 1995 she was working at the Roxbury Court. She hadn't yet met Mike Dannow and she had never heard of Lindsey Kern.

CHAPTER FIFTEEN

One of the most crucial pieces of a forensic evaluation is the comparison between the official version of the alleged crime and the self-report of the defendant. The degree to which the defendant's story matches the accounts provided by others goes directly to her state of mind at the time of the crime and to her propensity to manipulate both the truth *and* the psychologist. Suki was particularly concerned with the latter issue in Lindsey's case.

Yesterday afternoon, before taking her futile cruise around Witton, Suki had managed to squeeze in an hour reviewing police reports from the scene of Richard Stoddard's death as well as transcripts of the trial. In this type of case, it was often necessary to interview witnesses, but as there had already been a trial, Suki was hopeful the witnesses' sworn testimony would give her enough data. In the field, it was generally assumed that a psychologist who charged more than thirty hours on a forensic eval, even one as complicated as this one, was pushing the envelope. Suki was not interested in getting that kind of reputation.

Suki hadn't planned to meet with Lindsey again until she had spent more time reviewing the official version of Stoddard's death, but the message from Superintendent Rizzo last night had caused her to reconsider. She drove to the prison first thing in the morning without even calling the front control to ensure she would be able to interview Lindsey. Suki knew the shift changed at seven and that breakfast was at eight, so neither of those would be a problem, and, as she had permission to see Lindsey whenever she wanted, she figured it was worth the risk—even if she had to wait in the visitors' area with the squalling babies and exhausted grandmothers.

She needed to find out how Lindsey had managed to get her home number on the PIN—and convince the authorities it had been on there for five years. Suki wondered if Lindsey had ever done any secretarial work in the superintendent's office. It wasn't uncommon for prison administrators to fill their employment gaps with the "better people."

She didn't like the idea of leaving Alexa home alone, but couldn't see any way around it. Alexa hadn't wanted to go to school, and Suki hadn't forced the issue. As she closed Alexa's bedroom door, Alexa had curled away from her into a fetal position, and Suki had wondered about the hourly rate home tutors charged and the tuition at private schools. After what had happened last night, she wasn't sure she wanted Alexa to go back to Witton High. If she had to dip into Alexa's college fund, so be it.

The officer allowed her right through, and she was led into an unfamiliar interrogation room containing a beat-up wooden desk, two chairs and a barred window overlooking the concrete exercise yard; it had apparently been someone's office not very long ago and was hot and stuffy. Suki opened the window then sat down at the desk, pleased with the setup; it gave her a physical position of authority, and she was always more comfortable when there was a desk between herself and an inmate. Suki checked to make sure the police reports and trial transcripts were in her briefcase. She didn't plan to bring up the PIN list until after Lindsey had given her self-report of the crime. Anything else would be foolish.

Lindsey apparently didn't understand this, for as soon as she entered the room, she said, "I'm sorry about calling your house last night. I wouldn't have done it if I didn't think it was absolutely necessary."

"Apology accepted." Suki waved Lindsey into the chair in front of the desk. "But let's keep that on hold for the time be—"

"But if I can't tell Alexa," Lindsey interrupted, "I have to tell you."

"I want to talk about what happened ten years ago," Suki said. "On the afternoon of May tenth, at two forty Beacon Street."

Lindsey blanched, as if hearing the address of the house in which Richard Stoddard had died was a physical blow. "Isabel's house," she muttered.

"Do you think you could tell me about it?" Suki asked.

"No one ever believes me."

"Give me a shot. Just narrate the events, tell it like you'd tell a story around a campfire." Suki wanted Lindsey to lose herself in the telling, so she could watch Lindsey's facial expressions, her body language, listen to what she chose to reveal as well as what she chose to leave unsaid. Suki hoped not to have to interrupt or ask leading questions. "I won't listen with any preconceived notions if you don't talk with any," she added.

Lindsey snorted. "What are we, if not a bundle of preconceived notions?"

"Look," Suki said, sitting back in her chair, "you're a smart, educated woman, and so am I. We can continue to play these linguistic games, wasting both your time and mine—but only *your* mother's money—or we can get some work done."

Lindsey's sigh was large and dramatic. "Richard and I were standing on the top of the stairs, arguing, holding a carton full of my stuff," she said in a long-suffering voice. "Richard had one end—he was backing down the stairs—I had the other. I was mad, so I told him to leave and let go of the box. Isabel saw her opening and gave him a push—the weight of the box did the rest. He fell. She won. I lost."

"I see how you lost," Suki said, "but how did Isabel win?"

"Remember the other day when I was telling you how possessive ghosts are? Well, after I moved in, Isabel and I really connected. We were together all the time. We went for walks, played practical jokes on Edgar—we both thought he was a self-impressed jerk." A smiled played across Lindsey's face at the memory, then she sobered. "When I met Richard, I guess I stopped spending as much time with her and she got jealous."

"Jealous of you as a girlfriend?"

"Not a girlfriend in the sexual sense," Lindsey said. "A girlfriend in the friend sense. You've got to remember, Isabel had been alone for a long, long time. And even when she was alive, I don't think she had any friends."

Suki watched Lindsey closely. Her words were bizarre yet clearly heartfelt, and she spoke as if completely confident of her reasonableness. "So Isabel killed Richard to get your friendship back?"

"Pretty effective, huh?" Lindsey's smile was fast and fleeting. "There's not much else to tell. You can read all the gory details in the trial transcript. About how I told Richard to get out of my life. About how Edgar was standing at the bottom of the stairs and claimed *I* pushed Richard, although it was clear there was no way he could actually see. About how Richard broke his neck and was probably dead before he hit the bottom." Lindsey swung her head as if to throw off the image, but her eyes were dark and haunted, and it was apparent this recounting was painful.

Once again, Suki had the thought that Lindsey hadn't killed Richard, and, once again, she chastised herself. Lindsey's mental state at the time of the crime was her only concern. "Richard was a nice guy, huh?"

Lindsey didn't say anything.

"How long had you known him?"

"Can't you get Mike to give you the transcripts?" Lindsey asked. "Everything you want to know is in there."

Suki could feel Lindsey's resistance, as hard and as strong as the bars on the window. "You never testified," she said. "The transcript won't tell me your story. It'll only tell me everyone else's."

Lindsey narrowed her eyes. "You already have it—you've already read it."

Suki felt professionally bound to tell the truth. "Yes," she said, "but it didn't tell me what I want to know."

"And what exactly do you want to know?"

"I want to know what happened for you," Suki said. "What you were feeling and thinking."

"Before? During? After?"

"I've got time for them all."

Lindsey explained that Richard was helping her pack because he didn't think it was safe for her to live alone any more. "When I told him Isabel was going to kill me—or him—he said I should move to his apartment. That it would be safer for me."

Suki rested her elbows on the table and listened carefully. If Richard had thought Lindsey was incapable of taking care of herself that was another point for Mike: inability to handle the tasks of daily life is sometimes a symptom of mental illness.

"It was Isabel's moment of victory," Lindsey continued. "All along, Edgar said she wanted her house back. I never believed him, I used to laugh at him, but in the end, he was right."

Suki nodded.

Lindsey described how Isabel had the power to get inside her brain and make her see visions of whatever Isabel wanted her to see. She declared the hallucinations that afternoon to be the most vivid and scary Isabel had ever created: man-size knives, ceiling-high balustrades, Richard transformed from flesh to mahogany. Isabel had laughed inside Lindsey's head as Richard was tumbling down the stairs, as Richard was dying. "It was a gleeful sound," Lindsey said. "Full of triumph."

"What do you mean when you say Isabel could get 'inside your head'?"

"She could make my mind part of her mind. I would see what she imagined, hear what she wanted to tell me."

Suki wrote notes furiously and watched Lindsey as closely as she could. There was no doubt these were some serious delusions. "And what about afterward?" she asked gently. "After you realized Richard was dead. How was it for you then? What were you thinking? Feeling?"

"Isabel followed me into the hotel room where the police took me that night because I was afraid to stay alone in the apartment," Lindsey answered. "She brought her journal, even though I had purposely left it behind. I shoved the journal in back of the bureau, to hide it, before I went to sleep. But in the morning, it was out again. And that's when I knew."

Suki sat silently and waited for Lindsey to finish. When Lindsey had picked all the lint off of her pants and inspected each of her fingernails, when it became apparent she wasn't going to say any more without prompting, Suki reluctantly asked, "When you knew what?"

"When I knew I had to call Alexa and warn her."

Suki wasn't surprised by Lindsey's swift change of topic; her patients' logic chains were often missing a few links. She didn't allow any emotion to cross on her face. She didn't move a muscle. She watched Lindsey with the same thoughtful expression with which she had been watching her for the past few minutes, and she noted, not for the first time, that being a psychologist was a lot like being an actress.

"Alexa's in danger—and so are you."

"We were talking about Richard," Suki reminded her gently. It didn't take paranormal powers to know that Alexa was in danger—and by extension, Alexa's mother.

"But it's true," Lindsey cried. "I can see the aura."

"Lindsey," Suki said. "I appreciate your concern, I really do, but—"

"I've never done any secretarial work in the superintendent's office," Lindsey interrupted.

Suki was caught off guard by this topic shift, and she could feel herself stiffen in surprise at Lindsey, once again, answering her unasked question.

Lindsey grinned. "It was just like Rizzo told you. I wrote down your telephone number when I first gave them my PIN list. I didn't know who you were, but I knew I'd need you some day." She crossed her arms. "Like those forced-choice precognition experiments I was telling you about. I saw a event before it happened in linear time—or maybe more correctly, I *sensed* the presence of a possible future event."

Suki had checked on Lindsey's facts, and sure enough, Honorton and Ferrari had done a meta-analysis of over three hundred precognition studies and discovered that approximately thirty percent of them did conclude that prescience was demonstrated by the subjects. The odds of this result happening by chance were about one in 10^{25}. She didn't say anything.

"You don't believe me."

"I didn't say that."

Lindsey's eyes suddenly filled with fear. "You've

got to believe me," she cried, grabbing one of Suki's hands.

Suki reached toward the panic button with her other hand, but she didn't press it. Something told her to wait, and she was always attentive to her instincts.

"You have to tell Alexa that the man she's afraid of is the one who will ultimately free her." Lindsey's fingers pressed tightly into Suki's flesh. "That she has to let him run his course. If she interferes, all may be lost."

"You need to let go of me," Suki said calmly. "Please let go of my hand."

Lindsey released Suki immediately. She looked at her own hand as if she were surprised at what it had done. "Sorry," she mumbled. "I was just trying to help."

Suki stood. "I'm sure you were, and as I said, I appreciate it, but it's inappropriate and we can't do it." She walked to the door and rapped for the officer. "I think we'd better stop for today."

"But you're all alone in this," Lindsey cried. "You're trusting the wrong people, and if you don't take my advice, if you let Alexa's misplaced—"

The officer burst through the door, but when he saw Lindsey sitting in the chair, he visibly relaxed.

Suki turned to Lindsey. "I've arranged for you to undergo a series of neurological tests. The scheduling has to be worked out through the superintendent's office, but it'll probably be sometime early next week. Possibly sooner."

Lindsey clenched her jaw and Suki thought she was going to protest the testing, but instead, Lindsey said, "You need to go with this man. It's the only way you'll find what you're looking for."

"More of your witchy bitchy New Age act, Kern?" the officer said with a sneer. He obviously wasn't as fond of Lindsey as Darla was. "Hope this one's better than the one about Billig."

Lindsey stood and with great dignity said, "Billig's time just hasn't come yet."

That night, Suki slept poorly. She was plagued by nightmares interrupted by bouts of insomnia and didn't know which was worse, the anxiety-ridden hours of sleeplessness, every one of her fears enlarged in the psychotic darkness, or the dreams. Each time she woke, gleeful, triumphant laughter rang in her ears. At four-thirty, she climbed out of bed and sat down at her desk to compare the official version of Richard Stoddard's death with the story Lindsey had told her. She needed to engage her mind. Fill it. Wrap it around a puzzle.

The Kern case did that, and more. For, aside from the delusions Lindsey described, and the fact she claimed a woman who had been dead for almost one hundred years was the murderer, the various accounts of the events surrounding Stoddard's death were remarkably consistent. Edgar Price's story was just as Lindsey had described it, and the police report, although sloppy and littered with holes, concurred on the basic details. Other testimony verified that Richard was indeed helping Lindsey move from her apartment into his, and that Lindsey and Richard had been involved in a serious relationship.

A friend of Lindsey's—who appeared to be Babs of the four-dimensional apple—claimed they were planning to be married, but this couldn't be verified.

Suki pulled out the notes from her meeting with Lindsey, then referred to her forensic checklist, although, if Lindsey was telling the truth, the issues usually considered at this point in an evaluation were moot. If Lindsey hadn't killed Richard, had never even considered killing Richard, then her remorse, premeditation or awareness of the wrongfulness of the crime were all irrelevant. She hadn't used any weapons, nor did it appear she had ever considered an alternate strategy to bring about Stoddard's demise, and "the cop at the elbow" test—the question of whether she would have done the same thing if a policeman were standing next to her—was clearly a useless concept. If Lindsey was telling the truth.

It was just as plausible that Lindsey had made up the entire story in the hope of getting out of Watkins. If Lindsey had read books on psychosis and temporal lobe epilepsy, if she *had* pushed Richard Stoddard down the stairs, *had* killed him in cold blood as a jury had found, if now she was acting and lying and prevaricating, then the checklist issues suddenly became applicable and Suki's report quite straightforward to write.

On the other hand, it was also feasible Lindsey honestly believed Isabel had been standing on the stairs with her that afternoon, that Isabel was the one who pushed Richard, the one who laughed inside her head. This would support the contention that Lindsey was psychotic, that she was "suffering a substantial disorder of thought, mood, perception, orientation or memory which grossly impairs judgment, behavior [or] capacity to recognize reality. . . ." This was the threshold for determining legal sanity as outlined in the Code of Massachusetts Regulations, 3.01.

Suki stared out the window as fingers of dawn began to streak the sky. Of course, there was another possibility: that Lindsey believed Isabel had done all these things and was completely sane.

CHAPTER SIXTEEN

Alexa was not pleased when Suki told her she was going to have a neurological test, and even less thrilled to find out it was an MRI. "I heard it's really gross," she complained as they drove to Kendall Radiology, the facility in Cambridge where the test was to be performed. "Kendra had to have her back checked after she was in that car accident with her dad, and she said she thought she was going to die of suffocation."

"It's just a big magnet that takes pictures of your brain," Suki explained. "All you have to do is lay there. It doesn't hurt at all."

"But I have to get inside the machine, right? Kendra said it was incredibly claustrophobic. Like being in a coffin."

"If you want, I'll ask the doctor to give you something to help you relax."

Alexa stared out the window. "This is ridiculous," she muttered. "Just because you're a psychologist, just because you see diseases that aren't there, *I* have to take all these stupid tests."

"Humor me, please," Suki said. "Just be a good sport."

"You're the one who thinks something's wrong with my brain because of what happened to Jonah, not me."

"These tests don't have anything to do with Jonah," Suki said, striving for patience as she battled the morning traffic heading into Boston. "This is because of your headaches, your nightmares. It's more to rule out any neurological problems than because I really think you have any." She slammed on her brakes, barely missing a car illegally merging from the right into the Fresh Pond rotary. The other driver flipped her his middle finger, accelerated, then slammed on his own brakes as he barely missed a car illegally merging from his right.

"But what about my chemistry test?" Alexa whined. "I've been studying all week."

Suki reminded herself that nothing would be gained by fighting with Alexa, and that much could be lost. She pictured the quiet beach where she and Stan used to go on Key Biscayne. The old lighthouse rising above the rocky precipice that formed the southern tip of the island, the scurrying sandpipers, the soft pounding of the gentle surf. "We'll have you back at school by lunch."

"Chemistry's second block."

"Do you want me to come in and talk to your teacher?" Suki offered. "I'll explain that this was the only time we could do this, and ask him if you can stay after school and make it up." She imagined she was a bird, gracefully flying above the warm ocean, riding the tropical updrafts.

"Forget it," Alexa grumbled. "Just forget it."

Suki drove along Memorial Drive, past Harvard, toward MIT. The sun sparkled on the Charles River, and the trees on the Esplanade were in full leaf, the bright chartreuse of spring. Multicolored sails bobbed in the water. Alexa stared out the window, her jaw clenched and her eyes narrowed, as if she were viewing a scene of nuclear destruction rather than urban beauty. Suki let her stew.

Cambridge is one of the few cities in the world where taking three lefts in a row will never return you to your starting point. And, to make matters worse, there are no signs designating the street you are on, only the one you are crossing. Predictably, Suki got lost, even though she was looking for Second Street, a place that in any other town would be easily accessible once having found First and Third.

In the middle of their second loop under the Longfellow Bridge, Alexa said, "I don't want to go to private school."

Suki had attempted to discuss the topic of changing schools last night, but Alexa had refused to talk about it, claiming she had a headache, she was too tired, she needed to go to her room. Suki wondered why she was willing to talk about it now. Probably because she knew her choice was not her mother's.

"I'm going to stay at Witton High," Alexa declared.

"If that's what you want to do, I suppose it's all right with me. I just worry about the kids—about how difficult they can make things for you. Someone like Warren Blanchard won't always be around when they start in."

"You were holding his hand the other night—for a long time."

"I think it was an appropriate gesture under the

circumstances." Suki could have kicked herself for mentioning Warren. She glanced over at Alexa who was staring straight up, as if she could see through the roof.

"I had a dream last night that we were living somewhere else," Alexa said. "New Hampshire or Vermont or somewhere. And there was a strange man there. Living with us."

"I'm sure we'll hear from your father any day now."

"It wasn't about Dad," Alexa said. "I just didn't like the mountains."

Suki thought about the dream Alexa had just related. Of course it was about Stan. Suki put her hand on Alexa's knee. "About the last thing I'm interested in right now is a date. I'm only interested in trying to get you out of this mess."

Alexa sniffled and turned to stare out the window.

Suki finally saw the sign for Kendall Radiology and pulled into the parking lot. Although she had referred many patients here, she had never visited the facility. She looked up at the blue-tinted glass cube that housed millions of dollars of high-tech equipment and was staffed by Harvard-affiliated doctors. She was glad she knew the system well enough to get Alexa the best care.

Alexa was far from impressed. She climbed from the car as slowly as was humanly possible, then stood with her back to the entrance until Suki was forced to put her hands on her shoulders and turn her around. She grudgingly followed Suki into the office, then dropped into one of the leather director's chairs ringing the waiting room and stared at the large modern oil painting on the wall across from her, her face set in a mask of weary irritation.

Suki ignored Alexa, scribbling on a clipboard as she carried on a friendly discourse with an elderly woman named Molly, who sat down in the chair on the other side of her. Molly was here for a PET scan. "That stands for positron-emission tomography." Molly giggled like a young girl. "Sounds like something out of *Star Trek,* doesn't it?"

The waiting room was busy and, even this early in the morning, the staff appeared to be running behind schedule. Suki offered a year-old copy of *People* magazine to Alexa, who refused it, then began to thumb through the pages herself: announcements of weddings that had already ended in divorce, Broadway plays that had opened and closed. She dropped the magazine back on the table and listened as Molly cheerfully described her symptoms.

Molly was well into the details on her latest EEG when Suki sensed that Alexa was no longer staring at the painting. She turned and saw that Alexa's face was animated, interested, alive; for the first time in days, the girl looked like her old self. Suki patted Alexa's arm encouragingly. "I'm sure it'll only be a few more minutes."

Alexa didn't respond. Her eyes were focused on the door. She was watching a tall woman in an orange work shirt and pants enter the waiting room. The woman was Lindsey Kern. Darla held one elbow, an officer Suki didn't recognize held the other. There were no handcuffs.

Suki was momentarily baffled. Yesterday, she had told Lindsey that her private life was her own, not up for discussion or interference. So what was Lindsey doing here now? Then rationality kicked in: Lindsey was here for the tests she had ordered, the same tests Alexa was having. What incredibly bad timing.

Lindsey smiled. "Hi," she said to Suki, as if meeting her had always been part of the plan.

Suki nodded stiffly, then reminded herself that this wasn't Lindsey's fault. If it was anyone's fault, it was her own. "Hi," she said. They must have allowed Lindsey out without handcuffs on the assumption that she wasn't a danger to the public. Still, Suki was surprised.

"Good morning, Dr. Jacobs," Darla said. The other officer nodded.

"*Dr.* Jacobs?" Molly leaned closer, and Suki was overwhelmed by the smell of rouge. "You're a doctor?"

"A psychologist," Suki said. Molly's face fell.

Lindsey turned to Alexa. "I'm Lindsey Kern." She held out her hand. "You're Alexa."

Alexa's eyes were bright with excited anticipation. She extended her hand and grinned the way she grinned when her grandfather showed up unexpectedly. "Glad to meet you." She paused and tilted her head to the side. "Do I know you from somewhere? You look familiar."

Lindsey flashed Suki a wicked grin. "Could be," she said to Alexa. "I get around."

Before Suki could stop her, Darla pointed to the empty chair next to Alexa. "Sit there," she said to

Lindsey. "I'll get you checked in." The other officer sat down on Lindsey's right, his hand still clamped to her elbow.

Alexa leaned toward Lindsey. "How do you know my mom?"

Suki was relieved when Lindsey looked to her for guidance. "Through work," Suki told Alexa. "We know each other through work."

"You and I haven't met in this lifetime," Lindsey said to Alexa. Suki threw her an exasperated glance, but Lindsey pretended not to notice.

Alexa took in Lindsey's faded outfit, the illegible stenciling over her left breast. She turned and watched Darla talking with the receptionist. She started to speak, then she closed her mouth.

Molly, who had been eavesdropping without embarrassment, leaned across Suki. "Do you believe in reincarnation?" she asked Lindsey.

"Yes," Lindsey told her. "Along with more than half the people alive on the face of the earth."

"That can't be right." Molly shook her blue curls. "What about all the Christians? The Jews?"

"Just a piece of the world's population," Lindsey said. "But there have also been a lot of Christians who believed in reincarnation—the Cathers, for example. And Jesus did, too."

"That's ridiculous," Molly sputtered.

Lindsey was unfazed by Molly's skepticism. "Apparently the apostles—principally Saint Paul, I think—decided to keep this particular part of Jesus' teachings out of the New Testament. But Jesus was supposed to have said something like, 'To be reborn, all one has to do is remember.'"

"That doesn't mean he believed in reincarnation," Molly argued.

Alexa was listening intently.

Lindsey shrugged. "Voltaire and I both think it's no stranger to live once than to live twice," she said. That shut Molly up.

"I believe there are lots of things, like reincarnation, that everyone thinks aren't true, but are," Alexa said to Lindsey.

Lindsey appraised Alexa, her beautiful gray eyes probing and intelligent. She smiled. "At one time 'everyone' thought the world was flat and that human beings would never fly to the moon. It's never easy to defy conventional wisdom. No one respects it. No one respects you. They think you're crazy or they lock you up—sometimes both." She raised an eyebrow at Suki.

"Do you think a person can know something's going to happen before it does?" Alexa asked Lindsey.

"Of course," Lindsey said, turning back to Alexa. "Happens all the time—as you well know."

Alexa leaned closer. "Does it happen because you see it, or would it happen anyway?"

"Leave Ms. Kern alone, Alexa." Suki stood and walked to the receptionist's window. "We had a nine o'clock appointment," she informed the young woman behind the glass. "My daughter needs to get back to school as soon as possible."

"This is more important," Alexa interrupted before the receptionist could answer. She looked hard at her mother. "I want to hear what she has to say."

The receptionist quickly appraised the situation. "Please, come right this way," she said, standing and opening the door to her left. "We're just about ready for you."

As Suki steered Alexa through ahead of her, Alexa turned back and stuck her head through the doorway. "Maybe some other time," she called to Lindsey.

Before Lindsey could respond, Suki pulled the door closed behind her.

Suki had thought Alexa was hostile and uncommunicative on the drive down to Cambridge, but just a few minutes into the trip home, she realized she hadn't begun to plumb the depths of Alexa's hostility or reticence. When this girl was mad, the girl was *mad,* and she was going to make sure Suki knew it.

Suki's attempts to ask about the MRI were met with a stone wall; they drove entombed in icy stillness. Dr. Smith-Holt had not been at the lab, and Suki was informed that he wouldn't be able to review Alexa's scan until next week. Even when Suki gave them her credentials, the technicians would tell her nothing, claiming they didn't know how to read the results. Although Suki knew this was probably not the case, there was nothing she could do about it.

They were almost back in Witton before Alexa broke the silence, startling Suki. "I was supposed to talk to Lindsey Kern."

"It was time to go in for the test," Suki said.

"But she knew about *me*. She knew what happened."

"Lindsey Kern spends her days locked up in a tiny prison cell," Suki said. "What she knows is what she reads in the newspaper."

"Don't you get it?" Alexa cried. "I need to talk to someone who believes me! Who understands what I'm going through."

Suki took a deep breath. "Alexa," she said, "I can see how appealing the idea is, but I'm afraid Lindsey's just playing with you. Messing with your head."

"You're wrong," Alexa said. "You think you're so smart. That you know everything. Well, you don't. Lindsey has something to tell me. Something that will help me, I know she does."

The familiarity with which Alexa spoke Lindsey's name filled Suki with dread. "I don't think so, honey. Really I don't. Just because you want something to be true, doesn't mean it is."

"And just because you *don't* want something to be true," Alexa retorted, "doesn't mean it isn't."

After dropping Alexa at school, Suki drove right to the farmhouse, arriving fifteen minutes before her first patient's appointment. No one was in the suite, so she went into her office and called Kenneth at the police station. He was there, but she sat on hold for five minutes before he came to the phone. This gave her more than enough time to consider all the possible reasons why he hadn't called for two days.

"Something's wrong, isn't it?" Suki asked, as soon as she heard Kenneth's voice.

"I'm fine, thanks, and you?"

Suki couldn't help it; she laughed. "Sorry, but I'm a bit edgy these days."

"Let me call you back on a line that isn't monitored."

"There really is something."

"I'll call you right back."

When the phone rang, Suki picked it up and said, "Tell me quick."

"Charlie's taken me off the case."

Suki was simultaneously relieved and horrified. She had expected Kenneth to tell her that an arrest warrant was being issued, that she and Mike should be ready to bring Alexa to the station. This was both better and worse. She still had some time, but she no longer had Kenneth. "Can he do that?" she asked.

"He's the chief."

Suki turned her chair and stared at the rolling farmland edged by a thick forest of oak trees. Oaks came in late, and the web of delicate branches still held more brown than green. "Is this because you pushed?" she asked. "Because you were trying to find out something that he doesn't want you to know?"

"I've been reassigned," Kenneth said, and Suki could hear the care with which he was choosing his words. "It happens all the time, but that doesn't mean I'm letting this go." He lowered his voice. "I'm still with you, although it'll have to be unofficially."

"Kenneth, I really—"

"I can't talk now," he interrupted. "But I'll try and call you from home tonight. It's important you understand Charlie's going hard on this. He said the fact that they haven't found the gun isn't going to hold him back, that the only thing keeping him from typing up the warrant is lack of clear motive—but that he's willing to use the jilted lover angle if he has to."

"But that was over six months—"

"Listen to me," Kenneth hissed. "He's at the high school right now. Trying to find a kid who'll give him a reason why Alexa might have wanted to kill Jonah now. If he comes up with someone, even just one girl with a grudge because Alexa's prettier than she is, it's all over."

"Everyone knows Alexa did it," Parker Alley's taunting voice reverberated through Suki's head, through her body. *"Everyone knows why."*

CHAPTER SEVENTEEN

Suki was fortunate in being surrounded by love all her life. As a child, she was adored by her parents, and in return, she loved her mother more than life itself and thought her father the most perfect man in the world; she still did. With Stan, she shared a passion she wouldn't have thought possible, and she had loved, and continued to love, grandparents and cousins and dear friends. But when Alexa, still slippery from birth, was placed on her abdomen and the baby had opened her wide blue eyes and wisely studied the labor room, Suki was pierced by love as she had never felt it before: the love of a mother for her child. The strongest, most powerful, most unconditional love there is. A love that is a given no matter what else may occur. A love that can coexist with any other state—even hate.

For Suki hated Alexa at this moment, as she drove from her office to the rec center, as she planned what she would say to Parker Alley, as she tried to figure out what she could possibly do to save the child she so desperately loved. Neither emotion was negated nor reduced by the reality of the other.

As she followed River Road toward Witton Center, Suki averted her eyes from the spot where Jonah had been shot. But she didn't turn away quickly enough. She saw a single bouquet of flowers resting in front of an unremarkable cluster of maple saplings.

"Damn her!" Suki yelled into the empty car. "Damn her! Damn her!" How could Alexa have done this to herself? To them all? How could she have been so stupid, so careless? Suki started to slam the dashboard, but thought better of it. She didn't have the luxury of anger. She had to concentrate. Focus. Think.

According to Parker Alley, everyone knew Alexa had killed Jonah, and everyone knew why. Suki could care less if the entire student body of Witton High believed Alexa was a murderer—she knew that wasn't true—but she *was* concerned about who thought they knew why. If Alexa's pregnancy and abortion were common knowledge, Charlie Gasperini might find someone willing to tell him about it. And once Charlie got his hands on that information, Alexa was as good as arrested.

Suki touched the pager hooked over the waist-band of her skirt. It was set to vibrate when receiving an incoming call, and it hadn't moved all afternoon. If Charlie had typed up the warrant, Kenneth would have surely phoned. That meant Charlie hadn't discovered anything—or that Kenneth hadn't been allowed to call. Kenneth. She had the feeling she was going to miss him more than she knew. Damn that Charlie Gasperini. Damn him and his slimy cronies. Again, she caught herself. Focus. Think.

Varsity soccer practiced Monday, Thursday and Friday afternoons. Parker was on the team, as was Brendan, and although Parker wasn't first-string, he played well enough to allow Becky to brag about him—her favorite pastime. Suki drove through town and turned up the hill to the rec center. She checked her watch and then pressed her foot to the accelerator. She needed to catch Parker before practice started. And when she did, he was going to explain exactly what he had meant by "everyone knows why."

She stationed herself outside the boys' locker room and waited as the pride of Witton's soccer moms changed into shorts and ran through the open gym door to the field. Warren was nowhere in sight, but he had his team trained well; with a minimum of horsing around, the boys started their warm-up calisthenics. No one took any notice of her; these kids were used to parents hanging around.

Parker was one of the last to leave the locker room. Suki grabbed his arm. "Hi," she said.

He turned with a smile that Suki guessed meant he thought she was a particular girl. When he saw it was Suki, his smile disappeared. "Hi," he said, allowing her to maintain her hold on his arm. The confident, strutting Parker of the other night was gone, replaced by the tentative boy Suki remembered, the one who had cried in terror as he stood at the top of their backyard slide, the one who was afraid of clowns.

"I need to talk to you." Suki's voice was cool and crisp. She recognized an opportunity when she saw one. "Now."

Parker looked around, as if for help, then nodded.

She let go of his arm and leaned against the doorjamb.

He looked down at his feet and played with the

ripped piping on the right leg of his shorts. "Sorry about the other night," he mumbled.

"I was very surprised, Parker," Suki said as if he were still that scared child perched atop Alexa's slide. "I wouldn't have expected that kind of behavior from you."

Parker shrugged, and Suki saw that despite his six feet and the stubble on his chin, in many ways, he still *was* that child. He tugged so hard at his shorts that the piping ripped off in his hand. He shoved it into his pocket. "If you want, I'll apologize to Alexa." He looked longingly out the gym door at his friends on the field.

"I think that would be a good idea, a nice gesture, but there's still something I need to know. I need to know what you meant by claiming everyone knows why Alexa killed Jonah—when you and I both know she didn't."

"I'm sorry, Mrs. Jacobs. Really I am." He raised his eyes and Suki saw he was scared—and ashamed. "I don't know why I did it. Really I don't. I guess I was just showing off."

Suki believed him, and felt sorry for him, but she was not here to exonerate him. "What did you mean when you said 'everyone knows why'? Why did you say that?"

"Nothing." Parker clenched his jaw. "I didn't mean anything special."

Suki narrowed her eyes and scrutinized the boy closely. He knew something, but he wasn't talking. No one liked a snitch. This could be good.

"I told Chief Gasperini the same thing," Parker added.

Suki's heart began to pound and the questions poured out. "Chief Gasperini knows what you said the other night? He was asking you what you meant? When? Was he at school? Today?"

"He was at school," Parker said. "But no, I mean yes. Yes."

"Well, which is it?" Suki demanded. "Yes or no?"

"Well, uh . . ." Parker swallowed hard. "No about what I said, but yes that he was asking questions."

"And what exactly was he asking about?"

"Just if I knew why anyone would want to kill Jonah."

"Anyone?" Suki was astounded by the hope rising within her. "Not just Alexa?"

Parker shrugged again. "Mostly Alexa, I guess."

Suki's hope died as quickly as it had emerged, and she was chagrined by her naïveté.

"Hello, Mrs. Jacobs."

Suki whirled around at the sound of the familiar voice, unable to believe she was hearing correctly. Brendan Ricker stood before her. He too looked scared and ashamed, but more in control than Parker.

"I gotta go," Parker mumbled. He didn't move, and Suki could almost feel his muscles straining toward the open door. "Coach likes us to be finished with warm-ups by the time he shows up."

She nodded, knowing she wasn't going to get any more out of him, and he fled. She turned to Brendan.

Brendan flushed, but met her eye. "No one knows about the pregnancy," he said softly. "Not even Kendra."

Suki blinked.

"I heard what you were asking Parker."

"So what did he mean when he said everyone knew why?"

Brendan inspected his soccer shoes and cleared his throat. "I'm not sure."

"Don't give me that." Suki had been a psychologist long enough to recognize a lie. "You know exactly what he was talking about—and you're going to tell me."

Brendan shook his head.

Suki wanted to grab him by the shoulders and shake him. She clenched her hands into fists. "You're going to tell me exactly what Parker was talking about, Brendan Ricker. You're going to tell me because you owe me. Because you owe Alexa—you owe her big for throwing her to the wolves just to save your lying skin."

For a moment Suki thought she had gone too far, then Brendan mumbled, "He was talking about the drugs."

Suki was glad she was leaning against something. She flashed on the image of rolling papers and drug paraphernalia stuffed into the back of the locker at the boathouse. She had forgotten, actually forgotten, what she had seen there. Just when things got as bad as she thought they could get, they got worse. "Drugs?"

"It started out just as something to help us study. Just a couple of us did it once in a while—to help on tests and stuff. Get through the heavy reading."

"Get through the heavy reading," Suki repeated, as if saying the words would increase her comprehension.

"But we didn't get it from a drug pusher or anything like that. It was all clean—from an adult who knew what he was doing. It was never supposed to get to the point that it did," Brendan's words flowed out in a rush. "Then other kids started finding out—I don't know how, but they did—and they wanted some and, and well, you know how that can be. . . ."

"Some adult gives you drugs?" Suki asked. "Who?"

"I don't know." Brendan looked down at his feet.

"Does Alexa know?"

Brendan shook his head. "No one knows," he said.

"Aren't you supposed to be doing warm-ups, Ricker?" Warren came striding down the corridor toward them. "Hi, Suki," he said. "Are you two finished? Can I send him out?" When she nodded, he turned back to Brendan. "Get to the field. You're late."

Brendan got to the field.

Suki stared at Warren as she tried to integrate what Brendan had said. No one knew anything about the pregnancy, but they knew about the drugs. Alexa and drugs . . . Jonah and drugs . . . Clean drugs they got from some adult . . .

"Are you all right? Suki?" Warren was asking. His voice sounded as if it were coming from far away. "Do you want to sit down in Finlay's place? How about some water?"

"Finlay's place," she repeated stupidly. Although there was a new custodian, Suki had lived in Witton long enough to recognize that the room would always be referred to as Finlay's place. "Sure, sure."

Warren took her arm and gently led her into the tiny room. He pulled a bundle of lacrosse sticks off

the chair and motioned for her to sit. Suki sat. It
didn't make any sense. Alexa didn't do drugs. Sweat
prickled under Suki's arms as she realized she had no
idea what Alexa did and didn't do.

Warren disappeared and then reappeared with a
paper cup in his hand. "Drink."

Suki took the cup. The water was cold and wet
and a piece of her felt better for it, while most of her
wasn't even aware she was drinking. She suddenly
realized she hadn't spoken to Warren since the night
of the play. "I've, ah, I've been meaning to call you,"
she stuttered. "To thank you for your help the other
night. At the high school . . ."

He waved away her gratitude. "What just happened?" he asked. "Did Brendan do something to
upset you?"

"I . . . He . . ." Suki threw her hands in the air. If
Alexa was indeed mixed up with drugs, "upset" was
an understatement. "Yeah," she said. "I guess he did."

Warren sat on the edge of a stack of cardboard
cartons. "Was it about Jonah?" he asked. "Something I should know?"

Suki shook her head. "I've got to think. Let me
think. Talk to Alexa. I've got to talk to Alexa." She
knew she was barely coherent, that she needed to be
alone. "Go to your practice, Warren. To your team.
I'll be fine. Really I will."

"Suki," Warren said, "please let me help you. Tell
me what's going on."

She forced herself to stand and smile. "I'm all
right," she said. "Really I am. I'll call you in a couple
of days. I promise I will."

Warren looked at her dubiously. "Okay," he

said, "if that's how you want it. But you've got to remember that this isn't just about Alexa—this is about Jonah, too. That helping you is helping me. And helping Darcy."

Suki touched his arm as she walked from the cramped room. "Thanks," she said. "Again."

"So Alexa's okay?" Warren called after her. "Nothing broken?"

Suki whirled around. "Alexa's fine. What are you talking about?"

"Matt just told me in the locker room that Alexa fell off a piece of apparatus in gym today. That Carla had to take her to the hospital for X rays."

Suki stared at Warren in disbelief. "No one called me," she cried as she yanked at the hem of her sweater so she could see the readout on the pager hooked to her skirt.

"If no one called, Matt must have gotten Alexa confused with some other kid," Warren said. "Most likely he just got the story wrong."

But Suki saw that most likely Matt had gotten the story right. Her pager was turned off.

Suki raced to her car phone and punched the speed dial button for home. Kyle answered. "Is Alexa there?" The words burst from Suki's mouth before Kyle had finished saying hello. "Is she all right?"

"Where you been, Mom?" Kyle asked. "They've been trying to reach you all afternoon. Is—"

"What happened?" Suki interrupted. "Is Alexa hurt? Is she home?"

"She's here. She's all right," he said quickly. "It

was just a sprain. She's got an Ace bandage. You want to talk to her?"

"Of course I want to talk to her, Kyle," Suki said. "What do you think?" As soon as the words were out of her mouth, she was sorry. None of this was Kyle's fault. He was being great. She was the one who wasn't thinking. "I'm sorry, honey, Kyle," she said. "Sorry."

But it was Alexa on the other end. "I'm okay, Mom. Really, I'm fine."

"You went to the hospital?" Suki asked again. "Saw a doctor?"

"Ms. Amato took me to Emerson. They tried to call you. Is your pager broken?"

"What did the doctor say?"

"She said it was just a sprain. That I'll be fine."

"What's her name?" Suki demanded. "I'll call her."

"Relax, Mom." Alexa's voice reverberated with annoyed teenager, and Suki was relieved to hear her sound so normal. "You're making way too big a deal out of this. It's nothing. An accident. Really."

"Are you sure?" Now that she knew Alexa was all right, Suki could wonder about causes. Had it just been an accident, or had Alexa been careless, distracted by her meeting with Lindsey, by all that was happening to her? Cold fingers squeezed Suki's stomach. Could Alexa have hurt herself on purpose? Or could this be another spiteful act like the bottle through the window? "Tell me exactly what happened."

"I don't want to talk about it," Alexa said in the

tone she used when she was hiding something. "I'll tell you later."

"No," Suki said. "I need you to tell me now." Could McKinna be behind this, too? Even with all he had done, Suki found it hard to believe.

"I fell."

Suki didn't need to see Alexa to know the sulky pout on her lips, the defiant edge with which she was holding her shoulders. "And exactly *how* did you fall?" she asked, her fear biting into each word.

Alexa didn't say anything for a long moment. "I was doing the horse." Her voice was slow and plodding, as if she were speaking to a not-too-bright child. "And when I went to jump, the handle came off in my hand."

"And then?"

"I fell."

"Who was on the horse before you?" Suki asked. "Was there anyone hanging around the equipment?"

"What are you talking about?" Alexa was really annoyed now. "I don't get what you mean."

"Were you feeling okay?" Suki asked, switching tacks. "Did you have any residual effects from the test this morning? Dizziness? Nausea?"

Another long pause. "And if I did it would all be your fault."

Suki had had enough. "You stay right where you are, young lady," she ordered. "I'm on my way home—and when I get there you're going to tell me exactly what went on this afternoon." She punched the END button without saying good-bye and felt good about it.

• • •

Alexa was in a major snit when Suki got to the house. "You hung up on me," she cried as soon as Suki walked into the family room. "You can't treat me like that. I'm a person too!" She stood in front of Suki, her hands on her hips.

Suki eyed the Ace bandage wrapped around her daughter's left wrist; it looked fairly innocuous. "Calm down," she said, trying to control the edge in her voice as her concern for Alexa's safety ebbed and her anger returned. "I'm sorry I hung up on you, but you can be a bit annoying, you know."

"And so can you!" Alexa fired back as Kyle slipped from the room.

"Sit," Suki ordered, pointing to the couch.

Alexa swept her arms outward and dropped into the couch with an exaggerated curtsy. "Yes, your majesty."

The anger that had been building within Suki all day boiled over. "Don't you dare talk to me like that!" she exploded. "Don't you understand what's going on here? What we're contending with? Do you know that Chief Gasperini was at school today? That he was asking about you. About Jonah and a possible motive. Motive! Motive!" Suki had never spoken to either of her children like this, but she was beyond restraint. "And as soon as he gets someone to give him a motive, you're arrested! In handcuffs. In jail!"

Alexa was not impressed. "Chief Gasperini's an asshole," she said as if her words negated Suki's. "He's stupid."

"Don't underestimate the man, young lady,"

Suki advised. "He's dangerous and he's smart and he's got a mission."

"No one's gonna talk to *him*," Alexa said defiantly. "He'll never find out anything."

"Which anything?" Suki demanded. "The pregnancy? The abortion? Or the drugs you and Brendan and who knows who else have been doing or selling or whatever it is you little liars have been up to."

"I haven't been up to anything!" Alexa screamed and jumped up from the couch. "You don't believe me. You believe some stupid cop and Brendan and Devin before you believe your own daughter! Well, fine! I'm done with you. I don't want any more of your help. I don't want any more of you!" She burst into tears and flew up the stairs to her room. The door slam shook the house.

Suki got up early the next morning to work on the Kern evaluation. Politely worded second notices—"if your check has been mailed, please disregard with our apologies"—had arrived yesterday from both the telephone company and the plumber, and Mike had asked when he could expect the next installment of the evaluation. It was Saturday. The kids were asleep. The house was quiet. But instead of being able to escape into work, as she had hoped, Suki was consumed with worry. With each passing day her worries shifted and changed, but never diminished. Sometimes the huge and hulking concerns of morning became removed by afternoon, nothing, in light of new, more terrible revelations. Yet, the earlier worries still persisted, always hovering, always there.

Suki stared at the materials spread on her desk—the social, medical and legal debris of Lindsey Kern's life—and she realized why she was unable to escape within them. This case wasn't just a job she had taken, a means to an end, a check, a mortgage payment, an entrée into another job; this case was about her daughter, her mother, and about Suki herself. About what was possible—and what wasn't.

Suki stared through the small window over her desk. And now she had drug abuse to add to her list of worries. Alexa. It was as if the girl who had been a piece of her, a part of her heart, her being, for seventeen years, had vanished, a new, unknown girl left in her place. Suki threw down her pen and stood up. She needed to look at Alexa, to see that she was indeed the same girl she had always been.

Suki climbed the stairs and slowly pushed Alexa's door open a crack. She peered into the darkness. Then she threw the door open wide and flipped on the light. "Alexa?" she called into the room she saw did not contain her daughter. She went to the window overlooking the carport. The car was gone. And so was Alexa.

Suki raced down to the kitchen to see if Alexa had left a note, but there was none. She whirled around, stared at the colorful poster board still pasted in the window, turned back to the table. Where had Alexa gone? Suki's mind flew to every possible disaster from an overdose of drugs, to a psychotic break, to depression-induced suicide.

Suki thought of Jen's walking wounded, the haunted kids who sat, staring at nothing, as they waited for their appointments. She thought of all the teenagers she had seen when she worked in Roxbury, all their fear, anger, hopelessness. All their suicide attempts. Cut it out, she scolded herself. Yesterday's fall had just been a fall. Alexa had probably gone for a ride. Just in case, she would call the police to find out if there had been any accidents. But when Suki looked at the boarded-up window, she knew the police were not the answer. Maybe Alexa was at Kendra's. She reached for the phone book.

Alexa walked in just as Suki was dialing Kendra's number.

Suki slammed down the phone. "Where have you been?"

"I went for a drive." Alexa pulled a leaf from the bottom of her jeans and threw it in the trash. She didn't meet her mother's eye. "To Hayden Park. I walked in the woods. I needed to be outside. To breathe."

"Did it ever occur to you to write a note? To let me know where you'd gone?" Suki asked, her voice rising with each word. "To think about someone beside yourself?" she added before she could stop herself. She braced for an explosion.

Instead, Alexa dropped into a chair at the kitchen table. "Sorry, Mom," she said softly. There were twigs caught in her curls. "It was thoughtless, I know, really thoughtless. I won't do it again. I promise."

Suki's anger dissipated in the face of Alexa's apology and distress. She sat down next to her daughter. "I guess we're all a little stressed-out, huh? I'm sorry I've been yelling so much."

Alexa twisted the silver ring on her thumb.

"So you went for a walk?"

Alexa twisted the silver ring on her forefinger.

"Was it nice?" Suki turned so she could see out the dining room window. "It's a nice morning. Good time to be out."

"I had a really bad nightmare."

Suki could see a vein pulsing at the right side of Alexa's forehead. "Is that why you left?"

Alexa nodded.

"Do you want to tell me about it?"

"No," Alexa said, shaking her head. "Yes."

Suki reached out and pressed her daughter's cold hand between her two warm ones. Alexa's fingernails were dirty.

"It was like I was awake and asleep at the same time," Alexa finally told her. "Like I was dreaming and not-dreaming."

Suki didn't say anything. She held Alexa's hand.

"Lindsey was in my room."

Suki jerked back in surprise.

Alexa looked at her mother with frightened eyes, and Suki gave her hand a quick squeeze. Alexa sighed a shuddering sigh, then continued. "She was there and not-there. Kind of see-through. Floating, hovering like a ghost. She motioned to me, and even though she didn't say anything, I could hear her. She told me to come with her."

Suki nodded.

"Then I started floating, too. Out of my room, out of the house." Alexa shook her head and her hair fell in clumps around her face. "But it didn't feel like a dream—and I don't remember it like a dream. It seems more like something that really happened. Like a memory." Alexa's description matched the report of precognitive dreams in the parapsychology textbook.

Suki pushed her chair closer to Alexa's and wrapped her arms around her as she remembered Lindsey talking about how she enhanced her powers of precognition and clairvoyance through astral projection, how astral projecting was her way of "getting out of prison." Suki pressed Alexa closer. "Dreams come in all types," she said. "Some are fragmented. Some are clear."

"That's not the bad part," Alexa whispered.

Suki played with a limp curl on Alexa's forehead. Her hair used to be so springy, shiny with youth and life. Now it was dull, sluggish. Just like Alexa. She let go of the curl.

"We went to the cemetery. The one where . . . where . . ." Alexa took a large gulp of air and then hiccuped.

"I know," Suki said soothingly. "I know."

"There was a funeral going on. It was, it was—" Alexa buried her head in Suki's breasts. "I can't tell you, I can't," she wailed. "I don't want to say it."

"It's okay, baby. It's okay. You don't have to say anything you don't want to say."

Alexa cried quietly for a long time. Then she raised her tear-streaked face to Suki. "It was Chief Gasperini's funeral," she said. "His wife and daughters were crying. They were each carrying a white rose."

Not another precognitive vision, Suki thought. Not another death. Not another person whom Alexa had reason to want dead. "Just because you dreamed it," she said, "doesn't mean it's going to come true."

But that afternoon, when Kenneth phoned to tell her Charlie had been killed in an early-morning boating accident, Suki wasn't all that surprised.

CHAPTER EIGHTEEN

Suki didn't know how to tell Alexa. Or what to tell Alexa. She knew she was going to have to tell her that Charlie was dead, that there had been an explosion on his boat involving gas fumes and a great deal of fire, that there *would* be a funeral at which his wife and daughters cried and carried white roses. It was how to tell it so Alexa suffered the least. But even as she worried about her phrasing, Suki recognized the problem wasn't in the words she used to recount the incident—it was in the part of the story she didn't have to tell. In the underlying truth implied by the events: that once again, Alexa had foreseen the future. A future that held death.

Suki raised her eyes to the ceiling of her study. Alexa was upstairs in her room with Kendra; Suki could hear their muted words, the pounding bass on the CD they were playing. Just a few feet away. A lifetime away. For, as was true with Jonah's death, after Alexa heard about Charlie's, her life would never be the same. From that moment on, Alexa would live in a world in which all the rules were changed. Where nothing was for certain. A world Suki had entered when she picked up the phone and heard Kenneth's voice.

Kenneth had been distraught. "I can't believe it," he kept repeating. "How can it be true? I can't believe Charlie's really dead." Despite his disagreements with his boss over how Jonah's case was being handled, Kenneth was genuinely fond of Charlie—*had been* genuinely fond of Charlie. So had Suki, for that matter. Before Jonah, Charlie had been a family friend, a colleague at the library, a fishing buddy of Stan's—and Alexa's.

Alexa and Stan had gone fishing with Charlie almost every Saturday morning between March and December. Kyle had never shown any interest in the sport, but Alexa had loved these adventures. She had been fascinated by the speed and agility of *The Chief*, Charlie's sleek powerboat, and Charlie, whom she had idolized, had taught her everything about his craft—from the mechanics of the engine to the best way to tow a water skier. Charlie. Another entry on the growing list of men who had betrayed and abandoned Alexa.

At yet, Suki realized it was quite possible that Charlie's death was going to be good for Alexa. What were the chances the new chief would be a friend of Ellery McKinna's? That he would be as easily intimidated by the DA's office? It seemed quite possible that another chief, a different man, unburdened by friends and political obligations, would see that Alexa hadn't killed Jonah. Maybe this new chief would even begin looking for the real murderer.

The bass above her head gave a powerful beat, and Suki pushed herself from her chair. She walked slowly up the stairs and knocked on Alexa's door. No response. She knocked again. Louder. Harder.

Alexa pulled the door open and looked at her warily.

"We need to talk." Suki nodded at Kendra, who was sprawled out on the carpet.

"But, Mom—" Alexa started arguing, as if by reflex, then stopped.

Kendra was already on her feet. "I've got to get home anyway," she said. "I promised my mom I'd get a few things at the Stop and Shop." She gave Alexa a quick hug and whispered, "Call me later." Then she slid out the door, obviously glad to be going.

Suki came into the room and sat on the edge of the bed. She didn't bother to close the door. Kyle was at a soccer game. They were alone.

Alexa pulled herself to her full five feet. "Am I going to be arrested?"

"No," Suki said, and Alexa visibly relaxed. "But it's not good."

Alexa gripped her hands together; her knuckles were white. "Tell me."

"Charlie Gasperini was killed this morning."

Alexa's jaw dropped and her eyes opened wide. For a moment, Suki was reminded of Edvard Munch's painting *The Scream*. "It was a boating accident," she continued, as if Alexa had asked, as if this conversation was about an accident that had happened to a casual acquaintance—not an accident loaded down with the baggage of arrest and murder and Alexa's dream. "Not far from the boathouse."

Alexa slid down the wall, melting into a heap of gray sweatshirt. She stared up at Suki. "I killed him," she whispered.

Suki knelt down. "What are you saying?"

"I killed him," Alexa repeated stiffly, as if a puppeteer was moving her vocal cords, pushing the air through her lungs. "I killed him just like I killed Jonah."

Suki was aware of the carpet nubs beneath her hands, Alexa's clock ticking on the bureau, the sweet-smelling breeze wafting through the window, the hollow pinging sound of someone down the street bouncing a basketball.

Alexa's teeth began to chatter. "It's my fault," she whispered. "I see it and they die." Her voice grew louder, more high pitched. "They die because I see it!"

Suki closed the window and ripped the spread off Alexa's bed, trying to figure out the best thing to say. If she acknowledged Alexa's dream was related to Charlie's death, would she be encouraging Alexa's delusions, perhaps even causing more dreams and visions? And if she denied any connection, would she lose credibility in Alexa's eyes? "Don't say such things," she said as she wrapped Alexa in the black quilt. "Don't think them. Don't say them. Don't say them to me. Don't say them to anyone."

"But it's the truth! I see them die in my mind and then it happens. I make it come true. I do. Even though I don't want to. Even though I don't want to, I do!" Alexa was becoming hysterical. "I want to and I don't, I want to and I don't. I don't I don't I don't . . ."

Suki pulled Alexa into a prone position on the floor and then stretched out alongside her. She put her arms around her daughter, tucking Alexa's head under her chin, making sure her legs were making contact with Alexa's, her feet with Alexa's feet.

"Hush, baby," Suki murmured as she nested the small quivering body within her own. "Hush."

Suki had learned this from her father when she was a child. He had explained that when a person begins to lose mental touch with reality, it's important to put them into physical touch. To help them reconnect. He had done the same with her mother. Rocking her, consoling her, hoping the feel of his body would bring his wife back to him.

"Hush, baby," Suki whispered. "Hush."

Frank Maxwell, who headed up the small detective bureau of the Witton Police, was named acting chief. He was an up-through-the-ranks kind of guy: basic, straightforward, reticent. He was close, if not at, retirement age, had neither political connections nor aspirations—and he wasn't a friend of Ellery McKinna's. Mike arranged a meeting with him first thing Monday morning.

"Chief Maxwell," Mike began, "I know how busy and overwhelmed you must be, and I want you to know that we really appreciate you taking the time to talk with us." He was speaking in smooth, complete sentences. A mode of speech he used in a courtroom, not a police station. This was obviously a planned performance.

"Yup," Frank said.

"I think your daughter Rorie went to school with my husband, Stan. Stan Jacobs?" Although she had promised Mike she would let him do the talking, Suki found herself blabbering. "Graduated from Witton High in sixty-eight?"

"Rorie graduated in sixty-eight," Frank said.

"Same year as Stan."

Mike gave Suki a reassuring wink and then turned to Frank. "Can I be candid here?" he asked.

Frank looked at Mike from under his bushy white eyebrows. He didn't say anything.

"I'm sure you're quite familiar with the Ward case . . ." Mike paused for a moment and, when he didn't get a response, continued, "And I'm sure you know that Chief Gasperini had a prime suspect . . ."

Again, no response, neither verbal nor facial from the policeman.

". . . a prime suspect he was pursuing despite the large body of evidence supporting her innocence."

Frank appeared unimpressed with Mike's candor.

"Are you aware of the evidence?" Mike asked.

"Yup," Frank said.

Suki couldn't stand it any longer. "Frank," she said, leaning forward. She didn't know him all that well, but his grandson had been on the swim team with Kyle, and she had stood with Rorie and Frank in many overheated, chlorine-scented pool enclosures, cheering the boys on. "Alexa didn't kill Jonah."

"Chief," Mike interjected smoothly, "it's a fact that Devin McKinna, Brendan Ricker and Sam Cooperstein initially lied about their whereabouts on the night of Jonah Ward's murder. There is no reason to assume that the new story they concocted, the one in which they profess that Alexa shot Jonah, holds any more truth than their first pack of lies."

"Yup," Frank said again.

"So you see the problem?" Suki was filled with

hope, although she was well aware a "yup" from Frank didn't necessarily mean he agreed with the statement preceding it. "And you think you might look into the whole thing a bit more? Or differently? Now that Charlie's, ah, well, you know, now, that . . . that things are different." She bit down on her lip to keep herself from saying anything else.

Frank looked impassively at Suki, and she felt chastised. She slumped back into her chair.

"Having lied once, it's highly likely the boys will lie again." Mike's voice was assured, confident, as if no one in his right mind could possibly disagree with him. "It's obvious all three have something to hide."

"Haven't found the gun yet," Frank said.

"Alexa doesn't even know how to shoot a gun," Suki cried. "She never fired one in her life. So does it make any sense that the first time she does—without any training, mind you—she manages to shoot so well that she kills her target? Isn't that a bit hard to believe?" Suki felt Mike's hand on her arm, but she didn't want to stop. "And where would Alexa get a gun, anyway? How could she possibly fire it and drive at the same time? She was on the other side of the car, for God's sake. They found the powder burns on the passenger side. And Alexa was driving! She was driving!" Suki slapped her hand on the arm of her chair.

Suddenly, the room was thick with silence. The men glanced at each other, and when they turned back to Suki, they both looked at her with sympathy. She put her hands in her lap and took a deep breath. "Alexa was driving," she repeated more softly. "You can't drive and shoot from the passenger seat at the same time." She tried to smile. "It's a physical impossibility."

"Could have slid over," Frank said. "Car was stopped."

"And then there's the motive problem," Mike said quickly. "Alexa had no reason to kill Jonah Ward." He threw his hands in the air. "No motive and no opportunity. Doesn't sound like a very good suspect to me."

"To me either," Suki said before Frank could bring up the two girls who had heard Alexa say she wished Jonah was dead. She wondered if Charlie had discovered anything at his visit to the high school, if Frank knew more than they thought he did. "Seems like there are lots of better suspects around," she added.

"Quite a few strong suspects, in fact." Mike nodded sagely. "Much stronger than my client. Boys with knowledge of, and access to, guns. Boys who have admitted to being at the scene of the crime. Boys who have lied, who have motive. It appears there are many places to look for Jonah Ward's murderer. Don't you think, Chief?"

"Yup."

"So you'll try to find out who really killed Jonah?" Suki asked.

"Case is on hold," Frank said.

Suki and Mike exchanged glances.

"Got another case taking up my manpower."

"On hold?" Suki asked, unable to believe their good fortune. "What other case?"

"Seems there's evidence someone may have been tampering with the gas tank on Charlie's boat."

"You think someone killed Charlie Gasperini?" Mike asked. "Killed him because he was chief?"

"Don't know much for sure yet," Frank told them.

"Wow," Mike said.

Suki didn't say anything. She could only think of Alexa, returning home Saturday morning from an odd, early walk, leaves and branches caught in her clothes and hair.

As they walked to the parking lot after their meeting with Frank Maxwell, Suki didn't mention Alexa's dream about Charlie's death or her absence the morning of the accident. It was obvious Mike was wondering why Suki wasn't happier, why she wasn't more relieved, so she tried to pretend she was delighted with the results of their conversation, but her words sounded flat to her own ears, and she knew her smile was thin.

Mike was exuberant. "Maxwell's going to be the best thing. Best thing ever happened," he declared as they walked to the parking lot behind the station. "See him listening? Hear what he said? He thinks Charlie was going about it all wrong. I can tell. Even with all that silent brotherhood crap. He may not be saying anything now, but later on, when he's in the driver's seat, old Frank's not going to be doing things Charlie Gasperini's way."

"Yeah," Suki said, trying to follow his words, to respond appropriately. "I think you're right. Sure, you're right." But she kept hearing Alexa's voice: *"I make it come true. . . . Even though I don't want to, I do. . . ."*

Mike leaned against the front of her car. "Get any of those test results on the Kern eval?"

"Not yet." Suki fished in her purse for her car keys. "But the rest's coming along. I've got almost all I need, and, with a bit of luck, I might only have to go out to Watkins one more time."

"Getting around to forming an opinion?"

Suki busied herself unlocking the door. Usually at this point in an evaluation she would have no doubts as to her final assessment. But this case was tough, tricky and heavily loaded.

"Suki?" Mike was asking. "You okay?"

"Yeah," she said, straining to smile. "It's just that this has all been a bit much. I haven't been sleeping too well."

"Sure," Mike said. "Understood. Be fine if you get that final report to me the day before you're scheduled to testify."

Suki was surprised. Evals were usually due at least a week before testimony; the report had to be shared with the other side—as a part of the discovery process—and few attorneys allowed their experts to take the stand without an hour or two of pretrial preparation.

"Not a problem," Mike said, in answer to the question she didn't ask. "I'll handle the DA, and I know you can handle the testimony. Your slot looks to be sometime early next week. That workable?"

Suki nodded and dropped into the driver's seat. This was really decent of him, but unfortunately, she needed the money—yesterday. "Let me see if I can wrap it up sooner. I should be able to get you the versions of the alleged crime in a day or two."

Mike pushed off and headed for his silver BMW. "If you think you're coming down on the side of sanity," he called over his shoulder, "make sure you let me know ASAP."

Suki gave him a mock salute. How long would it take to sort it all out? Sanity. Insanity. Truth. Lies. Guilt. Innocence. And she wasn't thinking about Lindsey.

The previous night, when Suki had told Alexa she wanted her to stay home from school for a few days, for once, Alexa didn't argue. She had just nodded—or more precisely, barely nodded, lowering and raising her chin with such a small movement that Suki wouldn't have caught it had she not been watching closely—and continued to lie on her bed, staring silently at the ceiling.

Alexa was completely devastated by the accident, neither sleeping nor eating nor showering nor speaking to anyone since hearing the news. She hadn't even stirred when her grandfather came to visit, sitting on the edge of bed, full of bad jokes and unconditional love. If Seymour couldn't reach Alexa, than no one could. Where was Alexa? Suki wondered as she drove home from the police station. And who was she? Was Alexa the girl Suki thought she knew, or was that girl just the daughter Suki wanted her to be?

Suki pulled into the carport and stared at the flakes of paint peeling off the side of the house. Stain wasn't supposed to peel, but the stain on this house did. It was Stan's guess that someone had put a coat of latex on it years ago, and then tried to cover the deed with stain. He said it would never be right until all the paint was scraped off. Fat chance that was ever going to happen. Suki still owed the plumber for the broken toilet three months back.

The thought of her debts caused her to think of Lindsey, who had permanently slid from Suki's professional life into her personal when she insinuated herself into Alexa's dreams. Was it their common paranormal interests that drew Alexa to Lindsey—or something else? Suki climbed out of the car and slammed the door.

But as soon as she got into the house, Suki forgot her questions. Alexa was huddled in the corner of the family room, still wearing the same gray sweatshirt she had had on Saturday. She was curled into a fetal position. Rocking.

"Alexa?" Suki said, softly, kneeling by her daughter.

Alexa swatted her away.

"Let me make you a cup of tea," Suki offered. "How about some nice wild berry zinger? I know how much you like it." Suki stood and tugged gently on Alexa's hands, but she refused to rise and pulled herself more tightly into her ball of pain. Suki squatted down again.

"I'm afraid to see," Alexa mumbled. "Afraid." She twisted herself into an even smaller space, although it didn't seem possible. "If I see, it comes true."

"Is that why you haven't been sleeping?" Suki felt as if her heart were breaking. "So you won't dream?"

"If I don't see it, it won't happen." Tears squeezed through Alexa's closed lids.

"Alexa," Suki said, "honey, you know the world doesn't work that way. Things don't happen because you see them, things happen because things happen."

Alexa shook her head furiously, her eyes still shut, her body still rigidly fetal. "I keep seeing this symbol," she said into her chest. "It's bad. Dangerous, I think."

Suki was filled with a powerful apprehension, almost a premonition, that she shouldn't ask what Alexa meant. But she had to know. "What kind of symbol?"

"It's like a letter," Alexa said. "But not an English letter, another alphabet. Different. Hebrew maybe. I think it might be a ring."

Suki pressed her hands together. "Do you know whose ring it is?"

"No!" Alexa's eyes flew open and she flung her arms outward; Suki rocked backward to avoid being hit. "I just know the ring and the symbol have something to do with Jonah and a fire and . . . and . . . you. It's scary and it's about you!" She burst into tears and lunged at Suki. "I can't see it! I can't see it! I won't."

"Just because you see a symbol doesn't mean something bad is necessarily going to—"

"Yes it does!" Alexa cried. "If I see it, it's going to happen!"

"If you don't want to see it," Suki said soothingly, "you don't have to see it. I know how scary this whole thing is for you. What it must be like—"

Alexa flung herself away from her mother. "You

have no idea what it's like!" she screamed, jumping up and standing with her hands on her hips. "You don't even believe me. You've never dreamt that someone would die and then they did. And it happened to me twice. Twice!"

Suki winced. One of the first lessons a therapist learns is never to tell a patient you know what it feels like to go through what she's going through; she's the only one who can know. Why was her training so useless when it came to Alexa? Why couldn't she use what she knew, use her carefully honed skills to help the one she loved most? Suki pulled herself up slowly. "You're right, honey. I don't know. I can't know, no one can. But I can try and empathize—"

Alexa suddenly stood completely still. Her tears stopped and her expression became more composed, as if she were tapping into a reservoir of strength. "Lindsey Kern knows."

"I don't think—"

"I'll talk to Lindsey."

Suki started to say no, then stopped herself. "Why do you think Lindsey can help you?" she asked.

"You heard her at the doctor's office," Alexa said. "She knew exactly what had happened to me. What's happening to me. She'll know how to keep the visions away."

"Do you understand that Lindsey Kern is a convicted murderer?" Suki asked. "Do you know that she's serving a life sentence at MCI-Watkins for killing her boyfriend?"

"She didn't do it."

"A jury of her peers said she did."

Alexa would have none of it. "Well, they were wrong, and it's irrelevant anyway. I need to talk to someone who understands. I have to be with someone who believes in me—not someone who thinks I'm crazy."

Suki remembered her mother saying almost the exact same words to her father. She reached out to Alexa. "I don't think you're crazy."

Alexa turned away. "Or that I'm a murderer."

"That's ridiculous," Suki said quickly. "I know you couldn't kill anyone." But if she was so sure of this fact, why hadn't she told Mike about Jonah's note or about Alexa's dream of Charlie's funeral?

"You don't believe anything I've been telling you." Alexa stared at Suki, her eyes gleaming with hatred. "You don't believe in what I've seen, you don't believe in me. Lindsey's the only one. Only Lindsey can help me."

There was something about Alexa's words, about the look in her eye, that caused Suki to snap. "I'm doing the best I can here, Alexa," she said sharply. "And I can't imagine Lindsey Kern will be able to do any better. Lindsey's in prison and Lindsey is most likely out of her mind."

"Nice talk for a hotshot psychologist."

"I don't want you talking to Lindsey Kern." Suki reached out and grabbed Alexa by the shoulders. She gripped her so hard she could feel the unyielding bones under fingers. "That's all there is to it. Do you understand? Have you got that?"

"I've got nothing," Alexa spat. "Nothing, because I've got you for a mother. A mother who won't see me, who can't give me what I need. I'm going to talk to Lindsey and you can't stop me!"

Suki dropped her hands; they were trembling. "Over my dead body," she said softly.

"Don't you understand? Don't you see?" Alexa cried as she raced up the stairs. "That's just what I'm afraid of!"

CHAPTER NINETEEN

First thing the next morning, Suki stopped at her office before going to Watkins for what she hoped would be her final meeting with Lindsey. She needed the fax machine to send Mike the alleged offense section of the evaluation—which she had finished somewhere in the dark hours between 3:00 and 4:00 A.M.—and to receive the results of Alexa and Lindsey's neurological tests, which Dr. Smith-Holt's secretary had promised to fax. Suki needed Lindsey's test results for their meeting, and she desperately wanted to see Alexa's. As soon as she walked in, she checked the fax machine, then her mailbox. Nothing from Smith-Holt. She punched Mike's fax number on the pad and fed her pages into the machine.

Jen was in their office with a patient, so Suki sat down at the receptionist's desk to review her plan for Lindsey's interview, sans the necessary test results. She hit her pen on the desk blotter. Damn. She had photocopied a symptom checklist for temporal lobe epilepsy, hoping to use Lindsey's self-report, in conjunction with the MRI, to make a preliminary diagnosis. Now she would just have to go through the checklist with Lindsey and hope the test results were waiting for her when she returned. It wasn't ideal, but it would have to do.

Just as she was preparing to leave for the prison,

the phone at her elbow rang and a whiny voice informed her that Dr. Smith-Holt's office was calling with patient test results. After giving Suki a cryptic summary, the whiny voice faxed over the reports, along with the phone number where the doctor could be reached if Suki had any questions.

Suki scanned the report on Alexa. Just as the secretary had said: completely and perfectly and beautifully normal. EEG, MRI, even the blood work and vitals they had measured. Although Alexa had appeared unconcerned about the tests, Suki guessed her nonchalance was feigned and called home to give her the results; Alexa didn't pick up the phone, so Suki left the good news on the machine.

Suki was much relieved, although she knew that in some ways, a neurological diagnosis would have provided a simple and easy explanation for so much that was unexplainable. And she was even more heartened by the fact that Lindsey's tests contrasted markedly from Alexa's—anything that differentiated Alexa from Lindsey was welcome.

For while Lindsey's results didn't give Suki the definitive diagnostic tool she would have liked, they couldn't be classified as normal. Yet they weren't quite abnormal either. The tests looked just as inconclusive as the ones Lindsey had taken ten years ago. As was to be expected, despite the tremendous changes in her life over the past decade, Lindsey's brain had remained stable.

Suki pulled Lindsey's old test reports from the file and compared them to the ones she had just received. The EEG showed the same spiking in the temporal region of the brain, the same abnormal slowing in nonfocal areas. The MRI detected increased tissue density, a bit of atrophy and slightly enlarged ventricles. All possible indications of temporal lobe epilepsy. None conclusively so.

A clear-cut depiction of brain dysfunction would have been powerful evidence in support of an insanity defense. Especially with a multicolored MRI image. Juries just ate up that kind of thing. Suki compared Lindsey's test results to Alexa's with an eye to a slide presentation in court: normal brain on one side, Lindsey's brain on the other. She could use a pointer to show the anomalies: density, atrophy, enlargement. There was no doubt about it, Lindsey's brain *did* look odd. But was it odd enough to convince a jury? Odd enough to convince herself?

Stuffing the reports into her briefcase, Suki reminded herself that although this was a tough quandary to be in so late in an evaluation, at least Alexa's brain was the one being used for comparison. It could be much worse. For, despite the fact that Alexa was still not eating or sleeping, and would speak only to Kendra, the entrance of Frank Maxwell into the investigation was clearly auspicious. After weeks of having everything go wrong for Alexa, something was going right. McKinna's reach finally appeared to have been exceeded—as long as the police didn't put together exactly how auspicious Frank Maxwell's entrance might be.

Suki placed a quick call to the testing service where she had sent Lindsey's MMPI to be scored. After a long wait on hold, the clerk, who sounded all of twelve years old, informed her that the results had been mailed out yesterday. No, she was told, the clerk was not authorized to divulge test scores over the phone. She would just have to wait. Again, not such bad news. With any luck, the scores would arrive tomorrow. Time enough to integrate the results into the section of the evaluation that still remained to be written: the all-important Discussion-and-Conclusions, the section that linked the data to her opinion and outlined the logic behind that linkage.

Suki planned to get the last of the necessary information from Lindsey today and then begin to write up the discussion, which included a summary of the first two sections of the report. Often, the process of synthesizing and condensing helped her sort out her thoughts, and she hoped that would be the case now. "The law's black and white," one of her favorite professors used to say. "Unfortunately, people are many shades of gray." And Lindsey was more shades than most.

As Suki left the office and climbed into her car, she was well aware of the clock ticking down to Lindsey's trial. She threw the car into gear and drove, too fast, toward the prison, trying to sort through the evidence and begin to formulate an opinion. But hard as she tried, she couldn't keep her mind on Lindsey; it kept straying to Alexa. When she tried to conjure up a picture of Lindsey's brain, she saw Alexa's healthy one instead. When she ran through the series of questions necessary to derive a valid conclusion on Lindsey, she found herself asking these questions of Alexa.

Suki pulled into the Watkins parking lot and climbed from her car. The building's massive concrete walls, topped by observation towers and electrically charged wire, rose into the sky. She heard the angry barking of guard dogs and the clanking of leg irons as a line of inmates filed out a steel door and into a white van. She was here to see Lindsey Kern, but she couldn't stop seeing Alexa.

"Do you remember if you had any head injuries as a child?" Suki asked Lindsey when they were once again seated in the interrogation room. "Falls? Car accidents?"

"Got the MRI results, huh?" Lindsey appeared especially chipper this morning, bright-eyed and connected. "Same thing Naomi asked me."

"And you answered . . ."

"No head injuries. No accidents. No falls." Lindsey smiled disarmingly. "But you know the Tegretol didn't work."

The effectiveness of Tegretol was known to be erratic, and the fact that it hadn't reduced Lindsey's symptoms was yet another inconclusive bit of evidence to add to the growing body of inconclusive evidence. "So you think that means you don't have TLE?" Suki asked.

"Well, apparently, my right temporal lobe is kind of screwy, and, if you want to look at it that way, I do have lots of the symptoms. Isabel could just be one of those pesky little 'Lilliputian hallucinoses.' And I guess nightmares, headaches and memory lapses are all pretty common."

"I see you've done your homework." Suki wasn't surprised by Lindsey's grasp of the implications of her symptoms. There was no doubt the woman was very bright. Unfortunately, high intelligence often made cases more difficult to diagnosis. A smart person is much more capable of effective manipulation than a dumb one. "But you didn't answer my question."

Lindsey shrugged. "And I guess the MRI didn't either."

Suki pulled the TLE symptom checklist from her briefcase. She wanted to get through it before Lindsey closed up—and some of the signs were already evident. Suki quickly scanned the list: headaches, sleep disturbances, memory problems, aggression, violence, hallucinations, hypergraphia, hypersexuality, compulsiveness, head turning, stuttering, inability to take a full breath, transient weakness in the limbs . . .

"Although precognition and clairvoyance aren't abilities neurologists usually associate with TLE," Lindsey broke into Suki's thoughts, "some of the historical figures who had it were also known to have these skills." Lindsey lifted her hands palm-up. "What's a great prophet, but one who can predict the future?"

Suki noticed that whenever Lindsey spoke about the paranormal, her diction and language changed. She became more precise, more academic, as if she were lecturing to a class, rather than talking to just one other person—or as if she were speaking lines she had memorized rather than believed. "Who do they think had TLE?"

"Moses and Mohammed, for two," Lindsey said. "And did you know that Julius Caesar's epileptic seizures were one of the reasons his men followed him into battle? They thought it meant he was 'touched by the divine.'"

Under other circumstances, Suki would have loved the opportunity to discuss historical notions of epilepsy with someone so knowledgeable on the subject, but she just didn't have the time now. She looked down at the symptom checklist and cleared her throat. "I'm sorry, Lindsey, but I'm really under a time crunch here, and we've got to get through these questions today," she said. "Can you tell me how long you took Tegretol?"

"Can't remember." Lindsey shrugged again and Suki could see the sulk forming around her eyes. "Not long."

"Did you notice any difference in your symptoms when you took it? Did you see Isabel any less? Have fewer headaches or nightmares?"

Lindsey looked out the window, through the crosshatch of bars, into the concrete exercise yard below. "I heard the chief of police in Witton was killed over the weekend."

"Lindsey," Suki said gently. "You realize your trial starts in just a couple of days? That my testimony is going to be a very important factor in whether you spend the rest of your life in prison?"

"Did you know him?" Lindsey asked. "This Charlie Gasperini?"

Suki sat back in her chair. Maybe if she gave Lindsey what she wanted, Lindsey would return the favor. "Yes," she said. "I knew him."

"Did Alexa know him?"

"We're not here to talk about Alexa," Suki said evenly. "We're here to talk about you."

"You know," Lindsey said, "there really are only two possible explanations when a person correctly predicts a future event. Either she's precognitive or she's going to make the event happen herself."

Suki flipped her pen around between her fingers.

"It's not a vision," Lindsey added, "it's a plan."

Suki didn't like either alternative, yet, like those sticky logic problems she had hated in graduate school, one of the two answers appeared to be true. Except in a case like Son of Sam, where both answers were true: Berkowitz had had visions *and* developed a plan. "Did you predict that Richard was going to die?"

Lindsey blinked and, once again, Suki saw the pain in her eyes. If she were a betting woman, she would bet that Lindsey hadn't killed Richard Stoddard. "I worried about Richard dying," Lindsey said. "I was afraid Isabel might kill him, but no, I never 'saw' it the way I've seen things since then. At that time, the only thing I could 'see' was Isabel."

"Was she small? Did you see her as very tiny?"

"Still pushing that Lilliputian hallucinosis stuff, huh?" Lindsey snorted. "Isabel Davenport was a very small woman, so it only makes sense that she would be a very small ghost."

Suki glanced down at her list. Hypergraphia. "You once told me you were a writer. Is this something you were driven to do? Are you compulsive about it?"

"We get a lot of time in here," Lindsey said, her eyes on the exercise yard.

Suki turned slightly so she, too, could see out the window. The yard was vacant, silent. Weeds pushed out through the cracks in the crumbling concrete. Life where there was none.

"Empty time." Lindsey was drifting, following

her mood wherever it took her. "Hours and hours of nothing to do. Open, empty hours. Huge hours that go on forever. I read in the hours to fill the gaps and think a lot about things I never had time to think about before." She focused once again on Suki. "I was reading William James the other day. *The Will to Believe and Other Essays*. Have you read it?"

Suki shook her head.

"He was a smart man—a very smart man. Forward-thinking. Let me see if I can remember this right." Lindsey stared up at the water-stained ceiling and began to quote, "'The ideal of every science is that of a closed and complete system of truth.'" She paused and then started again. "'Phenomena unclassifiable within that system are therefore paradoxical absurdities and must be held untrue.'" She lowered her eyes and grinned at Suki. "Pretty good, huh? A paradoxical absurdity, that's me."

Suki watched Lindsey watching her. "Is that how you perceive yourself?"

"For a smart woman you sure can be dumb sometimes." Lindsey steepled her fingers and gave Suki a long, probing look. "It's not how *I* see myself, it's how *you* see me—and how you see what I can do."

Suki knew when she was beat. She put her pen down on the table and said, "Tell me more about what you can do. Explain to me how you can do it. How it works."

Lindsey nodded, as if she had expected this all along. "The truth is, my abilities are minimal. There are many people much more sensitive, more talented, than I am. The real skill, the real gift, is in the control. I can't make it start, and once it's started, I can't make it stop. Sometimes I see a picture—a vision, a place or a person, or two things linked together that have a meaning because of their linkage. But most of the time, like I told you, it comes in dreams."

Suki sat quietly, barely breathing. She had only had time to skim the library books, but according to what she had read, images did seem to be the most prevalent mode of receiving extrasensory information, dreams the most common vehicle. There had been successful precognitive image experiments at Princeton involving the works of famous artists, solid ESP card research at Duke, and dream studies by the Maimonides group in which slides from a graduate student's trip to Europe were used as the picture targets. Even Sigmund Freud had noticed that sleep enhanced telepathic ability.

"But sometimes, it's more of a feeling," Lindsey continued. "A feeling of fear. Or of danger." She tapped Suki's arm. "As it was with you. I felt an aura of danger around you. Around Alexa, too—I still do." Lindsey paused and when Suki didn't respond, said, "Sometimes what I see isn't important at all. Like last week. On Wednesday, I saw the opening credits for the movie they were showing on Friday night." She shrugged. "Who cares about that?"

A furry ripple of fear flowed up Suki's backbone. Her mother used to play a game with her when she was a little girl in which Harriet would guess which movie was coming the next week to the Central Theater. Harriet was almost always right. "Are you always right?" Suki asked.

"No," Lindsey said, "and that's the problem. Sometimes I get visions that have nothing to do with anything. They're full of people I don't know, all jumbled and impossible to decipher. They just don't make any sense. Or I'll have a very specific vision: like of a small blond boy with brown eyes who has a scratch on his forehead, hiding in the woods. And then I'll watch the news to see if anyone's been lost, but no one has."

Suki was both relieved and nonplused by Lindsey's admission. On one hand, Lindsey was acknowledging failure, on the other, there was something about the declaration that increased her credibility—like her timing mistake with Finlay. Suki reminded herself of all the ESP research that had come up empty, of all the departments of parapsychology that had closed over the years, of how often her mother had predicted events that never occurred. She would have to ask Kenneth how frequently Doris Sheketoff's guesses were off the mark.

Lindsey scrutinized Suki intently, as if she were the psychologist under pressure to make a forensic assessment. "Other times, the visions are just obtuse. Skewed. Like someone's playing a game and I'm 'it.' I'm the one who's supposed to solve the riddle."

Suki pulled at the collar of her blouse. "Did you ever have a vision that someone was going to die?"

Lindsey smiled shrewdly. "And then it happened?"

Suki nodded.

"Once." Lindsey's face fell at the memory, "I had a vision of a big shadow over my sister-in-law's lung. She died of lung cancer six months later."

"Did she smoke?"

"Not a day in her life."

"Did you tell her about it?" Suki asked. "Did you try to get her to see a doctor?"

"You want to know about free will and determinism."

"I guess," Suki said slowly. "I want to know if you believe that what you see has to happen." She paused. "If you don't see it, do you think that'll stop it from happening? Or do you think what you see can't be changed? That it's a given?"

"A lot of questions for an agnostic."

"This isn't about me, Lindsey."

"I'm well aware of who this is about." Lindsey folded her hands in her lap.

Suki picked up her pen; two could play this game. "Have you ever suffered from any transient weakness in your limbs?" she asked. "Ever had a problem with stuttering?"

Lindsey threw her hands upward in an exaggerated gesture of defeat. "I think my visions are a picture of the way things will be if nothing changes: the road ahead given the path being followed. But I also think that by altering behavior, you can change what is foreseen." She smiled. "Free will *and* determinism."

"But what if you don't see it?" Suki asked. "If you stop yourself from seeing the vision, will that make the vision not happen?"

"Doesn't make a bit of difference," Lindsey said emphatically. "The future's going to be the future whether I see it or not. No matter who sees it—or doesn't." She paused. "That's what I have to tell Alexa."

"Lindsey," Suki began, "Your concern about Alexa is touching, and I do appreciate it, but she's—"

"Alexa needs to know. She *has* to know."

Suki pulled at her collar again. Why was it always so warm in public buildings: schools, courtrooms, prisons? So much waste. A waste of money, energy. She looked at Lindsey. So much waste.

"If you don't let Alexa learn what she needs to learn," Lindsey warned, "it's going to backfire on you."

"I told you before, we're not here to talk about my personal life."

Lindsey crossed her arms over her chest. "But that's all I'm willing to talk about."

"It's your call." Suki stood and rapped on the door, then busied herself gathering her things. When the officer arrived, Suki turned to Lindsey. "I think I've got all I need," she said. "I'll see you next week in court."

As Suki wended her way back past the trap and into the waiting room, she thought of Lindsey's words: *"There really are only two possible explanations when a person correctly predicts a future event,"* Lindsey had said. *"Either she's precognitive or she's going to make the event happen herself."*

Suki shivered in the overheated air. Which would she rather believe: that her daughter was a murderer or that the paranormal was possible?

CHAPTER TWENTY

When Suki got back to the farmhouse, the results of Lindsey's MMPI were waiting for her. Almost an hour remained before her first appointment, and as both inside offices were in use, Suki sat down at the reception desk and pulled the computerized scoring sheets from the envelope. The Minnesota Multiphasic Personality Inventory was the most widely used personality assessment test; hundreds of experiments involving MMPI protocol were published every year, and all this research had created a huge body of correlational data for both diagnosis and prognosis. Although, as Suki was well aware, accurately interpreting MMPI results was really an art form. She was a bit rusty, but had had years of tutelage in the lab of Chanley Hathaway, the man generally considered to be the worldwide expert on MMPI analysis.

The computerized sheets spread out in front of her contained Lindsey's scores on each of ten standard clinical scales, four special scales and three scales that assessed validity. Although the standard scales attempted to measure mental illnesses like depression and schizophrenia, a high score on any given scale didn't necessarily mean a person suffered from that disease. Rather it was how the scores combined, the pattern they created, that gave the clues to underlying pathology. "Look to the clustering," Hathaway was always saying. "Look to the clustering."

Suki looked to the clustering and was amazed at the profile the scores presented; it was not what she had expected. After listening to Lindsey's answers that day at the prison, Suki had guessed Lindsey would score low on all the psychopathology scales and high on the validity scales measuring malingering. But this was not the case. Lindsey's three highest scores were on scales that measured schizophrenia, anxiety and repression, respectively. This was a cluster usually indicative of fairly substantial psychosis. And her scores on the validity scales fell within normal ranges, albeit toward the high end. Suki checked the name and the ID number at the top of the printout to make sure this was indeed Lindsey's test result. It was.

Suki had to admit that Lindsey did exhibit the incident-independent lability—wild mood swings not obviously based on events—often associated with psychosis, and her brain scans were clearly not normal. There were also strong indications she was not in touch with reality; after all, the woman was convinced she could see into the future as well as free her spirit from her body at will. But still, these results indicated a more severe illness than Lindsey presented.

Suki sat back in her chair and considered the results. She sketched the cluster picture Hathaway had taught her to draw. Then she turned the drawing to view it from various angles. This was clearly a pathological configuration. It was also clear that although she prided herself on her ability to maintain an open mind during a forensic evaluation, she had not done so. Her surprise at the scores was an unmistakable indication that she had prematurely concluded that Lindsey Kern was sane.

"A single test cluster is *not* a diagnosis," was another of Hathaway's favorite lines. "It's only a data point. The clinician must analyze the scores within the full spectrum of the patient's life history and behavior in order to render an accurate diagnosis." Right, Suki thought. Within Lindsey's life history and behavior. A life history which contained very few instances of, or correlates to, mental illness, behavior which appeared amazingly sane—until Isabel Jessel Davenport had arrived on the scene.

The door behind Suki swung open and a teenage girl, wearing a tiny black dress and shoulder-high lace gloves, sauntered across the room in platform shoes that must have been at least five inches high. Suki did appreciate Jen's patients' sartorial displays. At least this one's hair wasn't blue. The girl floated out of the office as if she were Scarlett O'Hara on her way to the ball.

"Yo!" Jen yelled from inside the office, and Suki wondered how she could possibly know she was there. "How goes it, pal?"

"Good," Suki said, then remembered Frank Maxwell. "Really good."

"Really good, like *really* good?" Jen leapt into the outer office. "Did something change over the weekend?" she demanded. "Is Witton finally coming to its senses?"

"Looks like we may not have as much business

as you had hoped." Suki told her about the accident.

Jen's eyes widened as Suki related the story. She had been at the Cape since last Thursday and wasn't a big newspaper reader. "I can't believe Charlie Gasperini's dead," she said, dropping into the old couch across from Suki. "I never really liked the guy all that much, but dead. Jesus."

"Charlie wasn't such a bad guy."

"But this has all worked out in Alexa's favor?" Jen asked, her antenna picking up the relevant point.

"Frank Maxwell's acting chief, and he seems to think Charlie was wrong about Alexa." Suki looked down at the MMPI scoring sheet. "He didn't exactly say it, but both Mike and I are pretty sure he's going to go after the boys."

Jen vaulted from the couch and gave Suki a hug. "That's terrific. Really terrific—although I'm sorry Charlie had to die to make it happen."

Suki swallowed hard, not trusting herself to speak.

Jen scrutinized Suki's face, then looked at the papers on the desk, catching, as always, that Suki had said all she wanted to say on a particular subject. "Now that your problems are over, can I go back to giving you shit?"

"I wouldn't say my problems are exactly over. . . ."

"But I'm going to give you shit anyway." Jen pointed at the printouts. "What the hell are you doing with these stupid paper-and-pencil tests?" She shook her head with exaggerated distress. "The numbers may be useful for the rat-lab contingent, but they aren't worth a hill of beans to us."

Suki twisted her head and looked at Jen. "They don't give rats MMPIs."

But Jen didn't even crack a smile. "You know the only way to know anything is through face-to-face. You're a fabulous therapist, incredibly intuitive. What the hell are those scores going to do for you? They're all correlations anyway. Just like intelligence and height." Jen grabbed her hat off the coatrack. This hat was a deep crimson with a wide band of velvet: as outlandish as Jen's headgear always was. She raised her eyebrows at Suki. Come on, she seemed to be saying, fight me on this one.

But Suki didn't want to fight. She knew the intelligence-height argument: if you gave intelligence tests to a random sample of the population and matched their scores with their height, you would consistently discover that the taller someone was, the smarter they were. And although this was true, there was an important variable missing from the equation: age. "Do you ever wonder about the paranormal?" she asked instead. "Do you think any of it could be true?"

Jen's hat stopped midway between the coatrack and her head. "You mean ESP and mediums who can put you in touch with the entity of some famous dead person?"

"More like being able to predict the future."

"Oh, crystal balls and palm readers and fortune cookies. Sure," Jen said. "I believe in them all."

"I'm serious."

"Why?" Jen twirled her hat on her finger.

Suki hesitated. "It's complicated," she said. "I'd just like to hear your honest opinion: do you think it's possible that some people might have the ability to tap into future events? That there are more senses then just the five we know of?"

"Hello! Hello!" Jen leaned over and knocked on the desk in front of Suki. "Anyone home?" she asked. "How the hell can you tap into something that hasn't happened yet?"

"Well, what if everything were going on at the same time? You know, like a fourth dimension?"

"Oh, so now you're talking six senses *and* four dimensions. Soon you'll be discovering past lives and astral projecting your family to a fab vacation in Disney World."

"I know it seems kind of out there, but how can you be so sure it's not true?"

Jen patted her hat onto her head, then tugged at the brim, setting it at a jaunty angle. "Because if it were true, don't you think someone would have figured out how to use it to make a killing on the stock market by now?" She winked. "Great news about Alexa. When this is all over I'm taking you out for a celebration dinner and we'll drink a shitload of champagne." Jen blew Suki a kiss. "Until we puke," she added, then slipped out the door.

Suki put the MMPI printout in the file with Smith-Holt's report on Lindsey's EEG and MRI, thinking that Jen, in her inimitable way, had managed to refute Suki's two current theories: Lindsey was *not* crazy and the paranormal was *not* possible. She didn't want to think what this might imply for Alexa.

Instead, Suki focused on what the MMPI scores implied for Mike. Despite what Jen had said about personality tests, these scores were exactly what the defense attorney ordered. Although the prosecutor was sure to argue that Lindsey's mental status in the present had nothing to do with her mental status the afternoon Richard died, Mike could counter that Lindsey's MRI and EEG were identical to the ones administered at the time of the death. This assertion would again be contested, by the state's forensic expert this time, who was likely to inform the jury that the link between neurological brain function and psychopathology could not always be made. Still, the power of the simultaneous presentation of Lindsey's abnormal EEG, MRI and MMPI results was not to be underestimated.

Suki glanced at her watch. Just time enough to talk to Mike. They hadn't spoken since their visit to the police station yesterday, and Suki was anxious to know if, upon reflection, Mike still thought the meeting with Maxwell had gone as well as he had indicated in the parking lot. Although she expected that he would, she wanted to hear him say it.

As she stood to go into her office and call Mike, the phone on the receptionist's desk rang. It was Kenneth, and Suki now knew Kenneth well enough to recognize from the timbre of his "hello" that something was wrong. "What?" she demanded.

He sighed. "I wish I wasn't always the bearer of bad news."

"They've decided Charlie was murdered," Suki guessed.

"Huh?" Kenneth was clearly surprised, and Suki could have shot herself for her stupidity. "No," he said slowly, "nothing's new there. It's something else. About the Ward case. I didn't want you to hear it from the news, or hear it and not understand what it really meant."

Suki's heart sank. "Just say it. Quick."

"The boys are going to be arrested, but it's not what you—"

"Why, that's fantastic," Suki cried. "Fabulous."

"No, it's not," Kenneth said. "That's what I'm trying to tell you."

"What do you mean?" Suki held her breath.

"They're making a deal with Sutterlund's office. The boys will plead guilty to accessory-after-the-fact charges, and in return for turning state's evidence against Alexa, they'll get off with a few months' probation."

"I . . . I don't understand." Suki dropped into the chair. "When Mike and I talked to Frank Maxwell yesterday he seemed to realize, he *did* realize, he knew, that Charlie was wrongly pushing for Alexa's arrest. Frank knew—I know he did. I saw him. I saw his face."

"Apparently, what Frank believed yesterday and what he believes today are two different things."

"But he said the case was on hold," Suki argued, even though she knew Kenneth was on her side. "That his manpower was all tied up with Charlie's."

"I guess he's worked out his staffing problems."

"McKinna," Suki growled. "I'll kill the bastard."

"Take it easy, Suki. We don't know that he—"

"Like hell we don't!" she interrupted. "Ellery got to Frank, and I'm going to prove it."

"Don't waste your time."

"We're talking about my daughter," Suki said. "That's not what I consider a 'waste of time.' "

"If it was my daughter, I'd go after that missing witness."

"But what if I can prove Ellery's screwing Alexa to keep Devin out of trouble? That he's lying, creating false evidence. That he and Teddy Sutterlund are in cahoots—"

"The deal's all locked up, Suki." Kenneth's voice contained real sorrow. "I'd say that the witness is about the only hope you've got."

"But what if—"

"Listen," Kenneth interrupted. "I've got to run, but I'll give you a hand however I can."

Suki's patient walked into the waiting room. "Thanks," she said brightly, too loudly. "I'll call you back later." Suki replaced the receiver in its cradle and smiled at Ronnie, a trim older woman who had survived a fiery car crash that her daughter and grandson had not.

Somehow, Suki managed to get through the next three hours and three patients. But after she had walked her last patient to the door, she dropped back into her chair and closed her eyes. How could she keep fighting when everything and everyone seemed to be working against her? If one of her patients came in with such a claim, she would assume they were overly paranoid, but in her own case she knew it wasn't paranoia, it was reality.

The witness, Kenneth had said. The witness was her only chance. But how did she go about finding some unknown person who was obviously trying very hard to remain unfound? She had bombed out on the car. Where did she go next? To Lindsey Kern?

One of the books on the paranormal Suki had borrowed from the library was in her briefcase. She pulled it out and flipped to the index, searching for precognition. There was an entire chapter, which she skimmed. The gist of the chapter was that precognition was a real, research-substantiated phenomenon. But as Suki reread the pages more carefully, it became clear that "research-substantiated" did not have the meaning any of her professors would ordinarily attribute to it.

While the authors proclaimed that successful, systematic precognition research had been going on since the early thirties—as Lindsey had said, when J. B. Rhine first instituted his ESP-card experiments at Duke University—a closer analysis of the data indicated that almost three-quarters of the studies had serious methodological flaws. The footnotes and endnotes detailed the facts: the famous Honorton and Ferrari meta-analysis had used a database so heterogeneous as to render it virtually useless for combined analyses, subjects had been preselected by the experimenters in the Cleveland studies, shady claims and fraudulent conclusions were rampant. Despite their obvious prejudice in favor of the paranormal, the authors were forced to conclude that "precognition in forced-choice testing is a weak effect," and that their most important finding was that the data offered "a clear signpost for the future direction of paranormal research." Maybe Jen had a point.

Suki closed the book and stared at the painting of a futuristic, alien-looking man on the cover. He was naked and deathly pale; multicolored geometric shapes circled his head. If a book on parapsychology professing to be the most "authoritative, comprehensive and up-to-date" on the subject could say nothing more definitive than that precognition was a weak effect, how real could it be? And if precognition wasn't real, then how had Lindsey known all she had?

Suki thought back to the things Lindsey had predicted—that an emergency phone call might be trouble at home, that Suki would want to find someone, that Finlay was near trees and water, that there was an aura of danger around Suki and Alexa—and she realized many of Lindsey's predictions had either been vague or been something she easily could have learned from another source. The prophecies were like the astrology column in the *Globe,* like the little strips tucked inside fortune cookies that foretold great wealth or great disaster: Nothing more than hazy statements which could be read by the gullible as meant especially for them. But then there was the dead boy's hand, the PIN number . . .

Suki pushed herself up from the desk. She couldn't think about Lindsey now. She had to focus on Alexa, on the witness. The witness she had no idea how to find. Kenneth had said he'd do what he could, but Suki was afraid he was going to get his hands tied pretty quickly by Frank Maxwell. Her thoughts turned again to Warren Blanchard, to how he had offered to help. But what could Warren possibly do? He was a nice man, so genuinely concerned that day at the rec center, so worried about what Brendan had told her. What Brendan had told her.

She froze, her hand halfway to the coatrack. About the drugs. Jesus. The drugs. There was so much going on, she had completely forgotten about the drugs.

She sat down, dialed the Witton Police Station and asked for Kenneth. When he came on the line, she didn't bother with small talk. "Have you heard anything about kids selling drugs at the high school?" she asked.

"You really shouldn't call me here." Kenneth's voice was low, tight.

Suki hadn't thought about how her calling might affect Kenneth's job—or his chances of being able to help her. She sat down in the chair. "Sorry," she said, and she was. "Do you want to call me back?"

"Work or home?"

When Kenneth was once again on the line, he asked, "What's this about drugs? Don't you have enough to worry about?"

"Maybe it's all the same worry." Suki turned her chair and squinted out over the open fields. The sun was clear and strong, and the grass glowed in its warmth. It hurt to look at it.

"You think Alexa and the boys are mixed up with drugs?" Kenneth interrupted her thoughts. "That it has something to do with Jonah's murder?"

She turned so she couldn't see out the window. "You don't sound surprised."

"I'm a cop. There's not much that can surprise me."

"So there *are* drugs at the high school?"

"There've been drugs at the high school since the sixties. Maybe earlier."

"How about something that's being used by so-called 'good kids' to help them study?" Suki asked. "Some kind of speed? Methamphetamine maybe?"

"Sure, meth's the kind of stuff they'd think would help them study, but in reality, it just fries their brains."

"I was told it was 'clean'—supplied by some adult 'who knew what he was doing.'"

Kenneth chuckled. "It's always supplied by some adult who knows exactly what he's doing."

"Do you think the boys could have been doing meth that night? That maybe Jonah was, too? Has anyone ever looked at the autopsy report? Was a tox screen done?"

Kenneth hesitated. "They almost always do a tox screen, but now that you bring it up, I can't say I remember anyone ever mentioning any results. Too touchy—or maybe the family quashed it."

"This could be it," Suki cried excitedly. "It really could. The drugs were why the boys were fighting. It all fits together, makes sense. And maybe the witness is involved somehow, too." She tapped her finger on the desk. "Maybe that's why the witness didn't want to be found. Maybe he *is* the one pulling the strings—the one selling the drugs. Why else wouldn't he come forward?"

"Whoa," Kenneth said. "Slow down there. My experience with meth is from my New York days. Far as I know, there hasn't been any around Witton yet. What gives you the idea there is?"

Suki explained what Brendan had told her.

Kenneth was silent for a long moment. "Does sound like it. But you're making quite a leap there to pull in all the boys—not to mention the witness."

"Leaps are about all I've got left."

"Tell you what." Kenneth said, lowering his voice again, "Let me see what I can find out. I'll keep it separate from the Ward case. Just tell Frank I got a tip—and it's the truth: I did just get a tip."

"And I'll see if I can dig anything up on my end."

"I know it was me who suggested you check into this witness thing," Kenneth's voice was stern. "But if by some long shot you're actually right about this connection, you could be treading in some real dangerous waters. Why don't you just sit tight until you hear from me?"

"Sitting is a luxury I can't afford."

Kenneth's sigh was resigned, but he gave it one last try. "Brendan may think he's dealing with some 'clean grown-up who knows what he's doing,' but let me tell you, people who deal drugs are never clean. They're mean and easily angered—and they're often armed."

CHAPTER TWENTY-ONE

Suki drove home from her office, Kenneth's warning reverberating in her ears. She was anxious to see how Alexa was doing. Despite the positive result of their meeting with Frank Maxwell yesterday, Alexa had spent most of the night awake, prowling the house, watching old movies, playing computer games in the basement. She had been disheveled at breakfast, her expression blank, so wounded she was unable to integrate good news. Suki knew that no matter how this all ended, for Alexa, it was never going to go away.

Suki was the first car in line when the crossing guard stopped traffic in front of the middle school. While she waited, she compiled a mental roster of places she could search for information on the missing witness: TeenScene, the rec center, the mall, the hangout tree near the high school. Brendan had said Alexa didn't know who sold the drugs, that he didn't either; for the moment, Suki would take his word. She watched the kids, full of just-released-from-prison energy, so young, so innocent, as they danced and punched and flirted their way across the street. But were they as untainted as they appeared?

Of course they were, she told herself. They had to be. These were middle schoolers; they were only eleven, twelve, thirteen. Surely, "tainted" was not an appropriate adjective. But when Suki thought of all she had learned over the past weeks, about guns and sex and drugs, about the underbelly of teenage life, she wasn't so certain.

Suki blanched as a young girl in a T-shirt and overalls, her heavy backpack slung across her shoulder, crossed in front of the car. The girl looked as Alexa had looked two, three years ago: slight, blonde, pretty, full of optimism. What to do? What to do for a daughter whose world had become so wretched that it couldn't be lightened by hope? For a girl who feared she had the power to kill people with her thoughts—or one who was consumed by guilt?

Alexa had resisted the suggestion of counseling whenever Suki raised it, but maybe now was the time to insist. It was clear Alexa was depressed, that she needed to talk to someone—and she sure wasn't talking to Suki. She might even need medication. There were wonderful meds on the market, serotonin-specific reuptake inhibitors—Prozac, Zoloft, Paxil and the like—that had been producing spectacular results with depressives. Although Suki was aware that in more than a few cases, the SSRIs had been so successful in alleviating the depression-related lethargy that the patient had found the energy to climb out of bed and commit suicide.

Of course, Alexa wasn't suicidal. Suki pressed her foot to the accelerator, speeding toward home, toward Alexa who wasn't suicidal. The girl might not be sleeping or eating or talking, but these were symptoms of depression, not self-destruction. Suki thought of Harriet and took the turn into Lawler

Road without downshifting. Her tires squealed in alarm.

Breathless, she burst into the house. "Alexa?" she yelled up the stairs. "Alexa!"

"Up here, Mom," Alexa called in her "before" voice. Before Jonah. "In the kitchen."

The house was filled with wonderful aromas. Of baking. Of vanilla and sugar and all things resonating to home and family and love. Alexa was fine.

When Suki got to the kitchen, Alexa was bent over the open oven, inserting a toothpick into a cake pan. Her face was flushed and a finger of flour streaked her left cheek. She had obviously slept and showered: her hair fell in soft curls and her eyes were bright and awake. She grinned at her mother. "Surprise!"

"Is it my birthday?" Suki asked, thrilled to see the old Alexa.

"Better," Alexa said. "It's your appreciation day."

Suki walked over to her daughter and kissed her brow, which was slightly damp with her exertion. Suki couldn't resist wiping the flour from her cheek. "Sounds like my kind of celebration."

Alexa carefully closed the oven door and set the timer. She turned to Suki. "I was up all night thinking," she said. "Thinking about all you've been doing for me. Thinking about how awful I've been."

"Oh, don't worry about it, honey. It's not a big—"

"No," Alexa interrupted. "I do worry about it, and I want to apologize. I need to apologize."

Suki sat down at the kitchen table. She didn't say anything. She just let Alexa talk.

Alexa ran her fingers through her hair, leaving a dusting of flour on the curls at her forehead. "You've been so great. Greater than any mom could be. And now that it looks like this is finally going to be over, now that the police are going to stop harassing me and go after the guys, now that everything's going to be all right, I just wanted to say how sorry I am for being so awful—and to thank you for all you've done." As her voice began to crack, Alexa turned and gestured grandly toward the oven. "So I'm making you your favorite vanilla-and-lemon layer cake." When she turned back to Suki, her eyes were glistening. "I walked to the store and got all the ingredients." She bit at the cuticle on her left thumb. "I didn't know what else to give you."

"Oh, honey," Suki said around the lump in her throat. "This is perfect. A perfect gift. I'm happy to accept your apology, and I really appreciate the cake—although my hips won't." She held open her arms. Alexa knelt down and put her head in her mother's lap. Suki silently played with Alexa's hair. How could she tell Alexa that it wasn't close to over, that unless she found the witness—and soon—things were about as far from "all right" as they could get?

TeenScene was billed as a "safe, alternative hangout and resource center" for the teenagers of Witton. It had been the brainchild of two fed-up mothers in the early nineties. The two had rallied the town into donating a warren of rooms in the basement under town hall and then rallied the community into donating enough money and hand-me-downs to partition and furnish the space. TeenScene was now on most Witton residents' charity lists.

The ceilings were low and the windows small, but the rooms burst with color and light and noise. The neon yellow room held two pool tables and a Ping-Pong table, the crimson one was filled with battered desks and hand-me-down computers. Green-and-white stripes formed the background of the "movie room," which was dominated by a large television and VCR, while a narrow room furnished with a mishmash of couches and overstuffed chairs was royal blue. The bright walls were plastered with movie and music and antidrug posters; boom boxes were everywhere. TeenScene was staffed by "peer leaders" from the high school, supervised by a parent or teacher, and was open from 3:00 to 9:00 on school days, 12:00 to 12:00 on weekends. It was usually packed.

But it wasn't all about fun. There was a teen hotline: "When things get rough you can fall back on us," an on-staff social worker three afternoons a week, and a Witton policeman came by to just "hang out" on a regular schedule. Pamphlets about contraception and drugs and AIDS filled a rack next to the front door.

Suki stood in front of a bulletin board packed with notices of math tutors and odd jobs and therapy groups for abused children of alcoholics. As she scanned the board, she wondered why, when she wrote her annual check to TeenScene, she had never thought to question its necessity. She wasn't discovering the heretofore uncovered underbelly of teenage life in Witton; it had openly existed all along. She just hadn't wanted to see it.

And now, despite Kenneth's warning, she was going to confront what she had refused to see. She would stare this unpleasant reality in the eye, look directly into the black abyss of its soul, if that's what it took. She checked for drug pamphlets on methamphetamine, but if there had been any, they were all gone. Marijuana, cocaine, crack, LSD, ecstasy, heroin—she hadn't even known kids were still doing heroin—but no speed.

She stuck her hands in her pockets, glad she had changed into jeans, and ambled through the rooms. No one appeared to notice her, although she felt whispers in her wake. It was four-thirty in the afternoon and the rooms were full: kids were playing games, listening to music, doing homework, flirting, watching *Casablanca*. Suki recognized many of them, but no one would meet her eye.

"Can I help you with something?" A young girl with round glasses and a wide streak of purple in her hair smiled at Suki. According to her badge, her name was Kimberly and she was a peer leader. She looked like a freshman.

Suki wanted to ask Kimberly about the dark abyss, but instead she said, "I'm just looking around. That's okay, isn't it?"

"Sure," Kimberly said, her voice as perky as her name. "Make yourself at home—and let me know if there's anything I can do for you."

Suki continued to wander, but the place was too small for her to wander for long. The kids didn't look like drug dealers or killers, they looked like kids had always looked, hanging out and screwing around on a Tuesday afternoon. But Suki knew if she was going to help Alexa, Alexa of the vanilla-and-lemon cake, she had to push beneath the surface.

She walked up to Kimberly, who was sitting at a desk, her purple-striped hair falling over an open algebra book. "I'm a writer," Suki said, "doing an article on teens and drugs. I was wondering if you'd be willing to talk with me for a moment."

"A writer?" Kimberly's eyes opened wide behind her glasses. "Like Mary Higgins Clark? Her books are just awesome," she gushed. "Have you ever met her?"

Suki shook her head, both in answer to Kimberly's question and in disbelief that she could lie so effortlessly. "I'm not that kind of writer," she said. "I do pieces for newspapers, professional magazines—this one's for a psychology journal."

"Oh." Kimberly's face fell, then she perked up again. "And you want to interview me?" She looked around to see if any of the other kids had heard. Then said loudly, "Sure. Glad to. Awesome. Really awesome."

Suki sat down at the desk next to Kimberly's and pulled out a small pad and pen from her purse. A real writer would have a much bigger notepad, but Kimberly didn't seem to notice. "Now Kimberly, this can be an anonymous interview, or we can use your name. Which ever you prefer."

"Oh, we can use my name. It's Kimberly, Kimberly Kitteridge. Would you like me to spell it?" Kimberly spelled it before Suki could answer. "I don't do drugs," she said. "That's why it's okay to use my name."

"Good," Suki said. "That's very good. But what about other kids? Do a lot of kids in Witton do drugs?"

"Well, I don't know if I'd say a lot. . . ." Kimberly paused. "But I guess there are a lot. Depending on what you call a lot, that is, of course." She blushed slightly.

It occurred to Suki that Kimberly might be lying—or that she had already decided to lie about something Suki hadn't asked yet. But, then again, maybe the kid was just uncomfortable talking with an adult about drugs.

"And what kind of drugs do they like to do? What's everyone's favorite?"

Kimberly shrugged. "I, ah, I'm not really sure. Beer. Lots of beer. And pot, I guess."

Suki wondered if beer was considered a drug, but knew she had to stay on point. "How about other drugs? Do kids use cocaine? LSD? speed?"

A shadow fell over Suki. "What's going on here, Kimberly?" a stern voice demanded.

"Oh, ah, hi, Mrs. Gasner," Kimberly stuttered. "This is, this is, ah, a reporter. She's doing an article."

"Hi, Abby," Suki said. Abby Gasner was on the library board with her. Her son, Jonathan, was the same age as Alexa. Suki thought she remembered that Jonathan played basketball, that he had been a teammate of Jonah's.

Abby turned to Suki, her blue eyes as cold as glacial ice. "May I speak to you alone for a moment, please?" Her voice was just as frigid.

Suki stood and rapped on Kimberly's desk. "Thanks," she said. "You've been a big help."

"What the hell do you think you're doing?" Abby hissed as she pulled Suki into a corner. "Why are you here?"

"I'm trying to find out the truth," Suki said, standing her ground. She and Abby had been on the same side of the acquisitions argument at the library last year; working together, the two of them had persuaded the board to add five hundred, instead of three hundred, new books to the library's collection. "Trying to save my daughter."

"You just can't come in here and start badgering the kids." Abby crossed her arms over her ample chest, but her eyes seemed to subtly soften.

"Abby." Suki touched Abby's sleeve. "Do you know anything about a drug called methamphetamine? It's a kind of speed. Have you heard any of the kids talking about it?"

Abby took a step backward. "I'm sorry, Suki, but I'm going to have to ask you to leave. It's not that I don't sympathize with you, I do, but I sympathize with Darcy more. Her child is gone. You still have yours."

"This isn't an either-or thing," Suki began to argue, then she caught herself and lowered her voice. "You don't have to pit us against each other. We're both suffering. We're all suffering."

"Perhaps." Abby pointed toward the door and motioned for Suki to precede her. "This way."

Suki did as Abby indicated, but turned when they reached the entryway. "Alexa didn't kill Jonah," she said softly, "and I have to talk to people, adults as well as kids, to get the information I need to prove she's innocent."

Abby held open the front door. "You're a nice woman, Suki, and I'm sorry for your problems," she said. "But if I were you, I'd get someone else to do my digging." At Suki's surprised look, she added, "The way this town is feeling right now, I don't think too many people are going to be willing to talk to you."

Suki drove home, went into her study and closed the door. She dialed Watkins and asked to speak with Lindsey Kern; it was time to establish the veracity of Lindsey's claim once and for all. A surly officer informed her there had been trouble in Lindsey's pod and all inmates had been confined to their cells.

"I'm authorized for unrestricted access to Ms. Kern," Suki explained. "Check with the superintendent's office, if you have to, but I need to talk to her right away." Suki couldn't quite believe she was calling a women incarcerated in a maximum security prison to help her find someone on the outside, but on the other hand, she didn't have too much to lose.

"We'll have to get back to you on that."

"Transfer me to the superintendent's office, please."

After a long wait, Rizzo's secretary finally came on the line. When Suki explained why she was calling, she was immediately switched over to the superintendent.

"It's not possible for you to talk to Ms. Kern right now," Rizzo said.

"Is she all right?" Suki asked, thinking of Lindsey's black eye.

"She's in solitary at the moment, and in restraints—

but it's all for her own good—Dr. Hollerand expects she'll be back in her cell before bedcheck." Dr. Hollerand was the prison physician and a well-known incompetent.

"What happened?"

"I'm really not at liberty to discuss this, Dr. Jacobs, but I can tell you she had some kind of spell before breakfast this morning. According to an officer who was there, she went pretty wild."

Suki hung up and called Warren Blanchard. Abby Gasner had said Suki needed a front person, and with Lindsey out of the running, it looked like it had to be Warren. Everyone knew and liked Warren, and they would trust Jonah's uncle.

As the phone began to ring, Suki hoped Darcy wouldn't answer. But Darcy did. Suki pitched her voice low and asked for Warren.

"He's at the rec center right now." Darcy was friendly and open, most likely assuming Suki was a new romantic interest. "But he should be home any time now."

"That's okay," Suki said quickly. "It's nothing important."

"I'm sure he'll be happy to return your call." Darcy definitely thought she was a potential date.

"No, really. I'll—"

"Who is this?" Darcy interrupted. She suddenly sounded cautious, on guard.

"No one," Suki said quickly. "I'll catch him some other time."

"Hey—" Darcy began.

Suki dropped the receiver back into its cradle. Darcy had recognized her voice. She knew it. The poor woman, probably just feeling the full brunt of her grief now that the initial numbness had worn off. Looking for answers. Looking for someone to blame. To hate. How would she cope with the pain and the horror? The emptiness?

Suki sat at her desk, thinking about all she had lost and all she still had. How each hurt in its own way. Her child was still alive, that was true, but Alexa would forever be wounded. Suki forced back the tears that threatened and went upstairs.

Alexa was layering cheeses and vegetables for eggplant parmesan with the speed and agility of a master chef. She flashed a quick smile, then resumed her rapid-fire layering. "I think I'll go to school tomorrow," she said. "I'm feeling much better."

Suki hadn't yet told Alexa that the boys were turning state's evidence, and although she knew she must, the thought of Alexa's spiraling back down into that black depression was, at the moment, just too unbearable. Instead, she told Alexa she thought going to school was a good idea, then she went downstairs to peek in on Kyle. He, as usual, was at the computer, playing Sim Tower instead of writing his English report. She didn't chastise him, just rested her hand on his shoulder as he added another suite of offices to his building. He watched her warily as she left the room.

Suki wandered back into her study and called Mike. She wasn't surprised when he was unavailable, nor was she encouraged when Betty promised he would return her call in the next few hours. She placed the phone back in its cradle and stared through the small window over her desk. What else had she wanted to speak to Mike about? She knew she had to talk to him about Alexa, about what the boys' plea bargain was going to mean, about their counterattack. But there was something else, something tickling at the edge of her brain.

She looked around the room and noticed her briefcase standing in the corner. Lindsey. Of course. She needed to tell him about Lindsey. About her aberrant test scores, about what had, or hadn't happened at the prison this morning. It crossed Suki's mind that if she determined Lindsey was indeed insane, she would make more money than she had projected when she expected her verdict to be sanity. Evaluations with conclusions in opposition to the client's expectations did not result in court testimony—which could run up to ten hours, including pretrial prep, waiting time and testimony. At one hundred dollars an hour, every hour counted.

As Suki calculated how many additional hours this might entail, the phone on the desk rang. She picked it up immediately, hoping it was Mike. But it was Warren. He told her that Darcy had recognized her voice.

"I'm sorry if I upset her," she said.

"It's not your fault," Warren assured her. "She's having a real tough time. It doesn't take much to upset her."

"I bet."

There was an uncomfortable silence, and then Warren asked, "So, what can I do for you?"

"Oh, right," Suki said, "I called you, didn't I?" She managed a short laugh, and started again. "Remember the other day when you offered to help me?"

"You're having a tough time, too, huh?"

Suki knew Warren's question was rhetorical, so she continued, "I'm calling to take you up on your offer." Then she quickly explained what Kenneth had told her about the boys' deal with Teddy Sutterlund.

"Those guys are all slime wads," Warren said, his voice full of disgust. "What can I do to help?"

Suki described her methamphetamine-witness theory and then told him about her visit to Teen-Scene.

"I'd be glad to help you, Suki," he said after a long hesitation, "but I can't imagine that this is the route to go. How likely is it that this witness is connected to the drugs? Seems like a real long shot to me. And, if by some wild coincidence, he—or she—is, then it's too dangerous." He paused again. "I suppose the police are useless."

"Kenneth Pendergast said he'd check around about the meth, but that he'd have to keep it separate from Alexa's case."

"Pendergast's a good guy," Warren said. "We've coached together, and he's not like the others. I'll bet he also told you not to do any investigating on your own, didn't he?"

Suki chuckled despite the bleakness of the situation. "Touché," she said.

"Well, maybe you should listen to him."

"As I told Kenneth, I don't have the luxury."

"So what are you going to do?" Warren asked.

"I'm going to go out and find the truth," Suki said, aware as she heard her own words that she sounded self-righteous and rather obnoxious. "I mean, I've got to find out what really happened. It's Alexa's only chance."

"But what if no one's willing to talk to you?"

"Oh, I'll get someone to talk to me," Suki said. "I'll find out what went on the night Jonah was killed. You can bet on it."

Warren sighed and Suki could hear in the long rush of air that the man was exhausted, worn out by grief—his own and everyone else's. "Okay," he said, "How about tomorrow afternoon?"

They made plans for Suki to pick him up at the commuter rail station, as his car was in the shop, discussed a few details, then hung up. Suki stretched her arms to the ceiling and turned around in her chair. She froze.

Alexa was standing in the open doorway. Her cheekbones cast deep shadows over her face, and her skin was so bloodless it was almost translucent. Suki could see a narrow blue vein pulsing next to her right eye. "Am I going to be arrested?" Alexa asked in a hoarse whisper.

CHAPTER TWENTY-TWO

Kyle and Suki had cold eggplant parmesan for breakfast. It was overcooked and chewy. Kyle ate three helpings anyway, indifferent to everything but filling his hollow teenage-boy stomach, while Suki wrestled with sinewy pieces of blackened cheese. Alexa had gone into her room after overhearing Suki's conversation with Warren last night, and she had not appeared since. Suki knew they had to talk. She was fortifying herself for the encounter with black coffee and burnt provolone.

When Kyle was finally satiated, he pushed back his chair and stood up, sending it to the floor with a crash. He righted the chair and told Suki he had a soccer game after school. "Scott's mom is taking us to McDonald's after and Scott said she could bring me home when we're done."

Suki ripped another piece of cheese off the top of the casserole and watched Kyle shifting awkwardly, biting the inside of his cheek. The poor kid. All his friends knew what was going on. How bad things were. "She's quite the supermom," Suki said. "This Mrs. Fleishman."

Kyle shrugged. "She just likes soccer." He worked the toe of his sneaker into the floor, closely observing how the shoe flexed under the pressure.

Suki observed, too. Both the sneaker and Kyle.

He seemed taller than the last time she had bothered to notice, thinner, older. Alexa was aging them all. "What is it, honey?" she asked. As if she didn't know. "What's bothering you?"

"Nothin'," he said, still engrossed in his foot.

"It's going to be all right, Kyle. I promise. I'm not going to let anything happen to Alexa."

"It's not that."

"I've been trying to reach your dad," she said. "Almost every day. I'm sure he'll call soon." Thoughtless, self-centered son of a bitch.

Kyle looked up at her for a second, then looked back down.

"Is it Dad?" Suki felt as if all the nerves in her body were being stretched toward their breaking point. She strained to keep her voice even, not to take out on Kyle what Stan and Alexa had done. "Is that what's bothering you, honey?"

He shrugged again.

"I can't help you if you won't talk to me." Suki was unable to control the frustration that colored her words.

He patted her shoulder. "I just wanted to tell you that you're a good mom, too." Then he grabbed his backpack and was gone.

Suki stared at the empty doorway for a long time, then she took a final swig of coffee and slowly climbed the stairs.

Alexa was awake, lying fully clothed on her bed, staring at a piece of black chiffon hanging over her head. She had attached it to the ceiling with masking tape. Alexa didn't acknowledge either Suki's knock or her presence when she stepped into the room.

The room smelled faintly of patchouli incense, and Alexa had moved her candle collection from her bookshelves to the floor. An elongated semi-circle, constructed from three dozen candles of varying heights, widths and colors, ringed the bed. The grouping was disturbing. Suki raised her eyes and regarded her daughter. She couldn't just let Alexa lie here, surrounded by unlit candles and self-pity, contemplating an old piece of cobwebby material.

"Do you feel up to school today?" Suki asked cheerfully.

"Will I be sent to the same prison Lindsey's in?" Alexa answered.

"You're not going to prison." Suki sat down on the bed and took Alexa's hand. Alexa let her, but the hand lay there, limp and unmoving. Suki put it back down and said, "Honey, you've got to believe me, I promise you, I will not let that happen, and neither will Mike Dannow."

Alexa continued to stare at the ceiling. "Mike Dannow didn't do a particularly good job of keeping Lindsey out of prison."

"That was a completely different situation," Suki said. "And Kenneth Pendergast is working on a lot of angles, too. These are good people who believe in you. Who are going to help you get out of this mess."

Alexa didn't respond. The black gauze undulated in the breeze from the open window.

"And I've got an idea for how we're going to get the boys to admit the truth." Suki said. "You want to hear how?"

Alexa shook her head almost imperceptibly.

"I can't do this alone."

Alexa moaned softly and Suki recognized the pain in her eyes: Alexa was thinking of her father. Damn him. Damn him. Damn him.

"I need you to be there with me," Suki said. "To help me."

"I thought you had Mr. Blanchard to help you."

"Is that what this is all about?" Suki asked softly. Alexa *was* thinking about Stan. As if the kid didn't have enough to worry about.

Alexa twitched her shoulder.

Suki turned and stared out the window, at the weeds choking her garden, at the asphalt crumbling at the end of the driveway, at the morning sun climbing the sky. "I'm sorry if this is upsetting to you, honey, but the truth is, we need Warren Blanchard. And when I asked him to help, he was nice enough to agree." The front lawn needed mowing. She turned to her daughter. "We *have* to let him help us, Alexa. We've got no choice."

"I'm afraid," Alexa whispered.

As a child, Alexa had been overrun with fears. Fear of the night. Fear of fire. Fear of strangers and beaches and swings. Suki and Stan had worked hard to rid her of these anxieties, using Suki's variation of desensitization and lots of coddling. When, at age twelve, Alexa had taken off by herself down an expert ski slope, Stan and Suki had decided they had been *too* successful.

"I'm scared of what might happen."

Suki could see that Alexa was truly afraid. But what was she afraid of? Another death, or her mother getting involved with another man? What the hell, Suki thought and sat down on the bed.

"Lindsey Kern told me to tell you that the man you're afraid of is the one who's going to save you."

Alexa sat up. "Lindsey said that?"

"I think that's what she was trying to tell you at the doctor's office, too. Remember? She told you to let me get the help I need?"

Alexa shook her head. "Lindsey was talking about knowing things—about seeing things before they happen, about how she and I believed in things other people didn't, like reincarnation and precognition. I don't remember her saying anything about you."

"Well, she did," Suki said. "And she also told me to give you that message about the man you're afraid of."

"When? When did she say that?"

"I don't remember exactly, but it was before the doctor's."

Alexa jerked herself into a sitting position. "Mr. Blanchard's got something to do with the symbol. Don't you remember?" she demanded. "I told you about the symbol. A Hebrew letter on a ring?"

"But honey," Suki said, striving to remain reasonable in the face of Alexa's growing irrationality. "Warren Blanchard's not even Jewish."

"He could still have a ring," Alexa insisted. "I know what I know."

"But what about what Lindsey knows?" Suki demanded. "According to her, Warren Blanchard's the way to make this all go away."

"I don't care."

Suki slapped her hands on her thighs and stood up. "It can't work that way, Alexa. You can't believe when it's convenient, and then, when it doesn't suit your purposes, decide you don't believe anymore." As she headed for the door, she realized that on some levels, she was guilty of the same thing. She turned around. "I'm sorry if you think it's a mistake, honey, but I have to do what I think is best."

Alexa stared at the ceiling. "And I'll do what I think is best."

Suki turned and left Alexa alone.

Suki parked in the small lot adjoining the Ayer train station, although "train station" was a bit of a misnomer: "concrete slab partially enclosed by dirty Plexiglas," would be a more apt descriptor. She was early and the station—what there was of it—was deserted. Although Ayer wasn't all that far from Witton, Suki had never had reason to come here before, so she had allowed more time than was necessary to drive the country lane that led to the tiny hamlet. Now that she had seen the main street of Ayer, its two blocks of tilting 1930s buildings in desperate search of a new coat of paint, she figured it would probably be a while before she returned. She leaned back against the headrest.

It had been a long day already. Her first patient had experienced the worst of human unkindness as a child. Her second couldn't reconcile what he had done in Vietnam with who he was now. Her third was an ex-therapist burnt out from dealing with other people's catastrophes. Those three had been followed by a kick-off meeting for a new competency-to-stand-trial case and a quickie preliminary interview for a forensic eval on a spousal abuse claim. Then she had had an unrewarding phone call with Dr. Smith-Holt. Now she sat waiting for Warren Blanchard's train. It was due in fifteen minutes.

Suki leaned forward and punched Mike's number on the car phone. They had been unable to connect over the past few days, and she didn't expect to reach him now. But she did.

"Sorry we keep missing," he apologized before she even said hello.

"You got my message about Frank Maxwell?"

"Had Betty check it out."

"And . . ."

"Unfortunately, your information was correct."

Suki was surprised by the sick feeling that soured her stomach. She knew Kenneth's information had to be correct, so why was she so upset when Mike confirmed it? Apparently, she had been hoping for some kind of reprieve. "The boys are going to be arrested?"

"In the next day or two."

She swallowed hard. "And how do things look for us after that?"

"We'll take that as it comes," Mike answered cautiously.

Suki stared at the wild flowers growing in between the rusty tracks. There were clusters of a delicate, white flower and shoots of a sturdy-looking blossom that was an amazing deep yellow. How did these tiny wisps of tender life develop and propagate when they were run over by a train at least a dozen times a day? One would think the noise alone would destroy them.

"—know my track record," Mike was saying. "Once we get into the courtroom I'll rip those boys to shreds."

Suki snapped back into reality. Courtroom. "Kern eval," she said. "I got the test results."

Mike cleared his throat. "I was thinking that maybe it would make more sense if you—"

"You're going to be pleased," Suki interrupted before he could complete his thought. She told him about the MRI, the EEG and the MMPI. Aberrant alphabet soup.

"That's great," Mike cried, his voice warming despite what she knew was his concern that she would be unable to deliver the evaluation on time. "Got any of those multicolored brain images?"

Suki felt the approaching train before she heard it. "I think we could work up some pretty impressive slides," she said as the distant thunder of metal-on-metal reached out to her, an almost visible presence.

"You haven't told me your conclusion."

"I haven't made it yet," she yelled over the advancing noise. "But I'm getting close."

"Are you close?" Mike yelled back.

The double-decker silver train pulled to a stop with a powerful screech of brakes. A wide band of purple was barely visible under the layers of grime along its side. "I've got to go," Suki shouted. "Maybe I'll have more to tell you tomorrow—about both Alexa and Lindsey."

Mike said something she couldn't catch, and then the phone went dead. As she was fitting it back into its housing, Warren Blanchard stepped from the train, a worn backpack slung over his shoulder.

"Hey." He climbed into the car and threw his pack into the back seat.

"Hey, yourself."

"Thanks for coming all the way out here to get me," Warren said as he settled into the seat. "Damn car lives in the shop."

Suki patted her dashboard. There was a big chunk missing from the time Stan had yanked Kyle's car seat too hard. "I know all about old cars."

Warren raised his palms skyward. "At my age I'm supposed to have outgrown these problems, but it turns out that graduate school is more expensive than I thought—or to be more exact, not having a real income is more expensive then I thought." He went on to describe his money and housing problems with charming self-deprecation, and Suki was horrified to find she was wondering what it would be like to kiss him.

"I think it's great that you're taking the risk of going after a new career at this point in your life," she said, then felt her face flush. Was he going to think she was flirting?

"You mean, it's impressive for an old fart like me?"

"That's not what I meant at all," Suki said, flustered. "We're just about the same age."

Warren laughed and then abruptly sobered. "I know I agreed to help you, Suki, but I've got to tell you, the more I think about this thing, the more I feel you're going about it all wrong."

Suki turned the key and concentrated on backing up the car.

"Especially this drug connection thing," he continued. "Explain to me again why you think the drug dealer is the missing witness."

"Who else would leave a boy to die alone on the road?" she asked.

"Someone who was buying drugs?"

Suki glanced at Warren. His hands were resting on his thighs, and she saw that he was wearing a ring on his right hand. It was a large ruby encircled in gold. A high school or college ring. Nothing even close to a Hebrew letter. A sigh escaped her lips.

"Okay, fine," he said, misreading the meaning of her sigh. "A deal's a deal. Where to?"

Suki cleared her throat. "How about the rec center?" she suggested. "Maybe talk to some of the kids—although Brendan claims no one knows who the dealer is."

"Who is this guy? David Copperfield?" Warren shook his head. "I don't think you're going to get what you need that way. No kid's going to tell an adult—especially a coach—where he gets his drugs."

"But Brendan was the one who told me."

"Still," Warren said, "I think we should try getting our hands on some information first. Something that'll convince the boys we already know what they're up to. Then it'll be in their best interest to tell us what we want to know."

Suki liked the sound of his logic and was glad she had overridden Alexa's objections. Especially now that she saw Warren wore a ruby college ring. "Such as?"

"Well," Warren said slowly, "I was thinking that maybe we should start with the school. Talk to someone over there who knows what's going on."

Although Warren hadn't taught at the high school for a few years, because he continued to coach, he still knew everyone on staff.

"Davio?" Suki asked. Dale Davio was the vice principal, the one who worked most closely with day-to-day student issues: bus passes, failing grades, skipped classes.

Warren tapped his finger on the arm rest. "No one confides in the person in charge of detentions," he said. "I think we should try guidance."

"I've never run into anyone in guidance who appeared to have any brains," Suki said dubiously.

"All too true," Warren agreed. "Except for Nancy Lansky. Know her?"

Suki didn't.

"She's pretty young—mid-thirties—and hip compared to the rest of us," Warren said. "The kids talk to her because she doesn't remind them of their parents."

Suki turned and headed for Witton High.

"Want me to go in on my own?" Warren offered. "I can scout Nancy out without any of the sticky stuff you're worried about."

"No," Suki said. "I'd really like to hear it all with my own ears."

"But don't you think, given the circumstances, that I'd be—"

"I appreciate it, Warren," Suki interrupted, "but, no thanks. I really want to be there. I *need* to be there."

The strained silence that filled the car reminded Suki of the ride she and Warren had made to Sunderland to find Finlay. A disastrous day. As they pulled into the long drive leading to the high school, Suki remembered the night Warren had helped them deal with Parker Alley. Now he was helping again. She parked. "Thanks," she said.

"Haven't done anything yet." Warren climbed out of the car quickly, as if to head off any more gratitude. They started toward the entrance.

School was out for the day, and the lobby was quiet. The guidance office was through a maze of corridors, and Warren followed the twists and turns with ease. They walked into a tiny square office, off of which two even smaller offices opened. A woman with the stereotypical steel gray hair of a schoolmarm sat behind a stereotypical steel gray desk. She dropped her reading glasses, which were held against her large bosom with a stereotypical chain, and looked at Suki. Her thin lips grew even thinner, although Suki wouldn't have thought it possible. Then she shifted her glance to Warren and her face transformed. "Warren Blanchard," she cried. "I didn't get a chance to talk to you at the funeral."

Warren walked over and gave the older woman a hug. "How you doing, Libby?"

She placed a hand on her arm. "I'm so sorry about Jonah."

Warren ducked his head in thanks and pointed at Suki. "Do you know Suki Jacobs?"

Libby mumbled something about being "pleased to meet" and kept her hand on Warren's arm. "Terrible thing," she said. "Terrible, terrible thing."

"We're looking for Nancy," Warren said. "Is she around?"

Libby patted Warren's arm. "I think Nancy's

talking to Dale. Go take a seat in her office, and I'll page her for you. Would you like some coffee?" she asked Warren, ignoring Suki.

Warren shook his head and led Suki toward Nancy's office. "Libby's actually a very nice woman," he said when they sat down in the two chairs facing a steel gray twin of Libby's desk. "A bit provincial, maybe."

Suki nodded as Libby's page blared over the PA system. Then they waited in another uncomfortable silence until Nancy appeared. She was not at all what Suki had anticipated. From Warren's description, she expected Nancy to be cute and pert and very cool, dressed in clothes from the Gap, her hair long and pulled back with funky clips, or cut stylishly short. Instead, Nancy wore no makeup, and her hair hung limply to her shoulders. Her shoes could have belonged to Suki's Aunt Sayde.

"Nancy," Warren cried, jumping up from his chair. "What's wrong?"

"You haven't heard?" Nancy's voice was empty of emotion. When Warren shook his head, she said, "It's Mark."

Warren wrapped Nancy in his arms. "Is he okay?" he asked, but Suki could tell he already knew that Mark, who Suki guessed was either Nancy's son or husband, was far from okay.

Nancy closed her eyes and pressed her cheek against Warren's chest. "Brain cancer," she whispered. "We just found out last week."

"I'm so sorry," Warren said as he led Nancy to her chair. "I never would have come by today if I had known."

Nancy's eyes filled with tears. "And I'm sorry about Jonah."

Warren waved a hand at Suki. "This is Suki Jacobs."

"Sorry about all this, Suki," Nancy said with a sniffle. If she knew about Suki's relationship to Jonah and Warren, nothing in her demeanor revealed it. Nancy Lansky might be the only person in Witton who just didn't care.

"And I'm sorry about your . . . your . . . ?" Suki began.

"Husband," Nancy said. "Mark's my husband."

When Suki and Warren left Nancy's office a half hour later, Suki was not surprised that no mention had been made of methamphetamine. She was disappointed, yes, but even more than disappointed, she was depressed. Depressed by the sheer volume of sorrow in the world, by the number of people whose lives were destroyed by a moment of accident or violence or unchecked cell division.

She sat in the driver's seat and stared out the windshield into the woods. The leaves on the trees were now almost fully open, and she couldn't see the field that she knew lay only a few dozen yards beyond the edge of the parking lot. It came and it went: life, luck, happiness.

"Sorry," Warren said, interrupting her thoughts. "Guess that was pretty much of a bust."

"Not your fault." Suki watched the woods.

"Hey," he said gently. "You want to call it quits for the day? Try again some other time?"

She pulled herself from her reverie. "Let's do something," she said loudly, too loudly. "Anything," she added more softly. "The center? TeenScene again? The mall?"

"The mall might work," Warren said. "We could go to Video Haven—you know, that awful video arcade on the second floor?"

Suki knew all about Video Haven. It was Kyle's favorite place in the world—and her least favorite. "I thought you wanted to talk to some adults before we hit the kids?"

"That idea panned out well," Warren said with a straight face.

Suki was surprised she could laugh. "To the mall."

Video Haven was even worse than Suki remembered. It seemed as if twice as many machines now filled the long, narrow space, which meant twice the kids, twice the noise, twice the flashing lights, twice the headache. The walls, the floor and the ceiling were all painted black, but this lack of color was atoned for by the arcade games themselves: streaks of pink and purple neon soared from "Soul Edge"; "Sega Virtua Cop 2: Guardian of Virtua City" blinked orange and white and then orange and white again; two pulsing red car seats raced along the winding highway of "Cruis'n USA"; Roman gladiators held guns in one hand and round shields outlined by flashing lights in the other, an anachronism Suki was sure no regular patron had ever noticed.

It was jammed. Kids stood three and four deep in front of every machine, pushing buttons, shooting guns, rotating joysticks. Here and there a group of girls played, or a parent stood behind a small child, but mostly, Video Haven was populated by teenage boys. "I'm killing him!" a voice cried next to Suki. "Shit, I'm dead!" moaned another. "Yeeh, ha!" It smelled like stale Fritos.

"This time I bet you'll be more than glad for me to go it alone," Warren yelled in Suki's ear.

She shook her head and yelled back, "I'm ahead of you." For a while, the two tried to carry on barely intelligible conversations with friends of Alexa's, friends of Jonah's, friends of Kyle's, boys Suki didn't know. No one was easily pried from the machines, and no one seemed pleased to see them when they were. Most of the boys were unable to hear the questions—or else they feigned deafness. When Suki's head began to pound in time to both the stampeding elephants of "Jungle Death" and the guns of the elite S.T.A.R.R. team of "Area 51," she told Warren she'd wait at the entrance.

Suki walked out of Video Hell and leaned her head against the cool tiles that lined the walls of the mall. She stared into the blinking eyes of "Mystic Lady: She Knows All," a mechanical palm reader perched at the edge of the wide doorway. "Press your hand here to learn the truth," it said over Mystic Lady's turbaned head. If only it were that easy.

But she couldn't resist dropping a quarter into the slot. She pressed her hand to the metal electrodes and waited. A moment later, a piece of paper spit from Mystic Lady's mouth. "Stop wasting your time at the arcade," it said. Very funny, Suki thought, yet she couldn't help wondering if the advice wasn't apt.

Warren finally emerged from the dark. He

looked like he had a headache, too. "You want to go get a drink or something?" he asked.

"Do I need one?"

Warren took her arm and led her to the escalator.

As she rode down, Suki watched the rows of pulsating waterfalls erupt from chunks of marble. This mall had once been a one-story utilitarian shopping center, then the roof was raised, the floor covered with marble, the arty fountain and glass atrium installed. Now the stores charged twice as much.

When they got to the ground floor, Suki turned to Warren. "Tell me," she said.

He pointed to an empty marble bench near the wishing pond that edged the fountain. They sat. Warren stared at the coins sparkling in the sunlight. "I didn't get anything on the witness," he finally said. "I don't know if there isn't anything to get, or if no one's talking—but my guess is it's the former."

"What about the dealer?"

Warren stared into the waterfalls. He looked troubled, distant, almost afraid.

"Just say it."

"Marcus Bouchard, a good kid, a senior . . ."

Suki had never heard the name. "What did he say?" she asked.

"He said he wasn't sure who the big speed dealer was, but that he thought it was some kid from Boston."

Suki slumped on the bench. This was going nowhere. It was hopeless. Then she looked at Warren and saw that there was more.

Warren cleared his throat. "I'll give it to you

straight and fast: According to Marcus, Alexa has been selling methamphetamine in the girls' room."

Suki shook her head.

"Marcus said a friend of his bought some speed from her a few weeks ago. Before all of this."

"No," Suki said. "He's wrong."

"He's a pretty straight shooter."

"It's not possible." Suki stood up and began walking toward the exit. Warren followed her. "It's a lie." But even as she said it, she wondered why a kid would lie about such a thing. Maybe it wasn't the kid. Maybe it was Warren.

"It's tough being a parent," Warren said.

Suki was so angry she couldn't speak. First Warren accused Alexa of dealing drugs, then he condescended to her. Why had Warren been so willing to help anyway? What was his agenda? She hadn't thought to suspect his motives because he was Jonah's uncle, but that assumption might not be sound. She threw a glance at the man walking beside her, at his lanky hair, his scruffy clothes. He *did* work at the rec center with Ellery, and he *did* mentor Devin. Warren could easily be in on McKinna's plot to frame Alexa, feigning assistance while he monitored and impeded Suki's progress. She walked faster.

"There's a lot that goes on in this town that parents are oblivious to." Warren kept up with her pace.

No. It didn't make sense that Warren would be involved in a cover-up for Jonah's murderer. Maybe he actually believed Alexa *had* killed Jonah. Maybe he had agreed to help her as a way to punish them.

"Parents tend to see their kids as the innocent

children they once were," Warren continued, "but the world isn't innocent, and neither are the kids."

"I don't need you to tell me about being a parent," Suki reminded him. "I think I know my daughter a little better than you do."

"Maybe it *is* a lie," Warren began backpedaling. "Maybe Marcus got his story wrong, but that doesn't change the fact that things aren't always the way you want them to be."

Suki clenched her fists, but didn't say anything.

"I want to help you, Suki. Really I do. But like I told you before, I don't think this is the way to go about it. You're way off base on the witness-drug dealer thing, and scrounging around like this, you're just asking to find out things you don't want to know."

Suki turned and faced him. "What exactly are you implying here, Warren? That you think Alexa is a drug dealer? That she killed Jonah?"

"I'm not saying that. Not at all." Warren held up his hands. "I'm just trying to help. To keep you from wasting your time. From getting hurt."

"I think I can decide for myself what's a waste of my time," Suki said. "And if saving my daughter means I get hurt, then so be it."

As soon as Suki stepped into the house, she knew it was empty. She felt its stillness, its vacancy, with a sixth sense. She had spoken to Alexa at lunchtime and, although Alexa hadn't sounded great, her lethargic, monosyllabic answers to Suki's questions were nothing out of the ordinary; Alexa hadn't said anything about going anywhere. Suki called out, but was not surprised when she received no answer.

The answering machine in the kitchen was blinking, and Suki jammed the button with her forefinger. There was one message. It was from Superintendent Rizzo's office.

"I'm just calling to double-check on the note you sent in with your daughter, Dr. Jacobs," a voice coated with annoyance announced from the speaker. "The one giving her permission to visit Lindsey Kern?" There was a long pause. "Well," the voice continued, "seeing as how you're not there, and the note's signed and on your letterhead, I'll let Alexa in this one time. But in the future, we need both written and phone authorization for minor visitations. I thought you knew that."

CHAPTER TWENTY-THREE

When Suki got to Watkins, she found Kendra sitting in her mother's van, reading *Mademoiselle*. She sent the girl home. Wednesday evening was visiting night, and the lot was full. Two boys wrestled in the back seat of an old Chevy parked next to Suki and, on the other side, a little girl stared out her window and nibbled on a french fry. As Suki headed for the main entrance, a rangy mongrel barked at her from the back of a station wagon. A guard prowling the parking lot wished her a good evening. She was so angry she could barely give him a civil reply.

Suki opened the door and marched up to the front control. She had never seen the man behind the glass before, as she had never been here during the evening shift, and he looked at her with bored disdain.

"Name of inmate," he barked.

"Lindsey Kern," Suki said, "I'm—"

"Already got a visitor," the officer interrupted. "You'll have to wait."

"I'm not just a visitor. I'm the forensic psychologist evaluating Ms. Kern's case for Michael Dannow's office. I have a letter signed by the superintendent permitting me to see her any time I wish." Unfortunately the letter was in her briefcase at home.

"Don't matter, *miss*." He leered at her breasts, then waved to two rows of plastic chairs shoved into a tight corner of the room. The chairs overflowed with a not very happy humanity of crying babies, sullen adults and teenage boys who needed showers. "She can only have one visitor at a time. You've got to wait like everyone else."

Suki brought her face close to the mouthpiece. "My name is Dr. Suzanne Jacobs. Call Superintendent Rizzo's office right now and tell him it's an emergency. That I must speak with Ms. Kern immediately. He will authorize it."

"They're all gone for the day," the officer said, but he was much less belligerent, much more wary, after hearing his boss's name.

"Try anyway," Suki ordered, although it was past six.

"I know for a fact—"

Suki pressed her palm to the small shelf in front of the window. "The girl in there talking with Ms. Kern is underage," she said quietly. "She hasn't received the proper consents for the visit, and unless this is straightened out right away, someone could get into big trouble."

The man began fumbling with the sheets in front of him. A file and a few pens fell to the floor. "That can't be," he muttered to himself. "Can't be." Then he raised a piece of paper and waved it triumphantly. "Says right here that Alexa Jacobs, age seventeen, was verbally approved by the superintendent's secretary. And she had a letter." He crossed his arms over his chest and smirked at Suki. "Seems like she's got all the consents she needs."

"And who signed the authorization letter?"

The officer ran a nicotine-stained forefinger slowly down the columns. He squinted at the small writing. "A Dr. Suki Jacobs," he said before he recognized the name he was reading. Startled, he looked up.

For the first time since meeting Warren Blanchard in Ayer that afternoon, Suki felt a beat of triumph. "I rescind my authorization," she said sweetly.

But Suki's sense of triumph was short-lived. After being escorted through the metal detector and the trap, down a long hallway and up two flights of stairs, she was led into a large room divided in half by a wall of Plexiglas: the shadow box. On either side of the plastic partition were two dozen open cubicles, each set connected by a telephone, each set occupied. Husbands, children, mothers, lovers, sisters, nephews, friends: full, half, ex- and step. Every permutation of every possible relationship. It should have been noisy and chaotic, but instead, the air was tight and close, overheated and full of hushed urgency. Dusty sunlight filtered through the barred windows. Corrections officers stood behind every fifth prisoner and at either end of the visitors' row.

Suki immediately saw Alexa amidst the murmuring crowd, and her stomach clutched. Alexa looked like an illustration in an anorexia text, or a photograph to solicit donations for the Jimmy Fund. Alexa's right hand pressed the phone to her ear while her left pressed tight against the partition; Lindsey's hand mirrored hers from the other side. They were linked, finger to finger, palm to palm, and, Suki feared, soul to soul.

Suki walked over to Alexa. "You're out of here," she growled in her daughter's ear.

Alexa dropped the phone.

Suki grabbed the girl by her elbows and raised her from her chair. "My car is in the lot." Suki looked at the name tag of the officer who had accompanied her. "Ms. Knobe here will bring you outside. You are to get in the car and stay there until I'm finished."

"But I—"

"But nothing," Suki ordered, her anger coating every word, although her voice was soft. "We will discuss this later. Now go."

Alexa and Ms. Knobe went.

Suki sat down in the seat Alexa had vacated. At her right shoulder, the receiver hung by its cord, swinging like a lost soul from the gallows. She picked it up. "Just what the hell do you think you're doing?" she asked Lindsey.

Lindsey leaned her elbows on the table in front of her and watched Suki calmly. She kept the phone pressed to her ear, but didn't answer for a long time. "She came to me," she finally said without a trace of regret in her voice.

"You could have refused to see her," Suki snapped.

"No," Lindsey said. "I couldn't do that."

Now it was Suki who watched Lindsey. The woman was quite striking, even in her faded orange work shirt, without makeup, her hair pulled back severely. Her eyes dominated her face, so large, so intelligent, and, at the moment, so compassionate. Suki could see that in her own way, Lindsey wanted to help Alexa, and Suki's anger dissipated.

"She's just a child," Suki said, a wave of deep, searing sadness rolling over her. "A baffled child whose life is coming apart at the seams. She doesn't need any more confusion."

"That's why I couldn't refuse to see her."

"Lindsey," Suki tried again, "forget our professional relationship, just talk to me as the mother of someone you care about. Just listen to me, please."

Lindsey nodded. "Fair enough."

"I know my daughter, I've been with her almost every day for the last seventeen years—for almost every day of her life—and I'm telling you, it's not good for Alexa to talk to you, to be with you. It could be very dangerous for her mental health."

Lindsey appeared to consider Suki's words. "Why do you think that?"

"Because I'm afraid you'll reinforce her delusions."

Lindsey raised her eyebrows. "Even in your mother role, you sound like a psychologist."

"I *am* a psychologist," Suki said. "That's the way I think. It's what I know. And I know the crippling power of holding false beliefs. Especially when those beliefs go against everything you've been taught—against what everyone else thinks is true." Her mother's bruised, lifeless face rose before her, and Suki closed her eyes against the image. When it didn't go away, she opened them again.

Lindsey regarded Suki, her expression full of compassion. "Alexa believes she's responsible for the deaths, and she's afraid she'll cause another one."

"And that's why I can't have you encouraging her."

"If no one acknowledges the reality in Alexa's fears, she'll never be able to get through this."

"But I don't know if there *is* any reality to her fears."

"That's why she came to me," Lindsey said. "Because you can't, or won't, face the truth."

Suki stared at the rows of panels in the drop ceiling over her head. Some were water-stained. Some were missing. Voices rose and fell around her: "You can't do that no more. It just isn't fair." "We miss you, especially John. He's been in a bad way. A real bad way. . . ." "Get out of my life!" "Anna had her gallbladder out last week. . . ." "And then you want to hear what she went and fuckin' did?" Chairs scraped. A man sitting next to her sobbed softly, and Suki could smell the cheap aftershave he had used far too liberally.

"You're right about one thing," Lindsey was saying, "Alexa *is* confused. She's scared, full of guilt, full of questions and uncertainties. And she needs to share these concerns with someone she respects, to have them recognized as real and valid. You're denying her feelings."

"Who sounds like a psychologist now?"

Lindsey had the good grace to smile.

"But I don't deny Alexa's feelings," Suki argued. "I'm very aware of what she's going through, of how she's suffering. I can see that that part is real."

"When you reject the possibility of the paranormal, you reject Alexa."

A bell clanged loudly. For a moment, Suki thought it was an alarm, that there was a fire or a lockdown. Then a voice blared through the PA,

"Visiting hours are over in five minutes. Visitors must clear the room in five minutes."

"Alexa came here because she's afraid if she goes to sleep, she'll dream," Lindsey said. "And she knows if she dreams, she'll see your death. And if she sees your death, she thinks it will make it happen."

"I know, and that's the reason—"

Lindsey switched the phone to her other ear. "Alexa wanted my advice—needed my advice. She wanted to know how to keep you alive. She didn't know where else to turn."

"And what did you tell her?"

"I told her what I told you: that there's both free will and determinism."

"But what did you tell her *exactly?*"

"I told her what she saw was the future if it continued on its current course undisturbed," Lindsey answered. "And I also explained that seeing is a gift, not a curse. That by seeing, she has the power to change what she has seen—that she should feel empowered, not afraid."

"What did she say when you told her that?"

"She said it made her feel better."

Suki didn't know if this was good or bad news.

"It's good news," Lindsey said. "Believe me."

"So are you saying I'm really in danger?" Suki asked. "That all the other things are going to happen, too? Alexa's worries about fire and a Hebrew letter and Warren Blan—" Suki stopped. Alexa had warned her about Warren Blanchard.

"I don't know," Lindsey said. "I told you before that sometimes I see things that appear to be meaningless. Maybe Alexa does too. But what I can tell you is that I think you're in danger too—that the thing you fear most in the world is going to happen." She paused and narrowed her eyes. "And you must stop searching for this witness."

"Did Alexa tell you to say that?" Suki demanded, focusing on the witness rather than on which of her worst fears might be realized.

"About the witness?" Lindsey shook her head. "No. It's just something I sense."

"How did you know I was looking for someone?"

"I don't know that you are." Lindsey shrugged. "I just know you have to stop."

Suki remembered how, when Alexa heard that her precognitive warning was in opposition to Lindsey's, she had stubbornly insisted that hers was the true vision, ignoring the inconsistency in her logic. Now Lindsey was doing the same. But Suki also remembered that this was the fourth time someone had recommended she quit her search: Kenneth, Alexa, Warren, and now Lindsey. It didn't make any sense—or did it?

"These things don't always make sense the way you think of sense," Lindsey said. "It's like I once told you about turning sideways—"

The bell clanged again. "Visiting hours are over in one minute. Visitors must clear the room immediately."

Suki pushed her chair back. "What happened yesterday morning?" she asked. "Are you okay?"

"Up!" An officer behind Lindsey ordered her to stand.

Lindsey flashed Suki a quick grin. "Life on the inside," she said as she was led away.

Suki walked back down the stairs and through the long corridor, surrounded by a despondent crowd. Men, women, kids; people of every color, of every age, who shared the misfortune of having someone on the inside. They bickered, they cried, and some, like herself, trudged on in stony silence. Was this a glimpse into her own future? Suki wondered. When she would keep Wednesday evenings free to visit her daughter? Suki hadn't answered Alexa when she asked, but the truth was, if Alexa were found guilty of murder, she would be incarcerated at Watkins.

Alexa had been asleep for over twelve hours when Kenneth called the next morning. "I've got some information on methamphetamine that I thought you'd be interested in hearing," he said to Suki.

Suki was sitting at the kitchen table. Kyle had just left for school, and she hadn't come down early enough to hound him to clean up after himself. Two open boxes of cereal, a bowl, half an orange, donut papers, an empty milk container, two glasses and three spoons—she had no idea why he had needed three spoons—were strewn in front of her. Chaos. Just like her life. No napkins.

Last night, it had been Suki's turn to prowl the house, sleepless, while Alexa lay, unmoving, almost unconscious, on her bed. As Suki climbed stairs and stared out windows, she worked herself through just about every negative emotion on the chart. But when she was finished, when she had faced the anger and the guilt and the bewilderment and the panic and the worry and the inadequacy and the unbearable frustration, she realized that underlying each emotion—within it, above it and encircling it—was fear. Fear of what would happen next. Fear of the boundless consequences.

"Suki?" Kenneth interrupted her reverie. "Don't you want to hear this?"

Suki stared at the brightly colored poster board still taped inside her broken kitchen window. She had to get it fixed. Then she remembered what Warren had said about Marcus Bouchard—if there even *was* a kid named Marcus Bouchard—and sat up. "Tell me."

"It turns out your little informant was correct: we do seem to have a bit of a meth problem at the high school."

"No one knew this before?" Apparently, parents weren't the only blind adults in Witton: police, teachers and guidance counselors could now be added to the list. If nobody knew what was going on, anything could be going on. Lots of anythings.

"I guess this meth thing is pretty new," Kenneth was saying. "It seems to have happened over the last couple of months."

"Was it brought in from Boston?" Suki asked, thinking of Warren's story. If what he had said about the dealer was true, maybe there was a Marcus Bouchard, maybe there was some truth in the tale.

"Boston's the most likely source, but meth can come from just about anywhere. It's incredibly simple to make."

"You mean someone could have just whipped it up in their basement?" Suki asked.

"Sounds like it would be easy enough to pull off," Kenneth said. "Guess what the main ingredient is."

"Amphetamines?"

"Sudafed."

"The stuff you take for a cold?" Suki asked.

"Yup. All those over-the-counter cold pills have a drug in them called . . ." He paused and she could hear the rustle of papers. "Pseudoephedrine. And this pseudoephedrine is the active chemical in methamphetamine. It's easy to isolate and reengineer—and just as important, it's cheap. A five hundred dollar investment in Sudafed, iodine and some kind of phosphorous can bring a return of up to fifteen grand."

"That could buy a lot of replacement windows," Suki said glumly. Maybe she should start making meth. Then she'd be able to pay Mike's bill. And the mortgage. And the plumber.

Kenneth missed her witticism—or chose to ignore it. "I checked the Internet," he continued, "and there's lots of information. Warnings from the DEA. Academic papers on abuse trends. Newspaper articles on how these clandestine meth labs are cropping up all over the place. Everyone's wailing and moaning and talking about what a horrible problem it is, how awful it is for kids and police, and then I find that some asshole—excuse my language, but this guy *is* an asshole—posts the chemical formula and instructions on his Web site. 'Four Easy Steps from Sudafed to Methamphetamine,' he titles it. Can you believe anyone could be so stupid?"

Suki stared at the overturned cereal box in front of her. At the crumpled and browning orange peel, the globule of spilled milk, the used donut papers. Being stupid was easy. So was being blind.

"There's a couple other things. The first you probably already know: there's a strong link between methamphetamines and violence—both research and anecdotal. All that speed makes them edgy. No food and no sleep make Johnny an angry little fellow. There've been reports of more brawls and unprovoked assaults in cities where there's been an increase in methamphetamine use." Kenneth paused before he added, "And more homicides."

Suki did know about the speed-violence link; she just hadn't linked it to anything else. If Alexa was doing meth, selling meth . . . "Do you know a kid named Marcus Bouchard?" Suki asked, her voice a hoarse whisper. "He's a senior."

"Can't say that I do. But there's another name that keeps coming up in connection with meth at the high school." He paused again, and the silence felt heavy, laden with meaning.

Suki gripped the edge of the kitchen table. Her knuckles were white. Alexa had definitely been more irritable of late. She wasn't eating, wasn't sleeping. . . .

"Devin McKinna," Kenneth said triumphantly.

Suki let go of the table. She didn't realize she was holding her breath until it exploded from her lungs. "What have you got on him?"

"Not much."

"Anything that can help Alexa?"

"Unfortunately, nothing solid at the moment, but rumors are always a good place to start." When Suki didn't respond, he added, "It's important not to give up hope."

Suki focused on what a nice man Kenneth Pendergast was. On the bright sun outside the dining room window. How it threw brilliant bands of light across the shiny hardwood floor. "When are the boys going to be arrested?"

The line hung empty. As Suki listened to the distant static, she tried to concentrate on the sunshine. Finally Kenneth said, "It's already happened. All three are being arraigned in Concord later this morning."

"How long have we got?"

"It's hard to know," Kenneth said slowly. "Depends on Maxwell and Sutterlund and how long all the paperwork takes."

The light was so bright it was beginning to hurt her eyes. When she closed them, it still burned hot white across her retina. "Tell me."

"Could really be any time now."

Her fear expanded, fueling itself with itself. Suki tried to resist, but it filled her throat. White stars fluttered around the edge of her vision.

"Listen to me, Suki," Kenneth ordered. "You've got to keep fighting. This isn't over until you give up." His voice was tinny. High and far away. It sounded as if he was on the other side of a long tunnel. Or on the other side of the world.

"I'll try," she whispered. "I'll try." Then she hung up the phone, dropped her head to the kitchen table, and let the fear take her.

CHAPTER TWENTY-FOUR

Suki opened one eye and saw two cornflakes. The golden yellow flakes sat slightly askew, casting tiny lopsided shadows on the kitchen table, and she thought how nice it would be to be a cornflake. She hadn't felt this way since she was fourteen, when Richie Potter invited Maggie Marholin to the roller skating party after Suki had told everyone he was taking her. Suki lifted her head and squinted at the bright sunlight. Unfortunately, she couldn't transform herself into a cornflake; there were laws of physics to consider, after all. She pushed herself to a stand and began to clean the kitchen.

She put the dirty dishes in the dishwasher and returned the cereal boxes to their cabinet. She rinsed out the empty milk carton and threw it into the recycle bin under the sink. She dumped the half-eaten orange down the garbage disposal and the papers in the trash. Then she wiped the crumbs from the table and countertops, and poured herself another cup of coffee. All nice and tidy, she thought as she sat back down in the chair. Just like her life.

Suki knew her actions were a hollow effort to dupe herself into believing she could actually wield influence over something—anything. Great. She now had power over dirty dishes and cornflakes. A major victory. She grabbed the phone and called

Mike. He, of course, was not available and Betty, of course, promised he would call her back as soon as he could. Great. She walked into the dining room and stared out the window, pressing the warm coffee mug between her icy hands. Her early rhododendron bushes were in full bloom, and the sight of the bold balls of purple always lifted her spirits. Suki turned from the flowers, their exuberance an affront.

A primitive metal sculpture she and Stan had bought in Mexico sat in the middle of the dining room table. They had always assumed it was a depiction of a man wrestling a whale, but had never been sure as the artist had spoken very little English. "You like, you take, me happy," the tiny woman with copper-colored skin had kept repeating. "You like, you take, me happy." Her words had become Stan and Suki's stock response whenever one looked to the other for the okay to buy something he or she really wanted.

The sculpture was incredibly dusty. Suki leaned over the table and used the bottom of her T-shirt as a cloth. She rubbed until the statue was clean and shiny. Power over dust. When she finished with the man and the whale, she looked around for something else to attack with her T-shirt. As she approached the ceramic bowl on the breakfront, she stopped herself. Maybe she was giving up too easily. Maybe she could exert influence over more than she thought. There still might be time before the arraignment. She could find the witness, the gun, get enough proof to make the boys tell the truth and unmask Ellery McKinna as the lying bastard he was. Suki glanced at the clock and pushed her T-shirt into the bowl; a cloud of dust lifted into the air. She sneezed. Maybe she should stick to inanimate objects.

Suki wandered into the living room and straightened the throw pillows on the couch. When she dropped onto the couch, coffee spilled on her T-shirt, but she didn't bother to blot it up. Instead, she watched the brown stain spreading across the front of her shirt, mesmerized by the strange exotic creature. The coffee seeped through the threads of the shirt, quickly at first, then more slowly, then finally loop by loop, until it stopped. Fascinating.

The phone rang. It was Mike. "You heard about the arraignment?" he asked without preamble. Before she could answer he told her he was sending an associate to Concord, explaining that he was tied up negotiating an arrest arrangement with Frank Maxwell.

"Arrest arrangement?"

"Like I said before—no cuffs, no media, no front door."

Suki could barely breathe.

"Weekday morning only," Mike continued. "Get her out on bail that afternoon so there'll be no night in jail."

"But . . . but . . . what if there's some new evidence?" Suki stammered. "What if the boys change their minds? Or if the arrest doesn't happen?"

"I'm sorry, Suki," Mike said, his voice filled with sympathy. "But I'm afraid we're dealing with a 'when' here, not an 'if.'"

Suki realized that *this* was her worst fear. "When?"

"Probably sometime early next week."

"Isn't there anything you can do?" Suki begged. "Anything we can do?"

"Time's real short on this side of the arrest," he said. "But afterwards, there'll be more than enough."

"But then it'll be too—"

"Not at all. Their case is full of holes. You know that. You understand how all this works. They need the arrest to appease the media, but when they try to take this to trial, all hell's going to blow. The evidence's all circumstantial—what little there is of it. The boys aren't exactly credible, there's no witness, no murder weapon, and Alexa's as clean as they—"

"I don't want her arrested," Suki interrupted, not wanting to think about how "clean" Alexa was—or, more correctly, wasn't. "I can't care about what comes later yet, I can only care about now. The arrest is what's happening now, and we can't let it. It's too awful. She's just a kid. This could destroy her."

"Suki, listen," Mike said. "I understand where you're coming from, and we can talk about this later, but now I've got to run. Betty just buzzed. Maxwell's on the other line."

"But—"

"Know what? Forget about the Kern eval. I'll get someone else to finish up. Ask the judge for a few days' postponement. You've got too much to handle right now."

"No," Suki said more sharply than she meant to. "I can do it. I promised I would and I will. It's too late for you to get someone else, and I won't have you postponing because of my personal life."

"Your testimony's scheduled for Monday.

Today's Thursday. At the latest, I'd need your conclusion in writing by tomorrow, and the full evaluation by Saturday to get it to the DA on time. It was
going to be tight before all this—I just don't see how
you can do it now."

Suki willed her voice to be steady. "I appreciate
your offer," she said. "Really, I do. But I made a professional commitment to you, and I will see it
through."

"You're sure you're up to it?"

"To tell you the truth, I need to work. If I don't
have something to think about beside Alexa, I'll be
the one to go mad." Power over forensic evaluations.

"You're a real trouper," Mike said and Suki could
hear the respect in his voice. "I'll get back to you
after the arraignment."

Suki showered and dressed and forced herself to sit
down at her desk. She had told Mike she needed to
work, and she did. It was the only way to make this
horror go away—even if it was just for a few mental
moments. She pulled the materials from her briefcase and opened up the Kern file on her computer.
Although she had almost all the necessary factual
data collected and written up, facts were only about
a third of a forensic evaluation. The other two-thirds
were concerned with opinions and the logic linking
the facts to those opinions. As she hadn't formulated
her opinion yet, two-thirds of the evaluation was still
unwritten.

Suki leaned back in her chair and glanced at the
clock on her desk. After talking with Lindsey for

what could have been no longer than an hour, Alexa had been sleeping for almost fifteen. What should she say to her when she woke? Suki wondered. Should she confront her about her visit to Lindsey, a visit in direct opposition to explicit instructions? About Marcus Bouchard's accusations? They *had* to discuss the drugs; Suki needed to find out exactly what was going on, how heavily involved Alexa was. But maybe, at this point, it was just best to try to prepare her for what was to come.

Suki forced her eyes back to the computer screen and her thoughts back to her report. What did she think about Lindsey's state of mind at the time of Richard Stoddard's death? Was Lindsey criminally responsible? Suki opened the computer file that held forensic definitions, and read what she already knew by heart: the 1967 *Commonwealth v McHoul* decision. Wrongfulness and conformity.

Had Lindsey known killing Richard was wrong? Yes, she just claimed she hadn't done it. So wrongfulness was not an issue. But the law considered either wrongfulness *or* conformity to be sufficient. Was Lindsey capable of stopping herself from killing Richard? This was not so clear-cut. Nor was the definition of "mental disease or defect," a state that was legally necessary if a defendant was to be found not guilty by reason of insanity.

Suki read the definition for mental disease or defect: "A substantial disorder of thought, mood, perception, orientation or memory which grossly impairs judgment, behavior, capacity to recognize reality, or ability to meet the ordinary demands of life. . . ." Was Lindsey's judgment impaired? Seemingly so. Was her behavior? Possibly. What about her capacity to recognize reality? If Lindsey honestly believed Isabel Davenport was on the landing with them, and that it was Isabel, a woman dead one hundred years, who had pushed Richard down the stairs, then Lindsey's capacity to recognize reality did seem acutely diminished.

As for Lindsey's ability to meet the demands of ordinary life, wasn't Richard taking her to his apartment because he believed she was incapable of living alone? Hadn't a friend testified that Lindsey had been delusional and at times hysterical the week prior to Richard's death? Suki checked the trial transcripts for other reports of Lindsey's behavior that week. There were statements attesting to atypical absences from work, Lindsey's claims of murdered dogs and attacking snakes, not to mention her paranoid contention she was being stalked. It was amazing Mike had managed to *keep* Lindsey's precarious mental state from becoming at issue at the first trial.

Suki rolled her mouse around the mouse pad and watched the cursor zip across the screen. Did this mean she believed Lindsey was not criminally responsible that afternoon? That Lindsey had suffered from a mental impairment that affected her ability to recognize reality? If Suki objectively considered her responses, she had to conclude that she did. Unless, of course, the ghost of Isabel Davenport *had* been on the stairs. . . .

Suki had the itchy feeling she was being watched and whirled around in her chair. Alexa was standing in the doorway. Her eyes were swollen from sleep, and the pillowcase had etched creases in her cheeks. She looked like a frightened animal, ready to bolt.

"Hi," Suki said tentatively, carefully. "How are you feeling?"

Alexa eyes lurched around the study, as if looking for something she wanted, but knew she wouldn't find. She didn't say anything.

"I guess after fifteen hours of sleep you must be feeling better." Suki tried to put an upbeat lilt in her voice, but she could hear how false it sounded. She cleared her throat. "Would you like a cup of coffee?" she asked in a more normal tone.

Alexa nodded, but her expression was confused. As if she wasn't quite sure what coffee was.

Suki stood and put her hand lightly on Alexa's shoulder, turning her toward the stairs. Beneath Suki's fingers, Alexa felt so tiny and defenseless, and Suki knew there was no way she was going to confront Alexa about her duplicity or drug use. Alexa allowed Suki to lead her up the stairs and into the kitchen. She sat in her chair and watched Suki pour two cups of coffee as if Suki were performing an alien tribal ritual she had never witnessed before.

"How about a bagel?" Suki asked, placing a mug of black coffee in front of Alexa. "An English muffin?"

Alexa ran her fingers through her matted curls. She blinked at the mug, but didn't reach for it.

"English muffin it is then," Suki said as she forked the muffin into two pieces and slipped them in the toaster oven.

"I didn't dream anything last night," Alexa whispered.

Suki turned and leaned against the counter. "That's good, isn't it?"

Alexa played with the ring on her thumb. "I guess."

"Did you want to?"

Alexa shrugged.

"Did Lindsey tell you to dream?"

"Lindsey didn't tell me to do anything," Alexa said without the attitude she had been displaying since the day she met Lindsey at the doctor's office. Her voice sounded as if she didn't care what Lindsey had told her.

Suki took the raspberry preserves from the cabinet and made a show of twisting the top loose and searching for a knife. Could Alexa's visit to Lindsey have had a very different result than Suki had thought? "What did she tell you?" she asked nonchalantly.

"Things." Alexa spread her hands out on the table and inspected every ring she had on. There were seven. "Some very confusing things."

Suki opened the toaster oven. "Not ready," she muttered as if she really cared. "Trouble with English muffins." She closed the oven door, pressed the On button and turned to Alexa. "Confusing?"

"She didn't tell me to dream, but she said I would."

"And you didn't?"

"No," Alexa said. "I mean yes. I didn't dream. Yes." She looked as bewildered as her words sounded.

Suki longed to take the girl in her arms, to hug her, to console her, but she had been a psychologist long enough to know when to act and when to sit tight. Right now, Alexa needed to talk, to work through her feelings, more than she needed a comforting cry on her mother's shoulder. The bell on the toaster oven rang and Suki busied herself spreading jam on the muffins.

"I don't know what to think. . . ." Alexa said.

Suki put the muffins on the table.

"Some of what she said made me feel better, like that maybe I wasn't so crazy and maybe some of it wasn't my fault. . . ." She looked up at Suki and her eyes filled with tears. "Then she started babbling about flying around without her body and how someone she knew once turned into fire."

"I can see why you're confused," Suki said, sitting down.

"But she believed me—she knew all about it. She understood."

Suki took a sip of her coffee.

Alexa dabbed at her eyes with a napkin, then got up and threw the napkin into the trash. When she sat again, she seemed a bit calmer. "Do you think she knows what she's talking about, Mom?"

Suki stood and poured another dollop of half-and-half into her mug. She didn't want the coffee any lighter; she just needed to buy some time. It actually sounded as if Alexa wanted to hear her answer; for the first time in a long time, Alexa seemed to care about her opinion. Suki sat back down at the table.

"Do you?" Alexa pressed.

"Sometimes Lindsey says things that make a lot of sense," Suki began slowly. "Like one day, she was telling me how science puts blinders on our thinking. She explained how science likes a closed system in which everything fits according to its rules. And that that's why, when something comes along that doesn't fit, science has to say that it's wrong, that it's not true—but that doesn't necessarily mean it isn't true. At one time, science believed the earth was the center of the universe."

"That all sounds just great, something I can use in a philosophy paper some day." Alexa sniffled and turned the plate which held her untouched muffin. "It's just that if you follow it through to its logical conclusion . . ."

Suki broke off a piece of muffin and handed it to her.

Alexa took the muffin reflexively, and just as reflexively, dropped it back to the plate. "I mean, how far does it go? Like, does that mean the universe isn't expanding? That evolution didn't happen? That the sun isn't going to burn out in x million years?"

"Oh, honey, don't you know it's all gray?" Suki said, reaching across the table and taking Alexa's hands. "This whole line we give ourselves about true and false, good and evil, that isn't how the world is. It's a continuum. What's true changes. What's evil changes. It's hardly ever absolute."

Alexa squeezed Suki's hand, but she retained the stunned expression of an accident victim.

"It's like Lindsey," Suki tried again. "She's not always right or always wrong. Sometimes she makes a hell of a lot of sense, and other times she's mighty confused."

"I guess." Alexa dropped Suki's hands and took

her first sip of coffee. She picked up a piece of muffin and chewed it slowly. The food appeared to revive her, and she asked, "So did Lindsey kill that guy?"

"To be perfectly honest, I have no idea. I'm not sure anyone does—including Lindsey."

"You think she was so crazy she didn't know if she killed him or not?" Alexa asked.

"She thinks a ghost pushed her boyfriend down the stairs."

"So does that mean she's crazy?" Alexa argued. "What about what you said before about science?"

"Crazy is a complicated term," Suki said. "And legally, the way I have to look at it, it's even more complicated. Just because a person can carry on an intelligent conversation doesn't mean that they aren't suffering from a mental illness—and just because they don't always make sense doesn't mean they're insane."

"Lindsey told me that Jonah and Chief Gasperini weren't my fault."

"They weren't."

"And she said that what I see and what happens are independent of each other—that if I didn't see it, it would still happen."

"And I'll bet she's right about that, too," Suki said smoothly, although she hoped Alexa wouldn't question how she suddenly became an expert on precognition. "But, it's like I said before, that doesn't mean she's not mentally ill."

"Or me either?" Alexa kept her eyes on her coffee mug.

"There's no comparison," Suki said quickly. "Lindsey's had a long history of both psychological and neurological problems. She's got lesions on her brain, she's been violent, hallucinatory, and now she's convinced she can fly her spirit wherever she pleases. Does that sound at all like you?"

"Do you think she's crazy because she believes in the paranormal?"

Suki chose her words carefully. "That's a part of it, sure, but there are lots of people who believe in the paranormal. It alone doesn't make a person crazy."

"But you think Lindsey is?"

"I guess I do."

"Is that what you're going to say in court?"

"Yes," Suki said slowly. "I am." And as she spoke the words, relief flooded through her. At least she knew what she was going to do about something.

Alexa played with the crumbs on her plate, but didn't eat any more of the muffin. "I'm sorry I went to Watkins when you told me not to," she said to the table.

"I need to know when I tell you not to do something, that you won't do it," Suki said gently. "I need to be able to trust you."

Suddenly, Alexa jerked her head up. Her eyes opened wide and her body stiffened. She cringed away from the poster board in the window, her face a mask of true terror.

Suki whirled toward the boarded window. Someone was on the other side—every one of Alexa's nonverbal cues screamed it. Suki jumped up, her heart pounding. "Who's there, Alexa?" Suki cried. "What do you see?"

Alexa thrust her arms forward. "No," she moaned, pushing at something in front of her. "No."

Suki's heart beat even harder as she realized no one was on the other side of the window, that Alexa was seeing something completely different.

Suki knelt and pressed Alexa's cheeks between her hands. "Alexa," she said softly. "It's me, Mom. Alexa, honey, talk to me."

"Stop it!" Alexa screamed, pushing Suki with all her might.

Suki rocked backward on her heels and fell to the floor, her legs splayed out in front of her.

"I won't see it!" Alexa covered her eyes with her hands. "I can't."

Suki pushed herself up and knelt in front of Alexa. "Lindsey said that seeing it doesn't mean it's going to happen. That you have the power to change what you see."

Alexa slowly pulled her hands from her face; her eyes were dilated with fright. "But what if she's wrong?" she moaned. "You said she was crazy—that she was wrong about tons of things."

Suki searched for the right words. "I also said that sometimes she made a lot of sense."

Alexa slumped in her chair, as if all her bones had turned to cartilage. Her head dropped forward.

Suki reached up and pushed Alexa's hair from her forehead. It fell back to where it had been. "Are you okay?"

Alexa nodded.

Suki stood and poured herself more coffee, which she neither wanted nor needed, then sat back down at the table. She waited.

"I tried to fight it," Alexa whispered. "But it was too strong."

"What was, honey? What was too strong?"

"What I see. The visions," Alexa said dully. "Like in my dreams. Like Jonah."

"This happens a lot with my posttraumatic stress patients," Suki began. "And what you've gone through over the last few weeks certainly qualifies as traumatic. You haven't been sleeping or eating, so it's not surprising you're having hallucinations."

"It's not hallucinations. You just said I wasn't crazy—how could I be hallucinating?"

When you reject the possibility of the paranormal, you reject Alexa.

"Well, then," Suki said gently, "maybe it's not. Maybe it's exactly what you and Lindsey think it is: a vision of the future."

"You think so?" Alexa asked in a small, trembling voice. Suki wasn't sure whether she was asking if Suki believed it, or if it was indeed true.

"For argument's sake, let assume that it is," Suki said, feeling on much firmer ground: playing out a patient's worst fears was a common therapeutic tool. "And if, as Lindsey says, this vision of the future is a glimpse at what *might* happen, then let's focus on how to stop it. Now take a deep breath and tell me exactly what you saw."

"I'm . . . I'm not really sure." Alexa took a shuddering breath. "But it's a place where you're searching for something about Jonah. And there was the ring with the Hebrew letter, and . . . and fire."

"And you're worried these things are going to hurt me?"

Alexa bit her lip. "Yes," she whimpered. "I'm afraid."

"I know you're afraid, honey, but let's look at this rationally. There's no ring with a Hebrew letter on it that we know of, there's no fire, and look, I'm just fine."

"So were Jonah and Chief Gasperini."

Suki had walked right into that one, and she couldn't dispute it—not to Alexa and not to herself. "Lindsey told me that sometimes she sees things that never happen," Suki said, trying to regain lost ground. "She said it's likely this happens to you, too."

Alexa shrugged. "Maybe Lindsey's wrong."

"Exactly," Suki said triumphantly, although she wasn't certain what she felt triumphant about. Alexa disparaging Lindsey's opinion, she supposed. Except that in this particular instance, she wanted Alexa to accept Lindsey's viewpoint. What was certain was that she was becoming as confused as Alexa.

"This isn't a chess game, Mom," Alexa cried. "This is my life. Your life. And I'm scared."

"I'm sorry," Suki said, and she was. "You're right. Look, if you really believe I'm in danger, if it'll make you feel better, I'll lay low and stop looking for the witness. It's all come to pretty much nothing anyway."

Alexa flew at Suki and threw her arms around her. "Oh, Mom, that would be great," she said and burst into tears. "Just great."

Suki held her daughter tight. Just great, she thought. Things were just great.

CHAPTER TWENTY-FIVE

Alexa went upstairs to shower and Suki went downstairs to work. Although relieved that she had come to a decision about Lindsey, Suki was drained from her conversation with Alexa. She sat in her chair, staring at the flying windows on her computer's screen saver. When she fiddled with the mouse, the screen cleared, revealing her forensic definitions.

Alexa had seen something in the kitchen, of that Suki had no doubt. But what had she seen? A figment of her own imagination or a fragment of what was to come? Sane or insane. Guilty or innocent. Good or evil. Truth or lies. These concepts weren't opposites, weren't mutually exclusive. They were, as she had told Alexa, continuums of gray. But for both Lindsey and Alexa, it was ultimately all going to come down to black or white.

She called Mike's office and left a message with Betty that the Kern evaluation would be coming in the way he wanted. Suki didn't specify, and she didn't need to. Betty chortled happily and told her she'd let Mike know as soon as his meeting was over. Black or white. She returned to her flying windows; the windows were blue and red and yellow and green. Each window started, dead center, as a tiny mass of wavy lines, growing larger and larger until it flew off the screen. Gone. Then it started all over again. A never-ending succession of multicolored flying windows.

Suki looked up and saw Alexa watching her watch the windows. She had no idea how long Alexa might have been standing there. The girl smelled of lavender soap, and wet curls hugged tight to her head. But Suki could tell something bad was coming. Another never-ending succession.

"We need to talk," Alexa said.

Suki stood. Somehow, somewhere, she would find the strength for this. "Sure." Suki waved toward the couches in the family room, and they sat down opposite each other.

"I have something to say." Alexa twisted each ring on her left hand. "It's not very good ."

Suki ran her fingers through her hair and tried to smile. "I'm getting to be an expert at 'not very good.' "

"I, ah, I . . ." Alexa swallowed and tried again. "I heard you were at TeenScene the other day. Video Haven, too."

For a moment, Suki was confused. She had gone to Video Haven only yesterday afternoon, and hadn't mentioned it to Alexa. Then she remembered that Kendra always carried a cell phone—and that Kendra was at school with all the kids she had seen at the arcade. Alexa had called Kendra after her shower. "No secrets in a small town, huh?"

Alexa twisted her thumb ring, looked up, then twisted the ring again. "I guess I haven't been all that honest with you."

Suki could have told Alexa she was well aware she was quite an accomplished liar—lying about where she was going, who she was with, what she was doing. Instead, Suki said, "That's not all that uncommon between mothers and teenage daughters."

Alexa flinched, then blurted, "I've been doing some drugs. A few, not a lot. Just once in a while . . ."

Suki stood and turned away from Alexa. She stared out the window into the carport. At her old Celica, the car from which children had fired a gun. An event, a short month earlier, which would have been impossible. Just like this conversation.

"I don't have a problem—or anything serious like that," Alexa added. "I mean, I'm not addicted or anything."

Suki was suddenly very cold. She wrapped her arms around her chest, but could not stem the chill. Not addicted. How many times had she heard a patient make this same claim? How often was it a lie?

"I can stop any time I want."

She had heard that one, too.

"And I will—as of right now."

Suki kept her back to Alexa, engrossed in watching Esther Isenberg pull her station wagon into her driveway. Esther's daughter was at Duke. Premed. Her own daughter was doing drugs. Suki repeated this grim reality to herself, but somehow, she couldn't feel its horror. Instead, she noticed Esther had been to the mall. She had shopping bags from Filene's and The Gap. Suki wondered what Esther had bought. Esther was a trim, tiny woman; everything looked great on her. Her daughter was doing drugs. It was as if it were happening to someone else's child. Esther's child, perhaps.

"You knew, didn't you?" Alexa asked.

Suki turned. She felt as if she were moving under

water, in slow motion, held back and supported, shielded from the glare—but not nearly enough. She nodded awkwardly, as if her chin were too heavy, too disconnected, to move on its own, and was reminded of a study she had read about teenage drug use. About parents and kids. It seemed so long ago. Maybe only a month, maybe years. Either way, it was another lifetime.

"I never meant to start doing it so much," Alexa was saying.

Suki nodded again. The study's most interesting finding was the difference between the parents' perceptions of their children's behavior and that behavior. Parents consistently underestimated their kid's drug use—especially parents of top students. "Good grades are no guarantee of good judgment," the authors had concluded. At the time, Suki had accepted the validity of the findings, but it had never occurred to her that they might apply to Alexa.

"The stuff just worked so great."

"Methamphetamine?" Suki asked. Warren had been telling the truth. Marcus Bouchard was a living, breathing boy.

"Yeah, meth," Alexa said. "It makes it easy to study—and fun. I started doing better in school, and you were so happy, and we started talking about Princeton and scholarships, and well, I just got afraid that if I didn't keep doing it, my grades would drop and then, and then it would be all over."

Suki gazed at Alexa in disbelief and, for a moment, it was as if Alexa *were* someone else's child. Suki blinked. "What would be all over?"

"Well, you were so pleased and so proud," Alexa

tried to explain. "And even though you ragged on me about not eating, I knew that you really liked that I was so thin. That you thought I looked—"

"Now wait just a minute," Suki snapped. "Are you trying to tell me that you were doing drugs to make *me* happy?"

"No, no," Alexa amended quickly. "I was just trying to explain. To help you understand." She looked down at her hands. "I'm sorry, Mom. I know how bad this is. How upset you must be."

Suki slammed her fist into the wall; it hurt and she was glad. Alexa had no idea how upset she was. Upset with Alexa's lies, her deceit, everything she had done and then pretended she hadn't.

"Mom—" Alexa began.

"Don't," Suki snarled in a barely controlled whisper. But she knew she was also to blame. She, with her self-congratulatory blindness. She, who had seen only what she wanted to see. The grades. The popularity. And yes, even the thinness. "Did you ever sell the drugs?"

"Of course not," Alexa protested, her voice filled with righteous indignation. "Just because I told you I did meth a few times, now you think I'm some kind of big dealer?"

"You never sold any methamphetamine to anyone in the girls' room at school?"

Alexa's indignation was replaced by fear. "Well, ah, a couple of times Devin did ask me if, ah, if I could give an envelope to these seniors for him. . . ."

Suki was ashamed. Ashamed of Alexa and ashamed of herself. She mentally apologized to Warren. He wasn't one of McKinna's henchmen; he had no hidden agenda. He had just wanted to help. She felt no relief from the knowledge that Alexa's prophecy had been wrong, only an unrelenting shame. "Devin was the dealer?" she asked.

Alexa shook her head. "The dealer is some guy Devin knows. Some straight adult or something. Devin would never tell anyone who it was."

Suki balled her hands into fists. "So let me get this straight," Suki said. "Some adult gives Devin the methamphetamine, then Devin sells it at school, and sometimes you helped him—but neither you or Devin are dealing drugs?"

"You don't understand." Alexa's eyes filled with tears. "We were just going to do it ourselves, but then somehow people knew, and everybody wanted some, and well, it, it just got out of hand."

Brendan had used almost the exact same words as Alexa. There was no doubt, despite all she had lied about, that Alexa was telling the truth now. Suki supposed it was about time, but that was small consolation in the light of Alexa's revelations. Suki dropped into the couch. "Out of hand," she repeated.

Alexa reached into the back pocket of her jeans and pulled out a small baggie. She threw it on to the coffee table. "Here," Alexa said. "I never even opened it. You take it. I'm done with it."

Inside the baggie was a smaller baggie, and inside that was a white powdery substance. Suki stared at the baggie inside the baggie. At the methamphetamine inside the baggie. At the desiccant inside the baggie. How professional it looked. Packed like that, with the desiccant to keep the moisture out, probably weighed to the exact milligram. Someone knew what he was doing. Exactly what he was doing. And Suki hated him for it.

"Take it," Alexa insisted.

Suki eyed the baggie as if it were a poisonous snake, poised to strike. That's just what it is, she thought: poison. She couldn't bring herself to touch it.

"There's something else," Alexa said quietly.

Suki closed her eyes.

"That's where we were going that night," Alexa whispered. "And I'm afraid the police are going to find out."

Suki's eyes flew open.

"We were dropping Devin off so he could cop the meth."

Suki winced at Alexa's street language. "Are you saying Devin was on his way to meet the dealer the night Jonah was shot?"

Alexa hung her head.

"Alexa," Suki said sharply, and Alexa's head snapped up. "Do you think the witness, the person who called nine-one-one, could have been the dealer?"

"I guess," Alexa said slowly. "I suppose it's possible. Devin never said . . ." Then her eyes widened in fear as she realized what she had done. "No!" she practically shouted. "It wasn't. You're wrong. No. I'm sure it was someone else." Alexa threw herself to the floor and grabbed Suki's knees. "You can't go out and try to find him," she cried. "You promised. You promised!"

Suki didn't answer. She untangled herself from Alexa's grasp, grabbed the baggie and walked from the room.

• • •

Suki knew she was going to have to spend the major-ity of the next three days at her office: she had no laser printer, no fax machine and no Internet access from her house—all things she needed to complete the evaluation. She also knew she probably had only the next three days, four or five at the outside, to find the witness and stop Alexa's arrest. It was not an attractive prospect, but Suki focused on the end product: a completed job and an exonerated daugh-ter. She had to believe that both were possible.

When she got to the office and explained the sit-uation, Jen was more than happy to turn over the desk for the duration. She didn't usually come in on Fridays and hadn't planned to work over the week-end. She offered to help Suki in any way that she could, but Suki turned her down. Jen was a bit too over-the-top to be an effective detective, and child psychologists were not well versed in forensics. Jen hugged Suki tight and cast a worried glance over her shoulder as she left.

After seeing two patients, Suki sat down at the computer to write Mike a fax stating the conclusion of her evaluation on Lindsey Kern, and promising the full report no later than Saturday afternoon. She poised her hands over the keyboard, but her eyes sought the sweeping vista of the meadow outside her window: two weather fronts were warring along the ridge that rolled off to the west. The clouds were odd, narrow fingers stretching from midsky down to the ground. Like a platoon of billowing ghosts, they marched eastward, their progress slowed, but not halted, by the dome of high pressure that had been protecting the area for days. So real, so powerful, yet only water vapor. Nothing but fog.

So hard to know what was real, what was illusion, Suki thought. So hard to know. Were Lindsey's beliefs so wrong, so deranged, that they qualified her for the label of insanity? Or was Suki just a victim of science protecting its world view? *"It's either a vision or it's a plan,"* Lindsey had said. If Lindsey was indeed insane, if the supernatural was untrue, what did that mean for Alexa? Suki watched the clouds, undersides dark with rain, pressing, pushing, asserting themselves, unaware they were only fog.

This wasn't about Alexa, Suki reminded herself. And it wasn't about the paranormal. This was about Lindsey and her aberrant MMPI and EEG and MRI. About nightmares and headaches and hallucinations stretching back to Lindsey's early childhood. Never before had Suki allowed her personal life to leak so disastrously into her professional—and vice versa. It was unprincipled, unconscionable, unprofessional. It was over.

Lightning flashed in the belly of one of the farther clouds. Suki turned from the window and began to type.

I, Suzanne Jacobs, Ph.D., a forensic psychologist certified by the Commonwealth of Massachusetts, conclude that, due to a substantial disorder of perception which grossly diminished her capability to recognize reality, Lindsey Kern was significantly impaired in her ability to conform her conduct to the requirements of the law at the time of the death of Richard Stoddard.

I shall so state, under oath, in the forthcoming trial of Lindsey Kern, and shall submit to you, prior to my testimony, the completed forensic evaluation detailing the data and logic chain from which this opinion is derived.

Before she could change her mind, Suki clicked on the Print icon. As soon as the page dropped into the printer tray, she fed it into the fax machine, punched in Mike's number and watched her words slide under the scanner. Then she left the office and drove to the rec center.

Varsity soccer practice was this afternoon, and Suki planned to corner Brendan and get him to tell her about the drugs and the dealer and what had gone on the night Jonah was killed. Now that she knew Devin was involved, Suki also knew Brendan had lied to her: Devin McKinna would never be able to keep something as juicy, or as image-enhancing, as the name of his drug dealer a secret. And Brendan was his best friend. He had talked to her before; she would make him talk again.

As on the afternoon when she had waited for Parker Alley, Suki stationed herself outside the boys' locker room. She couldn't believe that with all she had done since that day, she was still just as far, if not farther, from clearing Alexa. And now, the clock she had heard ticking in the distance was up close, pounding in her ear. It sounded a lot like the clanking of steel doors.

There was a loud clap of thunder and Suki

jumped. Thunder, she told herself, not clocks, not prison doors. *"You've got to keep fighting,"* Kenneth had said. *"This isn't over until you give up."* She would never give up. Never. While it was true Alexa had lied—admittedly, more than just lied—this did not make her a murderer. Suki could acknowledge that her daughter might be much less, or much more, than she had thought, and that she herself might have been blind to Alexa's faults, yet the other just didn't fit. Couldn't fit. Despite the pregnancy. Despite the drugs. Despite Jonah Ward and Charlie Gasperini.

Still, Suki began to lose heart as boy after boy raced from the locker room and Brendan was not among them. Perhaps he was sick, she thought, then remembered: He had been arraigned today. How could she have forgotten? Obviously, Brendan would not be coming to soccer practice.

Suki glanced at her watch. She should go back to the office, but she also needed to check on Alexa, who had been home alone all day. They hadn't talked about Alexa returning to school; it seemed a hollow discussion. Either Alexa would be arrested next week, and catching up on schoolwork would be the least of her worries, or she would be cleared and would return to classes. A world where Alexa's major concern was making up term papers and missed quizzes now seemed idyllic fantasy.

Suki turned from her post at the locker room door. She would run home for a minute and then go to the office. She needed to check the Internet for a few legal opinions and organize her notes before she could begin writing. As she headed down the hallway, she literally bumped into Warren Blanchard.

"Hey," he said, grabbing her by the shoulders.

"Hey yourself." Suki stepped away awkwardly, almost losing her balance. Warren reached out again, but she sidestepped him, righting herself by resting a palm against the wall. "I, ah, I meant to call you," she said. "I wanted to tell you I'm sorry I was so testy yesterday. It was uncalled for—you were only trying to help." Suki felt the heat rushing to her cheeks and was thankful that he didn't know the motives she had attributed to him, how she had made him a scapegoat to avoid seeing a truth she couldn't face.

"No need to apologize," Warren said. "It's already forgotten."

Suki played with the strap of her purse and wondered if Warren was aware of the boys' arraignment, if he and Darcy were kept up-to-date on the latest details of the case, if he might even know when Alexa would be arrested.

"What are you doing hanging around here?" he asked. "Is Kyle doing another sport?"

"No sport." Suki shifted from foot to foot. She felt she owed Warren something for misjudging him so. But she didn't know what exactly it was she owed him. Nor how to repay it. "Just on my way home," she added. "Going to my office." She had always been a poor liar.

He raised an eyebrow. "Which is it?"

"Both," she said. "Neither." She smiled sheepishly. Maybe what she owed him was honesty. "You were right about Alexa. I was wrong."

"I'm sorry, Suki," he said. "I wish it had been the other way around."

"Me, too." She pushed off from the wall. "I've got

to run. On top of everything else, I have a report to finish that's going to keep me in my office for the next three days straight."

"Work can be a great escape—take it from me."

Suki hesitated. How much honesty did she owe him? "Alexa told me some interesting things about the witness," she said. "My theory may not be as half-baked as we thought." Then she described her conversation with Alexa.

As Warren listened, his jaw tightened; it was obviously difficult for him to hear details of that night. When Suki finished speaking, he nodded slowly. "So you were waiting to talk to Brendan?"

"He didn't show up."

"I wouldn't have expected him to."

"Believe it or not," Suki said. "I forgot about the arraignment."

"Suki," Warren said softly, kindly, "you said you've got a ton of work to do. Alexa and Kyle need you. Why are you doing this now?"

"There's nothing more important than keeping Alexa from being arrested." Suki heard the stubbornness in her tone and, not wanting to repeat her mistake of yesterday, added, "She's my daughter. I've got to protect her." She thought of the baggie she had hidden under piles of paper in her desk drawer.

"And you really believe searching for this missing witness person is the best way to do that?"

She tried to smile. "Have you got a better suggestion?"

Warren glanced through the gym door and out to the soccer field. His boys were doing push-ups and sit-ups under a rapidly darkening sky. "Let me run out and check on them for a sec," he said. "Then there's something I need to tell you."

Suki didn't like the set of his mouth. "A better suggestion?" she asked, although she knew it wasn't.

"I'll meet you in two in Finlay's place," he said as he jogged toward the door.

Suki walked slowly across the gym and into Finlay's place. She wondered where Finlay was. How Lillian was doing. She didn't hold a grudge; Finlay had done what he needed to do for someone he loved. She could understand that. Unless it had been something more.

If meth was at the high school, meth was at the rec center. Maybe Finlay was the dealer. He definitely had the access, as well as the nice-guy reputation, and he was definitely in the "adult" age group. His name hadn't been on Phyllis's printout, but it would have been easy enough for Alexa to get the car models confused. Suki tried to remember what kind of car had been parked at the fishing cabin, but all she could remember was the rain.

Suki dropped into the only chair in the room and noticed that the place had been cleaned up a bit. There actually was a desk and enough clear floor for a person to stand, maybe even two. One never really knew: the world changed and people did things you would never expect of them. Maybe the drug dealer was Ellery McKinna himself, or Warren, or Kenneth. If it could be Finlay Thompson, it could be anybody.

Warren came in and perched on the edge of the desk. "I wasn't planning on telling you this—never would have occurred to me, actually—but now that you're here, and I see what you're doing, what you're going through, well, I just think it's the right thing to do. At least, I hope it is."

"Shoot," Suki said, before she realized what she was saying. She looked up at Warren, but he didn't appear aware of her callousness.

"The DA's office keeps us pretty well informed about what's going on," he began slowly. "Sometimes they tell us things before the Witton cops even know about them."

Suki's heart sank.

"There's been another development."

"Something about Alexa?" The clamor of steel slamming against steel filled Suki's ears.

"I'm afraid so."

Suki wanted to press her hands to her ears, to block out the sound of the prison doors, to block out Warren's words. But she had made the mistake of not listening to him once. She wouldn't do it again. "Tell me quick."

He cleared his throat. "The state cops found the gun. They dredged it out of the river yesterday."

"The gun that killed . . ."

"It was McKinna's—just like the boys said."

"Alexa, too."

Warren nodded. "Alexa, too."

The first thought that crossed Suki's mind was that this was good news, but when she saw Warren's face, she knew it was not. "Why is this bad for Alexa?"

Warren looked down at his hands. He spread his fingers wide, contemplated his ruby ring.

"Why?" Suki could hear a touch of hysteria in her voice.

"They got a fingerprint." Warren still wouldn't

meet her eye. "Apparently, it's not all that difficult—something about skin oils."

Suki remembered Kenneth talking about prints being viable even after a gun had been underwater for years. She leapt from the chair and stood directly in front of Warren. "Are you trying to tell me that Alexa's fingerprints are on the gun? None of the boys'—just Alexa's?"

"That's what Teddy Sutterlund told Darcy." Warren continued to study his hands.

"Well, I don't believe it for a minute," Suki said. "And neither should any thinking person. How exactly could that happen?"

"I—"

"What did Alexa do?" Suki continued before Warren could answer. "Go into Ellery McKinna's house and take his gun from wherever he kept it? How did she know where it was? Or even that he had one? And I suppose neither Devin nor Brendan touched it the whole time? Does this make any sense to you?" she demanded. "Well, does it?"

Warren placed his hands on her shoulders, and Suki resisted the impulse to twist away. "They're not saying the boys never touched the gun," he said. "They're just saying the only good print they got was Alexa's."

Suki sat back down in the chair and took a deep breath. She tried to match her breathing to Warren's. Calm to calm. This wasn't his fault. He was just the bearer. "The prints aren't Alexa's."

Warren sighed. "You told me you were wrong about Alexa yesterday, you could—"

"Don't you see that this is completely different?"

Suki interrupted. "This fingerprint thing is a setup, a frame-up, whatever you call it. There's a conspiracy going on here. The Witton police are involved—and who knows who else. Someone's been out to pin this murder on Alexa from day one, and the fingerprint is just another example of his, or their, handicraft."

"I shouldn't have told you," Warren said. "I wasn't thinking. It's not as if you don't have enough to worry about, enough to do."

"You did the right thing," Suki assured him. "I may have a report to write, and I may have to cook dinner and clean the toilets and hold my children's hands while their world falls apart, but none of that, none of it, is more important than fighting this." She stood up and swung her purse over her shoulder. "Nothing's more important than finding that witness and getting whoever is trying to get Alexa."

"It was stupid of me." Warren shook his head. "Stupid. I thought I'd be saving you time, trouble . . ."

"I don't care about the time, and it's no trouble at all, believe me," Suki said. "You've energized me, reinvigorated me. And I'm thankful to you for it. Really, I am." She surprised herself, and Warren, by leaning over and kissing his cheek. Then she walked across the gym and out of the rec center.

But Suki didn't go to find the witness, and she didn't go to her office, and she didn't cook dinner or hold her children's hands. She went home and climbed into bed. When the rain and the darkness and the thunder came, she welcomed it.

CHAPTER TWENTY-SIX

The storm raged all night, and Suki heard most of it. Her billowing ghosts were more than just fog after all; they were wind and rain and powerful rakes of lightning. She lay on her back and watched light and dark do battle on her ceiling. When the dawn finally broke, all was silent. And all was gray.

Kyle left for school, Alexa slept and Suki sipped her coffee. She tried to read the newspaper, but it made no sense; she understood each individual word, but when she tried to put them together, the sentences were meaningless. A second cup of coffee did little to improve her comprehension. Both Mike and Kenneth had left messages on the machine, so she called them back, hoping against hope that Warren had been wrong. Mike wasn't in the office yet, but Kenneth was at home. His news, as she had feared, was not good.

"I've been trying to reach you," he said as soon as he heard her voice. "State forensic guys dredged McKinna's gun out of the river." He snorted. "Piece of luck."

"Luck?" She caught hold of his last word. Now there was something she probably wouldn't recognize if it smacked her between the eyes.

"Lots of river," Kenneth told her with uncharacteristic reticence. "Small gun."

"Did, ah, did you hear anything about finger-prints?" Suki held her breath.

"Should I have?" Kenneth asked.

The line hung open and empty. The sky outside the dining room window seemed to pulse between gray and grayer.

"Do you know something I don't?" he pressed.

"I heard they got a fingerprint off the gun."

"Where did you hear that?"

"Teddy Sutterlund told Darcy Ward."

"Really?" Kenneth asked, and Suki could hear the surprise in his voice. "Sutterlund's getting pretty deep into this case."

Suki thought back to Kenneth's tale about Sutterlund's botched murder trial and political aspirations. "So you think that means it isn't true?"

"Did he say whose prints they were?"

Suki swallowed hard. "Alexa's."

"No," Kenneth said. "I don't believe it."

"You don't?" Suki was foolishly filled with hope.

"Figure of speech," Kenneth corrected quickly.

Although quite familiar with the extensive documentation on the resiliency of the human spirit, Suki knew she was pushing hers to its outer limits. It's true. It's not true. It's true. It's not true. She was living on a roller coaster of hope and despair. He loves me. He loves me not. "So you think it's true?"

Kenneth cleared his throat. "I didn't say that either."

Suki closed her eyes. He loves me. He loves me not.

●   ●   ●

Suki worked at home on the evaluation while Alexa slept. She had rescheduled her Friday patients and appointments so that she had the day free for the evaluation—and a few hours in the late afternoon to hunt Brendan down. Her plan was to work at home today so she could be with Alexa, and then tomorrow, when she could enlist Kyle to keep his sister company, she would go to the office and do the final editing, printing and faxing. Both Mike and the prosecuting attorney had to have the report in their hands no later than Saturday afternoon.

Given the complexity of the case, Suki felt she was in relatively good shape. She had all the data sections completed and just needed to put the finishing touches on the precise language necessary for the opinion section. It was the all-important data-opinion linkage that was proving problematical. On one level, Suki was glad: delineating exactly how she had concluded Lindsey was mentally ill, anchoring each piece of her reasoning process with a specific data set or precedent, was an intricate and mind-consuming task, and right now, mind-consuming was good. On the other hand, to complete this section she needed the details of the legal opinions she'd failed to get yesterday, and for this she had to have access to the Internet.

Alexa was still asleep when Suki left for the office. She wrote a cheerful note and propped it up next to a glass of orange juice on the kitchen table. In the note, she promised Alexa she would be back in an hour, but it was almost three before she was able to return. An unreliable Internet server, a patient suffering a panic attack and a massive traffic jam all conspired to keep Suki longer than she had planned.

Despite her frustration and continuing anxiety, as she drove toward home, Suki was feeling more optimistic than she had felt in days. Once she got on-line, she easily found the briefs she needed. She calmed her panicky patient and helped his sister find his meds while instructing her to keep him out of subway stations. And she spoke with Mike, who had given her a mixed bag of information on Alexa's arrest.

From her reaction to Mike's phone call—relief tinged with distress, rather than distress tinged with relief—Suki realized she now accepted the inevitability of the arrest, that she had moved on to the next level: getting Alexa through the ordeal. And that's where Mike's news was welcome. Late yesterday, he had successfully negotiated a deal with Frank Maxwell to go what he termed "low-profile." There would be no media notification, no handcuffs, no jail cell, no police cars at the house. First thing Wednesday morning, Mike, Suki and Alexa would drive themselves to the Witton police station. There Alexa would be "processed"—Suki appreciated Mike's careful use of that word—then immediately taken to the Concord courthouse, where she would be arraigned, bailed and released. Mike estimated a total of four hours at the outside. It would be painful, of that Suki was certain, but at least Mike was making it as painless a painful as was possible.

When she thanked him, Mike had waved off her gratitude. And when she promised him the Kern evaluation by fax tomorrow afternoon, he said he didn't want to talk about it—although she knew he did. Mike was the kind of lawyer who cared deeply about his cases, about his clients, and Suki was well aware he felt as strongly about helping Lindsey as he did about helping Alexa. As Suki waited to make her left onto Lawler Road, she almost believed, as Mike had said, that this too would pass, that they *would* win in the end.

The first thing she saw when she turned the corner was the strobing blue lights. Had there been a fire? she wondered. An accident? Then, slowly, it registered that the lights were attached to a swarm of police cars—and that the cruisers were clustered in front of her house. Suki slammed on her brakes and stared, immobilized. A television news van was parked haphazardly on the grass, reporters and photographers with minicams on their shoulders littered the front lawn, uniformed cops and plainclothes cops lined the walk to the front door.

But nothing, not what was happening in front of her, not her worst nocturnal imaginings, prepared her for what happened next: for the specter of Alexa, pale and terrified and tiny, being led from the house, her hands cuffed painfully behind her back.

The lightbulbs flashed and the minicams whirled as Suki raced toward Alexa. This wasn't happening. Her foot slipped on the sand at the side of the road and she went down on one knee. She threw herself up and forward. "Stop!" she shouted. This wasn't Wednesday. This wasn't low-profile.

"Stop!" she yelled again as she lunged toward

Alexa. "You can't do this. There's been a mistake." Someone grabbed her, but she twisted away, moving forward. Must go forward. Her arms reached out.

"Mommy!" Alexa wailed, using a word she hadn't spoken in at least five years.

Suki threw herself at Alexa, but just as her fingers brushed against Alexa's sleeve, Suki was yanked backward. Hard.

"I'm sorry, ma'am," a low voice said in her ear, "but we've got a warrant for your daughter's arrest."

"That's not possible," Suki told the young policeman, pressing her face almost into his. It was Norm Wolbrom. His mother was on the library board. "There's been a mistake. Call Frank Maxwell. He'll tell you." She whirled toward Alexa. "Alexa, honey," she cried, stretching her arms out again. She needed to touch her; Alexa needed to be touched. But Norm held her fast. She struggled against him, but could feel the futility of the match in the insignificant bit of effort he expended to restrain her.

Suki continued to fight as Alexa was led past. Suki kicked Norm in the shins, and he let go of her in surprise. In that nanosecond of opportunity, Suki drove for her daughter. The policewoman holding Alexa's arm hesitated. Maybe it was out of compassion, or maybe she was just caught unaware, but the woman stayed still long enough for Suki to grab hold of Alexa, to whisper in her ear that she loved her, that she would take care of this, that they would be home soon. Then she was seized by two policemen. It took both of them to wrench Alexa from her arms. Alexa sobbed uncontrollably, but Suki maintained her composure.

"I'm with you!" she called to Alexa's retreating back, to the tiny hands held in large silver cuffs. "I'll be right with you." Then she turned to Norm, who was holding her by both shoulders, and said calmly, "I have to go with her—she's just a child."

Norm shook his head. "I'm sorry, Mrs. Jacobs, but you can't do that. It's standard that—"

"I demand to speak to your boss," Suki interrupted. "You are making a drastic mistake here, and Frank Maxwell will not be happy when he finds out what you've done." Out of the corner of her eye, she saw the policewoman help Alexa into the cruiser. At least she didn't push her down into the back seat by the head, the way they did on television. "I'm coming!" Suki called out as the door slammed. "I'm coming!"

A man in a suit walked up to them. "The chief signed the warrant." He handed her a blue piece of paper, and Norm let go of her shoulders.

"That's impossible," Suki declared, but she wasn't as sure of herself as she had been. "Chief Maxwell just spoke with my lawyer. They made a de—had an arrangement." She tried to read the paper, but her vision blurred. The fingerprints. Alexa's fingerprints on the gun must have broken the deal. Suki's hands began to tremble so badly the warrant fluttered to the ground; she let it lay. She sensed, rather than saw, the cruiser pull away. "I have to go," she said to the cop.

He nodded and leaned over to pick up the warrant. Suki raced to her car and sped to the police station. The Channel 7 minivan was right behind her.

• • •

According to the now-defunct agreement Mike had hammered out with Frank, Alexa was to enter through the back door to avoid the media. When Suki got to the station, she saw why Mike had wanted this arrangement. The grassy knoll in front of the building was completely filled with men and women scribbling notes and photographing a spectacle sure to gladden the hearts of television news directors and newspaper editors all over the commonwealth: a pretty, teenage girl with no record, cuffed, a cop at each elbow, being led into an affluent, small-town police station to face a murder charge.

Suki put her head down and ran toward the front door. She ignored all comers, elbowing a willowy woman in a red suit out of her way and butting a man with her shoulder. Proper etiquette was not high on her priority list at the moment.

On the way over, Suki had almost driven off the road trying to steer and call Mike from her car phone. She was barely able to do one thing at a time, let alone two, but neither could wait. At a red light, she had finally managed to punch the correct numbers and reached Betty, who promised to beep Mike and have him meet her at the police station. He was in Concord—at Lindsey's trial, Suki knew—so he wasn't far. Betty estimated he would be there in less than half an hour and asked if Suki could hold down the fort until then. Suki assured her she could, but had begged her to tell Mike to come as soon as was humanly possible. As she ran up the stairs, she prayed Kenneth was on duty.

He was, and he was waiting for her. As she was buzzed through the door, Suki flashed on the first time they had met, the night of Jonah's murder, when Kenneth had stood on this same spot and reached a long-fingered hand to her, a smile on his face. He wasn't smiling now; his face was all angles and reminded her of photos of Abraham Lincoln during the desperate days of the Civil War.

"She's in processing," Kenneth said, taking Suki's arm. "Downstairs." He led her along a narrow corridor lined by a wall of windows overlooking a bank of computers: the emergency center. But if there was an emergency, it was not being attended to: everyone behind the glass was watching her.

Suki turned to Kenneth. "Frank made a deal with Mike," she told him as she tried to catch her breath. "We were supposed to bring her in on Wednesday. It wasn't supposed to be—"

He hushed her with a finger to his lips. "Not here."

"Is it because of the fingerprints?" Suki demanded. "Is that why?"

Kenneth shook his head. "Listen, under normal circumstances no one's allowed at a booking, but I made a pitch for an exception in this case—for you to stay with her, given her age and the, ah, the severity of the circumstances."

"Can I see her now?"

"Your lawyer's on his way?"

"Where is she?" Suki demanded, fear sending her voice up two octaves. "I have to see her!"

Kenneth stopped at the top of stairs and gripped Suki's shoulders. "You've got to listen to me," he urged in a fierce whisper. "If you get the least bit hysterical, cause Alexa to get hysterical, they'll yank you out of there before you can say 'boo.'"

"But I'm her—"

"I told them you were a forensic psychologist," he interrupted. "That you were used to dealing with the legal system—that you were calm and together, and you'd help ease the process for both them and Alexa. It wasn't an easy sell, so if you want to be with her, you've got to be who I said you were."

Suki took a shuddering breath and looked down at the linoleum floor. "Thank you," she whispered. Her eyes filled with tears, at Alexa's predicament, at Kenneth's kindness, but she blinked them back furiously. Later, she would cry. Later there would be plenty of time. She raised her chin and squared her shoulders. "Let's go."

When they got to the bottom of the stairs, Suki scanned the area for Alexa. To her left were three barred cells; Suki averted her eyes from their cold barrenness as soon as she saw they were empty. To her right was a closed door. Straight ahead was the processing area: desk, computer, camera, fingerprinting equipment, breathalyzer machine, milling cops. No Alexa. Suki whipped her head around to recheck everywhere she had already looked. She grabbed Kenneth's arm. "Where is she?"

"She's probably in with the matron," he said gently.

The matron. Alexa was being searched. Her possessions taken away, her body violated. "No," Suki moaned, closing her eyes as a wave of nausea rolled through her. "No."

"Suki." Kenneth turned her toward him. "I know this is hard, but you've got to be strong. You've got to do it for Alexa. I'm here, and I'll stay here. I'm with you both all the way, but you've got to get a grip on yourself. You can't come apart now."

Suki swallowed the bile that filled her throat. She thought of all the difficult moments she had survived in her life: her mother's death, Stan's abandonment, the past three weeks. And although none of those events could touch the horror of this moment, she knew she could survive this, too. She opened her eyes. "I'm . . . I'm all right," she managed to say. "I'll be fine."

"I'll get you a glass of water."

Suki nodded gratefully as he led her toward the processing area. She leaned against the cinder block wall while she waited for his return. She pressed her hot cheek to the cool bricks and took a series of deep breaths. She would survive this. And so would Alexa.

Kenneth returned and handed her a funnel-shaped paper cup filled with water. He glanced over his shoulder at the door at the bottom of the stairs. "It shouldn't be much longer," he said.

Suki downed the water in a single gulp and turned away from the closed door, toward the processing area. She couldn't think about what was going on in there. What was happening to Alexa. She focused on the activity in front of her. A uniformed cop sat behind the desk, typing with two fingers on a computer keyboard. Setting up the booking form, Suki knew. She realized she knew too much. She knew the Murphy bar attached to the front of the desk, with a single pair of handcuffs dangling from it, was to restrain agitated prisoners. She knew the mounted camera in the corner would record the entire process, that the video screen to its right would display it. She knew the still camera attached to the desk was for the mug shot, that Alexa would be seated on the swivel chair, and that due to a recent court decision, there would be no height lines behind her, no placard in front of her. Suki knew the lockers were for personal possessions, the large black drum for fingerprints. She turned away.

Suki wasn't sure how long she stood there, her eyes riveted to the row of metal lockers on the wall in front of her, not wanting to turn right, not willing to turn left. She thought of the beach at Key Biscayne. Of the quiet park. Of the tiny sandpipers scuttling along the water's edge.

She was yanked from Key Biscayne by the sound of an opening door. She jumped and started toward it, but Kenneth held her back.

"Stay here," he hissed in her ear. "You can't go to her. You have to stay here."

"But Mike isn't here yet," Suki said. "They can't do this without her lawyer."

"It's legal to book without counsel," Kenneth said, and of course Suki knew this was true. "It shouldn't take too long."

Alexa emerged from the door, followed by the policewoman who had been at the house. The handcuffs had been removed and, from a distance, she looked strangely ordinary in her jeans and T-shirt, like her everyday self. But as she approached them, Suki could see the glazed look in her eye. When

Alexa saw her mother, she nodded. "Mom," she said, her voice emotionless.

Suki's arms ached with their emptiness, and she gripped her hands into fists. "They're going to let me stay with you, honey," she said. "Right here the whole time. Right here."

Alexa gave Suki a vacant smile as the policewoman led her to the Murphy bar. Suki understood that Alexa had removed herself also, that she was in her own Key Biscayne.

The processing began with the Miranda rights, which Alexa acknowledged in a barely perceptible whisper.

"You'll have to speak up, young lady," the policeman behind the desk barked at her.

Alexa jumped back. "I understand," she said a bit more loudly, the tremor in her voice as audible as the words.

The policewoman turned and motioned to Suki. Suki looked up at Kenneth and he nodded. She went and stood next to Alexa. She took her hand. "Thank you," she whispered to the policewoman.

The policewoman, whose name tag identified her as Karen Adler, leaned over and turned the television so that it faced away from them. Suki would be forever grateful for Karen's kindness.

The policeman behind the desk glared at Karen, but she smiled sweetly and took up position on the other side of Alexa. "Name?" he snapped. As if he didn't know. He continued on in this manner, asking questions in a cold tone that bordered on rude. Alexa answered softly, but calmly, in her somewhere-else voice. Suki held her hand tight.

As Suki had known she would be, Alexa was photographed, face forward and face sideways. Then she was fingerprinted. Fortunately, it was Karen who rolled her fingers across the old machine and then pressed them to the recording sheets. There was one set for the FBI, one set for the commonwealth and one set for Witton. Thirty times Karen rolled Alexa's fingers. Thirty times Alexa allowed her limp fingers to be rolled; it was obvious she was not really present.

When the processing was complete, Suki and Kenneth followed Karen and Alexa back down the corridor to the room at the foot of the stairs. When they got to the doorway, Karen put her hands on Alexa's shoulders. "I need to put you in the cell now," she said gently. "I'll be in the room right outside, the door has a big window, if you need me, just wave."

Alexa looked at her blankly, but Suki jumped forward. "Is that really necessary?"

"I'm afraid it is," Karen said. "But as I told Alexa, I'll be right here with her, and the room has just been renovated. It's very clean. Would you like to see it?"

Suki had no desire to see the cell into which they were going to lock her child. It was about the last thing she wanted to do. "Yes," she said.

Karen waved all three of them ahead of her into a square room with a desk. Off the room was the cell. There were no bars. The door was glass, like those doors leading to decks in contemporary houses. Suki and Stan had once discussed putting a similar door in their house. Now she knew they never would. Stan, she thought, not with her usual anger or disgust, but with sympathy. He was going to be devastated by this.

"—only for women," Karen was saying. "The men's cells were on your left as you came down the stairs." She spoke with a sense of certainty and a touch of pride, and Suki knew part of Karen's job was to lead schoolchildren on tours of the police station. "Take a look," Karen offered.

Suki forced herself to peer through the glass. She caught her lip in her teeth. The cell was tiny, eight feet by eight feet at the most, and everything in it had rolled edges and was made of stainless steel. A single stainless steel sink-toilet unit—no seat—stood in one corner, and a stainless steel bench formed a bed along the far wall; it was covered by the kind of mat used on outdoor chaise lounges. A video camera with a wide-angle lens was mounted in the corner, and Suki knew it would be running all the time, as would the fluorescent lights on the ceiling. There would be no privacy, even for the most personal activities. Alexa couldn't stay here. She could not. She would not.

Suki spun around. "My lawyer should be here any second," she explained to Karen. "And we're going straight to the arraignment as soon as he arrives. Do you think there might be some other place Alexa could wait until then? Some place not so . . . so cold? It won't be more than a few minutes, I'm sure." She reached for Alexa's hand and held it tight. "I can't imagine what's holding him up."

Karen glanced up at Kenneth and didn't answer Suki. She busied herself looking for something in one of the desk drawers.

Suki squeezed Alexa's hand encouragingly and turned to Kenneth. "That would be okay, wouldn't it? You can arrange it, can't you?"

Kenneth looked at his watch and shook his head slowly. He rubbed a finger to the bridge of his nose. "I'm sorry, Suki," he said, avoiding her eyes. "I wish there were something I could do."

Suki stared blankly at Kenneth for a moment. He had been so great, so supportive, right from the beginning. Why was he backing off now? Had her early suspicions been correct? A small moan escaped her lips as Kenneth's meaning became clear. She pulled Alexa to her. It was late Friday afternoon. There would be no arraignment today. Nor tomorrow. Nor the next day. The courthouse was closed, and would remain closed, for the weekend.

Her baby was going to be locked inside that cold, hard cell until Monday morning.

CHAPTER TWENTY-SEVEN

Stan had once decided he wanted to write screenplays and began taking courses at the Cambridge Center for Adult Education. It turned out that he didn't have the discipline—surprise, surprise—but it took about a year of classes before he admitted this. One night, about midway through his creative-writing phase—he also dabbled in jewelry design, hang gliding and underwater photography—he came home all excited about a new concept he had learned: the bleakest moment. The bleakest moment is the point in a movie when the main character hits rock bottom, when everything is as bad as it can be, when the character appears doomed. And that was exactly how Suki felt now. She had reached her bleakest moment. She was within it, surrounded and consumed and subsumed by it. Just as Lindsey had predicted: her worst fear had been realized.

Suki stared out her office window at the beautiful spring day beyond. But it *was* beyond: unable to touch her, to warm her, to soothe her. Her bleakest moment was beyond relief. She had just left her daughter in a jail cell, locked behind a glass door, surrounded by rolled stainless steel. A jail cell where Alexa had spent the night. A jail cell where she was going to spend two more.

Last night, after Mike had arrived at the police

station and was unable—although he tried valiantly—
to get Alexa released, Suki called her internist, Larry
Starr. Larry phoned in a prescription for a strong seda-
tive for both Suki and Alexa. Kenneth ran to Witton
Drug to pick up the pills. According to Kenneth, who
stayed with her until midnight, and Karen, who
stayed with her until morning, Alexa had slept like a
log. Suki had, too, although now she felt groggy and
fuzzy. Better, perhaps, than being too cognizant.

She turned back to the computer. She had to fax
the evaluation to Mike in two hours. Although he
had told her to forget it, she couldn't. She wouldn't.
She had made a commitment and she would honor
it. Even she knew she was being stupid. But what else
did she have to do?

Kenneth had finally convinced her to leave the
jail; as much as she wanted to be with Alexa, Suki
could see her presence was little comfort. Suki
couldn't go into the cell, and Alexa couldn't come
out. So Suki had to sit at the matron's desk, Kenneth
at her side, staring through the glass door. Sometimes
Alexa stared back, once she had even waved, but for
the last couple of hours she had curled herself up on
the bench, back to the door. Suki had thought about
giving her another sleeping pill, but knew it had to
wait until evening. Just as she, too, must wait until
evening for her escape. It would be too easy to begin
drugging themselves against the pain. And who knew
when all this would end.

"Go," Kenneth had said. "I'll stay with her."

"I can't," Suki told him. But she finally had. She
went home and checked on Kyle, who assured her he
was doing fine, although she could see that he wasn't,

then showered and came to the office. She called Kenneth as soon as she arrived, and he assured her that Alexa was doing fine, although Suki was certain that she wasn't either. Kenneth said they were having an interesting discussion. Suki wondered if they were talking about Doris Sheketoff.

Kenneth had also helped with Stan. He managed to get through to some frontier patrol in New Zealand and convince them to launch a search. No promises had been made—apparently finding a small party in the outback was a needle-and-haystack game—but at least someone was looking. Suki was extremely grateful to Kenneth. And to Karen Adler, whose kindness had only begun at Alexa's processing. Karen had stayed in the cell with Alexa until she fell asleep, talking to her, soothing her, making her feel as safe as she could feel under the circumstances.

Suki tried again to focus on the computer screen, on the conclusion of the evaluation. She imagined she smelled something burning, got up and checked the cold coffee pot and returned to her desk. This section synthesized all the previously presented data and the opinions derived from it: a summary of her logic chain, akin to the proof for a complicated algebraic equation. Although this was usually her favorite part of an eval, and even with the pressure of the deadline lying heavy across her shoulders, Suki couldn't concentrate. She really could use some coffee. She could swear she smelled smoke. She thought she heard rustling outside. She stood and peered out the window.

There was no one about. The building was empty; she could feel it, despite the imagined rustling. Anyone with any sense wouldn't be at work anyway, they would be out, relishing the day. On the far side of the park there were probably plenty of people: playing tennis, eating picnic lunches, swinging on swings. On this side there was no one but she. Suki promised herself that if she ever got her life back, if normalcy ever returned, she would savor those moments of simple happiness, those afternoons in the sun. So trivial. So important.

"No," she said to the empty room. She would not succumb to despondency and self-pity. It served no good purpose and could easily serve a bad one. Alexa would be home in two days. At the trial, Mike would show those boys to be the lying bastards they were. Then it would be over. They would survive and go on to enjoy the sun.

Suki sat down and read the last sentence she had written. It was in support of her contention that Lindsey was mentally ill.

> Ms. Kern's hallucinations and delusions have been documented by mental health professionals since her early childhood, and were particularly apparent in the weeks preceding the death of Richard Stoddard when she claimed to speak with ghosts and to be threatened and stalked by inanimate objects.

Slowly, she began to type:

> These events have continued into the present. In conjunction with aberrant scores on recent batteries of psychological and neurological tests, during

the last month, Ms. Kern repeatedly expressed her belief that her spirit could leave her body, that she could visualize lost items and find missing children, that she had the power to see into the future.

Suki reread her words but wouldn't let herself think about them. What they meant. What they didn't mean. She had to finish the evaluation. Complete her obligation. Get her check. She bent over the keyboard and commenced typing. It was just a job, she told herself. Just a job.

In a few minutes, she held the completed report in her hand: Lindsey's ticket out of Watkins. An all-expenses-paid visit to Bridgeriver State, Massachusetts' guest house for the criminally insane. Another kind of hell. Suki remembered a lecture from one of her law courses. "A forensic psychologist doesn't fire the gun," the professor had said. "He or she just supplies the bullets." It was the jury who would pull the trigger. She had done what she had to do. Her job was over.

The automatic feed on the fax machine was broken, so Suki had to guide each sheet through by hand. She should have felt relief, watching the pages disappear and reemerge, knowing they were reaching their destination an hour before the promised time. But all she felt was exhausted. Exhausted and haunted. Haunted by what she had written—and by what was left unsaid.

She scooped up the last page as it slid from the machine and sat back down at the desk, staring at the report lying before her. She had used Lindsey's belief that she could see into the future as evidence of her mental illness. Suki shivered, although a wide swatch of sunlight was falling across her body, for she could still hear Lindsey's words: *"There really are only two possible explanations when a person correctly predicts a future event. Either she's precognitive or she's going to make the event happen herself."*

Suki dropped her head to the desk. This was indeed the bleakest moment.

Suki was awakened by her own coughing. She opened her eyes, disoriented. It was foggy, yet light. Familiar, yet foreign. Was she still asleep, dreaming? She blinked as her thoughts moved sluggishly toward understanding. Her office. She was in her office. She jumped up from her chair. It was dusk. She had slept the entire day away. She had to go to Alexa.

Suki's throat hurt and her chest felt constricted. She began to cough violently. She looked around for the jug of spring water and realized she was dizzy. Tears poured from her eyes, and when she blinked them away, she saw it wasn't the shadows of dusk darkening the room, it was billows of smoke. She heard crackling inside the walls. Felt the heat. Fire.

Suki tried to remember what you were supposed to do. Stay low. Feel doors before you opened them. Wrap your head in a towel. Breathe into a handkerchief. But she did none of these things. She stood, frozen, immobilized by the thought that this was no accident. Fire. Fire and danger and a ring with a Hebrew letter on it. Smoke pushed under the door and the room was incredibly hot. Suki dropped to the floor, then jumped up again and grabbed the phone. It was dead. Someone had cut the wires. Set the fire. Someone who wanted to keep her from discovering what had really happened the night Jonah died.

Suki began to cough. Out. She had to get out. The antique farmhouse was made completely of wood. Lots of old wiring. Old insulation. It would go up in a flash. She didn't have much time. She thought of Alexa and Kyle and scrambled on all fours through the outer office to the hallway door; she pressed her palm to it. It was hot. Very hot. If she opened it, she would pull in the flames.

She rose and started to run to the window behind her desk, but as soon as she stood, she was racked by a coughing fit and immediately dropped down again. She pressed her hand over her nose and crawled, coughing, toward her office. A fire escape. There was a fire escape off the window in the second office. She switched direction. The smoke was thicker. It was difficult to see. Harder to breathe. She pushed forward, sucking in as much oxygen as she could between coughs. Crawling. Coughing. To the window. To safety. To air.

Nauseated and dizzy, she kicked the office door closed with her foot and threw herself at the double-hung window. She twisted the latch, but it didn't move. It was painted shut. Her breath was coming in short gasps. Sweat ran in rivulets down her face. Her eyes burned.

Suki looked around for something, anything, to use to break the metal fastener. She grabbed a stapler off the desk and began pounding the latch. She managed to chip off some of the paint, but the latch wouldn't budge. She would have to break the window and squeeze herself through—although the window was no larger than two feet by two feet.

She hit the latch with one final, desperate smash. It flew open and the top window dropped slightly. She shoved the window up, punched out the screen, and threw herself onto the fire escape. The air was so sweet, so clean. She closed her eyes and gulped at it like a greedy child, collapsing onto the metal railing. Sirens in the distance. People yelling, running toward her. But Suki couldn't move. She could only breathe.

Footsteps pounded on the fire escape. Hands grabbed her. "Are you all right?" a female voice asked.

Suki opened her eyes and looked into the face of a pretty woman, her dark hair pulled back in a ponytail. She had probably been doing exactly what Suki had imagined earlier: enjoying a picnic lunch and playing with her children in the sun. Suki smiled and closed her eyes again. The air was so incredibly sweet.

"Come on," the woman said. "You can't stay here. It's too dangerous. My name's Helene. Take my arm."

Suki allowed herself to be led down the stairs. Danger and fire. She looked at Helene's hand. She wore a simple gold wedding band and a small diamond. No Hebrew letter.

When they reached the ground, the small crowd applauded. "Is there anyone else in there?" a voice called out.

Suki shook her head. "I . . . I don't think so," she managed to say, still leaning against Helene.

At that moment, two fire engines roared into the parking lot, and Suki went weak with relief. She was safe, and the fire would be taken care of. "Thank you," she said to Helene. "I'm fine." She pulled away and tried to stand on her own, but her knees buckled and Helene caught her.

"Better sit down anyway." Helene said, and they started toward a bank of grass that edged the parking lot.

As they crossed the asphalt, Suki peered into the growing crowd, searching for whoever had set the fire, whoever wanted to scare her, possibly kill her, the one who was willing to destroy a young girl's life to hide his own crimes. Suki knew enough about human nature to know he wouldn't be able to stay away. He was here. Somewhere close by. Watching her.

"Are you alone?" Helene asked. "Do you want me to call someone to take you home?"

Suki was distracted, scanning the faces, wanting and not wanting to know. "No," she said, "I mean, yes, but no, you don't need to call anyone. My car's right here."

Helene was unconvinced. "I don't think you should drive. . . ."

"I can drive her," a deep voice said from behind them.

Suki didn't turn. He was putting his arm around her. Pulling her to him. Assuring Helene he would see to it that Suki saw a doctor and got home safely. A violent tremor rocked her body.

"I'll take good care of her," Warren Blanchard said. "I promise."

"Oh, I'm so glad there's someone here for her." Helene smiled at Warren, then squeezed Suki's arm. "You take care now."

"Thank you," Suki said. "You were great, but please don't leave—"

"No need," Helene said with a wave. "You'd have done the same for me." Before Suki could say any more, she disappeared into the crowd.

Warren gripped Suki tightly. "What happened?" he asked, his voice full of concern. "Are you okay?"

Suki couldn't speak. She looked up into his face, hoping she was wrong, but the cold glint in his eyes negated his words, his actions; it told her everything.

Still holding her close, he rubbed soot from her cheek with his right thumb. "My car's right down the road. I think Darcy keeps a blanket in the trunk."

"Must . . . must talk to the firemen," Suki managed to gasp.

"That can wait," Warren said. "Let's wrap you up and get you sitting down." Dots of sweat were gathering on his upper lip, and he kept looking behind him.

Suki's skin crawled where he was touching her. She wanted to spit in his face, throw his arm off and pummel him with her fists. But he might have a weapon. He was probably powerful enough to kill her without one. She walked along with him, stunned, imagining she smelled gasoline, looking for Darcy's dark midsize late-model Chevrolet.

"Here we are," he said as they approached the navy blue Chevy. He led her to the passenger door, pressing her to him with one arm while he reached into his pocket with the other.

Suki struggled to contain her revulsion. His shirt was wet under the arm and the clammy dampness made her want to gag. She covered her queasiness with a cough and swallowed her nausea. Warren appeared unaware she knew what he had done. Acting normally was her only escape. She had to remain calm. Then run like hell as soon as he let go of her.

But he didn't let go. He continued to hold her. Firmly, almost frantically. He was strong, and Suki knew it would be both futile and stupid to resist. "Keys," he muttered to himself. "Keys." He looked back at the burning building, then down at his pocket as if he had never seen his pants before.

Maybe he was more aware than she thought. She would be a fool to underestimate him. "Thanks," she whispered so softly she feared he hadn't heard. "Thanks," she said again.

"Aha!" Warren raised a set of keys, and his eyes gleamed in triumph as he placed the key in the lock. A gold charm dangled from the key chain. A charm in the shape of a letter. A Hebrew letter.

Suki gasped.

"What is it?" Warren grabbed her by the shoulders. "Are you going to faint? You're completely white."

"Shock," Suki mumbled. "Shock."

He swung the door open and pushed her down into the seat. "Sit." He rolled down the window, shut the door and leaned in toward her. "Rest your head back. Get some air. Breathe deep." Before Suki could gather her wits, he was around the car and beside her in the driver's seat. He took her hand and slipped the key in the ignition. "I'm glad you weren't hurt."

Yet, Suki thought, I'm not hurt yet. She tried to smile. "I'm fine, really, I am." She had to convince him she felt safe, get him to lower his guard, let go of her hand. "That's . . . that's an interesting key chain."

Warren continued to hold her hand. "It's the Hebrew letter aleph," he said. "A mathematical symbol used in set theory. Order of numerousness, finite, infinite—that kind of thing." He shifted his gaze from her to the fire, which was now raging, then back to her. "Topic of my doctoral dissertation."

Suki couldn't take her eyes off the aleph; she began to tremble. "I'm . . . I'm fine," she said, although he hadn't asked again. "Really."

Warren looked at her oddly; his pupils were dark and dilated. "You're shaking." He reached across her and locked her door. "Don't want you to fall out." Then he kissed her.

Suki was revolted by his hot breath and the smell of his hair. She wanted to kick him and run as fast and as far as she could, but the vision of Alexa huddled in her stainless steel cell kept Suki in her seat. She sucked in her breath and tried to still the trembling of her hands. She had to get out. Away. As quickly as possible. Go to the police and have Warren arrested. Free Alexa.

She kissed Warren back, trying to ignore the horror of his lips on hers, to think of walking into that cell and taking Alexa home. But as he pulled her closer, she was filled with another horror: the police wouldn't arrest him on her word alone, and she had nothing else. What could she say? That she knew he was guilty because her daughter could see into the future? She needed proof, and she had none.

Warren moaned and thrust his tongue deeply into her mouth.

Suki couldn't help it. She pushed him away, more forcefully than she intended. "Blanket," she gasped. "Cold. Need a blanket. For the shock."

He dropped back into his seat, dazed, and blinked at her. "Sure," he said after a moment and reached down to press the trunk release. "I'll be back in a flash."

As soon as his wide shoulders disappeared behind the lid of the trunk, Suki slid across the seat and twisted the key. She smashed her foot on the gas pedal. As the car lurched forward, both the driver's door and the trunk slammed shut. She swerved into the sandy shoulder, yanked the wheel and managed to pull back onto the road.

Suki swiped her forearm across her mouth and risked a glance in the rearview mirror. Warren was running after her, his fist raised in the air. He was shouting something she couldn't hear. The bastard, Suki thought. Drug-dealing, lying, slimy bastard. And suddenly Suki realized she did have proof of Warren's guilt. It was at home, in her desk drawer, hidden beneath piles of paper.

She put both hands on the wheel and swung the car into a hard left turn. As the tires threw up a veil of gravel and dust, Warren was lost from view.

Suki brought the baggie of methamphetamine to the police station and told the dispatcher she had to see Kenneth right away. When Kenneth came upstairs, Suki dragged him into the interrogation room where Alexa had first told him about the shooting. She was somehow surprised to see that the children's drawings still adorned the wall. "I need your help. Fast."

He waved her into a chair. "What's all over your face?"

Suki pulled the baggie from her purse and threw it on the desk. "I want you to check the inside bag for fingerprints."

Kenneth pushed the baggie with the back of a pencil. He flipped it over. "Methamphetamine?" he asked.

"I know who the witness is. It's the dealer, like I thought. The person who sold this to Alexa. But we have to move fast. He could be destroying the evidence right now."

Kenneth raised his eyes from the meth and looked at her carefully. "Is that soot?"

She rubbed her cheek impatiently with the palm of her hand. "There was a fire at my office. He set it to try to scare me away from my search."

"Someone set the Hayden house on fire just to scare you?" Kenneth looked a bit skeptical. "Who?"

"Warren Blanchard."

Now Kenneth looked more than just a bit skeptical. "I've coached soccer with Warren for years. You must be mistaken."

"His fingerprints are going to be on that baggie," Suki insisted. "I know it. Please, there isn't time to argue."

"Are you saying that Warren was the one who called nine-one-one the night Jonah was killed?" Kenneth asked slowly, rubbing his beard. "That he left his own nephew on the road to die?"

"I know it sounds crazy, but I also know it's true." She bit her lip and ordered herself to stay in control. She had to make him believe her. "Maybe he didn't know it was Jonah. Maybe he was too busy trying to save his own skin."

Kenneth shook his head. "Warren making drugs? Selling drugs? It's a tough one to buy."

"He's a scientist." Suki was frantic. "He's got money trouble. Access to the kids. It makes sense, it does, in its own sick way."

"And you think he set the fire because you were getting too close?"

Suki could see that Kenneth thought she had finally gone over the edge. She took a deep breath, hoping that Kenneth's belief in the paranormal was strong enough to overcome his doubt about Warren. "Over the last couple of weeks, Alexa's been telling me she's afraid of Warren. She predicted he'd do something to harm me. Something that had to do with a ring with a Hebrew letter on it—and fire."

Kenneth's eyes widened. "You saw the ring?"

"It wasn't a ring. It was a key chain with a mathematical symbol. The symbol is a Hebrew letter."

"I thought you didn't believe in this stuff?"

"Lindsey said that the man Alexa was afraid of was the one who would save her."

"And you think Warren Blanchard's that man?"

"Couldn't you just please check the fingerprints?" Suki begged.

Kenneth opened up the small lab at the station and dusted the baggie, then placed it under an oblong magnifying light. As everyone in Jonah's family had been printed at the time of his death, Warren's fingerprints were on file. Kenneth pulled the file and stared at the two sets of swirls before him. Suki held her breath.

Finally, he raised his head and threw his reading glasses on the table. "Bingo."

• • •

Kenneth needed a warrant to search Darcy's house, but as it was Saturday, it wasn't going to be as easy or as quick as either of them would have liked. He told Suki to go home, that she couldn't come with him to the Wards' anyway, that it could be hours. But Suki refused to leave the police station. She sat outside Alexa's cell, wishing she could tell Alexa what had happened, but afraid this too might backfire, that once again, she would be bringing Alexa false hope. She wasn't going to say anything until she knew for certain that Alexa was free to go home.

Alexa still lay on the bench, knees pressed to her chest, back to the door. A reticent policewoman sat at the desk doing paperwork. Suki concentrated on keeping her mind a perfect blank. Every second was painful. Warren could disappear, he could destroy the evidence, all this could come to nothing.

"Ma'am?" a stocky policeman stuck his head into the doorway.

Suki jumped to her feet. It had been less than an hour; it felt as if it had been a lifetime. "Is Detective Pendergast ready to leave?"

"Already gone, ma'am. Said you should head on home. That he'd call you there."

Suki was not surprised Kenneth had slipped away. "I think I'll stay here."

The policeman shrugged. "Your choice."

The dispatcher brought Alexa dinner from McDonald's, which Alexa refused, but the police-woman ate. A janitor mopped the floor. Sirens came and went. A cop Suki didn't know told the policewoman that Charlie Gasperini's death had been officially declared an accident. Suki startled at the policeman's words, but then realized she wasn't startled at all. Doors slammed. Walkie-talkies crackled. Suki waited.

Kenneth sent another message that it was going to be a long night and Suki should go home, but she didn't. She called Scott Fleishman's mother and asked if Kyle could sleep over. Then she got in Darcy's car and drove to Darcy's house.

When she reached the modest ranch on the "less desirable" side of Witton, there was not as much activity as she had expected. Kenneth's unmarked car and a cruiser were parked in the driveway, but aside from the open front door, there was nothing to indicate that a police drama was taking place inside. There was no spectacle like the spectacle at her house yesterday, and Suki realized someone must have informed the media prior to Alexa's arrest.

She walked up to the open door and looked in. Kenneth was seated on the living room couch. No one else was visible. The house was eerily silent. This wasn't about lack of media, Suki thought, this was about lack of evidence. She slumped into the doorjamb, glad she hadn't said anything to Alexa.

"Suki!" Kenneth jumped up. "I told you to go home," he said as if he were sending a naughty child to her room.

"Where is everyone?" She forced herself to stand tall. "Did you find anything? What's going on?"

Kenneth frowned and shook his head, but Suki could see from the sparkle in his eye that he wasn't really angry.

"Tell me," she said as she strode into the small room, her hopes rising. "Did he confess?"

"No," Kenneth said, a slight smile playing beneath his beard. "No confession—lots of denial, as a matter of fact."

Suki stepped closer, trying to reconcile his words with his expression.

"But we did find a lab in the basement." Kenneth's face broke into a grin. "A laboratory Blanchard claims he uses for his schoolwork. Things are kind of a mess, as if someone had tried to clean it up in a hurry: empty containers, just-rinsed bottles . . ."

"He's into math," Suki said. "Mathematicians don't need laboratories."

Kenneth nodded. "Especially not ones stocked with large quantities of Sudafed, iodine—and what looks to be phosphorous." The ingredients in methamphetamine.

Suki threw her arms around Kenneth, and he hugged her back. "Where is he?" she asked, pulling away as heat raced to her cheeks. "Where's that slimy bastard now?"

"He's in the basement with Frank." Kenneth stepped back and shrugged with gawky discomfort. He ran his hand over his beard. "We're playing good-cop–bad-cop. Keeping it mellow so as not to freak him—he's jittery as hell."

"Has he said anything about Alexa?" she demanded. "About that night?"

"Not directly, but I think it's coming."

Suki dropped into a wing chair, its fabric shiny with age. She slouched within its comforting arms, afraid to believe this was actually happening, and afraid not to.

Kenneth knelt down next to her. "It might take days to wear Warren down," he said. "Or it might not happen at all. You've got to be patient."

"I can't be patient when my daughter's locked in a jail cell."

"You have to be," he said, slapping his knees and standing. "And you have to get out of here. It's probably not a good thing for Warren to see you—it could make it worse."

"I want to see him." Suki stood up and faced Kenneth, her hands on her hips. "I deserve that."

"Not now." His voice was firm. "Trust me, it's not a good idea. You need to go home, get some sleep, and let us take care of this our way."

"But—"

"No buts," Kenneth said and turned her toward the door.

"Can I at least see the lab?"

He started to shake his head, then hesitated. "Stay here."

Suki followed Kenneth to a doorway at the far end of the kitchen. Standing behind him, so his body blocked her from the view of anyone downstairs, she leaned in when he did. She didn't see Warren or Frank, although she could hear their voices. What she saw was a long workbench. It could have been any handyman's workbench, with its jars of nails and open coffee tins, except that on this bench stood a beam scale, a Bunsen burner and at least a dozen packets of Sudafed. Next to the Sudafed were boxes of baggies. Multiple sizes.

•   •   •

Suki didn't go home as Kenneth had suggested. She went back to the police station. She wanted to be there when they brought Warren in. It was late, so she gave Alexa a sleeping pill, but she didn't take one. She fell into a fitful sleep in the chair at the matron's desk and dreamed of sandpipers.

A hubbub outside woke her. She blinked, reoriented herself and slipped from the room into the shadowy hallway. They were bringing someone in through the rear entry. Suki went to the empty booking area and looked down the long corridor that led to the garage. It was surreal. The bright lights of the back parking lot. The middle-of-the-night stillness of the building. The smell of disinfectant. The low rumble of men's voices approaching the open doorway.

"Move it."

"This way, asshole."

"Where the hell's Smitty?"

Suki crept silently down the empty corridor, toward the voices. She pressed her palms against the cool cinder blocks and held her breath.

The hallway exploded with light and noise and commotion. Three uniformed policemen burst through the open garage door. They were followed by Kenneth, who had a tight grip on Warren's arm. When Suki saw that Warren was in handcuffs, her knees buckled and, as if in slow motion, she slid down the wall. She was sitting on the floor when Warren passed by. He lowered his eyes and whispered something that sounded like, "Sorry." She didn't dignify him with a response.

Kenneth turned Warren over to one of the other cops and knelt down next to Suki. He took her gently in his arms. "They never found any fingerprints on the gun," he said into her hair. "Blanchard made it up."

"So why was Alexa arrested?"

He shrugged. "Someone must have gotten Frank to break the deal."

"Did Warren confess?"

"Not quite yet, but he's willing to sign a statement that he saw Alexa driving that night. That it—"

Suki pulled away and stared at Kenneth. "He left Jonah?"

"He didn't know who had been shot—just like you thought."

Suki pressed her cheek to the lapel of Kenneth's jacket. "Thank you," she said. "For everything."

"Anytime." Kenneth pulled her more tightly to him. "Anytime at all." Then he lifted her gently from the floor. "How about we get Alexa out of that cell?"

Kenneth unlocked the door and Suki went in alone. She walked over to her sleeping daughter and sat down beside her. She touched Alexa's silky cheek. "Honey," she whispered. "Wake up."

Alexa groaned and rolled over. She opened her eyes and blinked up at her mother. "Huh? What?" she asked, her voice bleary with sleep.

"It's over," Suki said, tears streaming down her cheeks. "Let's go home."

CHAPTER TWENTY-EIGHT

Suki had never liked testifying at the Concord courthouse, officially known as the District Court of Central Middlesex County, although no one ever called it that. The low-slung building was modern enough and the clientele much less gritty than in many of the courts in which she worked, yet there was something in the hollow echo of the brick walls, in the sharp shadows cast by the halogen lights, in the cavernous spaces, that always made her wish she were somewhere else. But, at the moment, Suki was just glad she was in Concord for Lindsey's trial rather than for Alexa's arraignment. She was also glad to be here at all; she was almost half an hour late.

Everything had conspired against her this morning, and after the frenzy of the weekend, she had been a predictable loser in her battle with the clock. Kyle couldn't find his biology notebook. Alexa had a case of nerves about going back to school. The spark plugs on her car got wet and she had to dry them, one by one, with the towel she kept in the carport for that purpose. And then there had been an accident on Route 2 that tied up traffic for miles. Suki slammed the Celica's door and, without locking it, raced for the courthouse, the heels of her navy blue "testimony" shoes clacking against the concrete.

Mike had said to be there before nine, that she

was his first witness of the day. It was almost nine-thirty, and Suki hadn't thought about Lindsey Kern since she fed the last page of her evaluation into the fax machine on Saturday afternoon. Saturday afternoon. Two days ago. A lifetime ago.

As she raced across the courthouse anteroom, her echoing footsteps were a harsh admonition that despite all that had happened, all the good and all the bad, all the horror and all the relief, she still had work to do, a family to support. The New Zealand frontier patrol had been, as yet, unable to find Stan. Work, she reminded herself. Work. She tried to orient herself in Lindsey's case, in the MRI and EEG and MMPI, in the history of mental instability, in Lindsey's strange version of Richard Stoddard's death. Suki squared her shoulders and raised her chin. Although it wasn't ideal, she knew she could handle this without her usual compulsive pretestimony preparation. She was a pro.

Brick walls rose at least three stories to a brick ceiling over a brick floor. Mike had said the trial was in the small round courtroom, but Suki wasn't familiar enough with the layout to know which door led to which room. She pulled open the first door she saw, but the room was large, square and empty. She went to the next and opened it. Mike was standing at the defense table and when he saw her, he turned to the judge. "Your Honor," he said, "I call my first witness, Dr. Suzanne Jacobs."

Suki walked swiftly, but calmly, past the almost empty gallery pews, through the swinging gate, and into the well of the courtroom. A lone reporter fiddled absently with his notepad, one lanky leg stretched along the pew to his left. Suki smiled at him, and then at Lindsey, who looked startlingly attractive—and startlingly normal—in street clothes. Mike led her past the jury to the witness stand, a waist-high wooden enclosure in which she was to literally stand. She nodded to the judge, an unusually young man she hadn't met before. He couldn't be more than forty. HONORABLE MATTHEW F. JAFFEE, read the engraved nameplate before him. She looked around her; the courtroom had no windows.

Mike took her coat and threw it over the railing behind Lindsey. "Where the hell have you been?" he muttered.

"Accident on Route Two," she whispered as the bailiff came forward to swear her.

"Dr. Jacobs," Mike began when the bailiff retreated, "are you a duly licensed psychologist of the Commonwealth of Massachusetts?"

"I am."

The ADA stood. His name was Juan Gomez, and Suki had worked with him at Roxbury Court. He was a smart man with a good heart, and Suki was sorry to see he had transferred out: they needed all the good hearts they could get down there. "We'll stipulate the doctor's qualifications, if Your Honor please." Juan winked at Suki. She smiled in return, relaxing into the familiar game.

Judge Jaffee nodded. "Proceed."

"Now, Doctor," Mike said with all the deference to be expected of an attorney questioning his star witness, "did you have the occasion to examine Lindsey Kern, the defendant in this proceeding?"

"I did."

"When and where did you examine her?"

"At MCI-Watkins." Suki frowned as she tried to remember exactly how many times she had interviewed Lindsey. Damn. This was the kind of thing she always checked before testifying. "Five—no, six times over the past four weeks. Beginning on Thursday, April twentieth." April twentieth. The day Kenneth had found Alexa wandering by the side of the road, convinced Jonah was dead.

"Since that time," Mike said, "have you examined Ms. Kern's medical and psychiatric records?"

"Yes."

"Did you also review the police reports of the alleged incident and the trial transcripts from *Commonwealth v Kern*?"

"I did."

"And did you interview Ms. Kern to solicit her account of the alleged offense?"

"Yes, I did," Suki said. *Richard and I were standing on the top of the stairs. . . . Isabel saw her opening and gave him a push. . . .* Suki could, once again, see the pain in Lindsey's eyes. At the time, she had been so sure Lindsey was describing a delusion.

"Did you conduct a psychological assessment of Ms. Kern and petition for a battery of neurological tests to be performed?"

"Yes." Suki thought of Lindsey's inconclusive test scores, of the Tegretol that hadn't worked, of how fuzzy the line between sanity and insanity really was.

"Now, *Dr.* Jacobs," Mike paused for effect, "after studying the record, after interviewing Ms. Kern, after analyzing her test scores, did you form a conclusion based upon your own knowledge, training and years of experience in the field of forensic psychology? Have you formed an opinion as to Lindsey Kern's mental condition at the time of the alleged offense?"

Suki looked at Lindsey, seated at the defense table in her dark blue suit. Lindsey smiled at Suki and mouthed the words, "I'm glad about Alexa." She made a fist with her right hand and raised her thumb. Her left hand, attached to the right by a handcuff, flopped on the table.

Suki was wrenched by the sight of Lindsey in shackles. This was justice? She thought about PIN numbers and Finlay Thompson being found near water. She thought of fire and danger and the Hebrew letter aleph. She thought of Jonah and Charlie Gasperini.

Reality is at the edges of your awareness, you just need to let yourself turn sideways a bit to see it.

Based on Alexa's precognitive prediction, Suki had concluded Warren had seen Jonah's murder. And, although Warren still claimed he had nothing to do with the fire, he had confessed to making and selling methamphetamine, and admitted he had indeed witnessed the shooting. His sworn statement, affirming Alexa was driving and the gun was fired from the passenger seat, had led to Devin McKinna's arrest and Alexa's release. Apparently, after doing meth, Brendan had talked Devin into taking his father's gun and using it to scare Jonah in retaliation for what Jonah had done to Alexa—and things had escalated from there. Just as Alexa had said: Warren Blanchard was a man to be feared. And just as

Lindsey had predicted: the man who Alexa feared was the one who ultimately freed her.

There's so much happening beyond your field of vision. So much you just don't let yourself believe. . . .

"Dr. Jacobs?" Mike's voice pulled Suki from her reverie. "Have you, or have you not, formed an opinion as to Ms. Kern's mental condition?"

Suki opened her mouth, but couldn't find her voice. How could she change her mind now? That was certain death for her career—and her family's already precarious financial stability. A forensic psychologist who submitted a written evaluation with one opinion and testified to another, would be blackballed by every ADA and lawyer in the state. It was a small, closed community, and it was certain, if Suki did this, she would never be hired to perform a court evaluation again.

A knowing smile played around Lindsey's mouth. "Go with your gut," she mouthed to Suki. "Go with your gut."

"Do you think she's crazy because she believes in the paranormal?" Alexa had asked.

"There are lots of people who believe in the paranormal. It alone doesn't make a person crazy," Suki had replied.

"Dr. Jacobs?" Mike's voice was rising in alarm. He put his hands on the railing and leaned toward her. "Suki," he hissed. "What's going on here? Are you all right?"

Suki couldn't look at him. After all Mike had done, for both Alexa and for her, how could she let him down? She shifted her gaze over his shoulder, straight at Lindsey, who looked straight back, her wide gray eyes clear, full of compassion. Lindsey knew what she was going through.

Suki's mind raced. If she changed her testimony, she could very well be consigning Lindsey to Watkins, to ten more years of shackles, of being beat up by thugs, of no hope. But was Bridgeriver State really a better alternative? Lindsey didn't deserve either. She wasn't guilty of anything except believing the unbelievable.

"Let me refresh your memory, *Dr*. Jacobs," Mike said as he strode to the defense table and grabbed a file. "Did you, or did you not, write the following: 'I, Suzanne Jacobs, conclude that, due to a substantial disorder of perception which grossly diminished her capability to recognize reality, Lindsey Kern was significantly impaired in her ability to conform her conduct to the requirements of the law at the time of the death of Richard Stoddard.'" He marched to the witness stand. "Did you, or did you not, state that Lindsey Kern was legally insane at the time Richard Stoddard was killed?"

"I did." Suki kept her eyes on Lindsey, who smiled slightly and then nodded, as if giving Suki permission to go ahead. It was Lindsey sitting at the table across from her, but Suki also saw her mother and Alexa. And the Hebrew letter aleph.

Mike cleared his throat. "And did you not also write: 'I shall so state, under oath, in the forthcoming trial of Lindsey Kern.'"

"I did." Suki shifted her gaze to the jury, to the fifteen men and women who held Lindsey's fate in their hands. She knew her testimony could keep Lindsey in prison, send her to a mental institution, or maybe even free her. She had the power to load the gun with the bullets of her choice. Yet, Suki also knew her testimony wasn't about power, it was about truth and opening her mind to possibilities she had thought impossible. She hadn't believed her mother and she hadn't believed Alexa. It was time to believe.

Lindsey raised her elbows to the defense table and rested her chin on her manacled hands. She watched Suki intently, occasionally nodding her head, as if she were reading, and responding to Suki's thoughts.

"And this is your opinion as a result of your forensic evaluation of the defendant, Lindsey Kern?" Mike pressed.

"Just because we can't explain it," Kenneth had once told Suki, *"doesn't mean it didn't happen."*

Suki turned to the jury. "Reality is at the edges of your awareness," she said in answer to Mike's question. "You just need to let yourself turn sideways a bit to see it."

"And what exactly is that supposed to mean?" Mike snapped.

"It means," Suki grinned at Lindsey, who grinned in return, "that I've changed my mind."

EPILOGUE

Suki turned off the highway and drove up to Watkins. In the full spring sunlight, the metal fencing surrounding the prison didn't look all that intimidating, nor the turrets particularly menacing. The German shepherds scampering on the grass to the side of the parking lot seemed more like playful puppies than guard dogs. Attitude sure did define the world. She shot a glance at Alexa, who was sitting beside her, staring at the barbed wire and the turrets and the dogs, a stunned expression on her face; as Suki had feared, Alexa's trauma was not over—and might never be. "We can go home if you want," she offered gently. "I don't mind at all."

"They would've sent me here, huh?"

Suki pulled into a parking spot and turned to Alexa. "Yes," she said. "But no one's sending you here now. You say the word and we're gone."

Alexa shook her head. "I want to see Lindsey."

Suki nodded, although she wasn't crazy about the idea. Even though the jury *had* found Lindsey not guilty. Even if the paranormal *was* possible. This was something Alexa needed to do, and Suki respected that. She climbed out of the car and Alexa followed, but slowly. Suki turned and put her arm around her daughter. "No one will ever make you come here," she said. "It's over."

Alexa raised her eyes as the shadow of the boxy building fell over them. "It could've happened," she said. "Look at Lindsey."

Suki knew Alexa was right. In many ways, it had all been serendipity: Warren's arrest, Alexa's release, Lindsey's freedom. Or had it been something more? Suki didn't know, and probably never would, although she was now mindful enough to keep herself open to possibilities. She was also mindful that given a small change in an event here or an action there, Warren's and Alexa's and Lindsey's lives would now be on completely different tracks. And this was especially true of Lindsey.

After Suki's testimony, the courtroom had broken into pandemonium. Mike was enraged, the jury confused, Juan Gomez amused, and the bored reporter, who turned out to be from the *Boston Herald*, the city's tabloid daily, suddenly became quite engaged. Juan declined to cross-examine, and as Suki stepped down from the stand, Lindsey flashed her another thumbs-up. But as Mike handed her her coat, he had hissed under his breath, "You better find yourself a new profession, *Dr.* Jacobs, because I'm going to make sure this is the last courtroom you ever testify in."

Suki knew he had every right to be furious, every right to publicize her duplicity to the forensic community. "It came to me suddenly," she tried to explain. "Just when I was on the stand. I didn't know what to do, so I followed my heart."

"It's not your heart I'm concerned with," Mike snapped. "It's your ethics."

Suki had left the courthouse, both elated and

depressed, knowing she had done the right thing, fearing it would have horrible consequences. But the consequences never materialized. Mike switched to Plan B—attacking Edgar's credibility as a witness to raise the possibility that Richard's death was an accident—and, in an act of desperation-inspired brilliance, after recalling Edgar, he put Lindsey on the stand and went with "full disclosure": allowing her to reveal everything, without reserve, to the court.

And it worked. Lindsey's testimony was emotionally wrenching and powerful; Edgar's was weak. The combined result was that the jury decided that the commonwealth had not proved criminal intent beyond a reasonable doubt: they were just not convinced Lindsey was capable of calculated murder, nor that that was what Edgar had seen. Whether the jury believed it was an accident or that Isabel Davenport killed Richard Stoddard would never be known, but it didn't matter. All that mattered was that they had returned after a short deliberation with a full acquittal.

And now, at Lindsey's request, Suki and Alexa were on their way to escort her out of Watkins. Lindsey was being released—and she wasn't going to Bridgeriver State. After ten years, Lindsey Kern was going home. And she felt she owed this to Alexa and Suki.

The officer at the front control told them they could either stay in the waiting room or go into the prison and meet Lindsey on her way out. Alexa chose the waiting room. When they sat down, Alexa reached over and took Suki's hand. Alexa was still very fragile, even after Stan had finally been located and sent a telegram promising to catch the next plane "back to the States." Suki guessed he'd return with a New Zealand accent. She squeezed Alexa's fingers and they waited for Lindsey, hand in hand, in the uncomfortable plastic chairs.

Lindsey burst through the metal detector, along with her mother and brother. She was beaming. She was free. She hugged both Suki and Alexa. Her brother Joel retrieved the bottle of champagne he had left with the officer and popped the cork. They toasted Lindsey and freedom and Mike and Suki and Alexa with the paper cups Lindsey's mother dug up in the bathroom. Joel had forgotten to bring glasses. Suki wished Mike could have been here, but he was in court. They had had a long talk and worked it all out, and he had forgiven her, but warned her to never, ever, ever do anything like that to him again. She had promised she never would.

"I'm out of here!" Lindsey shouted, waving the empty champagne bottle in the air. The waiting room erupted in a loud cheer as Lindsey marched out the front door with her family close behind. They were immediately swallowed by a school of reporters waiting in the parking lot.

Suki squinted as she and Alexa walked into the sunshine. Watching Lindsey happily talking to the press, Suki realized she still didn't understand what had happened. Not what, not why and definitely not how. But she knew she had been changed by it. She didn't feel like some touchy-feely airhead, and she wasn't going to go out and try to relive her past lives or reach the astral plane, but on the other hand, she wasn't as sure as she had been that these were impossible endeavors.

"Things don't always make sense the way you think of sense," Lindsey had once told her. And Suki knew it was the truth.

"Hey," someone called. "It's the shrink!"

Suki was horrified to see a wave of reporters peel off from the huddle surrounding Lindsey and head toward them. Reflexively, she pushed Alexa behind her.

A young woman in a slinky pink dress reached Suki first, a photographer right behind her. The woman waved an open copy of the *Herald:* PSYCHIC SHRINK'S TESTIMONY FREES CONVICTED MURDERER, screamed the huge headline. "So you're the psychic shrink?" She shoved a microphone in Suki's face.

"I guess I'm the person the paper's referring to," Suki began. "Although I wouldn't say that I'm—"

"But you have a Ph.D.," the reporter interrupted. "You're a licensed psychologist. And you believe in ghosts."

Suki looked around for someone to help her, but there was only Alexa, and the girl just gave her a small smile and shrugged. "I am a licensed psychologist," Suki said slowly. "But I think I'd have to say that the ghost thing is an open question."

"Will you be taking on more cases like this, Dr. Jacobs?" Another microphone appeared before her. "What's next on your agenda?"

"What about the guy who claims he was abducted by aliens and they forced him to shoot his brother?" someone else clamored. "Will you vouch for him?"

"How about the reincarnation lady?"

Suki grabbed Alexa and headed for the car. "No comment," she called over her shoulder. But she figured she better come up with a comment shortly. She had the feeling this wasn't going to go away anytime soon.